STREETS OF GOLD

by Evan Hunter

EVAN HUNTER

STREETS OF GOLD

HARPER & ROW, PUBLISHERS

NEW YORK, EVANSTON, SAN FRANCISCO, LONDON

1817

STREETS OF GOLD. Copyright © 1974 by Evan Hunter. All rights reserved. Printed in the United States of America. No part of this book may be used or reproduced in any manner whatsoever without written permission except in the case of brief quotations embodied in critical articles and reviews. For information address Harper & Row, Publishers, Inc., 10 East 53rd Street, New York, N.Y. 10022. Published simultaneously in Canada by Fitzhenry & Whiteside Limited, Toronto.

FIRST EDITION

ISBN 0-06-012012-6

Library of Congress Catalog Card Number: 74-6980

This is for my grandfather—
Giuseppantonio Coppola

Let's all get up and dance to a song
That was a hit before your Mother was born
Though she was born a long long time ago
Your Mother should know—your Mother should know
Sing it again

JOHN LENNON and PAUL MCCARTNEY

1

I've been blind since birth. This means that much of what I am about to tell you is based upon the subjective descriptions or faulty memories of others, blended with an empirical knowledge of my own—forty-eight years of touching, hearing, and smelling. But paintings, rooms with objects in them, lawns of bright green, crashing seascapes, contrails across the sky, the Empire State Building, women in lace, a Japanese fan, Rebecca's eyes—I have never seen any of these things. They come to me secondhand.

I sometimes believe, and I have no foundation of fact upon which to base this premise, that *all* experience is secondhand, anyway. Even my grandfather's arrival in America must have been colored beforehand by the things he had heard about this country, the things that had been described to him in Italy before he decided to come. Was he truly seeing the new land with his own eyes? Or was that first glimpse of the lady in the harbor—he has never mentioned her to me, I only assume that the first thing all arriving immigrants saw was the Statue of Liberty—was that initial sighting his *own*, or was there a sculptured image already in his head, chiseled there by Pietro Bardoni in his expensive American clothes, enthusiastically selling the land of opportunities where gold was in the streets to be picked up by any man willing to work, himself talced and splendored evidence of the riches to be mined.

The villagers of Fiormonte, in the fifth year of their misery since *la fillossera* struck the grape, must have listened in awe-struck wonder as Bardoni used his hands and his deep Italian baritone voice to describe New York, with its magnificent buildings and esplanades, food to be had for pennies a day (food!), and gold in the streets, gold to shovel up with your own two hands. He was speaking figuratively, of course. My grandfather later told me no one believed there was *really* gold in the streets, not gold to be mined, at least. The translation they made was that the streets were *paved* with gold; they had, some of them, been to Pompeii—or most certainly to Naples, which lay only 125 kilometers due west—and they knew of the treasures of ancient Rome, knew that the statues had been covered with gold leaf, knew that even common hairpins had been fashioned of gold, so why not streets paved with gold in a nation that surely rivaled the Roman Empire so far as riches were concerned? It was entirely conceivable. Besides, when a man is starving, he is willing to believe anything that costs him nothing.

Geography is not one of my strongest subjects. I have been to Italy many times, the last time in 1970, on a joint pilgrimage— to visit the town where my grandfather was born and to visit the grave where my brother is buried. I know that Italy is shaped like a boot; I have traced its outline often enough on Braille maps. And I know what a boot looks like. That is to say, I have lingeringly passed my hands over the configurations of a boot, and I have formed an image of it inside my head, tactile, reinforced by the rich scent of the leather and the tiny squeaking sounds it made when I tested the flexibility of this thing I held, this object to be cataloged in my brain file along with hundreds and thousands of other objects I had never seen—and will never see. The way to madness is entering the echo chamber that repeatedly resonates with doubt: is the image in my mind the *true* image? Or am I feeling the elephant's trunk and believing it looks like a snake? And anyway, what does a snake look like? I believe I know. I am never quite sure. I am not quite sure of anything I describe because there is no basis for comparison, except in the fantasy catalog of my mind's eye. I am not even sure what I myself look like.

Rebecca once told me, "You just miss looking dignified, Ike."

And a woman I met in Los Angeles said, "You just miss looking shabby."

Rebecca's words were spoken in anger. The Los Angeles lady, I suppose, was putting me down—though God knows why she felt any need to denigrate a blind man, who would seem vulnerable enough to even the mildest form of attack and therefore hardly a worthy victim. We later went to bed together in a Malibu motel-cum-Chinese restaurant, where the aftertaste of moo goo gai pan blended with the scent of her perfumed breasts and the waves of the Pacific crashed in against the pilings and shook the room and shook the bed. She wore a tiny gold cross around her neck, a gift from a former lover; she would not take it off.

For the record (who's counting?), my eyes are blue. I am told. But what is blue? Blue is the color of the sky. Yes, but *what* is blue? It is a cool color. Ah, yes, we are getting closer. The radiators in the apartment we lived in on 120th Street were usually cool if not downright frigid. Were the radiators blue? But sometimes they became sizzling hot, and red has been described to me as a hot color, so were the radiators red when they got hot? Rebecca has red hair and green eyes. Green is a cool color also. Are green and blue identical? If not, how do they differ? I know the smell of a banana, and I know the shape of it, but when it was described to me as yellow, I had no concept of yellow, could form no clear color image. The sun is yellow, I was told. But the sun is hot; doesn't that make it red? No, yellow is a much cooler color. Oh. Then is it like blue? Impossible. The only color I know is black. I do not have to have that described to me. It sits behind my dead blue eyes.

My hair is blond. Yellow, they say. Like a banana. (Forget it.) I can only imagine that centuries back, a Milanese merchant (must have been a Milanese, don't you think? it couldn't have been a *Viking*) wandered down into southern Italy and displayed his silks and brocades to the gathered wide-eyed peasants, perhaps hawking a bit more than his cloth, Milanese privates securely and bulgingly contained in northern codpiece; the girls must have giggled. And one of them, dark-eyed, black-haired, heavily breasted, short and squat, perhaps later wandered off behind the grapes with this tall, handsome northern con man, where he lifted her skirts, yanked down her knickers, explored the black and hairy bush promised by her armpits, and probed with northern vigor the southern ripeness of her quim, thereupon planting within her a few thousand blond, blue-eyed (blind?) genes that blossomed centuries later in the form of yours truly, Dwight Jamison.

My maiden name is Ignazio Silvio Di Palermo.

Di Palermo means *of* Palermo or *from* Palermo, which is where my father's ancestors worked and died. All except my father's father, who came to America to dig out some of the gold in them thar streets, and ended up as a street cleaner instead, pushing his cart and shoveling up the golden nuggets dropped by horses pulling streetcars along First Avenue. Ironically, he was eventually run over by a streetcar. It was said he was drunk at the time, but a man who comes to shovel gold and ends up shoveling shit is entitled to a drink or two every now and then. I never met the man. He was killed long before I was born. The grandfather I speak of in these pages was my mother's father. From my father's father, I inherited only my name, identical to his, Ignazio Silvio Di Palermo. Or, if you prefer, Dwight Jamison.

My father's name is Jimmy, actually Giacomo, which means James in Italian; are you getting the drift? Jamison, James's son.

6

That's where I got the last name when I changed it legally in 1955. The first name I got from Dwight D. Eisenhower, who became President of these United States in 1953. The Dwight isn't as far-fetched as it may seem at first blush. I have never been called Ignazio by anyone but my grandfather. As a child, I was called Iggie. When I first began playing piano professionally, I called myself Blind Ike. My father liked the final name I picked for myself, Dwight Jamison. When I told him I was planning to change my name, he came up with a long list of his own, each name carefully and beautifully hand lettered, even though he realized I would not be able to see his handiwork. He was no stranger to name changes. When he had his own band back in the twenties, thirties, and forties, he called himself Jimmy Palmer.

There is in America the persistent suspicion that if a person changes his name, he is most certainly a wanted desperado. And nowhere is there greater suspicion of, or outright animosity for, the name-changers than among those who steadfastly *refuse* to change their names. Meet a Lipschitz or a Mangiacavallo, a Schliephake or a Trzebiatowski who have stood by those hot ancestral guns, and they will immediately consider the name-changer a deserter at best or a traitor at worst. I say fuck you, Mr. Trzebiatowski. Better you should change it to Trevor. Or better you should mind your own business.

For reasons I can never fathom, the fact that I've changed my name is of more fascination to anyone who's ever interviewed me (I am too modest to call myself famous, but whenever I play someplace, it's a matter of at least some interest, and if you don't know who I am, what can I tell you?)—a subject more infinitely fascinating than the fact that I'm a blind man who happens to be the best jazz pianist who ever lived, he said modestly and self-effacingly, and not without a touch of shabby dignity. No one ever asks me how it feels to be blind. I would be happy to tell them. I am an expert on being blind. But always, without fail, The Name.

7

"How did you happen upon the name Dwight Jamison?"

"Well, actually, I wanted to use another name, but someone already had it."

"Ah, yes? What *was* the other name?"

"Groucho Marx."

The faint uncertain smile (I can sense it, but not see it), the moment where the interviewer considers the possibility that this wop entertainer—talented, yes, but only a wop, and only an entertainer—may somehow be blessed with a sense of humor. But is it possible he really considered calling himself Groucho Marx?

"No, seriously, Ike, tell me"—the voice confidential now—*"why* did you decide on Dwight Jamison?"

"It had good texture. Like an augmented eleventh."

"Oh. I see, I see. And what is your *real* name?"

"My real name has been Dwight Jamison since 1955. That's a long, long time."

"Yes, yes, of course, but what is your *real* name?" (Never "was," notice. In America, you can never lose your real name. It "is" always your real name.) "What is your real name? The name you were born with?"

"Friend," I say, "I was born with yellow hair and blue eyes that cannot see. Why is it of any interest to you that my *real* name was Ignazio Silvio Di Palermo?"

"Ah, yes, yes. Would you spell that for me, please?"

I changed my name because I no longer wished to belong to that great brotherhood of *compaesani* whose sole occupation seemed to be searching out names ending in vowels. (Old Bronx joke: What did Washington say when he was crossing the Delaware? *"Fá 'no cazzo di freddo qui!"* And what did his boatman reply? *"Pure tu sei italiano?"* Translated freely, Washington purportedly said, "Fucking-A cold around here," and his boatman replied, *"You're* Italian, too?") My mother always told me I was a Yankee, her definition of Yankee being a third-generation American, her arithmetic bolstered by the undeniable fact that *her*

8

mother (but not her father) was born here, and she herself was born here, and I was certainly born here, ergo Ignazio Silvio Di Palermo, third-generation Yankee Doodle Dandy. My mother was always quick to remind me that *she* was American. "I'm American, don't forget." How *could* I forget, Mama darling, when you told me three and four times a day? "I'm American, don't forget."

In Sicily, where I went to find my brother's grave, your first son's grave, Mom, the cab driver told me how good things were in Italy these days, and then he said to me, "America is *here* now."

Maybe it *is* there.

One thing I'm sure of.

It isn't *here*.

And maybe it never was.

❖

The way my grandfather told it, Pietro Bardoni was always a braggart, a self-styled man of the world, a loudmouth, *uno sbruffone.* He had grown up with Bardoni, of course, and he knew him well; in a town with one main street and sixty-four houses built of stone and whitewashed stucco, it was virtually impossible not to have known everyone as soon as you were old enough to walk the cobbled streets. During the day, you worked in the vineyard. In the evening in the summer, you sat outside the town's only bar, sat at round metal tables painted red and yellow and blue, the men smoking guinea stinkers (My grandfather always smoked those foul-smelling twisted little Italian cigars. When I was young, I used to ask him why he smoked those guinea stinkers all the time. He would reply, and I record his fractured English as best I can, "Attsa no guin'a stink, Ignazio. Attsa *good* see-gah.") —smoking their good cigars in the awninged dusk and drinking grappa, a foul-tasting liqueur that is supposed to be good for the liver and also for removing paint from furniture, sat and smoked and talked about the grape and about the coming fall harvest.

9

Italy in those days—this was in the late 1880s before the grape blight—was the leading wine merchant to the world. It was only later, when the plant parasite phylloxera ("*la fillossera*," my grandfather called it, and invariably spat immediately afterward) destroyed most of the vineyards in southern Italy, that the French took virtual possession of the industry, and Bordeaux replaced Chianti as the most popular wine in Europe and abroad. *La fillossera* destroyed the crops and destroyed the economy as well; the land was the grape and the grape was the economy. But in the fall, when times were still good, the men would come home from the harvest and, without bathing first—there was no running water in Fiormonte, and the men bathed in well-drawn water in wooden tubs in the kitchens of their homes, and this was done in privacy, in the dark, Italian farmers unlike Scottish miners being very modest about such things as showing their privates to other members of the family, unless incest is their intent—without bathing first, the men would go to the bar, and sit outside under the blue-striped awning and talk about how good things were, and how blessed they were, and then caution each other about speaking of their good fortune aloud lest someone, God alone knew who, would put the Evil Eye on them.

When I was born blind, Mary the Barber ventured the opinion that the Evil Eye had been put on my mother when she was pregnant with me. Filomena the Midwife clucked her tongue and said No, it was my mother's experience with the Chinaman thirteen years ago that had been the cause of the tragedy attending my birth. It was my Uncle Luke who first told me about the Chinaman, but my grandfather was the one who later related the story to me in detail. My grandfather told me everything. To my knowledge, he never lied to me. I loved my grandfather very much.

He would sit with the men of the town in the good days—oh, he was perhaps fourteen or fifteen at the time; he did not come to America until 1901, when things became really unbearable—and

10

he would watch the girls go by in their long cotton dresses, and with the younger men of the town he would exchange secret desires, always careful never to impugn the reputation of anyone's sister, because in southern Italy, that was—and *is*—ample reason for murder. And yet the talk was there, the talk always rendered harmless by distance; the girls they wanted to fuck lived in Rome or Venice or Milan, but never in Fiormonte—though the girls of Fiormonte paraded with eyes downcast like nuns, contradictorily ripe asses twitching provocatively. My grandfather was a very handsome man, to hear him tell it, with black hair and dark brown eyes and a nose he said had Sienese influence (I knew the shape of his nose, I explored its contours with my fingers many, many times; it was not unlike my own, hawklike and thin; it could very well have had its origin in Siena—there goes my Milanese cloth merchant theory), and tall in comparison to the other men of the village, five feet eight inches. His father and his grandfather before him had worked the vineyards, and had he stayed in Italy, I would probably be working the vineyards now, though God knows what Fiormonte is like today. It may be bustling with machinery and factories, for all I know. It was not that way in 1970, when I went back to find my grandfather, and to find my roots.

I walked the cobbled streets, the same streets he had walked as a boy, and the August sun burned hot on my bare head, and I reached down to touch the cobbles. *What you walk on in the street. Here. Put your hand. Touch. Feel.* Ignazio Silvio Di Palermo, four years old, squats at the First Avenue curb outside his grandfather's tailor shop and sticks his hand down between scabby knees—which bleed when he picks them, he is told, though he cannot see the blood, and can only feel its warm ooze; you are bleeding, they tell him, and they tell him the color of blood is red, it is what runs through your body and keeps you alive—reaches down, his hand guided by his grandfather's fingers around his wrist, and touches the street. And feels. Feels with the four

11

fingers of his right hand, the fingertips gingerly gliding over the surface of the smooth, rough stones, and then circumscribing the shape of one stone, it is like a box, it is like the box he keeps the toy soldiers in, it is the shape of a box, and feeling where the next stone joins it, and the next, and forming a pattern in his mind, and his grandfather says *Do you see, Ignazio?* Now *do you see?* I walked that town from one end of it to the other, trying to pick out the locations my grandfather had described, finding the bar at which Bardoni had first broached the subject of leaving for America, sat there in the cool encroaching dusk as my grandfather must have done after a day's work, and smelled the familiar aroma of the guinea stinkers all around me, and heard the muted hum of the male conversation, and above that, like the strident shrieks of treetop birds, the women calling to each other from windows or balconies, and the counterpoint of peddlers hawking their produce in the streets, "*Caterina, vieni qua! Pesche, bella pesche fresche, ciliegie, cocomero,*" exactly as my grandfather had described it to me—or were these only the cadences and rhythms I had heard throughout all the days of my youth in East Harlem?

Brash young Bardoni had sat at a table here with my grandfather when they were still boys, boasting loudly of having *fatto 'na bella chiavata* in Naples, having inserted his doubtless heroically proportioned key into the lock of a Neapolitan streetwalker, while the other young men of the town, my grandfather included, listened goggle-eyed and prayed that San Maurizio, the patron saint of the town, would not be able to read their minds. In December of the year 1900, Bardoni walked my grandfather past this same café on Christmas Day, sunshine bright on cobbled streets, Bardoni dressed in natty American attire, striped shirt and celluloid collar, necktie asserted with a simple pin (Eliot's been translated into Braille), and told him of the streets over there in America, with all that gold lying in them, and further told him that he would pay for my grandfather's passage, and arrange to

12

have a job and lodgings waiting for him when he got to America, and he would not have to worry about the language, there were plenty of Italians already there, they would help him with his English. All Bardoni wanted in return was a small portion of my grandfather's weekly wages (twelve dollars and fifty cents a week! Bardoni told him) until the advances were paid off, and a smaller percentage of the wages after that until Bardoni's modest commission had been earned, and then my grandfather would be on his own to make his fortune in the land of the free and the home of the brave.

"But I will return to Italy," my grandfather said.

"*Certo*," Bardoni said. "Of course."

"When I have earned enough money."

"Of course," Bardoni said again. "*Italia è la sua patria.*"

It had been a barren Christmas Day in Fiormonte. I have tried hard to understand what life in that village must have been like, because I know for certain that the life transposed to Harlem, and later to the Bronx, and later to the town of Talmadge, Connecticut (where I spent more than thirteen years with Rebecca and the children), was firmly rooted in Fiormonte. The family, the *nuclear* family, consisted of my grandfather, his parents, his two sisters, and his younger brother. In musical terms, they were the primary functions of the key. The secondary functions were the aunts, uncles, and cousins who lived within a stone's throw of my grandfather's house. The *compari* and *comari* were the godfathers and godmothers (pronounced "goombahs" and "goomahs" even by my grandfather), and they combined with the *compaesani* to form the tertiary functions of the key; the *compaesani* were countrymen, compatriots, or even simply neighbors. Fiormonte enclosed and embraced this related and near-related brood, but was itself motherless and fatherless in the year 1900, Italy having been torn bloody and squalling from the loins of a land dominated as early as thirty years before by rival kings and struggling foreign forces. Unified by Garibaldi to become a single nation, it became

13

that only in the minds and hearts of intellectuals and revolutionaries, the southern peasants knowing only Fiormonte and Naples, where until recently the uneasy seat of power had rested. They distrusted Rome, the new capital, in fact distrusted the entire north, suspecting (correctly) that the farmlands and vineyards were being unjustly taxed in favor of stronger industrial interests. There was no true fatherland as yet, there was no sense of the village being a part of the state as, for example, Seattle, Washington, is a necessary five chord in the chart of "America, the Beautiful." The *patria* that Bardoni had mentioned to my grandfather was Fiormonte and, by extension, Naples. It was this that my grandfather was leaving.

He made his decision on Christmas Day, 1900.

He had been toying with the idea since November, when Bardoni returned in splendor, sporting patent leather shoes and tawny spats, diamond cuff links at his wrists, handlebar mustache meticulously curled and waxed. The economic system in Fiormonte, as elsewhere in the south of Italy, was based on a form of medieval serfdom in which the landowner, or *padrone*, permitted the peasant to work the land for him, the lion's share of the crop going to the *padrone*. (We call it sharecropping here.) Those carnival barkers who came back to the villages to tout the joys of living in America were *padroni* in their own right; a new country, a different form of economic bondage. They would indeed pay for steerage transportation to the United States, they would indeed supply (and pay for) lodgings in New York, they would indeed guarantee employment, but the tithe had to be paid, the *padrone* was there in the streets of Manhattan as surely as he was there in the big stone house at the top of the hill in the village of Fiormonte.

My grandfather's name was Francesco Di Lorenzo.

The house he lived in was similar in construction, though not in size, to the one inhabited by Don Leonardo, the *padrone* of Fiormonte. Built of stone laboriously cleared from the vineyards,

14

covered with mud allowed to dry and then whitewashed with a mixture of lime and water, it consisted of three rooms, the largest of which was the kitchen. A huge fireplace and hearth, the house's only source of heat and of course the cooking center, dominated the kitchen. The other two rooms were bedrooms, one of them shared by the parents and baby brother of young Francesco—it is difficult to think of him, no less write of him, as anything but Grandpa. But Francesco he was in his youth, and indeed Francesco he remained until he had been in America for more than forty years, by which time everyone, including Grandma, called him Frank. When I was a boy, people were still calling him Francesco, though every now and then someone would call him Frank. I'm hardly the one to talk about anglicizing names, being a ratfink turncoat deserter (Dwight Jamison, ma'am, I hope I am a *big* success!), but I have never been able to understand why we call Italy "Italy" and not "Italia," or why we call Germany "Germany" rather than "Deutschland." Who supplies the translation? Is there a central bureau in Germany that grants permission for the French people to call the fatherland "L'Allemagne"? I hate to raise problems; forgive me.

In any event, my grandfather eventually became Frank, and this curious metamorphosis is best revealed in the various documents my mother turned over to me when he died. A copy of his birth certificate had been requested for naturalization purposes in the early part of 1945, when the Germans were still clinging tenaciously to the northernmost portions of Italy. A duplicate certificate arrived from the south, mimeographed on a torn scrap of paper, the reverse side of which was a printed sheet of ration coupons for October of 1944—*pane, pasta, olio, zucchero,* and *generi vari,* the staples of the Italian diet, and most certainly much better fare than my grandfather had enjoyed back in 1900. *Comune di Fiormonte,* it read, *Provincia di Potenza.* And on the reverse, the requested information, listing the birth date of Francesco Luigi Di Lorenzo as the seventh day of July, in the year 1880. In New

York City, in the year 1901, a marriage certificate was issued to one Teresa Giamboglio (try *that* on your harmonica, Mr. Trzebiatowski) and the aforementioned gentleman of Potenza, except that this time his name was shortened to Francesco Di Lorenzo. His naturalization papers, dated the 27th day of April, 1945, state in ornate script lettering: *Be it remembered that Franco Di Lorenzo then residing at 2335 First Avenue in the City of New York, State of New York, who previous to his naturalization was a subject of Italy, having applied to be admitted a citizen of the United States,* and so on. *Franco* Di Lorenzo. And his death certificate (I can never think of that goddamn day last June without tears coming to my eyes) records that he died at Bronx-Lebanon Hospital in the intensive care unit after being there for less than nineteen hours. The time of his death was 11:50 A.M. on the morning of June 17, 1973. His age was recorded as 92 years, 11 months, and 10 days. His occupation was given as tailor. His name was recorded as Frank Di Lorenzo. Good old Grandpa. Yankee Doodle Dandy at last.

But Francesco he was in 1900, and it was he who shared the second bedroom with his sisters, Emilia and Maria, respectively fourteen and ten. Emilia snored, but he never told her this, lest it spoil the hours of pleasure her own reflection in the glass brought her. Her light snore filled the small room now. He put on his eyeglasses. It was shortly before dawn, and the paneless window high on the wall over Emilia's bed, covered with a stretch of goathide rubbed to translucent thinness, admitted enough early light so that he could see the beds of both his sisters, and the carved wooden chest on the wall opposite, and the wooden chair beside his own bed, and beyond that the open door of the archway leading into the kitchen, brighter than the bedroom now because its larger windows faced east, toward Bari and the Adriatic. He was twenty years old, but he leaped out of bed with all the excitement of a five-year-old, and went immediately to the arch and

16

looked into the kitchen. The *presepio* stood in one corner of the room. He went to it slowly, as though uncertain he had seen correctly (or, more properly, uncertain that what he had *not* seen was truly and validly not *there* to see), and then turned away in disappointment. Shivering, he went to the woodbox in the opposite corner and took from it the brush he had scavenged the night before. He lay this upon the grate in the old stone fireplace painted white and streaked with soot, and twisted under it a yellowed copy of the *Corriere della Sera* which his father had brought back from Naples two months ago, when he'd gone there looking for work.

Wood was scarce; well, *everything* was scarce. He carried three huge and treasured pine logs (but this was Christmas) to the grate and carefully placed them on the tinder to form a distantly related cousin to the *presepio* standing in the corner of the room, a skeletal isosceles pyramid with four shelves. The bottom shelf contained tiny wooden figures representing the Holy Family, which his cousin Renato had carved himself and brought as a gift three Christmases before, when times were better: Joseph and Mary and the infant Jesus, the Three Kings standing in the manger in adoration of the newborn Christ, shepherds and sheep and angels and a camel, all meticulously carved by Renato, who was excellent with his hands and could do such things. The three top shelves, reserved for gifts, were empty.

Francesco struck sparks from his flint into the nest of tinder, and then stood up and watched the spreading stain of fire on newsprint, heard the sharp crackling of the dried twigs, folded his arms across his narrow chest and stared at the flames as they grew like malevolent weeds around the pyramid of logs. His hair was black and curly, he had thick black eyebrows, and he wore rimless spectacles he had bought in the open market from the stall of Luisa Maggiore, about whom many rumors were spoken in the village—none of which he believed or repeated. He had picked

17

and searched through the mountain of eyeglasses on her stand, until he had found a pair which he felt added a touch of distinction to his face without robbing it of its handsomeness. He had worn glasses since he was four years old, but his eyesight stubbornly refused to improve; even the glasses he had bought from Signora Maggiore two years ago were now too weak for his faltering vision. He could not see five feet ahead of him in the morning unless he fumbled first for his glasses on the wooden chair beside his bed, and put them on before throwing back the coverlet and setting his feet on the cold stone floor.

The room was warming.

No longer chilled, he gave recognition to the hunger that had been gnawing at his belly long before he woke. It was still barely light outside, the sun was just rising, he supposed it was close to five in the morning. December in southern Italy, from what my grandfather told me, is normally a dismal time of the year, rain drenching the roads and turning the tiniest patches of soil into quagmires. The sky was clear that Christmas Day, the sun came blushing through the mountaintops as though embarrassed by its absence of the past few weeks. He had been hungry when he'd gone to bed the night before, had tossed hungrily in fitful sleep, had awakened hungry, and was still hungry. But he knew that all the food in the house had been jealously hoarded for this day of days, and he did not know whether he was supposed to touch even a crust of hidden bread. He trembled again, not from the cold this time, but instead from a feeling of helpless anger and frustration—why *la fillossera?* If there was truly a God, *why?* Hugging his slender arms across his chest, he stood trembling in his flannel nightshirt before the blazing fire, and wondered if his father would shout at him for having used the wood so early in the morning, before anyone else was awake.

His mother had been saving a handful of chestnuts for roasting with the Christmas meal. They were in an earthenware jar outside the largest of the kitchen windows, eleven of them; he had long-

18

ingly counted them. If he ate one of them with his early-morning porridge, would his mother realize there were only ten remaining when it came time to roast them?

Silently, thoughtfully, he went back into the bedroom to dress. Maria, the ten-year-old, was awake. "Francesco?" she said, and blinked at him.

"Yes," he answered. "Turn your back."

"Did he come?" She was referring to Father Baba, the Italian bearer of Christmas gifts, an old old man with long flowing robes and a white beard and a pack on his back, not unlike our own Santa Claus though rather scarecrowish in appearance, and certainly not rosy-cheeked or potbellied or jolly ho-ho-ho.

"Did he?" she asked, when Francesco did not answer.

"No," he said. "Go back to sleep."

He tightened his belt, and went out into the kitchen, and put the pot of *farinata* onto the hook, and swung it in over the blazing fire, and debated once more the theft of the chestnut. Maria came padding into the room. She was not his favorite person in the world since she still wet the bed at the age of ten, and between Emilia's snoring and Maria's stench, it was difficult to get a good night's sleep even if a man were not hungry all the time. The front of her gown clung limply to her now. Like a tiny galleon afloat on her own stale ocean, she flapped directly to the *presepio* and stared at it in disbelief.

"He didn't come," she said.

"I told you."

"Why not?" she asked, and turned accusingly, as though he alone were responsible for the absence of gifts in the house this Christmas Day.

"Because we are poor," he said flatly and cruelly, and then ladled hot porridge from the pot, and ate it without stealing the chestnut after all. Maria was crying behind him. He went to her. He gathered her into his arms, damp and smelling of her own urine, and he stroked her long black hair, and he whispered,

19

"*Non piangere, cara,* do not cry. He will come next year. I promise."

"Who are you to promise?" she asked.

"Why, your brother," he said, and grinned.

"*Vattene a Napoli,*" she answered, and pushed him away, and went back into the bedroom.

❖

He was not about to go to Naples, as his sister had advised. He was about to go to America. He had made up his mind the moment he decided not to steal the chestnut. He had never stolen anything in his life, and the very idea that he had even *considered* the theft appalled him. To steal from one's own family! No. It was not right to be so hungry. He would go to America, and make his fortune, and come back next Christmas with expensive gifts, as he had promised Maria. The thought of leaving Fiormonte excited him, and simultaneously filled him with dread.

My sons today think nothing of hopping into the Volkswagen bus and driving it out to Denver for the weekend. All of my children have been to Europe at least four times, Andrew having made the trip alone when he was sixteen. He is now in Greece, on the island of Samos, living with a girl from Baltimore. They plan to head east, to India, in search of a guru. (No, Dad, you don't understand. *You* don't find the guru, *he* finds *you.* Yes, son, bullshit.) The last time he went to India, lovely, disease-ridden, impoverished, starvation-gripped paradise (no offense, Madame Gandhi), he came back covered with lice, and with an open sore the size of a half dollar just above the arch of his right foot. I rushed him to the doctor and was told if he'd stayed away another two weeks, the foot would have developed gangrene and he'd have lost it. He'd been gone for eight months, dropping a line every so often, but never including a return address. I don't know what he was looking for. I don't think he found it because

20

he's heading back there again, come September. Nor do I think it's a guru he's seeking.

My grandfather knew what *he* was looking for, all right. He was looking for work. He was looking for money. He was looking for survival for himself and his family. He walked out onto those sun-silvered streets of the village on Christmas morning, determined to find in himself the strength and the courage to make the move. It would only be for a year, he told himself (the way Andrew told me his forthcoming pilgrimage would only take a year, after which time he will have found where his head's at, he said, and come back, and be ready to settle down and get some good work done). Francesco would send money home to Fiormonte to keep the family alive and well, meanwhile saving money for the return trip and for whatever enterprise the family decided to begin when he came home—for certainly they would be able to choose their own future and their own destiny once he came back to Fiormonte a rich man.

He did not go immediately to Bardoni; he was yet too fearful of making the final commitment. The streets of the town were empty, the sun burning off the early-morning mist. There was the aroma of smoke on the air, smoke coming from the chimney of his house, and from another house farther down the street, where another early riser doubtlessly had gone to the *presepio* in an almost identical kitchen and looked at its empty top three shelves in disappointment. He could see in the distance, growing wild in the hills into which the town was nestled, fields and fields of dry, thorny thistle. Signora Ruggiero was at the village well, drawing water. He passed her and touched his cap in greeting, and said, *"Buon giorno, Signora, Buon Natale,"* and she replied cheerlessly, *"Buon Natale, Francesco,"* and tugged at the rope holding the wooden bucket, and adjusted the black woolen shawl about her shoulders, black dress, black stockings, black hair, eyes so dark they appeared black, total limned blackness against the

21

bright cold hard wintry light. The sun had risen over the hilltops now to stun the unsuspecting streets; it had been gone too long, there had been only damp and dismal grayness for a fortnight. He walked.

His closest friend in the village was a boy his own age named Giuseppe Battatore. Unusually short, even for Fiormonte, chubby if not actually obese (in the dear dead days, at least), Giuseppe had from the time he was three years old been nicknamed with the diminutive Giuseppino, later abbreviated to Pino. He had lost a great deal of weight in the past several years, but he had not grown an inch since he was twelve. Nor had his generally cheerful disposition been changed by the bad times that had befallen the village. Black-haired and brown-eyed (was there anyone in all Fiormonte who was *not* black-haired, brown-eyed, and olive-complexioned?), sporting a mustache he had begun growing at the age of eighteen, but which still looked sparse and patchy though he groomed it and fussed over it like a household pet, Pino had the characteristically bulbous nose of the region (so unlike my grandfather's) and thickish lips with strong horselike teeth stained with tobacco from the guinea stinkers clamped between them day and night (it was my grandfather's contention that Pino went to sleep with a cigar in his mouth), quick grin breaking with such suddenness that it insinuated slyness or craftiness or guile or lecherous intent, all of which characteristics were alien to gentle, soft-spoken Pino Battatore, my grandfather's best friend. I knew Pino when I was a boy. He never spoke a harsh word to me— but then, hardly anyone ever speaks a harsh word to a blind person. That is a fact of life (*my* life, at any rate), and a rather nice one.

My grandfather talked earnestly to Pino that Christmas morning. They walked up the hill some distance from the house of the *padrone*, and sat with the gorse blowing wildly about them in the silver sunshine, and looked northward into the valley where the Ofanto rushed muddily to the sea. The Adriatic at

22

its closest point was only seventy-five kilometers away, and they had both been to Barletta, of course, had even been to Bari, farther down on the eastern coast, and gazed across those waters to where they knew Austria-Hungary and the Ottoman Empire began, but they had no notion of what those lands might be like. (They had seen foreign sailors in Bari once, but the Adriatic truly lacked any decent harbors, and such visits were rare.) Fiormonte was situated almost exactly midway between Naples and Bari, northwest of the arch in the Italian boot, due south of the spur in its heel. It was easier to get to Naples than to Bari because the roads were better, but the city itself cost more to visit, and besides, they always felt like farmers (which they were) when they got there. They talked now not of Canosa, the nearest town of any size, nor of Barletta on the coast, nor of the towns between there and Bari, nor even of the city of Naples, which was the largest city they had ever seen and certainly the most splendid. They talked of America. They talked of New York. Stultifyingly ignorant—neither of them could read or write their own language, but then again neither could ninety percent of the Italians in the south—blissfully naïve, desperately hungry, soaringly optimistic, they talked of undertaking a month-long voyage that would begin in a horse-drawn cart in Fiormonte, take them west to the bustling port of Naples, where they would board a ship that would steam out into the Mediterranean (and here their limited knowledge of the world's geography ended), through the Strait of Gibraltar, into the Atlantic, and across three thousand miles of ocean to a land more alien than any they might have imagined in their most fantastic dreams. The truth is they'd have been hopelessly lost even in Rome, only three hundred kilometers to the northwest, where the language would have fallen harshly on their ears, the food would have been too pallid for their coarser southern taste, the customs, the regional dress, the manners, and the mores all strange and frightening.

23

In less than an hour, they decided to go to America together and seek their fortunes.

It remained only to discuss financial arrangements with Pietro Bardoni.

❖

For my grandfather, America in the year 1901 was a hole in the ground and a room in a tenement flat. The hole was to become New York's subway system. The room was rented to him by an Italian family that had arrived five years earlier. My grandfather worked twelve hours a day, six and sometimes seven days a week. He left for work at five in the morning, and did not return to the building on 117th Street till seven at night. During those long winter months when he was learning the city and struggling with the language, and trying to make friends among the Italians already there, he rarely saw the sun. The room he rented was part of a cold-water flat, the last room in the railroad layout, its single window opening on an air shaft. There was a huge coal stove in the kitchen, but Luisa Agnelli did not bank its fires until she awakened at seven, long after my grandfather had left for work, at which time she would begin preparing her husband's breakfast. Her husband was a bull of a man who had grown olives near Taormina, and who now owned the ice station on 120th Street and First Avenue. His name was Giovanni, and he suspected that my grandfather was trying to make time with his squat and ugly wife, even though she was constantly chaperoned by three squalling brats who slept in the room next to my grandfather's, two of whom took delight in urinating into his shoes if he made the mistake of leaving them on the floor instead of sleeping with them under his pillow.

The neighborhood into which my grandfather moved was a ghetto in every sense of the word, though he never referred to it as such. To him it was *la vicinanza*, the neighborhood, nine blocks

24

long and four blocks wide, unless one chose to include the short stretch of Pleasant Avenue, a decrepit slum today, but aptly and justly named for 1901, a wide, tree-lined esplanade with a commanding view of the East River. *La vicinanza* ran from 116th Street on the south to 125th Street on the north, and was bounded on the east by the river and on the west by Lexington Avenue. Beyond Lex were the Negroes; Francesco quickly learned to call them "niggers," as part of the naturalization process, no doubt. The blacks were not to begin their own mass immigration northward till 1920, and in the following decade the population of Harlem (*their* Harlem) would rise by 115 percent. But they were there in 1901, too, and already they were niggers to someone who himself wasn't even a second-class citizen but merely an alien with a work visa.

The ghetto was not too terribly strange to Francesco. The language he heard there day and night was the same Italian spoken by the peasants in Fiormonte and the urban dwellers of Naples; the food he ate was the same food he had eaten when times were good in Fiormonte, the area crammed to bursting with grocery stores selling pasta and cheeses and salamis and fresh olive oil; chicken on the leg to be had at the market on Pleasant Avenue, seven cents a pound, claws tied together, bird hung upside down on the white-tiled wall, throat slit, white feathered wings flapping and splattering blood, cleaned and plucked by the poultry man; fresh pork sausage from the *salumeria* on 118th and First, ten cents a pound; *cannoli* and *cassatine* and *sfogliatelle* from the *pasticceria* on the corner of 120th Street—there was much to eat in this golden land (though it was not so golden to Francesco, who worked in the darkness twelve hours a day), and all of it was prepared in the coarse southern Italian style, heavy on the garlic and spices, *"bruta,"* as it was once described to me by a saxophone player in a Roman nightclub. The sounds were familiar, the smells were familiar, even the signs on many of the stores were in Italian, as foreign to him as were the signs in English

25

because he could read or write neither language. Except for the constant noise of the transportation facilities, which seemed to Francesco to express the tempo and the spirit and also the manners of the city—the jangling, rattling streetcars on First Avenue, the metallically clattering elevated trains rushing along ugly steel viaducts on Second and Third Avenues—he might have been living in a neighborhood in Naples.

The ordeal of the January Atlantic crossing was behind him, those terrible sick days in the hold of the ship with Pino cradling his head so that he would not suffocate in his own vomit, the cooking smells of the foreigners, the Russian Jews and Austro-Hungarians already aboard the ship when it steamed into the Bay of Naples, the babbling Spaniards they picked up in Málaga before they passed through the Strait, the handful of Portuguese in Lisbon, blankets hung from sweating steel bulkheads and overhead pipes, the sounds of mandolins and balalaikas, arguments in a dozen tongues, the fistfight between the small dark Spaniard who spit phlegm into every corner of the deck and the huge Russian peasant who would have killed him had not an officer of the ship come below with a billy and knocked the Russian senseless. The stench in steerage was overpowering. The passage was costing him twelve dollars, advanced by Bardoni, but for twelve dollars (sixty-two lire!) a man did not expect to be treated like an animal. At Ellis Island, he was penned according to nationality, examined like a horse or a mule, his mouth, his eyes, his nose, his rectum, heard English for the first time, questions fired in English, and stood with wide bewildered eyes while things were done to him or asked of him, commands accompanied by hand signals, thank God for Bardoni who was waiting for him and Pino when finally they were permitted to leave that terrifying place.

Bardoni had found lodgings for Pino with a bachelor who had been in America for only six months. Francesco was to live with Mr. and Mrs. Agnelli and their three children, in the back room of their apartment, for which he was to pay two dollars and fifty

26

cents a week. He did not know at the time, and Bardoni did not tell him, that a dollar of what he paid was going directly into Bardoni's pocket, or that the total *monthly* rent on the apartment was only seven dollars. Bardoni was a countryman, true, but he was not above collecting his rightful tithe, and Agnelli showed no open aversion to living rent-free at the expense of Francesco Di Lorenzo (who, anyway, was trying to fuck his wife, or so went his rationalization).

Ugly Luisa's only saving graces were a pair of large, purple-nippled breasts, one or the other of which she whipped out of her dress whenever her newborn son gave the slightest sign of needing sustenance or pacification. She was being neither seductive nor exhibitionistic. It was not unusual for the women of the neighborhood to nurse their children on trolley cars, or rocking on the stoops of their buildings, or chatting in their kitchens with cousins or aunts or goombahs or goomahs, junior sucking merrily away while the peaches were dipped in the wine. Luisa watched little Salvatore (for that was the darling's name, Salvatore, the Savior) as though he might explode into the kitchen if she did not stick an enormous boob into his mouth the moment he opened it. With alarming alacrity and frequency, she would slip one hand into the yoke neck of her dress, yank out a breast, and shove its nipple into the little Savior's puckered mouth. Between her infant and her husband, Luisa was kept busy; Giovanni had the habit of coming home from the ice station to compromise his lovely wife at the most unexpected hours, grabbing her from behind, both hands clutching at those prized beauties, her brewer's-horse ass wriggling against him in protest. There seems to have been some question as to who was doing exactly what to whom. Was my grandfather truly trying to get Luisa in the hay (his eyes were weak, but certainly not *that* weak) or was Giovanni trying to entice Francesco into making an open move, which he could then revenge in the Sicilian manner, by cutting off Francesco's balls and his own guilt-ridden, rent-free existence into the bargain?

27

Who knows?

My grandfather resisted all temptations. He was too busy down in the subway. He would refer to the Interborough Rapid Transit in later years as "my subway." Until I was ten years old, I actually believed he *owned* the goddamn thing, and wondered why I was not allowed to ride it without paying a fare. Now that I am forty-eight, I realize it *was* his subway. He built it. Or at least that part of it between the Brooklyn Bridge and Fifty-ninth Street. At the time, he felt no pride in its construction. He was digging a tunnel through the earth with no conception of where that tunnel would eventually lead. Even a mole, as blind as I, has a sense of direction; Francesco had none. He knew that a train would eventually run through this muddy hole, but he had never been farther uptown than 125th Street, nor farther downtown than City Hall Park, where he was dropped into the bowels of Manhattan each morning. West Farms, Bowling Green, Borough Hall, Atlantic Avenue, distant rumored destinations of the underground octopus, were names that meant nothing to him. Francesco blindly poked his shovel and his pick into the dripping earth, fearful that the city's streets would fall in upon him, workman's boots firmly planted in ankle-deep mud, which was at least *something* he knew from the old country. Hearing but only vaguely understanding the words of the Irish foreman, unable to answer him in his own tongue, he was rendered deaf and dumb as well, laboring at a muscle-wrenching job that made no sense except for the weekly pay check of fourteen dollars, more than Bardoni had promised but whittled down to ten dollars a week after repayment of the cost of passage, and Bardoni's commission, and Bardoni's "incidental expenses," never satisfactorily defined. From that remaining ten dollars, Francesco paid two dollars and fifty cents a week to the iceman, sent five dollars home, and kept two-fifty for himself—which was not bad in the year 1901, when a good roast beef dinner with buttered beets and mashed potatoes, chocolate layer cake and coffee cost no more than thirty-five cents.

28

Pino was less fortunate, and at the same time more fortunate. Because of his size, Bardoni felt certain Pino would be turned down for employment on the newly begun subway, and he was right. So he was sent to work in the garment district, where he earned seven dollars less per week than did Francesco, but where he worked aboveground and was able to see New York's spring that April when it broke with a belated delicacy that took his breath away. It was Pino who arranged for their first date with two "American" girls who worked downtown with him on Thirty-fifth and Broadway.

All that suckling in the Agnelli household, all those surprise visits by the clutching iceman must have stoked something of the old Mediterranean fire in Francesco's youthful loins, but what was one to do in a strange land where the only contacts were Italians with virgin daughters, and where the girls he saw on his rare excursions outside the ghetto spoke a language he barely understood? When Pino told him he had arranged the date, Francesco could not believe him.

"But what?" he said. "With two American girls? *Americans?*"

"Yes, Americans," Pino said, and that quick toothy smile flashed conspiratorially. They were both remembering Bardoni's story of the keying in Naples, and anticipating a similar adventure; it was common knowledge that American girls fucked like rabbits.

"And they said yes?" Francesco asked incredulously.

"Yes, of *course* they said yes. Would I be telling you about them if they said no? Saturday night. Eight o'clock. They live together on Twelfth Street."

"Alone?" Francesco asked. He could not believe his ears.

"Alone," Pino affirmed, and nodded. The nod promised galaxies.

"Do they speak Italian?" Francesco asked.

"No. But *we* speak English, *non è vero?*"

They were *not* speaking English on that Harlem rooftop where pigeons fluttered overhead in the April dusk; they never spoke English when they were alone together. They had, however, begun to feel their way around the language since their arrival, if only because they needed it to survive. Only the other day, underground, someone had shouted a command at Francesco, and had he hesitated an instant longer in obeying it, had there been the slightest gap between the shouted English warning and his immediate understanding of it, his head would have been crushed by a falling timber. I can only judge what my grandfather's English was like in 1901 by what it was like in later years, after I arrived on the scene. What it was like was atrocious, even though my grandmother had been born in this country, and probably worked hard trying to teach him. But English to him, before he met Teresa Giamboglio, was only a temporary necessity. He was going back as soon as he'd saved enough money. A year was what he'd promised himself. A year was a long enough time for a man to burrow his way through the stinking earth. A year without the sun was a long enough time.

He and Pino boarded the Second Avenue El at 119th Street, dressed in their Saturday-night finery, feeling very American, and immediately identifiable as greaseballs by every other passenger on the train. It was a beautiful balmy evening, the windows of the train wide open, the signs warning that fine and imprisonment would be the lot of any passenger foolish enough to try expectorating through them. Pino and Francesco sat on the cane seats side by side, each carrying identical corsages they had purchased in the flower shop on Third Avenue, each sitting stiffly in unaccustomed collar and tie, each wearing a straw boater rakishly tilted. Pino kept nervously stroking and patting his sparse mustache. Neither of the two talked very much on that trip downtown. Their heads were filled with images of dainty American underthings, petticoats and corsets, lisle stockings and perfumed silk garters—oh, this was going to be *'na bella chiavata.*

They had planned to take the girls to a restaurant suggested by the bachelor with whom Pino lived, inexpensive, with excellent food and wonderful service, where they were to be sure to ask for a waiter named Arturo, who spoke Italian. They had no plans for after dinner. Motion pictures had not yet burst upon the American scene—that was to happen two years later, with the introduction of *The Great Train Robbery*, an eleven-minute opus that changed the entertainment habits of the world. (I must tell you that I have heard nearly every motion picture ever made. I love the movies, and I have visualized scenes Pauline Kael has never dreamt of in her universe. I once went to the Museum of Modern Art to "see" a silent film because I wanted to imagine the whole damn thing just by listening to the piano underscoring. It was an exhilarating experience, even though the piano player must have studied under my grandfather's Irish foreman.)

Anyway, those two horny young wops had no plans for the evening's entertainment other than to take the ladies to dinner and to bed. The circus was in town, and they might have gone there or to any one of the vaudeville theaters along Broadway, but the boys had a different sort of entertainment in mind, and besides they didn't want the evening to cost too much. They got off the el at Fourteenth Street, and Pino reached into his pocket and took out the slip of paper upon which one of the girls—my grandfather told me her name was Kasha, but that sounds impossible to me—had scribbled the address. More and more of the city's gas lamps were being replaced by electric lights, especially in the downtown areas, and there was a new lamppost on the corner, and they stood under its glow, the Saturday-night city murmuring about them, a cool breeze blowing in off the river to the east, and they scrutinized Kasha's handwriting, and agreed upon what it meant, and walked downtown to Twelfth Street, and then over to Avenue A. The ghetto they entered was not unlike the one from which they had come—except that it was Jewish. (I have often toyed with the idea that Pino and my grandfather walked past the dry-goods store owned and operated by Rebecca's grandfather. The notion is far-fetched. But it persists, even now.)

31

The girls, as it turned out, did not live alone. Had Pino not automatically assumed that anyone who wasn't Italian was automatically American, he might have realized that *no* Jewish girl in the city of New York in the year 1901 lived alone. The girls were cousins. Kasha and Natalia. They had been in America for six months. They lived with Kasha's mother, father, grandfather, two brothers, a police dog who almost caused my grandfather to wet his pants, and a canary (my grandfather assumed it was a canary; the cage was covered for the night). More frightening than the police dog was Kasha's grandfather, a stooped and wrinkled tyrant who had lived through far too many pogroms to enjoy the enemy camp in his own parlor. He kept yelling in Yiddish all the while Pino and Francesco were in the house. Kasha's mother kept trying to calm him down, telling him in her own brand of English that this was America, this was different, they were nice boys, look how nice, see the flowers, what's the matter with you, Papa? In reply, Papa spat twice on the extended forefinger and middle finger of his right hand. Francesco knew a curse when he saw one; not for nothing had he been born in southern Italy. Kasha's father sat silently in a brown stuffed chair and busied himself with his Yiddish newspaper. The police dog was growling, fangs bared. Francesco's knees were shaking. The apartment smelled of the cooking smells in the hold of the ship that had taken him across the Atlantic. In another moment, he was going to be violently ill. Kasha's younger brothers sat anticipating the event with tiny mean smiles on their faces. Her mother saved the day, shooing the girls and their beaux out of the apartment in the nick of time. There was a strange piece of metal screwed to the doorjamb (a mezuzah, of course, though Francesco did not know what it was), and Kasha kissed the tips of her fingers and pressed them to it the moment they stepped into the hallway.

Francesco had decided Kasha would be his girl for the night. He had made this decision without first consulting Pino, and he had done so because he had already abandoned whatever fantasies he may have had of his date being a blond, blue-eyed, narrow-waisted American girl. He was now willing to settle for someone who at least looked Italian. Kasha had black hair, brown eyes, and a chunky figure; he might have been back home in Fiormonte. Pino's girl, Natalia, was tall and skinny, and had a habit of covering her mouth with her hand whenever she laughed, possibly because her teeth were bad. They must have made quite a pair that night, tiny fat Pino (he had regained a lot of weight since his arrival in America) and lanky Natalia with her hazel eyes and light-brown hair, hand flashing up to cover her giggle whenever anyone said anything even remotely comical. I normally despise attempts at recording dialect, possibly because it translates so badly into Braille, and I promise this will be the only time I'll try to capture the sound of immigrant speech. ("You have never kept a promise in your life," Rebecca once said to me.) But it seems to me the conversation among those four budding young Americans on that April night would lose most of its flavor and all its poignancy if it were rendered in any way other than it must have sounded. Bear with me, bear with them; they were trying.

"Whatsa matta you gran'pa?" Francesco asked. "He'sa craze?"

"He's ah *kahker*," Kasha answered, using the Yiddish slang for "old man."

"*Caga?*" Francesco asked, and tried not to laugh. *Caga* was Italian slang for shit.

"*Kahker, kahker,*" Kaska corrected. "He's *ahn alter kahker.*"

Pino, who now realized Kasha was talking about shit, burst out laughing, and then immediately sobered and tried to elevate the conversation to a more dignified plane. "Theesa two boys," he said. "They tweensa?"

"Tweensa?" Kasha asked, puzzled.

"*Gemelli,*" Pino said. "Tweensa. Tweensa, you know?"

"I don't know vot it minns 'tweensa.'"

"Tvintz, I tink is vot," Natalia said, and giggled and covered her mouth.

33

"Oh, *tvintz!* No, they nut no tvintz. The vun has ett, en' dudder has nine."

"I gotta one sist hassa ten," Francesco said. "An' dada one forty."

"Four-*teen*," Pino corrected.

"Sì, *quattordici*. Attsa home. Dada side."

"Vhere is det you from?" Kasha asked.

"Fiormonte. Attsa cloze by Napoli."

"Whatsa *you* home place?" Pino asked Natalia, and she giggled.

In such a manner did they manage to communicate, or to *believe* they were communicating, all evening long. The girls would not go to the restaurant that had been recommended to Pino because it was not kosher. (It suddenly occurs to me that the word "kosher" may have stuck in my grandfather's head, causing him to have recalled incorrectly the name of the girl who was his date. Every time I eat kasha knishes, I think of her. I wonder if she's still alive, I wonder what she'd have thought of Rebecca—my grandfather was wild about Rebecca—and I wonder what her real name was. Yes, but what's your *real* name, Ike?) My grandfather ate blintzes for the first time in his life that night—"Wassa like *cannelloni*, you know, Ignazio?"—and learned all about the *milchedig* and *flayshedig*, though I can't imagine how Kasha could possibly have explained the Jewish dietary laws in her broken tongue, or how he could have understood them with his tin ear. At ten o'clock, they took the girls home.

"Denks," Kasha said. "Ve hed a nize time."

"Denks," Natalia said, and giggled.

"*Buona notte,*" Pino said.

Francesco bowed from the waist, and said, "I'm enjoy verra much."

On Monday morning, in the tunnel he was digging under Manhattan, he almost got killed.

❖

There were four thousand Italians like my grandfather working on the New York subway. For the most part, they replaced the Irish and Polish immigrants, who had arrived years before and who were moving up to better jobs. But some of those earlier immigrants stayed on as laborers, either because they were indifferent to the possibilities of a fuller life in America, or simply because they were unintelligent, lazy, or incompetent. With characteristic territorial possessiveness, though, they resented the Italians coming in to do "their" jobs, suspecting the dagos of working for cheaper wages (which they were not), and fearful they'd eventually replace them entirely. The situation then was not unlike the white-black contretemps today. It always gets down to bread and the size of a man's cock. The Italians were stealing jobs, and were reputed to be great lovers besides. (You couldn't prove that by my grandfather, who was still a virgin at the age of twenty.) The Poles and Irishmen who worked side by side with these smelly wops were fearful, resentful, suspicious, and prejudiced. The wops were clannish, spoke an incomprehensible language, brought strange food to work in their lunchboxes, laughed at private jokes, and even, for Christ's sake, *sang* while they worked! The tunnel itself compounded the volatile nature of the mix.

I have since learned that the building of the New York subways utilized a method known as "cut and cover," meaning that first a trench was dug, and wooden plankings were laid down over it while the men continued to work belowground. But my grandfather's description of the tunnel made it sound like a mine shaft deep in the bowels of the earth (which it most certainly wasn't), and it is his description that lingers in my mind. Despite the facts, then—the subway's deepest point is 180 feet below the surface, at 191st Street, and my grandfather never got that far uptown—I shall describe that hole in the ground as it appeared to him, and as he subsequently described it to me.

The mud was sometimes knee deep, the ceiling of the vault dripping, the shoring timbers in constant creaking danger of collapse, the noise level shattering, jackhammers and drills pounding and stuttering, steel carts rumbling on rickety makeshift tracks, hauling dirt dearly paid for shovelful by shovelful, laborers sweating and coughing and belching and farting, foremen shouting orders in the lamplit gloom, half a dozen different languages and dialects creating a harsher din than that of a thousand picks striking sparks from granite. There were many fistfights, sometimes three and four a day, that might not have occurred had the men been working aboveground in the bright sunshine. But the tunnel was a tight, crowded, restricting place, and a closed crowd is a dangerous crowd because it cannot explode outward and can only turn upon itself.

Francesco was thinking only of home when it happened.

He was thinking that in April the wintry muddy waters of the Ofanto in the valley below rushed clear and sweet with torrents from the mountaintops. The banks rolling gently to the riverside would be covered with buttercups and violets, lavender and . . .

The voice that sounded beside him was intrusive. It brought him back to the dark reality of the tunnel; it made him conscious of the pick handle irritating the fresh blisters on his palms; it drowned the murmur of the river, allowed the reverberating noise of the tunnel to come crashing in again. The voice was Irish. I shall make no attempt (see, Rebecca?) to try for the brogue, or to counterfeit Francesco's labored English. In the end, the men understood each other. On a level more basic than language, they finally understood each other.

"What are you doing there?" the Irishman said.

"I'm working," Francesco answered.

"You know what I'm talking about, you fucking dago. What are you doing there with *my* pick?"

36

"This is not your pick."

He looks at the pick. It is surely his own pick. The handle is stained with mud and sweat, and the water from his blisters, and the blood from his hands. It is his pick. It is not the Irishman's.

"It is my pick."

Actually, the argument is academic. It is neither Francesco's pick *nor* the Irishman's. The pick belongs to the Belmont-McDonald syndicate, the subway's contractors. Each morning the workmen's tools are issued to them, and each night they must be returned. They are not debating actual possession, they are merely attempting to ascertain which of them has the right to work with this tool, this pick, this day. But the pick has not been out of Francesco's hands since seven o'clock this morning, he *knows* it is the one he has been working with all day long. So what is the matter with this Irishman? Is he crazy?

"It's your pick, is it, dummy? And what are those initials then on it?"

He does not understand the word "initials." What is initials? He looks at the handle of the pick again.

"I don't understand."

"No capish, huh, dago? Give me the pick."

Francesco hands the pick to the Irishman unresistingly. He knows there has been some misunderstanding here, and he feels certain it will be cleared up the moment the Irishman can *feel* the pick in his own two hands. He watches as the Irishman carefully examines the handle of the pick, reddish-blond hairs curling on the back of each thick finger, hair running from the knuckles to the wrists, turns the handle over and over again in his hands, searching, eyes squinched, what is he looking for, this man? The eyes are blue. They glance up momentarily from the scrutiny of the pick, look directly into Francesco's eyes, piercingly and accusingly, and then wrinkle in something resembling humorous response, but not quite, the mouth echoing the expression, the lips thinly pulling back, no teeth revealed, a narrow smile of eyes

37

and mouth that strikes sudden terror into Francesco's heart. He knows now that there will be trouble. The man is twice his size. He contemplates kicking him in the groin immediately, here and now, this instant, strike first and at once—before it is too late.

The Irishman is taking a knife from his pocket.

The lamps flicker on the steel blade as he pulls it with his fingernails from the narrow trench in the bone handle. The blade is perhaps four inches long, honed razor sharp, glittering with pinprick points of reflected light. Francesco is certain the Irishman intends to stab him, but he does not know why. Is it because of "initials"? Unconsciously, he backs against the wall of the tunnel. Muddy water drips from above onto his head and shoulders. He feels naked. He feels the way he felt at Ellis Island when the doctor poked his finger into his rectum, rubber glove slippery with jelly. He is very afraid he will soil himself. The Irishman squats on his haunches, laying the pick across his knees, tilting the handle toward the light. With the blade of the knife, he scrapes an area free of caked mud, up near the head of the handle, where the curved metal bar is fitted snugly onto it. Then, slowly and deliberately, he begins digging into the wood with the tip of the knife. Francesco cannot yet fathom what he is doing. His fear has dissipated somewhat, he is beginning to realize he was wrong about the Irishman's intent; he does not plan to cut him. But what is he doing to the handle of the pick?

And then Francesco understands. The man has carved a letter into the wood, the letter P, and after this he gouges out a small dot, a period, and then begins to carve the letter H, meticulously digging out each vertical bar, and then the crossbar, and then uses the point of the knife to gouge out another period. Rising, standing erect again, he closes the knife and puts it back into his pocket. Then he brings the pick close to his mouth and blows into the carved letters, sending fine minuscule splinters flying, and then passes his hand over the letters caressingly, and looks at Francesco, and grins.

38

"P.H. Patrick Halloran. *My* name, *my* initials, and *my* damn pick."

The Irishman continues to grin. Is there some humor here that Francesco is missing because of his scant understanding of English? There are so many words in English which sound the same, but mean different things. Is "pick" one of those words, and has he missed the entire thrust of the conversation from the very beginning? But no. "Dago" he understands, and "fucking" he understands, and yet he has heard these men jokingly calling themselves big fucking micks, which he knows is derogatory, so perhaps fucking dago was meant in the same way, perhaps a joke was intended, after all; perhaps the man was only being friendly, is that a possibility? He misses so many nuances because he does not understand; the subtleties of this land are overwhelming. But if it was all a joke, if the man is smiling now because a joke was intended, then why did he put his mark on a pick belonging to the company? Francesco knows it is the man's mark, he knows he is not mistaken about that because now that he has seen the letters gouged into the wood, the word "initials" makes sense to him, it is almost identical to the Italian word *iniziali*. Is it possible the man was only trying to introduce himself? Trying to tell Francesco his name? Carving his initials into the wood handle to facilitate communication? This appears ridiculous to Francesco, but so many things in this new country seem foolish to him. Would the man have damaged a pick belonging to the company merely to have his name be known? Does he not know the company rules? Does he not realize . . . and here a new fear seizes Francesco. This is the pick that was assigned to him this morning. A workman was responsible for his own tools, and had to pay for any damage done to them through his own negligence. Would he now have to pay for the damage this man has done to the pick handle by carving his initials into it?

"You have damaged my pick," he says. They are back again to

the question of possession, though now Francesco is not so sure he wishes to claim this damaged pick.

"I shouldn't worry about it," the man says.

"It is the pick I used all morning. The company will . . ."

"No, my friend, you're mistaken. *I've* been using his pick all morning. *You* were using the one over there."

Francesco follows the man's casual head gesture, squints into the gloom, and suddenly understands. A pick with a broken handle is lying half-submerged in the mud. The man's pick, broken in use. By claiming Francesco's pick, he is simultaneously willing to him the pick with the broken handle, so that the cost of replacing it will come from *Francesco's* pay check and not his own.

"No," Francesco says.

"No, is it? Ah, but yes. *This* one is mine, and *that* one is . . ."

He leaps upon the man before he realizes what he is doing. He has not been angry until this moment, but now a fury boils within him, and he gives no thought to the consequences of his sudden action. He knows only that the man is stealing from him, and by extension stealing from the family in Fiormonte. He seizes the handle of the pick, tries to wrest it away, but the man merely swings it around, with Francesco still clinging to it, pulling Francesco off his feet and dragging him sprawling into the mud, his eyeglasses falling from his face.

"*Ladro!*" Francesco screams in Italian. "Thief!" And gets blindly to his feet. And springs for the man's throat. The first scream goes unnoticed in the general din, but he continues to shriek "*Ladro! Ladro! Ladro!*" as his mud-covered hands struggle for a grip around the other man's throat. The man hits Francesco in the chest with the end of the pick handle, knocking him down again. The screams have finally attracted the other workers, most of them Italians who understand the meaning of the word that comes piercingly from Francesco's mouth in strident repetition: "*Ladro! Ladro! Ladro!*" He gets to his feet again, and again charges the other man. The man throws the pick aside, bunches his fists, and

40

begins to beat Francesco senseless, methodically breaking first his nose and then his jaw, pounding at both eyes until the lids are swollen and bleeding, splitting his lips, knocking out four of his teeth, and then kicking him repeatedly in the chest after he has fallen unconscious into the mud. The other men do nothing. It is the foreman who at last comes over, and says, gently, "Come on, Pat, there's no sense killing the little wop, now is there?"

My grandfather paid dearly for his encounter with Pat Halloran, and to his dying day he was to hate the Irish with undiminished passion. The broken pick handle cost him a dollar and a half, which was deducted from his weekly pay check. His hospital bill —they taped his broken ribs, applied poultices to his eyes, set and taped his broken nose, and took three stitches in his upper lip—came to twenty-four dollars and thirty-eight cents. The dentist who made his bridgework and supplied him with four false teeth charged him seventeen dollars. He lost two weeks' work at fourteen dollars a week, and did not return to the tunnel until the beginning of May. To honor his debts, he was forced to borrow money from Bardoni (at interest, of course), and it was Bardoni who suggested that there were men in Harlem who would be happy to take care of Halloran for a slight fee. My grandfather said he wished to have nothing to do with such men; he would take care of Halloran himself, in his own good time.

He did, finally, in the month of June—in a way that was entirely satisfactory and supremely ironic.

But before that, Pino Battatore fell in love.

❖

I don't wish to create the impression that nothing else was happening in America during that May of 1901. But according to my grandfather, at least, Pino's love affair with the neighborhood's undisputed beauty was far more fascinating to that band of wops in Harlem's side streets than were the politics, or economics, or quaint folkways and customs of a nation they did not consider their own. The Spanish-American War, for example, had not been their war, and the subsequent Filipino uprising against our military government, a struggle that had been raging for two years by the time my grandfather arrived at Ellis Island, was of little if any interest to them. Their letters home concerned the basic necessities of life, and not the trappings of power. They were not impressed with America's good and noble reason for declaring war against Spain (To Free Cuba from the Foreign Oppressor), nor did they understand the subsequent insurrection in the Philippines. (They did not even know where the Philippines *were!*)

Even those Italians who had been here before the war with Spain started were incapable of reading the English-language newspapers and had no idea that William Randolph Hearst and Joseph Pulitzer (who, like me, was blind—though *his* blackout didn't commence till 1889, when he was forty-two years old) had virtually started the war in tandem by publishing in their competing newspapers atrocity stories about the Spaniards' cruel colonial rule. Americans (but not immigrants) had told themselves, and eventually came to believe, that the United States was genuinely concerned over the fate and destiny of all those sweaty cane cutters and raggedy-assed fishermen somewhere down there off the coast of Florida. So the war with Spain began, and we threw millions and millions of dollars into it (three *hundred* million of them), not to mention more than five thousand young lives, and Hearst and Pulitzer sold lots of newspapers, and the ginzoes in East Harlem went right on eating their pasta and sending their money home. Eventually, we won the war. We always win our wars, even when we lose them. And finally, we managed to put down the insurrection as well, when Brigadier General Frederick Funston boldly raided Aguinaldo's camp and captured him in March—just before my grandfather had his teeth knocked out by Mr. Halloran of the disputed pick. Aguinaldo took an oath of loyalty to these here United States, and announced to his followers that the uprising was over. Another brilliant triumph for America, and Pino Battatore couldn't have cared less. Pino was in love. While near-hysterical praise rang out for Funston in the streets of New York, Pino's own rhapsodic paeans were reserved solely for one Angelina Trachetti, whom my grandfather in later years described as *"la bellezza delle bellezze,"* the beauty of beauties.

Angelina was five feet four inches tall, with jet-black hair and brown eyes, and a narrow waist and large, firm breasts—*"una bella figura,"* my grandfather said. She was nineteen years old, and had come with her parents from the Abruzzi two years earlier. Her working knowledge of English was good, and she was blessed with a wonderful sense of humor (somewhat ribald at times, according to Grandpa) and a fine culinary hand. She had been sought after by countless young Italians of heroic stature and discriminating eye, and the miracle of it all was that she had chosen Pino. There was but one thing that could be said against her, and this was the cause of the only argument my grandfather ever had with Pino: she did not wish to return to Italy.

"What do you mean?" Francesco asked. "She wants to stay *here?*"

They were strolling along Pleasant Avenue on a mild May evening, the sounds of the ghetto everywhere around them, so much like Fiormonte; even the East River reminded Francesco of the river back home, the memory jostled only by the incessant hooting of the tugboats. The Ofanto now would be swelled with spring floods, the valley would be lush and verdant. . . .

"*Here?* In America?"

"Yes," Pino said.

"You won't take her home to Italy?"

"No."

"To Fiormonte?"

"No."

"You'll stay here?"

"Yes."

"I don't understand," Francesco said.

He understood, all right. He didn't understand it on the deeper psychological level, the breakdown of the adolescent gang and all that Freudian jazz, but he understood it in exactly the same way that I did, years later, when my brother Tony wouldn't let me hear his record collection, and I considered him a traitor and a deserter and a ratfink bastard. Only the costumes and the geography and the languages change—the rest is eternally the same. They were both wearing striped shirts, those young men who had known each other from birth, the high-throated necks open and lacking the usual celluloid collars, the sleeves rolled up, braces showing under their vests and holding up their black trousers. They stomped along Pleasant Avenue with the gait of peasants, which they were, and my grandfather tried to control his anger at Pino's defection, while Pino tried to explain his deep and abiding love for Angelina—but no, my grandfather would have none of it, the betrayal was twofold: to friend *and* to country.

I have heard my grandfather in towering rages, especially when he was railing against his first-born son, my Uncle Luke, who invariably lost his own hereditary temper during poker games. I do not believe he was shouting at Pino that night. I think his voice must have been very low, injured, perhaps a trifle petulant. The song he hummed forlornly was "Wedding Bells Are Breaking Up That Old Gang of Mine," a lousy tune for a jazz solo, the essentially white chart starting with B-flat major and going to E-flat major, and a bit anachronistic for May of 1901, perhaps, when one considers that it was not published till 1929—but Grandpa was always just a bit ahead of the times. He was a little bit ahead of Pino just then, anger having fired his stride so that he was four paces in front of his friend before he realized he was carrying on a solitary monologue. He stopped dead on the sidewalk and turned to Pino and summed it all up, summed up the whole fucking adolescent severance of boyhood ties, maybe even summed

44

up the entire human condition in three short words: "What about me?"

"You?" Pino said. "But what does this have to do with *you*, Francesco?"

"You said we'd go back to Italy together, you said we'd go back rich, we'd take care of our families. . . ."

"But my family will be *here*," Pino said with dignity.

"And what about your family *there*?"

"I'll continue to send them money."

"Ah, Pino," my grandfather said, and sighed, and looked out over the river. A solitary silent tug was moving slowly downstream. He kept his eyes on the boat. He did not want to look again at Pino, not that night, for fear that he would burst into tears and reveal that his dreams of twinship had been shattered. Those daring explorers who had sailed three thousand miles across the Atlantic in search of treasure would *not* return *due a due* to the homeland, would not relate their adventures together, one interrupting the other in his excitement, words overlapping, augmenting and expanding upon each story the other told, the townspeople at their feet, mouths agape, as Pino and Francesco exhibited riches beyond imagination—Pino and Francesco, the Weber and Fields of Fiormonte. Now it would be Francesco alone.

In the neighborhood, opinion held the match to be ill-fated. To begin with, Pino was an ugly runt and Angelina was a beauty. But more important than that, no one had any real faith in this American concept of romantic love. In Italy, a man did not choose his own bride; she was chosen for him. Picking one's own wife was considered revolutionary, and don't think poor Angelina didn't get a lot of static about it from her father, who preferred that she marry the proprietor of the *latteria* on First Avenue and 120th—a man who, like himself, was from the Abruzzi. Her father finally acquiesced, perhaps because she was a strong-willed girl who argued with him in English, rather than Italian, thereby frustrating his ability to counterattack effectively. But even though

45

the American concept of *amore* was at last grudgingly accepted, Pino and Angelina were never left alone together. They were always shadowed by an *"accompagnatrice,"* usually one of Angelina's aunts or older cousins, or, on some occasions, her god-mother, a fearsome lady of substantial bosom and sharp eye, who was known to have shouted across First Avenue, *"Pino, non toccare!"* when Pino in all innocence tried to remove a coal cinder from Angelina's eye, the strident "Don't touch!" being the equivalent in those days of a bellowed "Rape!" Given Beauty and the Beast, then, given too this stupid unworkable foreign idea about "falling in love" (ridiculed by Papa Trachetti, but subtly supported by Mama, who kind of liked the notion), and given the strict supervision of a gaggle of fat ladies watching every move and censoring so much as a covert glance—how *could* this thing succeed?

Francesco, along with the rest of the neighborhood, hoped that it would not. Eventually, Pino would come to his senses and realize that this girl who did not wish to return to Italy was certainly not the girl for him. In the meantime, Francesco plotted his revenge against Halloran. While Pino and Angelina talked of whom they would invite to the wedding and the reception, Francesco plotted his revenge. While Pino and Angelina talked of what furniture they would need, and where they would buy it, and where they would live, and how many children they would have, Francesco plotted his revenge. His furtive scheming may have been a form of displacement, a way of venting all the frustration, anger, and disappointment he could not express to Pino. Who the hell knows? I'm a blind man. I can only visualize that morning of June the twelfth as my grandfather gleefully described it to me many years later.

It is raining.

It has been raining for twelve days and twelve nights; this June of 1901 will go down in the records as one of the wettest in the history of New York. The tunnel in which the men work is a veritable quagmire, but to Francesco it is resplendent with the sweet sunshine of revenge. He has planned carefully. In his native Italy, he could neither read nor write, but he has been diligently practicing English ever since his encounter with Halloran; or to be more exact, he has been laboriously tracing and retracing two letters of the alphabet—P and H.

He has rejected Bardoni's idea of hiring two Harlem hoods to bash in Halloran's skull, but he is not so foolhardy as to believe that he can handle Halloran by himself. The turn-of-the-century equivalent of Charles Atlas as a ninety-seven-pound weakling who got sand kicked in his face throughout all the days of my boyhood, my grandfather is no match (and he knows it) for a brute like Halloran. What is needed to defeat him is another brute, a similar brute, perhaps an identical brute. Francesco has carefully studied his fellow workers in the subway tunnel (while nightly pursuing his handwriting exercises at home—P and H, P and H) and has decided that the only true match for Patrick Halloran is a total clod of an Irish mick named Sean McDonnell. (Spare me your letters, offended Irishmen of the world; to a blind man you're all the same—wops, spics, kikes, micks, polacks, niggers; when you've not seen one slum you've not seen them all. And in any case, I am American to the core, a product of this great democratic nation. And that's what this whole fucking thing is *about*.)

McDonnell is a beast of burden. He is six feet four inches tall, and he weighs two hundred and fifty pounds. He speaks English with such a thick brogue that even his own countrymen can barely understand him. He is fifty-two years old, partially balding, with tiny black pig's eyes beneath a lowering brow, a bulbous nose he clears by seizing it between the thumb and forefinger of his right hand, holding the calloused palm away as daintily as though he is lifting a demitasse, and then snorting snot into the mud. He has a huge beer-barrel belly as hard as concrete, and is often daring the other men to punch him as hard as they can in the gut. He laughs

47

a great deal, but seemingly without humor, the laughter unprovoked by incident or event; he finds life either terribly comical or utterly mystifying. Because he is so stupid, he often cannot tell the difference between a well-intentioned compliment and an insult, and is quick to answer any supposed affront with his fists. He is a perfect foil for Francesco's plot.

The lunch hour comes at twelve noon. The foreman blows his whistle into the tunnel, and the men drop their picks, grab for their lunch pails, and begin to disperse. Even when the weather is good, they drift from their work areas to eat in other parts of the tunnel, the theory being that a change is as good as a rest. But this week in particular, when the mud is everywhere underfoot, they search out niches in the rock walls, higher stretches of ground, overturned wheelbarrows, the insides of carts, anything upon which they can spread their sandwiches and coffee safe from the slime. Francesco waits until all the men have wandered off, and then he moves swiftly to where McDonnell has dropped his pick —he has been watching McDonnell all morning, and knows exactly which pick is his. He lifts it from the mud, wipes the handle clean with the sleeve of his shirt, and takes a penknife from his pocket. Quickly, he carves the initials P.H. into the handle, and then drops the pick back into the mud. The explosion comes shortly after lunch.

"What's this?" McDonnell says.

Francesco, working some distance away, continues chopping at the solid rock wall of the tunnel. There is a sense of rising excitement in him, coupled with an uneasy foreboding. Suppose this backfires? But no, it cannot.

"What in holy bloody hell is *this?*" McDonnell bellows.

There is not a man in the tunnel who does not know of Francesco's run-in with Halloran two months back. With great relish they tell and retell the story of how Halloran carved his initials into the little wop's pick handle and then traded his own broken pick for the undamaged one. McDonnell is a notch above a moron, but he has heard the story, too, and what he sees staring up at him now from the handle of his pick are the initials P.H.

"Where's Halloran?" he shouts.

He does not ask Halloran for an explanation; he never asks anyone for an explanation. He knows only that Halloran has equated him with the puny wop and is trying to pull the same trick a second time. Francesco watches as McDonnell seizes Halloran by the throat and batters his head against the rock wall of the tunnel. He watches as McDonnell, one hand still clutched around Halloran's throat, repeatedly punches him in the face, closing both his eyes and breaking his jaw and splintering his teeth. He watches as McDonnell picks up the other man effortlessly, holds him over his head for an instant, and then hurls him some ten feet through the air to collide with the opposite wall of the tunnel. Then he watches as McDonnell takes the pick with its P.H. initials, breaks the handle over his knee, and drops the halves on Halloran's bloodied chest.

"It wan't comical," he says to Halloran, but Halloran does not hear him. Halloran is unconscious and bleeding and broken, and will in fact be taken to the hospital, not to report back to work till the middle of August, by which time Francesco will have left the subway-building business for good. In the meantime, he looks at Halloran lying in the mud, and he watches as the men begin to gather around him, and there is a tight grim smile on his mouth; he is from the south of Italy, and revenge is nowhere sweeter.

A conversation between my brother Tony and me, many years later. Tony is seventeen, I am fifteen. We are sitting on the front stoop of our house in the Bronx. Ten minutes earlier, I'd made casual reference to our grandfather's tale of revenge, which we'd both heard many times. Tony suddenly expresses a skepticism I can only link with his present anger at Grandpa. Tony wants to join the Air Corps; Grandpa has asked, "Why? So you can go bomb Italy?" But Grandpa has prevailed, and my mother has refused to sign the permission papers for enlistment. Tony blames

Grandpa for this, and now refuses to believe a story he has accepted as gospel since he was five.

TONY: It just doesn't ring true, Iggie, that's all.
ME: Grandpa swears it happened.
TONY: Why didn't McDonnell suspect that maybe *Grandpa* was the one who'd carved those initials into his pick?
ME: Because he was dumb.
TONY: He was smart enough to remember the story about Grandpa and Houlihan, and to . . .
ME: Halloran.
TONY: Halloran. He made *that* connection, didn't he?
ME: Come on, Tony, a caterpillar could've made *that* connection. The man's initials were carved into the pick! P.H. So McDonnell automatically . . .
TONY: . . . automatically went after Halloran and beat him senseless.
ME: Right.
TONY: I don't believe it.
ME: Well, I do.
TONY: What if I told you that June of 1901 was the sunniest June in the history of New York City?
ME: Grandpa says it rained for twelve days and twelve nights. It went into the records, he says.
TONY: Have you checked the records?
ME: No, but . . .
TONY: Then how do you know Grandpa wasn't lying?
ME: He never lies, you know that. Anyway, what's the rain got to do with the story?
TONY: I'm only trying to show you that if *part* of the story is a lie, maybe *all* of it is a lie.
ME: It sounds like the truth. That's good enough for me.

Which, in a way, is exactly how I feel about this narrative. If it *sounds* like the truth, that's good enough for me. *You* go check the records. I'm too busy, and I'm too blind. I haven't the faintest inkling whether June of 1901 was the wettest June on record or the sunniest. When you find out, let me know—though frankly, I don't give a damn. If you're willing to compromise, I'll say it was the *cloudiest* June on record, how's that? The floor of the subway tunnel was covered with *mist*, okay? The Spanish-American War took place in 1794, Pope John was a Protestant, we got out of Vietnam with honor, astronauts are lyric poets, and my mother is a whore. Who cares? The truth I'm trying to deliver has nothing to do with careful research meticulously sandwiched into a work of fiction to give it verisimilitude or clinical verity. The *only* truth I'm trying to convey is this: it's a lie. It's all a lie. *All* of it.

That's the tragedy.

❖

In contrast to the miserably wet June that year, the beginning of July was sunny and hot. The Fourth fell on a Thursday. Today, this would mean a four-day weekend, but in 1901, when men were working a six-day week, Independence Day was only a one-day respite from the almost daily grind. Francesco had been in America for the celebration of Lincoln's and Washington's birthdays (which meant nothing to him) and for Easter (which he had spent in the hospital recuperating from Halloran's attack). The Fourth was special to him only in that it promised widespread celebrations on the order of *La Festa di San Maurizio* in Fiormonte.

One of those celebrations was sponsored by the local Republican Club, and was announced in the newspapers (including *Il Progresso*, the Italian-language newspaper read by all literate Italians in the ghetto) as:

REPUBLICAN CLUB
GALA FOURTH OF JULY PICNIC
** FREE * FREE * FREE * FREE **
BEER   SANDWICHES   ICE CREAM
MUSIC   FIREWORKS
Jefferson Park—Noon to Dusk

Francesco awakened on the morning of the glorious Fourth to the sounds of the Agnelli children arguing in the room next door. He quickly checked under his pillow to make sure his shoes had not been spirited away and pissed into, and then glanced sleepily at the clock on the chair beside his bed. This was to be the most important day of his life, but he did not yet know it, nor would he come to know it for a long, long while.

I must get out, he thought, *I must go back*. He thought that every morning and every night, and yet he continued to work on the subway, and he continued to return to this dreary room in the apartment of the iceman and his family. There seemed little reason for Francesco to remain in America. He was more heavily in debt now than he had been on the day he'd arrived, and seriously doubted that he could ever repay all the money Bardoni had advanced to him. The weekly bite on his pay check had drastically reduced the amount of money he could send home to Fiormonte each week. He was weary most of the time; his bones ached from the labor he performed, his mind reeled from the babble of sound assaulting him most of his waking day. And now that Pino had defected, now that Pino had announced his intention to marry Angelina Trachetti and stay here in this barbaric land, where was there any sense in persisting? Was a man to be governed by his stomach alone? He would go back to Italy, he would return home. But each time he thought of returning, he was faced with new and seemingly insurmountable problems: where would he get the money for the return passage? Bardoni again? And how would the family survive in Fiormonte (where conditions were even worse now) if he returned? Whatever pittance he sent them from America was more than he could earn at home. Ah, *miseria*, he thought, and got out of bed, and put on his pants and his shirt.

The oldest of the Agnelli children, who had been picking up English in the streets, said, "Hello, cocksucker," as Francesco went through the room with his shoes under his arm. The door at the end of that room led to the bedroom of the *paterfamilias* and his wife, Luisa. Francesco eased the door open gently. The iceman had already gone to work, no rest for the weary on this Fourth of July, with picnics and celebrations all over the *vicinanza*. Luisa was alone in the bedroom, asleep in the double bed, one arm curled behind her head, hairy armpit showing. The sheet was tangled around her ankles; her purple-tipped boobs and dense black crotch were fully exposed. For a wild and frightening moment, Francesco considered hopping into the rumpled bed with her, as the iceman had feared he would do all along. The room stank of sweat and semen and cunt; Giovanni had undoubtedly enjoyed *'na bella chiavata* before heading out to cool the beer and soda pop of half the neighborhood. Francesco stood at the foot of the bed and silently contemplated Luisa's breasts and crotch. She turned in her sleep, thighs opening to reveal a secret pink slit that seemed to wink lasciviously. Is she awake? he suddenly wondered. Is she flashing her pussy in invitation? And was surprised to discover he had an erection. He hurried out of the room. If Luisa was beginning to look good to him, it was most certainly time to go back to Italy. But how? *Ah, miseria,* he thought again, and went into the kitchen, and sat on the floor, and put on his shoes.

The kitchen was hung with the iceman's blue work shirts, drying on a clothesline stretching from the wall behind the wood stove to the wall across the room, behind the washtub. It was in this tub that the family washed their clothes and also themselves, though not with the same frequency. A makeshift wooden cabinet had been constructed around the tub, serving as a countertop for scrub brushes and yellow laundry soap, drinking glasses, a blue enamel basin speckled with white. There were no toothbrushes; neither the Agnelli family nor Francesco had ever learned about brushing their teeth. A single brass faucet poured cold water into the tub, the plumbing exposed and bracketed to the wall. Wired to the cold-water pipe was a small mirror with a white wooden frame. A gas jet on the wall near the tub, one of four in the room, provided artificial illumination when it was needed. It was not needed on this bright July morning; sunshine was streaming through the two curtainless windows that opened on the backyard of the tenement. (I know every inch of that apartment. When I was growing up in Harlem, twenty-five years later, my grandfather lived in a similar railroad flat. Except for the by-then defunct gas fixtures, it had not changed a hell of a lot.) Francesco went out into the hallway to the toilet tucked between the two apartments on the floor, and shared by the Agnelli family and the people next door. Because of his erection, he urinated partially on the wall, partially on the toilet seat, partially on the floor, and then carefully wiped up wall, seat, and floor with a page of *Il Progresso*, which he ripped from a nail on the door. He pulled the chain on the flush box suspended above the toilet, stared emptily and gloomily into the bowl for several seconds, his hand still on the chain pull, and then went back into the Agnelli kitchen.

Luisa was at the tub. She was wearing only a petticoat and washing her armpits with the bar of yellow laundry soap. Their conversation was entirely in Italian.

"Giovanni's gone to work," she said.

"Yes, I know."

"Ah? How did you know?"

"I passed through your room."

"Ah," she said. "Of course. And you noticed." She glanced sidelong at Francesco, and then took a towel from a wooden rod nailed to the cabinet door. Studiously drying her armpits, she said, "I'm sending the children to my sister's. She'll feed them breakfast."

"Why?" Francesco asked.

"It's a holiday," Luisa replied, and shrugged.

"Then I'll go to Pino's," Francesco said. "He'll give me breakfast there." He paused. "So you can be free to enjoy the morning."

"I'll make breakfast for you," she said.

"Thank you, but . . ."

"I'll make breakfast."

The two oldest Agnelli children burst into the kitchen, fully dressed and anxious to start for their aunt's house, just down the block. Luisa gave the children a folded slip of paper upon which she'd scribbled a message to her sister, and kissed them both hastily. The oldest boy grinned at Francesco and said, "Good-bye, cocksucker." In the other room, the baby began crying.

"He wants to be fed," Luisa said, and again glanced sidelong at Francesco as she shooed the children out of the apartment. Francesco listened to them clattering noisily down the steps to the street. "Good," Luisa said. "Now we'll have some peace." She smiled at Francesco, and went to fetch the baby.

Francesco stood near the door to the apartment. Was he really about to be seduced by this pig of a woman? Was this how he was to lose his virginity? The stirring in his groin was insistent. In another moment, he would be wearing his second flagpole of the morning. And in another moment, if he was not mistaken, Luisa would carry young Salvatore into the kitchen, where she would bare her breast to his ferociously demanding mouth. Given his own appetite of the moment, Francesco doubted he could resist shoving the tiny savior away from that bursting purple nipple and usurping the little nipper's rightful place at the breakfast table. He argued with his hard-on, and made a wise decision.

He left the apartment and went to see Pino.

"My fellow Italian-Americans," the man on the bandstand was saying, "it gives me great pleasure to be able to address you on this Independence Day in this great land of ours. Do not make any mistake about it. For whereas many of you have been on these shores for just a little while, it *is* a great land, and it is *our* land, yours and mine."

The man was talking in Italian, and so Francesco understood every word. *Your* land, he thought. Not mine. *My* land is on the banks of the Ofanto. *My* land is Italy.

The bandstand was hung with red, white, and blue bunting. The man was wearing a straw boater and a walrus mustache, candy-striped shirt open at the throat, celluloid collar loosened, cuffs rolled back. The band behind him consisted of five pieces— piano, drums, trumpet, accordion, and alto saxophone. The musicians were wearing red uniforms with blue piping, white caps with blue patent leather peaks. On the face of the bass drum the words THE SAM RYAN BAND were lettered in a semicircle. The sky behind the bandstand was as blue as my own blind eyes, streaked with wisps of cataract clouds that drifted out over the East River, vanishing as they went. The trees were in full leaf, a more resound-ing green than that of the emerald-bright lawn upon which the picnic guests were assembled before the bandstand. They were, these ghetto dwellers, dressed in their Sunday-go-to-meetin' clothes because this was a celebration, and in their homeland a celebration was a *festa*, and a *festa* was by definition religious, and you dressed up for God unless you wished him to smite you from the sky with his fist, or to spit into the milk of your mother's obscenity. (How's that, Papa?)

The clothing exhibited on that lawn was a patchwork fancy of style and color, old-world garb mixing with new, yellows and pinks and oranges and whites in silk and organdy and cotton and linen, long dresses fanned out upon blankets in turn spread upon the grass, women holding parasols aloft to keep the sun off their delicate olive complexions, men fanning themselves with straw skimmers and mopping their brows with handkerchiefs cut from worn-out shirts, hemstitched, slurping beer foam from their mustaches as the man on the bandstand (an alderman, whatever the hell *that* was) went on and on about the glories of being a part of this wonderful nation called the United States of America, where there was freedom and justice for all, provided you didn't

56

run afoul of an Irishman's pick. After the speech, Sam Ryan and his grand aggravation played a few choruses of "America, the Beautiful" and then (out of deference to the audience, which consisted mostly of guineas from the surrounding side streets of Italian Harlem) played not "My Wild Irish Rose" or "I'll Take You Home Again, Kathleen," but instead played a rousing mick rendition of "'O Sole Mio!" followed by another all-time favorite (in Napoli, maybe) called "Funiculì-Funiculà." Nobody sang along.

The beer barrels had been rolled out long before the alderman began his heart-rending speech about that old Statue of Liberty out there holding the torch of freedom aloft for all those tired, poor, and huddled masses, and everybody had a mug in his hand or tilted to his lips, and many of the picnickers who were not yet accustomed to American beer had had the foresight to bring along some good dago red made in the basements of countless rat-infested tenements. So the ladies and gentlemen tippled an assortment of sauce (no hard liquor anywhere, except behind Sam Ryan's piano, in a pint bottle he swigged after each nerve-tingling number) and ate the sandwiches providently provided by the sponsors of this little outing, ham and cheese, or just plain ham, or just plain cheese on soggy rolls.

In those good old days of nineteen hundred aught one, contrary to today, when Republicans and Democrats alike give fund-raising dinners at a thousand dollars a plate, the vote of the common man was thought quite important, and both parties sought it avidly. Picnics and rallies were organized at the drop of a holiday, with free beer, sandwiches, ice cream, music, fun and frivolity for all, the only political hawking being in the form of buttons passed out for pinning to lapel or bosom, the equivalent of today's bumper stickers. It was understood that none (or at least very few) of these noisy wops were as yet entitled to vote in America since they were not yet citizens and (in many cases) did not *intend* to become citizens. But even Hitler recognized the beauty of

57

getting 'em while they're young, and so the wise politicians of yesteryear handed out their little buttons with the Republican eagle on them (at this particular picnic) or the Democratic star (at a picnic some few blocks away), hoping to begin a painless form of education that would guarantee the casting of the right vote in the near or distant future. A penny saved is a penny earned, and it's a wise man who knows his own father. Francesco took the button handed to him and promptly pinned it to Pino's backside, where it was later discovered by Angelina, who burst into delighted laughter. Her amusement impressed Francesco not one whit. She was the cause of Pino's defection, and Francesco wasn't about to forgive her simply because she had a melodic laugh and beautiful white teeth and sparkling brown eyes, and *Madonna*, maybe he *should* have stayed in Luisa's kitchen and sampled the cuisine!

Someone requested *"La Tarantella,"* which caused Sam Ryan to stare in goggle-eyed bafflement at his saxophone player, who shrugged and turned to the accordionist, an Italian who had been hired especially for this ethnically oriented outing. The accordionist nodded that he knew the tune, and he began playing it while the Irishmen faked along in less than spirited fashion. *"La Tarantella"* is a Neapolitan dance that presumably had its origins in the fitful gyrations of southern Italians "taken" by the tarantula spider. Attempting to expel the poison, the poor souls thus bitten by that hairy beast danced for days on end (or so legend holds), often to the point of complete exhaustion. A nice Italian idiom is *"aver la tarantola"* which literally means "to have the tarantula," but which translates in the vernacular as "to be restless." Those picnickers who got to their feet as the accordionist began *"La Tarantella"* and the sidemen hesitantly joined in really *did* seem to have the tarantula, *did* seem to have a hairy spider in their collective britches as they twisted and turned and rattled and rolled to the amazement of the Irish musicians and the calm acceptance of the accordionist, who kept whipping his dancing

58

fingers over the blacks and whites, and squeezing the bellows against his belly, and dreaming of a time when he was back in Positano dancing this very same *Tarantella* up and down the steps carved into the steep rock walls of what was then a quiet fishing village.

Into the midst of this snake pit on the bright green lawn, into this maelstrom of writhing bodies and sweating faces, there delicately walked an angel sent from heaven, side-stepping the frenzied dancers, a slight smile on her face, walking directly toward (no, it could not be true), walking in a dazzle of white, long white dress, white lace collar, white satin shoes, walking toward (he could not believe it), white teeth and hazel eyes, masses of brown hair tumbling about the oval of her face, she was smiling at (was it possible?), she was extending her hand, she stopped before him, she said in English, "Are you Francesco Di Lorenzo?"

He was sure he'd understood the words, his grasp of English after all these months was surely not so tenuous that he could not hear his own name preceded by only two words in English, he was sure he had understood. But did angels address men who worked in the subway mud? He turned to Angelina for translation. His eyes were filled with panic.

"She wants to know if you are Francesco Di Lorenzo," Angelina said in Italian.

"Sì," he said. "Yes. Sì. Son' io. I are. Yes. Yes!"

"I'm Teresa Giamboglio," she said in English. "Our parents are *compaesani*."

My grandfather had met my grandmother.

❖

I'm not a writer, I don't know any writer's tricks. At the piano, I can modulate from C major to G major in a wink and without missing a beat. But this ain't a piano. How do I modulate from 1901 to 1914 without jostling your eye? I know how to soothe

59

your ear, man, I simply go from C major to A minor to D seventh to G major, and there I am. But thirteen years and four children later? Thirteen years of longing for a tiny Italian village on a mountaintop? (I can only span an *eleventh* comfortably on the keyboard.) Thirteen years. If I play it too slow, you'll fall asleep. If I rush through it, I'll lose you, it'll go by too fast. I once scored a film for a movie producer who told me it didn't matter what the hell anybody put up on the screen because the audience never understood it, anyway. "It goes by too fast for them," he said. There's something to that. You can't turn back the pages of a film to find out what you missed. The image is there only for an instant, and then it's gone, and the next image has replaced it.

He wanted to go back, young Francesco. He was married in December of 1901, and his plan was to take Teresa back home within the year. But in October of 1902, Teresa gave birth to their first daughter, and the voyage home was postponed; you could not take an infant on an ocean trip in steerage, and besides, money was still scarce. My grandfather had quit his job on the subway a month after that fateful Fourth of July picnic, and had begun working as an apprentice tailor to Teresa's father, who owned a shop on First Avenue, between 118th and 119th Streets. When you talk about modulations, try moving gracefully from holding a pick to holding a needle. Teresa's father had studied tailoring in Naples, following a family tradition that had begun with *his* grandfather. He was quite willing to take Francesco into his thriving little establishment—he had, after all, known Francesco's father back in Fiormonte; they were *compaesani*. And besides, Francesco was soon to become his son-in-law, no? Yes. But Francesco, in the beginning at least, was a clumsy, fearful, inartistic, and just plain stupid tailor. Tailor? *What* tailor?

Old Umberto would show him how to trace a pattern onto a bolt of cloth, and Francesco would either break the chalk, or tear the pattern, or trace it onto a tweed instead of a covert— impossible. He was terrified of a pair of scissors; he opened them as though prying apart the jaws of a crocodile. Invariably, his hand slipped and he cut the cloth wrong. But even when his hand was steady, his eye was inaccurate, and one trouser leg would turn out to be longer than the other, a dress would be cut on the bias, a sleeve would not quite make a complete circle around a customer's arm. And his stitches! Very patiently one day (keeping his rage in check, reminding himself that this clumsy oafish dolt of a grape farmer was now married to his youngest daughter, his single most prized possession before she'd been spirited away by this ditch-digging greenhorn), Umberto told Francesco that with stitches such as these, spaced as they were, wildly crisscrossing the cloth as they did, with stitches like yours, Francesco, it would do better for you to pursue a career in the chicken market on Pleasant Avenue, where the task is to divest a bird of its plumage rather than to adorn it, to create a thing of beauty, a garment for a customer of this tailor shop to wear with pride! *Madonna mia*, do you have sausages for fingers? (My daughter could have married a *lawyer*, he thought, but did not say.)

Teresa Giamboglio Di Lorenzo could indeed have married a lawyer. She was some sweet lady, my grandmother. Not as beautiful as Angelina, the pride of the neighborhood and the recent bride of Pino Battatore (who'd married her the month before Francesco tied the knot with Teresa), she was nonetheless strikingly tall for a girl of Neapolitan heritage, and she carried herself with the dignity of a queen. She could silence an argumentative customer in her father's shop with a single hazel-eyed stiletto thrust that might just as easily have stopped a charging tiger. She spoke English fluently, of course, having been born in America, and she was aware that the Italian both her father and her new husband spoke was a bastardized version of the *true* Italian language, the Florentine. Her father had hand-tailored all her clothes from the day she was born, and she was still the most elegantly dressed young lady in the ghetto, coiffing her long chestnut brown hair herself, following the styles prescribed in the fashion magazines she avidly read each month—*Vogue, Delineator, McCall's,* and *The Designer.* She was quick-witted, short-tempered, and sharp-tongued, but I never heard her raise her voice in anger to my grandfather as long as she lived. Whenever she spoke to him, her voice lowered to an intimate, barely audible level; even in the midst of a crowd (and there were some huge crowds around my grandfather's table when I was growing up), one got the feeling that she and Francesco were alone together, oblivious of others, a self-contained, self-sustaining unit. I loved her almost as much as I loved him. And I'm glad she didn't marry a lawyer.

My grandfather once told me, in his scattered tongue, that for the longest time he would look into the mirror each morning and think he was twenty-four. Intellectually, of course, he knew he was no longer twenty-four. But the mirror image looked back at him, and although he was really twenty-five, or twenty-seven, or thirty, he thought of himself as twenty-four. Until suddenly he was *thirty*-four. I don't know why he fixed on twenty-four as the start of his temporary amnesia concerning the aging process. I suspect it was because he already had two children by then, with another on the way, and perhaps he recognized that raising a family in this new land was a threat to his dream of returning to the old country. Whenever he told me stories of those years following his marriage to Teresa, he would invariably begin by saying, "When I wassa twenna-four, Ignazio." It was some time before I realized that the event he was describing might have taken place anytime during a ten-year span.

When he wassa twenna-four, for example, the wine barrel broke in the front room. The owner of the tenement in which the Di Lorenzos lived refused to allow my grandfather space in the basement for the making of wine unless he paid an additional two dollars a month rent. Francesco flatly refused. He had finally paid off his debt to Pietro Bardoni, and he'd be damned if he was going to pay another tithe to another bandit. He set aside an area of the front room overlooking First Avenue, and it was there that he pressed his grapes, and set up his wine barrels, and allowed his wine to ferment without any two-dollar-a-month surcharge. When he was twenty-four, then (1905? 1906?), he was sitting in the kitchen of the apartment on First Avenue, playing *la morra* with Pino, and Rafaelo the butcher, and Giovanni the iceman, when the catastrophe happened with the wine barrel in the front room.

The Italian word for "to play" is *giocare*, followed by the preposition *a*, as in *giocare a scacchi* (literally "to play at chess"). When I was a kid and heard the men saying, *"Giochiamo a morra,"* I thought they were saying, "We're playing *amore,"* and wondered why the Italian word for "love" was used to label what I considered particularly vicious little game.

La morra is similar to choosing up sides by tossing fingers from a closed fist, except that it does not operate on the odds-or-evens principle. Not unlike a game played in France (the basis of a novel titled *La Loi*, which resonates with all sorts of Mediterranean undertones), the idea is to call out a number aloud while simultaneously showing anywhere from no fingers (a clenched fist) to five fingers. Your opponent similarly shouts a number and throws some fingers, and the winner of that round is the man who calls the number exactly matching the total number of fingers showing. *"Morra!"* is what you shout if the number you're calling is zero. If you shout *"Morra!"* and both you and your opponent throw clenched fists, you are again a winner. After a number of elimination rounds, the two men who've won up to that point square off, shout their prognostications, toss their fingers or fists, and eventually there's a single grand winner. This man is called *bossa*, an Italian bastardization of the word "boss." He promptly appoints a partner, usually his closest friend, and the partner is called *sotto bossa*, or "underboss." There is naturally a lot of yelling during the actual competition, which sometimes lasts for hours, but eventually there's a boss, and he chooses his underboss, and then the real fun begins.

63

The fun involves a five-gallon jug of wine. The boss, by dint of his having eliminated all competition in fair and strenuous play, is boss of nothing but the wine. It is he who determines who will be allowed to drink the wine. If he wants to drink all the wine himself, that is his right and his privilege. If he wishes to share the jug only with his underboss, that too is his prerogative. If he wants to give the entire jug to some *shlepper* who is a perennial loser, and who will gratefully accept glass after glass of strong red wine until he's consumed the full five gallons and fallen flat on his face, the boss can do that as well. The boss has absolute power concerning that jug of wine.

On the day of the catastrophe (when Francesco was twenty-four), he beat all the men at *la morra* and became *bossa*.

"Pino," he said, "would you like to be *sotto bossa?*"

"I would consider it a great honor," Pino said, and grinned.

"In that case, Pino, we will need a pitcher of wine and some glasses, please."

Pino went to where the five-gallon jug was standing on a chair near the kitchen table, and he poured a pitcher full to the brim and brought it back to the table together with four glasses. Francesco filled two of the glasses as the other men watched.

"Pino?" he said, and offered him one of the glasses. "I drink to our homeland," he said, and raised his glass.

"*Salute*," Pino said, and both men drank.

"Ahhh," Francesco said. "Excellent wine."

"Excellent," Pino said.

The other men watched. They were very thirsty after nearly forty minutes of throwing fingers and fists and shouting numbers.

"I think our homeland deserves more than one toast," Francesco said.

"I think so, too."

"Should we have another drink, *sotto bossa?*"

"Yes, *bossa.*"

"Do you think it is fitting that we should have another drink while these men, who I'm sure are thirsty, sit and watch us?"

"Whatever you wish, *bossa*."

"I think it is fitting," Francesco said, and poured two more glassfuls of wine. "Pino?" He raised his glass. "I drink to the beautiful village of Fiormonte in the province of Potenza, and I drink to the good health of our families and friends there."

"*Salute*," Pino said, and both men again drank.

"Ahhh," Francesco said. "Beautiful wine."

"Splendid," Pino said.

"But I feel we do a discourtesy to our homeland if you and I are the only ones drinking and toasting. We should have more than two drinkers, don't you agree, Pino?"

"I agree," Pino said. "If that is your wish, *bossa*."

"That is my wish." Francesco turned to the butcher. "Rafaelo," he said, "would you care for a glass of wine?"

"Well, that is entirely up to you, Francesco. You are the *bossa*." The butcher licked his lips. He could taste the wine, but he did not wish to appear overly eager, lest the boss change his mind.

"Pino?" Francesco said. "What do you think? A glass of wine for the butcher?"

Pino considered the question gravely and solemnly. At last, he said, "*Bossa*, he has to work tomorrow."

"That's true," Francesco said. "You'll cut the meat badly, Rafaelo."

"*Bossa*, tomorrow's tomorrow," Rafaelo said quickly. "And today is Sunday."

"I think he's thirsty," Francesco said, and winked at Pino.

"I think they're *both* thirsty," Pino said.

"So let's you and me have another drink," Francesco said. He poured the glasses full again, raised his in toast, and said, "To Victor Emmanuel."

"Are you drinking to the king without *us*?" Rafaelo said, appalled.

"To Victor Emmanuel," Pino said, and drained his glass.

"Ahhh," Francesco said. "Delicious." He looked at the other men critically, as though estimating their capacity for alcohol, and measuring their thirst, and judging whether or not they were good and decent men, and hard workers, and religious besides. A smile broke on his face. He turned to Pino. "Now, please," he said, "fill the glasses for our friends, and we will finish the wine together."

Agnelli the iceman let out a sigh of relief. "I like it when you're the *bossa,*" he said.

"Ah? And why?" Francesco asked.

"Because you have a soft heart," Agnelli said.

"A soft *head,* I think," Francesco said, and lifted his glass. "This time we drink to Italy together."

Solemnly, the other men raised their glasses. "To Italy," they said.

"To home," Francesco said.

"Francesco!" Teresa yelled, and came running into the kitchen, her white apron covered with what Francesco first thought to be blood.

"Oh, *Madonna mia!*" he shouted, and leaped to his feet. "*Che successe?*"

"The barrel!"

"What barrel?"

"One of the barrels!"

"What? What?"

"It's broken!"

"What do you mean? What is she talking about?" he asked Pino, who was as bewildered as he.

"Of *wine!*" Teresa said. "In the front room!"

"*San Giacino di California!*" Francesco shouted. "*Andiamo!*" he yelled to the other men, and ran out of the kitchen with the three of them behind him. The woman from downstairs knocked on the kitchen door, and when Teresa let her in she frantically told her there was wine on her ceiling, and it was dripping all over her

66

bed. Teresa sighed. Francesco ran back into the kitchen, bare-footed, his trouser legs rolled up, his feet stained a bright purple. He went immediately to the table and yanked the tablecloth from it.

"My tablecloth!" Teresa shouted.

"There's wine all over the house!" he shouted back gleefully, and was gone.

"It's dripping on my bed," the lady from downstairs said.

"Yes," Teresa said, looking somewhat distracted.

"We'll drown in wine," the lady said.

"Francesco will take care of it," Teresa said.

In the other rooms, the men were shouting, and laughing, and swearing. Teresa, her hand to her mouth, stood beside the lady from downstairs, and listened.

"Catch it there!"

"I got it!"

"*Mannaggia!*"

"A calamity!"

"There!"

Pino and Francesco backed into the kitchen on their hands and knees, followed by the iceman and the butcher, all the men clutching wine-drenched towels and sheets and pillowcases, trying to stem the flood of wine as it ran through the rooms, sopping it up, slapping down makeshift dikes. "To your right, Giovanni!" and the iceman threw down his sodden sheet and yelled, "*Got* him!" and Teresa shouted, "My linens! Look at my linens!" and Francesco turned over his shoulder and saw the lady from downstairs, and said, "*Buon giorno, signora,*" and she answered with her eyes wide and her mouth open, "*Buon giorno,*" and Rafaelo the butcher clucked his tongue and said, "What a sin!" and the lady from downstairs said, softly, "It's dripping on my bed," and Francesco said, "Get some peaches, and we'll dip them," and burst out laughing again. They built a barricade of linens across the kitchen doorway, and finally stopped the flow of wine from the rest of the apartment. Sitting on the floor, dripping purple, laughing as though they had just been through some terrible battle together and had emerged victoriously, they heard Teresa say, "Why don't you make your wine in the cellar, like other men?"

"What, and pay two dollars?" Francesco said.

Smiling, Teresa said, in Italian, "*Ma sei pazzo, tu.*"

"Let's all have another drink," Francesco said, and got to his feet. "Pino, I thought you were *sotto bossa*. Pour us some wine here." He put his arm around Teresa's waist. "Would you like a little wine, *cara mia?*"

"You're crazy," Teresa said, in English this time, but she was still smiling.

And when he was twenty-four (1907?), he came home from the tailor shop late one night, having worked till almost 4 A.M., and found his again-pregnant wife sitting in the kitchen with all the lights on, a bread knife on the table before her. She told him there had been odd knockings at the kitchen door, three knocks in a row, and when she called, "Who's there?" no one answered, and there was silence. And then, a half hour later, there were three more knocks, and again she called, "Who's there?" and again there was no answer. And then, just before midnight, the same three knocks again, and this time, when she called, "Who's there?" a voice whispered, "It is I, Regina," and she knew it was Regina Russo, who had been killed by a horse-drawn cart on 116th Street four years ago before Teresa's very eyes, and had reached out an imploring hand to Teresa even as the hoofs knocked her down to the cobblestones and the wheels crushed her flat.

Teresa had begun dabbling in the supernatural even before the birth of her second child, a boy she had named Luca in honor of her grandfather, and there were many occasions when Francesco would come home weary and hungry from the tailor shop only to find the neighborhood women clustered around the three-legged table in the kitchen, Teresa solemnly attempting to raise the dead,

68

imploring them to knock once if their answer was yes, twice if it was no, the table wobbling beneath the trembling hands of the women, its legs sometimes banging against the floor in supposed response from the grave. Francesco considered all of this nonsense, and not for a moment did he believe that whoever had knocked on the door was Regina, who was after all dead and gone. But it worried him that Teresa had been alone in the apartment with the three children, and expecting another baby, when someone had knocked on the door and refused to answer. (He dismissed the whispered "It is I, Regina" as a figment of Teresa's overactive imagination and her preoccupation with things supernatural.)

So he organized a group of men from the building, and each night they would take turns sitting in the hallway on one or another of the floors, and they did this for a week without result until finally on the very next night, when it was Francesco's turn to guard the building, he saw a man coming up the stairs in the darkness, and he bunched his fists and waited as the man approached the landing. He could smell the odor of whiskey, he realized all at once that the man was stumbling, the man was drunk. He waited. The man approached the toilet set between the two apartments and then very politely knocked on the door of the toilet three times, and when he received no answer, entered and closed the door behind him. Francesco waited. Behind the door, he could hear the man urinating. Then he heard the flush chain being pulled, and the torrent of water spilling from the overhead wooden box. In the darkness, he smiled.

When the man came out, he took him by the elbow and led him down to the street and told him he was not to use the toilets in this building again, they were not public facilities, he was not to go knocking on toilet doors in the middle of the night, did the man understand that? The man was old, wearing only a threadbare suit in a very cold winter, grizzled, lice-infested, stewed to the gills and understanding only a portion of what

Francesco said in his faulty English. But he nodded and thanked Francesco for the good advice, and went reeling along First Avenue, and then curled up in the doorway of the Chinese laundry and went to sleep. Teresa survived her pregnancy without any further nocturnal visits from girlhood chums already deceased.

And when he was twenty-four, on most Sundays they visited the home of Umberto, Teresa's father, the patriarch of the family. They would begin arriving at about noon, all of them: Teresa and her husband and the four children; and Teresa's sister, Bianca, who had not yet begun her corset business, and who was accompanied by *her* husband, who later ran off to Italy and forced her to fend for herself; and Teresa's other sister, Victoria, who was as yet unmarried but who was keeping steady company with a man who sold bridles, buggy whips, saddles, harnesses, and reins; and Teresa's brother, Marco, who sometimes came in from Brooklyn with his wife and three children; and assorted neighborhood *compaesani* and tailor shop hangers-on, who usually dropped by after *la collazione*, the afternoon meal, generally served at two o'clock by Teresa's mother and all her daughters.

That Sunday meal was a feast; there are no other human beings on earth (not even Frenchmen) who can sit down for so long at a table, or eat so much at one sitting. It began with an antipasto—pimentos and anchovies and capers and black olives and green olives in a little oil and garlic—served with crusty white bread Umberto himself cut into long slices from a huge round loaf. While the men at the table were dipping their bread into the oil and garlic left on their antipasto plates, the women were bustling about in the kitchen, taking the big pot of pasta off the stove—spaghetti or linguine or *perciatelli* or *tonellini*—straining off the starchy water, and then putting the pasta into a bowl, the bottom of which had been covered with bright red tomato sauce, ladling more sauce onto the slippery, steaming *al dente* mound, bringing it to the table with an accompanying sauceboat brimming and hot. "Somebody mix the pasta," Teresa's mother would

70

call from the kitchen. And while Umberto himself tossed the spaghetti or macaroni with a pair of forks, and added more sauce to it, the women would bring in more bowls, filled with sausages and meatballs and *bracìòle*, thin slices of beef stuffed with capers and oregano and rolled, and either threaded or held together with toothpicks. And then the women themselves would sit down to join the others, and Umberto would pour the wine for those closest to him, and then pass it to either Francesco or his other son-in-law, or his son Marco, but rarely to the buggy-whip salesman who planned to marry Victoria. There was celery on the table, and more olives, green and black, and there was always a salad of *arugala*, or chicory and lettuce, or dandelion, which was delicious and bitter and served with a dressing of olive oil and vinegar. And when the pasta course was finished, the women would clear the plates, and the men would pour more wine, and from the kitchen would come platters full of chicken or roast beef or sometimes both, roasted potatoes with gravy, and a vegetable—usually fresh peas or spinach or string beans prepared in the American manner, or zucchini cooked the Neapolitan way—and they would sit and eat this main course while filling each other in on the events of the week and the gossip of the neighborhood, and the latest news from the other side (they almost always referred to it as "the other side," as though the Atlantic Ocean were a mere puddle separating America from Italy), and then they would rest awhile, and drink some more wine. And then Umberto would go into the kitchen and take from the icebox the pastry he had bought on First Avenue, and usually Teresa's mother had made a peach or strawberry shortcake with whipped cream, and they would spread the sweets on the table, and only later serve rich black coffee in demitasse cups, a lemon peel in the saucer, a little anisette to pour into the coffee for those who craved it. There would be a bowl of fruit on the table, too, apples and oranges and bananas and, when they were in season, cherries or peaches or plums or sometimes a whole watermelon split in half and sliced, and there

71

would also be a wooden bowl of nuts, filberts and almonds and Brazil nuts and pecans, and hot from the stove would come a tray of roasted chestnuts, marked with crosses on their skins before they were set in the oven, the skins curling outward now to show the browned meat inside—there was much to eat in that decade when my grandfather was twenty-four.

Later, the men would break out the guinea stinkers, and the women would go into the kitchen to do the dishes and to straighten up, and still later they would come in to wipe off the table, leaving only the bowl of fruit and the bowl of nuts ("If anyone wants it, it's here"), and then all of them, men and women alike, would sit down to play cards, *settemezzo*, or *briscola*, or hearts (a new American game), or *scopa*, betting their pennies as though they were hundred-dollar chips, forming kitties for future outings to Coney Island or the beach, while the children chased each other through the house or crawled under the dining room table or whispered to each other dirty stories they had heard at school. My grandfather's children, all of them presumably born when he was twenty-four, had come in fairly rapid succession, or at least as rapid as one could expect, given the nine-month pregnancy span of the human female. Teresa had given birth to Stella (October 1, 1902), Luca (August 24, 1903), Cristina (January 29, 1905), and Domenico (May 17, 1907), and while she was producing all these new Americans, my grandfather was learning how to hold a pair of scissors, thread a needle, and make stitches that looked like those of a true tailor. He was twenty-four years old and he still wanted to go home to Fiormonte. But each time he was ready to make the trip, another baby arrived. And more expenses. And more ties to this country that was not his—by the time Domenico was born, for example, Stella was in kindergarten at the school on Pleasant Avenue and speaking English like President Teddy Roosevelt himself. And then one morning, Francesco looked into the mirror as usual, and began lathering his face preparatory to shaving, and the person who looked back at him was no longer twenty-four. He was *thirty*-four, and the year was 1914, and Francesco put down his shaving brush and leaned closer to the mirror and looked into his own eyes for a very long time, staring, staring, afraid that if he so much as blinked, another ten years would go by and he would not know where they'd gone or how he had missed their passing.

In July of the year 1914 (modulation all finished), my mother Stella, Italian for star, Stella my mother, Stella the All-American Girl ("I'm American, don't forget"), Stella by starlight, or sunlight, or the light of the silvery moon, Stella nonetheless, my mother (take a bow, Mom) Stella (enough already) was not quite twelve years old when two events of particular significance happened one after the other. Now I really don't know whether either of those events was traumatic, and caused her to become the kind of woman she grew up to be. (Rebecca hated her, and always described her as "a paranoid nut.") I can only surmise that they must have been terrifying to an eleven-year-old girl who, by all accounts (her own and my grandfather's), was imaginative, sensitive, inquisitive, extremely intelligent (*and* American, don't forget).

For an American, who had learned to recite the Pledge of Allegiance proudly every weekday morning at school, Stella was surrounded by more Italians than she could shake a stick at. Her classmates, of course, were all Italians, except for two Irish girls and a Jewish boy who had somehow wandered into the wrong ghetto. But in addition to her daily encounters with children who, like herself, were the sons and daughters of immigrants who could barely speak English, there was the family as well. The family was (in Stella's own words, oft-repeated) "a bunch of real ginzoes." She was living with her parents and her brothers and sisters on 118th Street and First Avenue, above the grocery store on the corner, just three doors away from the tailor shop. Within a six-block radius, north or south, east or west, there were perhaps four dozen aunts, uncles, cousins, goombahs and goomahs who

73

were considered part of "the family," the family being her mother's since Francesco's relatives were all on the other side. I don't think my mother quite appreciated their proximity, or the fact that she was eagerly welcomed into their homes.

When *I* was growing up, I looked forward to each loving pat or hug, knowing that I could walk four blocks to my Aunt Cristina's, where she would offer me some fresh-squeezed lemonade, or turn the corner to my Aunt Bianca's corset shop, where she would tell me all about dainty ladies' underthings. Bianca was a great-aunt, actually my grandmother's sister; her shop was on 116th Street, between First and Second Avenues, and she was known in the neighborhood as "The Corset Lady." My mother must have visited that same shop as often as I did, and at the same age, but she never spoke of it fondly, nor do I think she particularly liked Aunt Bianca, who to me (though I'd never seen her, and could only smell the sweet soapy lilac scent of her and feel her delicate hands upon my face) was a lady of great mystery and intrigue, fashioning ladies' brassieres as she did. My mother made similar family rounds, dropping in wherever she chose, always greeted warmly and lovingly, though she might have been there only hours before. And yet, the family did not seem to mean very much to her, their coarse southern Italian fell harshly upon her ears, their broken English rankled; she was American, Stella was.

I don't know why she was so drawn to Pino's wife. Angelina was most certainly beautiful, but her good looks were undeniably Mediterranean, and she still spoke English with a marked accent. To Stella, though, she must have seemed more "American" than any member of her own family, with the possible exception of her mother. As concerns the relationship between Stella and Tess, as she was called more and more frequently by everyone in the neighborhood, there seems to be little doubt that it was lousy. To begin with, Tess worked in the tailor shop alongside her father and Francesco, which meant that she had little time for house-wifely chores like cleaning or cooking. (My grandmother may have

74

been the first liberated woman in the history of America, who the hell knows?) Stella grudgingly inherited the running of the household, except for the preparation of breakfast, which Tess handled for the entire family before heading off "to business." Stella cleaned the four-room apartment, Stella prepared her own lunch as well as lunch for her brothers and sister when they came home from school at noon each day, Stella prepared dinner, Stella was the mother *her* mother should have been. ("My mother was a *lady*," she would say to me, almost as often as she said, "I'm American, don't forget." The word "lady" was always delivered sarcastically, and I could sense the curl of the lip, the angry flash in her green eyes. Was it coincidence that I later married a green-eyed girl? Must have been. Who the hell can tell green from blue, anyway, and really, who cares?) In any case, it was Stella who ran off to school each morning, feeling very American, and who came back to the apartment each afternoon feeling very Italian because it was she who did the donkey work. And I suppose she jealously guarded those moments when she could visit Pino's wife and become the inquiring bright child she had no opportunity to be at home.

Poking in Angelina's jewelry box, holding earrings to her ears for Angelina's approval, sampling Angelina's powders, sniffing at her perfumes, asking the hundreds of questions she could not ask of her absentee mother, listening to Angelina as she told stories of Francesco's and Pino's youthful days in Fiormonte, Stella enjoyed the most cherished hours of her childhood in that apartment on Second Avenue. Angelina had become pregnant again in January, after having miscarried nine times, the last having been particularly tragic in that she'd lost the baby during her fifth month. She, too, must have enjoyed Stella's visits in those final days of her pregnancy when, fearful of another miscarriage, she rarely ventured out of the apartment. It was on one of those visits that her time came.

Stella saw her clutch for her abdomen and heard her say, "Ooo,

75

sta zitto." The baby had been very active lately, each kick greeted with undisguised joy by Pino and Angelina—the child was alive, the prospective mother was healthy, this time all would go well. But this latest pang was something more than just another fetal kick; it was the beginning of labor. Angelina recognized it almost at once, and immediately sent Stella to fetch Filomena the Midwife. There were few telephones in Harlem in the year 1914. Umberto had one in the tailor shop, but telephones in the home were a luxury (they were *still* a luxury when I was growing up). Stella ran the six blocks to Filomena's building, her skirts and pigtails flying, and raced up the four flights to Filomena's apartment, and rapped on the door. There was no answer. She rapped again. A door across the hall opened, and an old man in his undershirt looked out at Stella.

"Where's Filomena?" she asked. "Where's the midwife?"

"*Che cosa vuole?*" the old man said.

"Filomena, Filomena," Stella said, and reverted impatiently to Italian. "*Dov'è Filomena? Dov'è la levatrice?*"

"*Non lo so. Hai provato il frigorifero?*"

"*Che?*"

"*Il frigorifero. Di Giovanni Agnelli.*"

What was he saying? The ice station? Mr. Agnelli's ice station?

"*Ma dove?*" she asked. "*Alla* First Avenue?"

"*Sì, sì,* First Avenue," he replied. "*Forse è la. Con Giovanni.*"

"*Grazie,*" she called over her shoulder, and ran down the stairs to the street. She could not imagine why Filomena had gone personally to the ice station, since Giovanni made home deliveries daily, shoving his huge blocks of ice along in a cart, chipping off smaller cakes with his ice pick, seizing them with his tongs, and tossing them into a wooden tub, which he carried up to his customers. Had the old man misunderstood her? Had she not explained herself adequately in Italian?

The streets were crowded and noisy. This was three o'clock on a Saturday afternoon in July. The weather was mild, and the

76

citizens of East Harlem had come outdoors to enjoy the bright untarnished day. Strollers thronged the sidewalk spumoni stands, bought ices and pastry, chatted with each other, admired babies in carriages; peddlers pushed their carts and shouted praise of their produce, the junkman's wagon rolled by piled high with newspapers and scrap metal, "I buy old clothes, I buy old clothes"; children roller-skated past on the pavement, old women shouted "*Stat' attento!*" and then returned to stoopside conversations; there was a sense of teeming life in those streets as Stella hurried to find the woman who would bring yet another life into the ghetto. On 119th Street, she waited for two trolley cars, passing from opposite directions, to rattle by, and then she ran across First Avenue to the ice station. Agnelli was nowhere in sight. She looked in the open yard where Agnelli's coal, piled shining and black in wooden stalls, had already been delivered in anticipation of consumer demand in the months ahead. Then she walked around to the back of the icehouse itself, and climbed the steps to the wooden platform, debated opening the heavy metal door, and decided to try instead the small shacklike structure Agnelli used as an office.

The office was some twenty-five feet from the back of the icehouse, and Stella ran to it as fast as she could, shouting, "Mr. Agnelli! Mr. Agnelli!" as she covered the short stretch of ground, and then threw open the office door, and saw first a calendar on the wall over a folding bed, and then Agnelli's very hairy backside, and then realized that a pair of pale white legs were wrapped around that backside. Agnelli turned his head for a look at the intruder, peering over his shoulder while just below him Filomena the Midwife poked her head around a tangle of arms and legs and whispered a silent prayer of gratitude to the good Lord Jesus for having sent but a mere child to discover her in such an indelicate and compromising position, rather than Agnelli's wife, Luisa, who was said to have a violent temper. Stella, for her part, stared first at Agnelli's ass, and then at Filomena's raised white legs (she had her high-buttoned shoes on, Stella noticed), and then realized that this was the man with whom her father had boarded when he first came to this country, this was Mr. Agnelli, the neighborhood's respected iceman, what was he doing on top of Filomena, who at this moment should have been in Angelina's kitchen, delivering a baby, instead of . . . instead of . . .

Well . . . fucking. Stella knew the word, she had seen it scribbled on tenement walls and fences, she had heard it whispered not so softly by boys at school, but she had never seen the word so vigorously demonstrated, and she had also never seen Mr. Agnelli's ass.

"*Che vuole?*" Agnelli shouted, without skipping a beat.

"*Basta, basta,*" Filomena said, and untangled herself with dignity, pulling up her bloomers and pulling down her petticoat and skirt. "What do you want, Stella?" she asked. Her shirtwaist was still open, she had apparently forgotten that the four top buttons were unbuttoned and that two pear-shaped breasts were staring at Stella, who stared right back at them speechlessly. Agnelli pulled up his britches, and went outside to check his coal.

"Well, what is it, child?" Filomena said. She glanced down curiously at her own breasts, sighed, and began buttoning her shirtwaist.

"Angelina," Stella said.

"What of Angelina?"

"The baby," Stella said.

Filomena was on her feet instantly. "Come," she said, and took Stella's hand. "And remember, you saw nothing. Else God will strike you dead."

The, only person God struck dead that day was Angelina Battatore.

❖

It's difficult to believe, in this day and age of sterile antiseptic hospital deliveries, that 679 women died of puerperal disease

78

during the year 1914, or that 6,617 babies were stillborn. In 1926, I myself was delivered in a bedroom of our Harlem apartment by a woman named Josefina, my grandmother's cousin, who, in addition to teaching English to new immigrants, *and* working for the Republican Club, *and* writing songs (all of which were terrible), *and* concocting an ointment called Aunt Josie's Salve (which was actually sold in some Harlem drugstores and which was reputed to possess curative powers for anything from boils to carbuncles), was a midwife in her spare time. My mother survived. I was born blind. Some you win, some you lose.

Angelina lost on that July day in 1914.

She lost after a monumental struggle that lasted for twelve hours and finally required the assistance of the neighborhood doctor, one Bartolo Mastroiani, who arrived at the Battatore apartment at a little past 3 A.M. on Sunday morning to find Angelina bleeding profusely and the baby's umbilical cord wrapped around its own throat, threatening strangulation each time Angelina struggled to squeeze the infant from her loins. Filomena the Midwife was utterly discomposed; the doctor unceremoniously pushed her out into the kitchen, where she joined some two dozen neighborhood ladies, all of whom were certain that someone had put the Evil Eye on Angelina. Mastroiani got to work.

He worked in a tiny bedroom with a single window opening on an air shaft, a naked light bulb hanging over the blood-soaked bed, the moaning in the kitchen assuming dirgelike proportions, Angelina shrieking in pain and pouring torrents of fresh blood from her torn uterus as he probed to unravel the unseen noose around the baby's throat, the baby struggling to be born and struggling against strangulation, Angelina contracting steadily and involuntarily while her life spurted out onto the bedclothes and onto the doctor's hands, awash in a pool of her own blood and sweat. He had studied medicine in Siena, had thought he'd become a surgeon, had practiced tying knots inside a matchbox, using only the thumb and forefinger of his right hand, working blind inside that confining space just as he now worked to free the stubborn cord around the baby's neck, hot blood spurting onto his hands, the walls of Angelina's womb closing and opening in convulsion around his fingers. The cord refused to unravel. In desperation, he cut it and tied both ends with string. The baby's triumphant cry shocked the kitchen women into silence. Angelina died six minutes later while Mastroiani was still working with clamps and sponges, fighting the impossible tide of blood— he had been a doctor for thirty-seven years and had never seen so much blood in his life. Later, he would go into the hall toilet to vomit.

Stella was in the kitchen with those wailing women. Stella heard the Evil Eye talk, and Stella heard the baby's victorious cry, and then waited while silence screamed as loudly as had the newborn child, silence bellowed in that kitchen, silence shrieked behind the closed door of the bedroom. And then the doctor came out, wiping his bloodstained hands on a white towel, and he shook his head, and the silence persisted for perhaps ten seconds more, and then the women began to wail again, and Stella saw the doctor go unsteadily into the hall, and heard him throwing up in the toilet outside. Someone went to get Pino. In those days, the mysteries of birth were thought best unseen by men, and he had been sitting in Francesco's kitchen (Tess, of course, was in the Battatore apartment with the rest of the women), nervously drinking wine while Francesco told him that everything would be all right, women sometimes had a very difficult time with their first baby, Tess had been in labor for six hours with Stella, everything would be fine. When Pino learned that everything had not been so fine, he fell unconscious to the floor, and Francesco took him in his arms, and wiped the sweat from his forehead, and began to weep for his friend.

Three days after the funeral of Angelina Battatore, the Chinaman made his pass at Stella—if legend and eleven-year-old girls are to be believed.

❖

The Chinaman— Stay, all ye Oriental Americans. In July of
1914, the guy who did the neighborhood laundry *was* called "The
Chinaman," or better yet, "The Chink." The Chinaman, then
(or the Chink, if you prefer), was a man named Chon Tsu, the
T-s-u being exceedingly difficult to pronounce unless you are yourself of Chinese extraction, in which case you would speak it as
though it were a cross between "Sue" and "She." In the neighborhood, they called him Charlie Shoe. Charlie was thirty-eight years
old, a short, slender man who still wore a pigtail and clothes he
had brought from his native province of Kwangtung, meaning that
he looked as though he were wearing pajamas and bed slippers in
the streets of Italian Harlem. He had been in America for two
years, having been one of those fortunate Orientals who'd smug-
gled himself into this gloriously democratic land after the Ex-
clusion Act of 1882.

Charlie worked eighteen hours a day in his laundry shop just
downstairs from where Stella and the entire Di Lorenzo brood
lived, his establishment being a two-by-four cubbyhole wedged
between the grocery store on the corner and the *salumeria* on the
other side, the tailor shop being the next in line on First Avenue.
It is doubtful that he even knew Stella existed before that afternoon in July.

There was, of course, a steady stream of customers in Charlie's
laundry, but to him all white people looked the same, and besides,
they smelled bad. Charlie had a wife and four children in Canton,
and he sent them most of his earnings, living at a bare subsistence
level in the back of his shop, where he washed the clothes and
ironed them and then wrapped them in thin brown paper, slipping
an identifying pink ticket under the white string, Chinese calli-
graphy and bold Arabic numerals, no tickee no shirtee.

He did not speak English at all well, his vocabulary consisting

81

of a scant hundred or so words, and he always looked harried and somewhat bewildered, and sounded rude or irritated because his words were monosyllabic to begin with, and delivered with a clipped Chinese accent usually accompanied by a frown that seemed to denote impatience but actually was a direct facial translation of utter confusion. He wasn't such a happy man, Charlie Shoe. There were very few Chinese women in America in the year 1914, and the Chinese like to fuck the same as anyone else, witness the population problem in Mao's thriving little commune over there. As inscrutable as Charlie may have appeared to the parade of wops who marched in and out of his shop with their dirty laundry, chances are he occasionally entertained the wildest fantasies of a sex life denied to him here in America. Have you ever seen any of those Far Eastern pornographic line drawings, tinted in the most delicate shades, and advertising the Oriental tool as one of truly remarkable dimensions—or at least so Rebecca described it to me, and mentioned in passing that the Chinese dong put my own meager weapon to shame. But what white woman in her right mind would even have entertained the thought of bedding down with a hairless, yellow-skinned, slant-eyed runt like poor Charlie Shoe?

Stella maybe.

I have no desire to probe too deeply into the fantasies of an eleven-year-old girl, especially when she happened to grow up to be my mother. I can only imagine what the sight of Agnelli and Filomena interlocked in interruptus did to fire the imagination of someone already hooked on the sloppy romances that were pouring out of the Hollywood dream factory and inundating the neighborhood playhouses. I have little or no respect for the theory that fiction triggers real events. But I cannot discount the fact that my mother was always a movie buff, and that her addiction started sometime in 1912 or '13, when films began to influence American life in a very important way. As a matter of fact, the two most significant changes in Harlem since the arrival of Francesco in 1901 and the initiation of Stella into the mysteries of tickle-and-grab in 1914 were the appearance of the automobile and the ascendance of the motion picture. It's difficult to estimate how many people in New York owned a tin lizzie, but there were nearly four million of the flivvers on the nation's roads, and it's safe to assume at least a goodly portion of them were clattering along the cobbled streets of the country's largest city. Where horses had once clopped upon and crapped upon the streets of New York, making it difficult to find the gold beneath all that manure, Henry Ford's new contrivance now rattled and clanked around every corner, adding to the general din that had so disturbed Francesco upon his arrival. New York was *never* a quiet place, but the advent and subsequent popularity of the automobile did little to restore my grandfather's sense of tranquillity.

To Stella, cars were exciting. She watched them jangling by, she dreamed of riding in one (it was rumored that her Uncle Joe, Tess's oldest brother and a gambler in Arizona, had bought one and, if he came east again this Christmas, might take her motoring), she bought all the paper-bound cheapbacks of jokes about the Ford car, and memorized them, and delighted her class-mates by reeling them off one after the other, with rapid-fire precision and nearly total recall. A label she saw pasted to the hood of one car—COME ON, BABY, HERE'S YOUR RATTLE—hinted at pleasures remote from the joys of motoring, promised delights she had not yet experienced except vicariously in the movie houses she frequented with her brother Luke every Saturday afternoon; Cristina and Dominick were still considered too young to spend hours in the dark watching what Francesco called, in the coined language of the immigrant, *garbagio*. The Italian word for "garbage" is *immondizie*, but in much the same way that Italian immigrants invented the word *baschetta* for "basket" (the choices in true Italian are either *paniere* or *cesta*), so did many other words come into half-breed existence. The funniest of these was probably minted by the earliest immigrants at a time when

83

toilets were still in backyards and not in the hallways of the tenements. The Italian word for "toilet" is *gabinetto*. But those poor struggling souls who had to race out to the backyard to sit upon a makeshift wooden seat in a tar-paper shack learned the word "backhouse," and immediately transmogrified it to *bacausa*, instant Italian-English.

The movies were *garbagio* to Francesco, and it was with great reluctance that he shelled out the admission price of fifteen cents apiece to his daughter and son each Saturday. On the particular Saturday that Stella was supposedly exposed to the rapacious intent of Charlie Shoe, she and Luke saw a winner called *Hearts Adrift*, starring Mary Pickford—

"Yes, but what's your real name, Miss Pickford?"

"Gladys Smith."

"Would you spell that for me, please?"

—*and* a Mack Sennett Keystone Kops two-reeler starring Ford Sterling and Mabel Normand, *and* the latest biweekly installment of the twenty-episode serial called *The Perils of Pauline*. Now here's where a little second-guessing comes in, not that Stella's story is to be doubted, you understand. (It had *better* be believed, or that poor hapless Chink suffered a southern Italian vendetta for no reason at all.) Such was the popularity of Pauline that, in addition to showing her continuing adventures on the screen once every two weeks, the episodes were also serialized in local newspapers, their appearance in print timed to coincide with the theater runs. But since Harlem wasn't Forty-second Street, and since the "chapters," as Stella called the filmed episodes, sometimes reached the Cosmo on 116th Street several months after the fictionalized accounts appeared in the newspapers, it's entirely possible that she had already read the episode she saw that day, and was conditioned to be excited by it, and therefore more susceptible to it than she otherwise might have been. It is a matter of record (go look it up) that on May 17, 1914, a full two months before Charlie Shoe reportedly lost his pigtailed head, the *New*

York American ran a fictionalized account of what happened to Pauline when she went to visit New York's Chinatown:

She fell beside the door. Strong arms seized her. For an instant she felt that she was saved. But she looked up into the lowering face of a man with tilted mustachios. From the wide, thick lips came threats and curses. From the passageway came the crashing of doors. She let herself be lifted . . .

And later, in that same published episode:

In the Joss House of the Golden Screens, the two Chinamen, dazed with opium, set of purpose, were arguing with a trembling priest. The door fell open and a white woman—with bleeding hands—fell at their feet. "Ha, she has come back!" cried one of the Chinese in his own tongue. There was the sound of steps in the outer passage. They lifted Pauline. They dragged her back. The priest hurried to the outer door and locked it.

Stella may not have read the episode when it appeared in the *American*, but that Saturday she *did* see the film upon which it was based, and you can bet your chopsticks the piano comper wasn't playing "Pretty Parasol and Fan" while that collection of Chinese dope fiends were gleefully having their way with perky Pauline (whose hands were bleeding), who was saved from their clutches only by the timely intrusion of her stepbrother, Harry, who also happened to be her suitor. (Bit of incestuous suggestion there? I digress.) Stella watched the film with rising excitement— Luke corroborated this later, said she could hardly sit still when them Chinks was picking Pauline up off the floor. Brother and sister both came out of the theater into blinding daylight; the fantasies were behind them in the darkness, there remained only the reality of Harlem in July. They walked from 116th Street and Third Avenue to where they lived on the corner of 118th and First. Cristina was skipping rope with four little girls in front of her building. Young Dominick, already wearing eyeglasses at the age of seven, was sitting on the stoop watching the other children. (*All* of the Di Lorenzo family—with the exception of Tess and Cristina—wore eyeglasses. Stella wore hers under duress, feeling they spoiled her good looks, which they probably did. She had not worn her glasses to the movie that day.)

"How was it?" Cristina asked.

"Good," Luke replied, and then sat down beside Dominick, and watched the girls without interest.

"What was it about?" Dominick asked.

"Lots of things," Luke said. He was a tall, skinny, shambling kid with unkempt hair, brown eyes magnified by thick, horn-rimmed glasses, one leg of his knickers falling to his ankle, shirt sticking out of the waistband. When Rebecca first met him, many years later, she said he looked as if he'd just got out of prison and was wearing the suit of clothes issued by the Department of Corrections. My memories of Luke are warmer. He was the soft-spoken man who pressed clothes in the back of my grandfather's tailor shop, always inquisitive about what kind of day I'd had at school, what subjects I was studying, how I was getting along. I can remember his long fingers tousling my hair. My interest in music was first encouraged by Luke, who began studying violin at the age of seven (at Tess's insistence) and who later dropped it in favor of playing the piano by ear. I now know that he was a hacker who played every song he knew in either C, G, or B flat. But there were times when I would stand alongside the upright in my grandfather's house and listen to Luke banging those keys, and Christ, to me he was making celestial music. It was Luke who chased me through the apartment one Sunday, after I kidded him unmercifully about a girl he was reportedly dating. I ran and hid under the bed, and he tried to flush me out with the straw end of a broom. He was mad as hell. It was Luke, too, who once threw his cards into the air during a poker game and yelled at my grand-father, "What the hell do you know about cards?" and then turned to me and said, "He draws to a goddamn inside straight,

86

and *fills* it!" I had no idea what he was talking about, but his voice was confidential, and I felt he was letting me in on the secrets of the universe. The last time I spoke to him was in 1950, shortly after I married Rebecca. His voice, as always, was tinged with a sadness that seemed to hint at specters unexorcised. "Hey, how goes it, Iggie?" he said on the telephone, and I could re-member again those long, thin fingers in my hair, and the smell of the steam rising from the pressing machine. "How goes it, Iggie?" I forget why I called him.

He sat on the stoop for perhaps ten minutes that July day in 1914, watching the girls skipping rope (Stella joined them at one point) and telling Dominick about the Mack Sennett short and the *Perils of Pauline* chapter, dismissing the Mary Pickford film as "lousy." Then he went upstairs to practice the violin. Dominick got off the stoop and walked over to the tailor shop to visit Umberto and Francesco, who was now a full-time partner and a fairly decent tailor. His rise to partial ownership was directly at-tributable to Pino, who still worked in the garment center, and who had brought to Francesco a large order for Salvation Army uniforms—a bonanza that guaranteed a basic income to the shop, a stipend that continued for all the years of my grand-father's life. Long after Umberto was dead, long after my grandfather became sole owner of the shop, those Salvation Army orders were there waiting to be filled each month. I can remember fingering the metallic S's and A's my grandfather sewed onto the collar of each uniform. It was the Salvation Army that got him through the Depression. And it was Pino, through his firm down-town, who first brought the business to his friend, Francesco.

Stella, weary of double-ee-Dutch, went back to the stoop and sat on it, chin cupped in her hands, and watched her little sister skipping under the flailing ropes while the other girls chanted. She rose suddenly, smoothed her skirt, and for no apparent reason walked into the laundry shop of Charlie Shoe next door.

RASHOMON

(titles cannot be copyrighted)

A play in three acts

by
Dwight Jamison

Act I

Stella Di Lorenzo, daughter to Francesco and Tess, aged eleven years, nine months, and sixteen days, speaking of the event to her parents, and her grandfather, and Pino Battatore, and unknowingly and inadvertently to her brother Luke, who is listening in the bedroom adjacent to the kitchen.

STELLA: I went in the laundry for lichee nuts. He has these lichee nuts he keeps on the counter, and when I bring in the shirts, or I go to pick up something, he always says take, and I grab a handful. That's why I went in the shop, because all of a sudden, I was sitting on the stoop watching Cristina and the girls, and I got an urge for some lichee nuts and I knew Charlie would give me some because he always gives me some when I go in there. Also, my hand was bleeding, it started bleeding in the movies when I was biting my nails, and I figured maybe Charlie had a bandage he could put on it or something. I didn't come to the tailor shop because I didn't want to bother Grandpa or you, Papa, and I didn't want to get blood on any of the clothes. I know how fussy Mama is about touching any of the clothes in the shop.

He looked kind of strange when he came out of the back. I think maybe he was smoking dope, they smoke dope a lot. His thing was open, his shirt, that silk Chinese thing he wears. The four top buttons was open. He said what did I want, and I told him did he have some lichee nuts? There wasn't none on the counter, they're usually on the counter. So he said no lichee nuts today, and I showed him that my hand was bleeding and did

88

he have something I could wrap around it, and he said come in the back. I didn't want to go in the back, but it was really bleeding, right near the cuticle. Also, I figured he really did have lichee nuts, they were in the back someplace, he once gave Mama a whole box of them when Uncle Joe was here last Christmas and she brought in a pile of his shirts. So I followed him through the curtain he's got hanging behind the counter, and he told me to sit down he'd see if he had something for my finger.

What he's got in the back of the store, it's this small room with this folding bed against one wall, and over the bed he's got pictures hung up of Mary Pickford and the two Gish sisters, and that lady who was in *Charity*, I forget her name, he's got their pictures tacked to the wall. And along the back wall, he's got these tubs where he washes the shirts and things, and he's got an ironing board set up where he does the ironing, and them shirts and things are piled on the floor, the dirty shirts. The ones he's already washed he's got on a table like the one Aunt Bianca has in her kitchen, with a white enamel top, he's got the clean stuff on that, ready to be ironed. And on the other wall, across from where the bed was, he's got shelves with soap on them, and also boxes of lichee nuts, and food and tea and stuff, and a little wooden icebox and one of them small gas stoves like the one Grandpa used to have near the toilet in the tailor shop, where he used to make coffee on it before he got that new one. Like that. What he did was say I should sit on the bed, so I sat down and looked at the pictures he had tacked on the wall—oh, and there was also a Chinese calendar with a picture of a Chinese lady on it and Chinese writing on it, even the days were written in Chinese.

He went to the shelves on the other side of the room, and he said what was my name, and I told him it was Stella Di Lorenzo, and he said Stella, Stella, saying it over to himself like it was a new English word he wanted to learn instead of somebody's name. He had his back to me all this time, he was looking around

89

the shelves there for I guess a bandage because what he brought over to the bed was it must have been an old sheet, I think it was an old sheet that maybe got ripped when he was washing it, that must've been what. So he stood in front of the bed and he tore the sheet up into strips, and he said how did I hurt myself and I said I was chewing my nails in the movies and he said okay, he was going to fix my finger up and then he would get me some lichee nuts. I was sweating, it was very hot back there. I said what a hot day it was, and how it must be great on a day like this to work in the ice station like Mr. Agnelli does, where he's got all that ice stacked up in blocks, you know, in the icehouse, and if he feels like it he can go in there and hide with all the ice and nobody'd know where he was or nothing. Charlie just nodded sort of dumb, I don't think he understood anything I was saying. He sat alongside me on the bed and took my finger in his hand and went tch-tch, you know, shaking his head and looking at where it was cut.

He didn't do nothing, not then, he just wrapped up the finger and then he tore the bandage, like up the middle, and wrapped the ends around my finger and tied a knot, and then he smiled and said okay, Stella? and I said yeah, that's nice, Charlie, thank you very much, and he said I was a brave little girl, and he went to get the lichee nuts. Then he came back with this whole box of them, with a picture of a Chinese girl on the cover, and he opened the box and told me to go ahead and take as many as I liked, and he sat down on the bed again next to me. And he said he had a little daughter like me back in Canting or wherever, I don't know, it was some Chinese name, I guess it's a town. And he asked me did I go to school, and he didn't do nothing, not yet, he just said did I like lichee nuts, and he said his daughter liked lichee nuts and in China you could also eat them fresh, that they were delicious fresh, and I said well, I like them this way, too, and he said how old are you, Stella?

I told him I was eleven going on twelve, I would be twelve in

October, and he said I was a big girl for my age, that in China the girls are smaller, but that in China when a girl was twelve years old, she was already married, that his wife had wrote to him last week saying she thought his daughter would be getting married soon. He was telling me all this in his funny way of talking, I could hardly understand anything he said, I think he *must* have been smoking dope because he really had this very stupid look on his face, I can't describe it, it was just *stupid*-looking. So I said wouldn't he like to have some of the lichee nuts, too, and he said no, he didn't care for none and then he put his hand on my knee and said I was a nice little girl. I didn't think it was nothing, his putting his hand on my knee, because he had a little girl my own age back home in China, and this wasn't like a stranger or nothing, this was Charlie in his shop, even though I know they smoke a lot of dope. I didn't think nothing of it until he put his hand under my skirt, and then I tried to get up off the bed, and slipped and fell, and he picked me up off the floor, and said shhh, shhh, don't be afraid, and put me on the bed and put his hand on my eyes, just put his hand on my eyes and when I looked again he had no pants on and I saw his heinie and everything and I got scared I would have a baby like Angelina, so I ran out of there and came upstairs and when Mama found me crying in the toilet and wanted to know what happened I couldn't tell her but I feel better now.

Act II

Stella Di Palermo, wife to Jimmy Di Palermo, mother of Anthony and Ignazio Silvio Di Palermo, talking to her youngest son in the year 1939 while the radio is telling of Hitler's invasion of Poland. Iggie is at the kitchen table eating chocolate pudding with whipped cream and a maraschino cherry. He is thirteen years old. His older brother is fifteen and has not yet come home from school—Evander Childs on Gun Hill Road. In 1942, Tony will be drafted into the Army. In 1943, he will be killed in Italy. Stella is thirty-seven years old, a bit thick in the middle, a few gray streaks already beginning to show in her brown hair. (Her father's hair has been completely white since 1932.) She is at the sink, washing red peppers which she will then roast over the open gas jet, later scraping off the black to produce miraculously succulent slices which she will serve cold with a little oil and garlic. For some reason, she has begun talking about that July Saturday in the year 1914. Perhaps the broadcast of Hitler's invasion has stimulated it. Iggie hardly listens to her. The war news is very exciting. He visualizes tanks and armored cars rumbling across the Polish landscape.

STELLA: They didn't believe me, none of them. They were my own family except for my father's friend Pino. He was there, too, and my grandfather, may he rest in peace, and I told them what happened with that lousy Chinaman downstairs in his shop, and none of them believed me. Am I a liar or something, have I ever lied to you, Iggie? That they shouldn't believe me? My own family, and I was telling them what that man did to me, and I could see my mother didn't believe it—well, she was a *lady*, you know, I guess she never dreamt in her entire life that anything like that could happen. That was for movies and books, you know, some Chinese dope fiend fooling around with her daughter. My grandfather yelled at her in Italian—you never met him, Iggie, he died before you were born, may he rest in peace. I was his darling, he liked me better than any of the other kids, even Cristina who was very pretty when she was a girl; it was my grandfather who took up for me. He said to my mother in Italian, what do you think she's doing, making this whole thing up? She just came from downstairs, you found her crying in the toilet, you think she could invent a thing like this? My mother said Charlie seems like such a nice man, I can't believe he would do something like this, and my father said Stella, are you sure you're telling us the truth?

92

You didn't make this up, did you, because this is very serious.

I said I didn't make it up, I saw him naked. You should have seen him, Iggie, he was the hairiest thing. I always thought Chinks were supposed to be practically hairless like albinos, isn't that true? Well, who knows? And those dirty pictures he had on the wall over the bed. He had this one picture of a dark-haired woman with her blouse unbuttoned, four buttons of her blouse, the top four buttons. I don't know what *she* was supposed to be, maybe one of those Chinese concubines, you know, like in *The Good Earth*; that was a really good movie. I also read the book, don't forget. They have six or seven wives, those Chinamen, you'd think it would be against the law. I don't think Charlie Shoe had more than one wife, but those pictures on the wall were of concubines or maybe Chinese actresses. All I can remember is the one who had her blouse open and showing everything, and practically naked except for high-button shoes.

It was a good thing I had the presence of mind to get out of there. I was only eleven, Iggie, well, almost twelve, and there he was babbling some kind of crazy English, I'm American, don't forget, I was speaking English from the day I was born, so how was I supposed to understand what he was saying? I was lucky, I'll tell you. Lying to me about his daughter, I'll bet he didn't even *have* a daughter, that was just his way of getting around me, you know? Putting me off my guard. He was doped up, Iggie, I'm sure of that, I don't want you ever, if anybody *ever* offers you anything, a cigarette, anything, I don't want you to *touch* it, do you hear me? You just say no, I'm sorry, I don't smoke, or tell them your father's a cop, make up any kind of story, but don't touch anything. I read in the *Journal-American* the other day that there's a lot of marijuana going around the city, that's how they get you, they could take you to China for all you know.

Maybe he would have done that to me, that's possible when you think of it. How would you like your mother to be dressed like a Chink in Hong Kong someplace or Shanghai and Paul Muni

93

comes in with his slanty eyes and says here's your dope, Stella, smoke all your pipe like a nice little girl. How do I know even those lichee nuts weren't doped up, he was feeding me enough of them. He could have gone to jail for fifty years, do you know that? Fooling around with a little girl? That's very serious, Iggie, they would've thrown away the key. Don't you ever fool around with any young girls, you hear me? I mean, when you grow up. What happened with Tina in the closet when we were still living in Harlem don't mean nothing, you were both little kids. But don't you never touch no little girls, he could have ruined my life, that man. And for what? So he could put his hand under my skirt? I don't know what he expected to find under there, I was only eleven. But of course, who knows where it would have stopped?

They had Dr. Mastroiani come up to examine me—that was my *mother's* idea, naturally, because she didn't believe her own daughter, she'd rather believe that nice little Chink downstairs— and Dr. Mastroiani didn't find nothing because he hadn't *done* nothing to me, of course, not that way. You don't know about these things yet, thank God, but it could have been very serious, he could have, well, penetrated me which Dr. Mastroiani said he didn't do, and which of course I knew he didn't do. All he done was put his hand on my leg and under my skirt, which was *plenty*. And then he put his hand over my eyes, and I think he warned me not to tell anybody about this because God would strike me dead. I guess that was why he put his hand over my eyes, that was like Chinese for you didn't see nothing, Stella. I'll *bet* that was it. Sure.

When you were born, you know, everybody said it was the Evil Eye, that when the Chinaman put his hand over my eyes like that it was some kind of curse, a Chinese curse, and that's what happended when you were born, though if that was the case, why didn't it happen to Tony? He was my first-born, right? Anyway, I don't believe in that greaseball stuff. I'm American, don't forget.

94

After the doctor got finished with me, the priest came upstairs, and I told him what had happened and he made me swear to God on the crucifix that I was telling the truth, and then I guess my mother finally believed me, and she looked at my father, and my father nodded, and then all the men went in the front room, my father and my grandfather and Pino, and then they went to get some other men—Mr. Bardoni who was also from Fiormonte, and Mr. Agnelli from the ice station, though I don't know why they bothered to call *him*, he was probably in his office behind the icehouse, who knows *where* he was? And also my cousin Ralphie, do you remember Ralphie, Iggie? He used to play accordion, he was a very good musician, you should get in touch with him now that you're doing so good with the piano. They all of them went downstairs to see the Chinaman, and what happened served him right.

Act III

Francesco Di Lorenzo, father to Stella, grandfather to Ike, in the intensive care unit of Bronx-Lebanon Hospital on the morning of June 17, 1973. He is ninety-two years, eleven months, and ten days old. He will die at 11:50 A.M. Ike has been alone in the room with him since ten minutes to ten the night before. His grandfather is in a semicomatose state, and much of his speech is incoherent. Ike, too, has been talking. Together and separately, they are trying to understand something. They do not always hear each other because sometimes they are talking simultaneously. But now, as his grandfather tells his version of what happened with the Chinese laundryman, Ike is silent.

FRANCESCO: He lives like a pig, this China man, *come un porco vero, capisci, Ignazio?* We go down, we come in the store, he say hello, hello, I say what you do my daughter? He's sweat, Ignazio, he's work in the back when we come inside, he look at us, he does no understand. I say my daughter, my daughter, what you do?

95

And Ralphie, he's big man, he takes the China man, he throws him in back through the curtain, and we go in. This is my daughter, no? I must believe, no? She swears to the priest, she puts her hand on the cross and she swears this China man he does things to her. But in the back, where is the bed? No bed, Ignazio. On the floor is a straw . . . *come si dice?* Mat? Mattress? *Come vuol' dire?* No bed. Only this skinny straw on the floor near where he irons the clothes. And Stella, she says there's movie pictures on the wall, pictures of girls, but where? No pictures on the wall. And a calendar where? No calendar with a Chinese lady, no thing like that. So where she gets this in her head? She makes it up? Or he hides everything when she runs away? He hides the bed, he hides the pictures, he hides the calendar? Ralphie says what you do to Stella? He says I bandage her finger. Ralphie says *I* give you finger, and push him against the wall, and the China man he's very scare, he looks at me, he looks at Pino and Giovanni and my father-law. I say *aspetta*, wait a minute, Ralph.

Because, Ignazio, tell me the true. If there is no bed and no pictures and no calendar, then maybe also there was no touch, eh? Maybe Stella don't lie, I don't think she lie, but maybe she think it happen what did not happen. So I sit down with the China man, and I say was my daughter here? My Stella? And he says yes.

And I say what you do to her, mister?

And he says I bandage her finger.

You touch her? I say. You put you hand under her dress? You cover her eye?

He says no. He shake his head. He says no again.

Ralphie says you a no-good lying bast, and he hit the man.

Then everybody is hit him, me too. And we go upstairs.

Ignazio, I don't know. I get very sick in my heart. I think, what is this America? A man's daughter is no safe two doors away? And to beat a poor man like myself? When maybe he is tell the true, but she swears on the cross? I decide to go home. This time I go home. This time I take Pino and his baby with me, there is no thing here for them, not no more, this time we go. I am thirta-four years old, it is enough. I promise you, Ignazio, this time I go home because I have been no more I wish to have this terrible things that happen, where in Italy, no, it does not, I will go home, I will tell Tessie, I will tell you grandma, I will say *no*, Tessie, we go home, you hear me, Tessie, I take you home now, I leave here, this place, we go home *now*, we *go*.

Grandpa, you might have made it. You just might have made it. If only the whole damn world hadn't decided to go to war the following week.

❖

It is to be remembered, by those who choose to ponder the ironies of alliances, that Italy was on the side of God (*our* side) in World War I. Japan was, too. And so was Russia, that dear good friend with whom we joined hands in a common cause again, less than thirty years later. War may be hell, and stupid besides, but that's not the point of this book, so let's not belabor the obvious. My grandfather recognized it as idiotic from the very beginning; as far as he was concerned, the world was conspiring to keep him from going home. When Italy entered the war in 1915, he shook his head in disgust and spat on the sidewalk outside the tailor shop.

But if Stella was undeniably American to begin with, she be-came even more so during World War I. It's easy for a girl entering puberty to become excited about all sorts of things, but war is the biggest thing going for pubescent girls and boys of all ages in *any* age, and World War I was the hugest spectacle that had come along in a long while, certainly the most extravagant (and onliest) since Stella's birth. For Stella, everything following World War I was simply old hat. World War II? So what? (Until she lost her eldest son in it, which senseless murder she justified with the

97

words "He died for America." You poor stupid woman, he died for *nothing*. And he was killed by a fucking wop; how did that sit with you, Mom? Did it make you feel even more American and less Italian?) Korea? Bush-league antics, and besides, they were killing Chinks, which served them right. Vietnam? Who ever heard of Vietnam before everybody started making such a stink about it? As wars go, Stella lived through the very best of them.

STUPENDOUS PRODUCTIONS, INC.
presents
The Great War
Cast of 8,528,831 (dead)
21,189,154 (wounded)

And for the first time ever in the history of warfare, the full-scale use of—heavy artillery, high-explosive shells, machine guns, barbed wire, *poison gas*, automobiles and trucks, armored cars and tanks, airplanes, and . . . SUBMARINES ! ! !

Now *that* was some war. That was a war you could follow with keen interest, even before America became involved in it. At times, Stella found it almost too exciting to bear. Now that the mundane events of her childhood were safely behind her—little everyday occurrences like walking in on the iceman and Filomena; or being in that kitchen when Angelina gushed out her life in the next room; or seeing Angelina laid out in a coffin in the front room of the Battatore apartment, Pino sobbing uncontrollably, a fresh burst of theatrical moans coming from the women in black whenever another relative entered the flower-bedecked room to pay respects; or watching Angelina's coffin being lowered into the ground in the Long Island cemetery, the day clear and bright in contrast to the solemn ritual, the priest from Mount Carmel intoning his elegy in Italian; and then just a few days later the Chinaman trying to get into her pants (dirty old Chink!)—why, my goodness, it had been a tumultuous and terrifically exciting couple of weeks that seemed to summarize and encapsulize all

98

the fun and adventure of growing up in a healthy, violent land that was beginning to test its muscle and gird its loins, stretch a bit, move out of its own childhood at just about the same time Stella moved out of hers. But *now?* Oh, good Lord, holy Jesus, Mary mother of God, here was a *war!* And *what* a war! Wow, you could follow that thing day by day in all the newspapers, and you could begin to take sides even before America itself began to take sides. You could study the maps and the battle lines as they shaped up, and wonder what it was like to be over there with bombs exploding all over the place and machine guns chattering and people screaming on the barbed wire and all. Wow!

During World War I, Stella's imagination soared. Cold print translated itself in her mind to the most vivid pictures in full color, Germans slicing off the hands of Belgian babies and raping nuns, and the English doing their own dastardly deeds, like putting strychnine in the coffee they served to German prisoners of war—it was almost *impossible* to imagine *all* the things going on over there, but Stella sure tried. She began to menstruate at the age of twelve (in the south of Italy, they sometimes start at eight), and this, too, was terribly frightening and exciting, unprepared as she was (Tess was too involved with going "to business" to notice that her eldest daughter was developing tiny little breasts, or to realize that if winter came, spring could not be far behind), and here it was—a virgin spring indeed, bubbling up out of the wells of her womanhood and scaring her half out of her mind. She ran to her Aunt Bianca's corset shop and told her she was bleeding to death like Angelina had, and Aunt Bianca calmed her (that dear, lovely, worldly woman) and introduced her to the mysteries of menstrual pads and the cycles of the moon. Stella must have felt enormously relieved when she left that shop, knowledgeable now, secure and somehow different. Being Stella, she probably felt more American as well, and undoubtedly walked a lot taller. For Christ's sake, she must have felt like John Wayne! (Stella Di Lorenzo, today you are a man!)

She wasn't John Wayne, nor was she even William S. Hart, his 1915 screen equivalent. She was just a little girl growing up, and the business of growing up was somehow connected in her mind to the ideal of growing up American. The ideal was, in many respects, pure and unsullied for her. It had a lot to do with the things she was being taught in the public schools of New York City, fantasies about George Washington chopping down the cherry tree, or Paul Revere riding his midnight horse through the streets of New England, or Patrick Henry knowing not what course other men might take, but as for him, baby, give him liberty, or Nathan Hale regretting that he had but . . . *whack*, the Englishman pulled the stick, and the trap door opened, and old Nathan was left hanging there in midair, kicking and twitching without ever having got out his last few words. Pop history. Who the hell knows if half those guys ever said a third of the things attributed to them? Can anyone imagine, for example, Jesus Christ himself, sitting before his disciples and spewing forth, nonstop, "To you it has been given to know the secrets of the kingdom of God; but for others they are in parables, so that seeing they may not see, and hearing they may not understand"? (Maybe you had to be there.)

Stella never quoted much from Jesus Christ, though she was learning her catechism three times a week at Mount Carmel on 115th Street in preparation for her First Holy Communion and her confirmation to follow. But she did quote a lot from the likes of John Paul Jones and Thomas Jefferson and Stephen Decatur and Abraham Lincoln. I got my first clue as to how she was taught when she recited two catch phrases that had been drummed into her head by Mrs. Pamela Frankel in the junior high school course on American History:

"Bull Run Number One, the Confederacy won.

"Bull Run Number Two, the Confederacy won, too."

She quoted these to me when I was six years old and in the first grade. Nothing much had changed in New York City's schools—I was being taught music appreciation the same way she'd been taught history. Until then, I had done most of my music appreciating in my grandfather's house, listening to my uncle bang away at the piano, pecking out one-finger melodies, searching for chords (invariably cacophonous) with his left hand, playing all the popular songs of the day, stuff like "Love Letters in the Sand" and "Out of Nowhere" and "Sweet and Lovely" (his choices now seem significant), all great old tunes which I myself still play. But they weren't teaching pop shlock when I was in elementary school, oh, no. For us little blind bastards, music appreciation was divided into twice-weekly sessions, one of them vocal, the other auditory, and both concentrating on stuff a little more profound than "Potatoes Are Cheaper." In the vocal hour, we were separated into Bluebirds and Blackbirds (not an ethnic breakdown since there *were* no blacks at my school) and we sang things like "The Lord High Executioner" from *The Mikado* or "By the Bend of the River" in four-part harmony. I was a Blackbird, and I hated the singing sessions. But I did enjoy listening to the records played on the wind-up phonograph in our school auditorium, and I guess I also enjoyed the "lyrics" Miss Alice Goodbody (that was her name; apt or not, I shall never know) wrote for the various compositions in an attempt to drill them into our heads. I'm not sure which philosophy of education was operating; I'm positive it wasn't John Dewey's. The following examples won't make much sense unless you know the melodies. If you *don't* know the melodies, then there *is* something to be said for the way I was taught them (and maybe for the way my mother was taught about the Civil War). Maestro?

> *Narcissus was*
> *A very good-looking boy.*
> *His image in the brook*
> *Would fi-ill him up with joy.*
> *He looked,*
> *And looked,*

101

> And looked,
> And looked,
> Until he turned
>   In-to a love-ly
> Flow-er.

Or . . .

> Dawn
> Over mountain and
> Dawn
> Over valley and
> Dawn
> While the shepherd is play-
>   ay-ay-ing his flute.

Or . . .

> Morning from "Peer Gynt"
> By Grieg the composer—
> Oh, morning has come
> And it's time to get up.

Or . . .

> Am-a-ryl-lis,
> Written by Ghys,
> Used to sell oranges,
> Fi-ive cents apiece.

One of my *mother's* favorites, which I'm sure she never was taught in school, and which I'm equally sure must have set my grandfather's teeth on edge each time she recited it, had no musical accompaniment; it was sheer soaring poetry:

> Julius Caesar,
> The Roman Greaser,
> Tripped and fell
> On an orange squeezer.

Understand, please, that Stella was simultaneously learning two seemingly contradictory things about America. In school, where all the pupils were the sons and daughters of immigrants (a fact appreciated and exploited by her teachers), she was being taught that America was a nation with a proud history of its own, nonetheless willing to welcome to its shores foreigners from many different lands (witness your own greenhorn parents, little darlings) who would eventually be absorbed into the mainstream, enriching the country and being enriched by it in turn. That's not a bad concept. That is, in fact, a damn fine concept. At the same time, in the ghetto, Stella was learning that the melting pot had hardly yet begun to boil. Charlie Shoe (who'd hastily moved to San Francisco) was a Chink. So was the man who'd taken over his laundry. They were both Chinks. In school, Stella could be told from dawn till sundown that Charlie was an American, or at least in the process of becoming an American, but you couldn't convince her that the man who'd reached under her dress was anything but a Chink. Nor did her terminology (and the stereotyped ideas *shaped* by it) have anything to do with her supposedly traumatic experience. The people who lived west of Lexington Avenue were "niggers" and a mysterious menace, and her feelings about them had nothing to do with the sanctity of her bloomers. (Or maybe so, come to think of it.) The bearded man who came around once a week taking orders for dry goods was "the Jew." Stella called him this to his face. He would knock on the door, and she would open it and yell, "Mama, it's the Jew." I don't think she ever knew his name. He was simply the Jew. The German family on the fourth floor were *i tedeschi*, the Germans. Her father (she knew this, she probably taunted him deliberately with the derogatory reference in her epic poem on the noblest Roman) was a wop, a dago, a greaser, a greaseball and a spaghetti bender—but he was not an American.

In Stella's mind, though (and *this* is what's amazing), there was no conflict between what she learned in school and what she

103

learned in the ghetto. For her it was extremely simple. The ideal was for everybody to be American. To be American was to be good, noble, pure, proud, brave, and capable of saying things like "Damn the torpedos, full speed ahead!" To be American meant studying French in junior high school. To be American meant lighting giant bonfires in the street on Election Day or roasting mickies in the empty lot on First Avenue and 121st Street. To be American meant being thrilled on the Fourth of July (tingling even down *there*) when you heard the band in Jefferson Park playing John Philip Sousa. To be American meant having a handsome suntanned uncle who was a gambler in Arizona and who spoke English with a drawl, and who did actually take you for a ride in his flivver when he came to visit at Christmastime in the year 1915. Unless you were all these things, and did all these things, and felt all these things, and understood all these things, you weren't American. What you had to do *then* was try very hard to get into this magic red-white-and-blue club, presided over by young Stella herself, who decided, unilaterally, on the entrance requirements.

Speaking English was, of course, the first and foremost of the initiation tests. Anybody who did not speak English as purely as Stella was automatically disqualified, maybe for life. (My mother still says "He don't want any," and pronounces "boil" as "berl," but she never says "ain't," which simply ain't American, by her standards.) But young Stella also took into account a person's appearance, whether or not one dressed according to the fashion dictates of the magazines Tess still slavishly subscribed to, or looked instead like somebody "fresh off the boat." If English was spoken well enough to please her, if clothes passed muster, she watched for other things—not for nothing was she the high priestess. Did a person, for example, know who had starred in *Judith of Bethulia* and who had directed the film? Did the aspiring American know the lyrics to "Take Me to the Midnight Cake Walk Ball"? How many Ford jokes were in his repertoire? Did

104

he know all the current comic-strip favorites, was he capable of differentiating between the work of Clare Briggs, for example, and Tad Dorgan? Was Hans the blond one in *The Captain and the Kids*? Or was it Fritz? Could the applicant speak French? (Her own French was limited to what she'd learned in one year at junior high school before the program was dropped as premature for children at that level. She learned quite useful sentences like "*Vite, vite, nous manquerons le match de football!*") Oddly, if someone could speak fluent Italian or German or Yiddish, this didn't make him an American. Only speaking French as well as she did (*Je suis américaine, n'oubliez pas*) qualified the petitioner for entrance.

She had a dream, Stella. When she was fifteen, she dreamed that everyone would one day be American—like her. No greenhorns anywhere in the streets of her golden city. Everybody talking English like mad (when they weren't talking French), everybody going to the movies every Saturday, and riding in Ford cars, and dressing like the people in *Vogue*, and making wisecracks all the time, and roasting mickies. America the beautiful.

I had a dream for America, too.

It was similar to my mother's except for one vital difference.

But neither of us ever realized our separate dreams.

❖

In April of 1917, when President Wilson and the Congress declared war against those Huns who were doing all sorts of atrocious things that simply incensed a devout American like Stella, she cheered her brains out and marched up the middle of 116th Street with four hundred other young American teen-agers like herself, chanting dire warnings and predictions to Kaiser Bill, who probably didn't hear her. She was fifteen, going on sixteen. The next few years of her life passed in a near delirium of excitement. Where the war had earlier been a remote fantasy translated from newspaper reports, it now became immediate. Everywhere around her, there was the activity of a nation gearing up to save the world for democracy.

The people running the war didn't have to try very hard to sell it; anti-German feelings were running high long before the formal declaration of hostilities, and patriotic fervor was almost hysterical. But nonetheless, they *did* have a product on their hands which was, by definition, lethal. And they decided they had better do something to make the product seem a trifle more palatable. The reasoning must have gone something like this: We are sending a lot of our boys over there to die on foreign soil because we want to make the world safe for democracy, which is an inspiring cause, to be sure, but mightn't someone (most likely a woman) ask a possibly embarrassing question such as "If my son goes over there to France and gets killed in a trench over there filled with poison gas and German bayonets, why then he will no longer be *in* this world, and how will it matter that he made it safe for democracy?" Now the way to avoid this question is to develop some sort of sales talk, some sort of pitch, native-born and inspired in concept, which we can shpiel at anyone out there who is likely to ask any questions about what this war is all about.

What we'll do is we'll organize bond rallies, so people will concentrate on buying bonds instead of on dying sons, put out these little Liberty Books, you know, where they can stick twenty-five-cent stamps in them, "Lick a Stamp and Lick the Kaiser," get some of our movie folk out there to push the bonds, maybe Doug Fairbanks wearing boxing gloves lettered with "Victory" on one glove and "Liberty Bonds" on the other, and have him knock out some Kaiser we can get from Central Casting, get them away from the prime question, you see, which is "*Why* are you sending our sons to be killed?" And we'll get old Herbert Hoover here, who's our Food Administrator, to ask for voluntary sacrifices on the part of all the people, ask them to hold off eating bread or other wheat products on Mondays and Wednesdays, and

106

pork on Thursdays and Saturdays, and any other kind of meat on Tuesdays—did we leave a day out? Idea is to get them thinking about their *own* sacrifices, you see, maybe even grumbling about them a bit, so they won't be able to think of their sons getting legs blown off or being sliced up the middle by some German bayonet. Get them involved *here*, you see, do you get the overall idea?

Stella had no trouble getting the overall idea because, in her case, it had something going for it that did not apply to the vast majority of Americans. Since most of the men immediately surrounding her—her father, her brothers, her uncles, cousins, and goombahs—were either too young or too old or not even American citizens, they were not required to go to Europe to have their brains blown out. They were safe. So what better way to enjoy a war? Not only did Stella have all those socks and sweaters to knit, not only did she have the thrill of seeing her favorite movie stars right there in New York City pushing the sale of war bonds, not only did she herself personally collect eight hundred and thirty-seven peach pits which she weighed on the grocer's scale downstairs (having been informed that it took seven pounds of pits to make a filter for one gas mask), she *also* was secure in the knowledge that nobody near and dear to her was going to be killed. War was fun.

The only person near and dear to her (though he wasn't near, and certainly not dear to her in the years between 1917 and 1919) who *might* have been killed was a stranger named Jimmy Di Palermo, my father-to-be. While Stella was collecting her peach pits for a filter, my father was throwing away his mask because the fucking thing didn't work, anyway—not against mustard gas.

❖

Giacomo Roberto Di Palermo was born on East 103rd Street in the year 1898. When America entered the war, he was nineteen

107

years old. In June of 1917, he walked over to P.S. 121 and registered for the draft. By August of the following year, he was getting shot at in France.

My father rarely talked about the war. Even when I was a kid, and he took my brother and me to pictures like *Dawn Patrol* and *What Price Glory?*, even then, walking home to our apartment on 120th Street, he refused to answer any of our questions about the war. "What was it *really* like, Daddy?" we would ask. And he would say, "Oh, it was okay."

Maybe it *was* okay. Maybe he'd lived through worse things than World War I.

In 1965, when one of my last record albums was being prepared for release, I was asked by the man compiling the liner notes to write something about the background of my parents, the idea being to show how they had influenced the music I make. (I think he had heard someplace that my father used to play drums.) I asked my father to jot down a few details, which I planned to edit before sending them on. This is what he wrote, on lined paper:

Dear Ike:

Here's my autobiography in part.

I came from Harlem in a prominent Italian section. My parents were Italian-born. I was born on the East Side around the 100's. I left school in the 4th grade because my father passed away and I went out to work to help my mother and the rest of our brood, consisting of two sisters and two brothers. I started as an errand boy of a delicatessen. From there I worked on the New York City Transit (trolley lines) in the repair shop. From there I worked in a laundry running all the machines. Then I worked in a florist, and really learned this trade. While here I suddenly was plummeted in the machine-and-beading line. My mother went into a partnership with a man who graduated Cooper Union in Art. He was the designer. My services and my younger brother's

108

were free because my mother went into this business without a penny. So our pay was put into the business until the amount was made up. I learned designing from this man and did very well.

Later my mother split up the business and we went on our own. I took care of the designing and drummed up the business. My mother took care of the girls inside of the store, also the home workers. While working here, I was compelled to take over a set of drums from one of our buddies on our block, so I may finish the payments. That's how I became a musician. I formed a five-piece orchestra known as "Jimmy Palmer and the Phantom Five." We did very well and got lots of work. Weddings, socials, baptisms, block parties, at most of the ballrooms in and around New York. I was still in the business of embroidery and crochet beading. At one of these functions, I met my wife Stella (it was at her sister's engagement party). After a short engagement, we were married in 1923. A year later, our first son, Anthony, was born. I took a summer engagement in Keansburg, N.J., at the palais de dance. That's where I formed a Dixieland band known as the "Original Louisiana Five."

When we finished this engagement, we went on the road with a show called the "Atlantic City Review." We were on the independent circuit. We lasted about 6 months on the road, but the one-night stands was too much for me. We were booked at the "Wm Fox" theatre at 107th Street and Lexington Ave but turned it down. We still took bookings around town, then I realized that our business was going out of style and we paid up our creditors and went out. My second son was born in 1926. Then I took a test for the Post Office dept. and was appointed a sub in Jan. 1927. Then came the stock market crash in 1929 and our list was frozen. That meant 8 yrs as a sub with puny wages. A job here and there in music really helped along. Finally I was made a regular letter carrier in 1937. I was appointed to Tremont P.O. I worked there two years and was transferred to Grand Central P.O. I worked there three (3) years and went to Wmsbridge P.O. in the Bronx. I worked here for 29-½ years

109

and retired in 1963. A total of 36-½ years for Uncle Sam. I am retired two years so far and really like it.

During my younger years when I was in my 20's I was a very good dancer. I gave exhibitions of Pat Rooney, Frisco, and a good imitation of the famous Charlie Chaplin. I now like to dab in art work, poetry and like to putter around my coin and stamp collection. My son is married and have three grandchildren, all boys.

This is my life.

J. R. Di Palermo

Rebecca, to whom I was still married at the time, read my father's "life" to me, and commented on his singularly beautiful handwriting. I began to cry. I cried because there was nothing in it I could use for the goddamn liner notes, and I cried because he had neglected to mention three significant things: that his first son was killed in Italy in the year 1943; that he himself had fought on the battlefields of Europe in 1918; or that he had spent two years of his life in a Catholic orphanage, where he and his older brother Nickie were sent when their father was killed in 1906. He was eight years old at the time.

❖

Giacomo wets the bed.

The nuns do not like this. When one of the children wets his bed, they send him out to stand in the sun with the sheets over his head until the urine has dried. Giacomo doesn't know why they do this to him. Wouldn't it be simpler to wash the sheets and then hang them up to dry? He does not understand a lot of things about this place. Most of all, he does not understand why he is here.

The nuns terrify Giacomo. They are always dressed in black, the way the women were dressed in black when Papa went to sleep. Papa was inside the box in the parlor, but they would not open the cover to let him see. His mother said there had been an

110

accident, *un incidente,* something with a trolley car, and that Papa had gone to sleep afterward, and the trolley car was why they could not open the box, they did not wish to disturb his sleep. They put the box in the ground. He wondered why they were letting his father sleep in the ground. Nickie said, "He's dead, dope."

There was talk in the kitchen. The uncles and aunts were talking in Italian to his mother. They could not send the girls away. Neither could they send the youngest child, Paolo, who was only four. They would have to send Giacomo and Nicolao. His mother explained it patiently afterward. There was not enough money. Even with help from the family, there was not enough money. He and Nicolao would have to go away for a little while. The nuns would take good care of them. They would be fed well. It would only be for a little while.

He does not want to hate the nuns, they are married to Jesus. But they make him stand with the sheets smelling of urine over his head, drying in the sun, and they beat him with a cat-o'-nine-tails when he can't remember his Hail Marys or his Holy Marys Mother of God, or when he does not make his bed to suit them. His sheets always smell of urine. They do not change the sheets except on Fridays, and he wets the bed almost every night, and in the morning he stands in the sun until the sheets are dry, and then tries to make his bed look neat again, making it up with hospital corners the way the sisters have taught him, but though he pulls the sheets very tight and tucks them in all around, they are always wrinkled and yellow and smelling of urine, and his bed never looks like the other children's beds, and the nuns are never satisfied, and they beat him because his bed is not right, and each time they beat him he remembers at night the beating that day, and becomes frightened, and wets the bed again, and still does not know why he is in this place. He does not even know where this place *is.* He was taken here in a bus. He got on the bus at Ninety-sixth Street, he said good-bye to his mother and his sisters

111

and little Paulie, and then he and Nickie got on the bus with the nuns, and now he is here and he does not know where he is, and does not understand why. The other children in this place have no mothers and fathers. Why is he here in a place like this? He *has* a mother, her name is Serafina, she lives on One Hundred and Third Street, Two-Two-Seven East One Hundred and Third Street, Apartment Four-A, he knows it by heart in case he gets lost. He *has* a mother.

Sister Rosalinda calls him *Pisciasotto*, which means "Pisspants."

"*Buon giorno, Pisciasotto*," she says, and smiles.

"*Buon giorno, Sorella.*"

He despises her.

She tells him of the Devil. She tells him that anyone who wets the bed as often as he does, with no regard for the comfort or health of those around him, subjecting others to the stench of his waste and his filth, anyone who has so little control over his bodily functions, is a prime target for the Devil, who can see what transpires on earth even as the good Lord Jesus can see, and who will surely come for Giacomo in the middle of the night if he does not stop wetting the bed, will come for him and lean over the bed with his glittering red eyes and breathe upon Giacomo a breath as foul as the stink of Giacomo's own waste, and clutch him into his hairy arms, his body cold and slimy though he comes from the depths of the inferno, clutch him to his chest and spirit him away to Hell, his giant black leathery wings flapping as they make the fearful descent to that place of doom where Giacomo will burn in eternal fires stinking of urine, and the Devil will laugh and claim him for his own. Giacomo is more afraid of Sister Rosalinda than he is of the Devil. Would the Devil make him stand in the sun with wet sheets over his head? Would the Devil beat him with a cat-o'-nine-tails in the small white room the sister shares with Sister Giustina, who limps?

One night, he has a good idea.

It makes him laugh just to think of it.

The other children have been taken out to the summerhouse behind the dormitory, where sometimes one or another of the sisters plays violin or flute for them, or tells a story of the horrors of Hell and the rewards of Heaven. This is Sister Rosalinda's night, and he knows she will be talking about the Devil; she talks so much about the Devil that sometimes Giacomo thinks she is married to *him* instead of to Jesus. He has been denied the pleasure of sitting in the summerhouse; he is being punished. Last night, he wet the bed again, and this morning he could not stand in the sun to dry his sheets because it was raining. So he has been sent to bed early, to sleep on the wet sheets and dry them with his own body warmth—unless he happens to wet them again, which he will most surely do. But he has an idea, and the idea causes him to chuckle out loud. He wishes Nickie were here so he could tell him the idea, but his brother is out with the other children, listening to Sister Rosalinda telling about what it's like to be with the Devil in Hell—you'd think she'd been there herself one time.

He creeps out of bed, oh, this is a good idea.

He steals through the empty dormitory, past the beds lined up in a row, the washstand and basin beside each bed, the tooth-brushes in glasses, the night light burning in the corridor outside. There is a nun sitting on a straight-backed chair at the end of the hall, engrossed in saying her beads, why are they always fingering their beads and mumbling to themselves? She does not notice him as he stealthily opens the screen door at the end of the hall and slips outside. The air is clean and fresh, he knows he is in the country someplace, but he does not know where, maybe as far away as the Bronx, maybe that is where they've sent him. He can hear crickets in the bushes, and can see fireflies flitting through the trees. He once caught a firefly and pulled off the part that glowed and stuck it to his finger like a ring, and Sister Giustina limped over to him and said that he would be punished for hurting one of God's creatures, and she took him to the room

113

she shared with Sister Rosalinda, and they beat him again that afternoon, even though he had not wet the bed the night before, and of course he wet the bed again after the beating. Why had God made such tempting creatures as fireflies, whose lights could be pulled off and made into rings? He had never seen a firefly before he came to this place, and no one had warned him that it was one of God's creatures. Didn't Sister Giustina slap mosquitoes dead, and were they not also God's creatures? Or did Sister Rosalinda later punish her in the small white room they shared? He had once spied Sister Rosalinda whipping herself with the same cat-o'-nine-tails she used on him, her habit lowered to her waist, flailing the leather thongs of the whip over her left shoulder, her bare white back covered with welts. Had Sister Rosalinda wet the bed the night before? He did not understand nuns.

He can hear her voice in the darkness as he crawls across the lawn, still wet from the day's rain. She is telling the children that in Hell there is no recourse, there is no one to turn to because the Devil presides and he is thoroughly evil and without mercy, and his assistants are as fiendish as he, and the people suffering in Hell are evil, too, which is why they were sent there in the first place, and wherever one turns there is only evil to be encountered in the flames, and one can expect no succor from those who have fallen from God's grace and who fear not the Lord and who have in their hearts no remorse for their evil deeds; he creeps closer.

The summerhouse is an octagonal-shaped building constructed entirely of wood, latticework covering the base, a screened wooden platform lined on all eight sides with benches upon which the children sit, columns supporting the roof. Giacomo crawls under the lattice and under the platform and covers his mouth with his hand to suppress a giggle. His initial idea had been to let out a moan from the depths of Hell, frightening and delighting the other children. But now that he is actually under the platform, he notices that there is a space between two of the boards, and he can see one of Sister Rosalinda's black shoes and the hem of her habit, and he has a better idea that suddenly comes to him from the text of her story and almost causes him to wet his pants with glee right there under the summerhouse. Sister Rosalinda is expanding upon her theme by telling the children that just as there is no recourse in Hell for those who are evil, so it is on earth for those who will not follow the teachings of the Lord Jesus. The Devil will seek out the sinners, he will reach up from the subterranean depths (oh, this is *such* a good idea, much better than the first), will reach out with his hairy hand to claim them as his own, seize them in his powerful taloned fingers . . .

It is here that Giacomo reaches up through the space in the boards, reaches up from the subterranean depths beneath the summerhouse, and clutches Sister Rosalinda's ankle in his powerful taloned fingers.

❖

My father was, and still is, an inveterate joker.

He tells that story with enormous relish, even though he insists Sister Rosalinda almost had a heart attack, and even though he was to regret his prank for the remainder of his stay at the orphanage—eighteen months and four days of a living Hell without mercy or recourse, just as the good sister had promised. She steadfastly maintained, incidentally, that after the hand reached up to grab her from below—and she let out a yell that must have alerted even Saint Peter up there at the pearlies, screaming, *"Il Diavolo, il Diavolo!"* while the children scattered and stumbled and shrieked in echo, *"Il Diavolo, il Diavolo!"* one of them crashing through the screen in his haste to get away from this infernal creature who had reached up to grab one of God's many wives (if he could grab a *nun*, who on earth was safe?)—she swore on a stack of Bibles, that smiling religious bitch who made my father's life miserable, swore that the imprint of the Devil's hand remained on her flesh for weeks after the episode, bright red against

115

the lily white of her virgin fields. Nickie told my father he was stupid for trying to buck the system. ("Don't buck the system," my Uncle Nick always said. "You try and buck the system, the system busts your head.")

My father hadn't been trying to buck the system. He was going for a laugh. I don't know when he began protecting himself with humor, maybe it *was* way back then when he was standing in the hot sun breathing in the stink of his own piss. I do know that he uses it the way other men might use anger or brute strength or guile. If things are getting a bit too serious (or even if they aren't), my father immediately tells a joke. Whenever I telephone him, he will answer my call (or *anybody's* call) in one of two ways: (1) He will disguise his voice and say, "Police Headquarters, Sergeant Clancy speaking," or "This is the Aquarium, did you want some fish?" or "Department of Sanitation, keep it clean," or (in a high falsetto) "This is Stella Di Palermo, how do you do?" (2) If he answers in his *own* voice, he will invariably say, "Your nickel, start talking," or "This one is on you," or sometimes, abruptly, and impatiently, and in mock anger, like a busy executive at General Motors called to the phone during an urgent meeting, "Yes, what *is* it?" (This one still gets a laugh from me, though he's done it perhaps ten thousand times.) He can calm a tense moment at the dinner table, and there were plenty of those between Rebecca and me, by suddenly tossing in a pun from left field, usually way off target but sometimes genuinely funny. I don't think I've ever had a serious conversation with him in my life.

When I called to tell him I'd left Rebecca, he answered the phone and snapped in his General Motors manner, "Yes, what *is* it?" I told him Rebecca and I were through. There was a long silence on the phone. Then he said, "Just a minute, I'll get your mother." Only months later did he say, "Ike, sometimes things work out for the best in life." That's the closest we've ever come to exchanging confidences. He used to talk to my brother Tony a lot. I can remember him and Tony having long conversations in the kitchen of our Bronx apartment. I never knew what they were talking about, and I thought at the time that I was too young to share such intimacies, that when I got older—like Tony —maybe my father and I could talk together the way they did. It never happened. (Once, and God forgive me for ever having thought this, I figured he didn't talk to me because I was blind.) The comic routines became more and more frequent after Tony was killed. He never mentions Tony now; it is as though his first son never existed. Except sometimes, when he turns away from the television and, forgetting for a moment, says to me, "Watch this guy, Tony, he's a riot," without knowing he has used his dead son's name, without realizing that each time he makes such a slip it brings sudden, unbidden tears to my eyes.

You fucking wop who killed him, I wish you the plague!

❖

As best I can piece this together, my father worked as an errand boy in a delicatessen only *after* he was released from the orphanage. By that time, his older sister Liliana had a steady job with the telephone company, and my grandmother figured she could safely afford to take her sons home. And, again filling in the gaps, I think he was drafted into the Army sometime after the jobs in the transit authority's repair shop and the laundry, and after the apprenticeship with the florist. In brief, he was working in the "business of embroidery and crochet beading" while simultaneously playing "weddings, socials, baptisms, block parties, at most of the ballrooms in and around New York" when he met my mother. And I estimate this to be in August of 1922, long after the armistice had been signed and the country was attempting a return to normalcy.

Now make of this what you will, analysts of the world.

The first band my father formed was called Jimmy Palmer and

117

the Phantom Five. Even given the enormous popularity of Griffith's film *The Birth of a Nation*, which had opened in Los Angeles at Clune's Auditorium in February of 1915 and had gone on from there to play to enormous crowds at theaters all over the country, a film that vividly depicted sheeted and hooded Ku Klux Klansmen riding the night; and given the resurgence of the Klan in the years immediately following the war (its membership would total four cotton-pickin' *million* by 1924!); and tossing in the arrest on May 5, 1920 (shortly before my father formed his band), of two immigrants named Nicola Sacco and Bartolomeo Vanzetti on charges of felony murder, and the attendant publicity given the case when it was discovered that both these ginzoes were anarchists and draft dodgers besides, which might very well have caused my father to pick the Anglicized *nom d'orchestre* Jimmy Palmer, and to further shield his true identity by hiding his face as well as his Italian background; even taking into account my father's penchant for disguises (his Charlie Chaplin imitation was a pip, he says), does it not seem passing strange that he would choose as the costumes for himself and his musicians (are you ready?) white sheets and hoods? I am not for one moment suggesting that standing in the sun for close to two years, with a piss-laden sheet over the head, warps the personality and causes paranoia. I am only stating a simple fact. My father's band was called Jimmy Palmer and the Phantom Five and they wore long white sheets with sleeves sewn into them, and they wore white peaked hoods with stitched eye holes, and they wore these costumes winter, spring, and fall, and also during the hottest summer in years—which was when my Aunt Cristina got engaged to the man who would become my Uncle Matt.

Stella didn't know which one of the Phantom Five was Jimmy Palmer; they all looked the same under those hoods with their eyes peering out of the holes like dopes. Also, was the name of the band strictly correct English? Since there were only *five* musicians, shouldn't they have called themselves Jimmy Palmer and the Phantom *Four?* Stella suspected, too, that the reason they were wearing those disguises was that they were lousy and afraid they'd be lynched in the streets afterward if anybody recognized them. She was, to tell the truth, altogether bored by Cristina's engagement party. She had been kissed and hugged by distant cousins and aunts and uncles and goombahs and goomahs she didn't know existed, some of them from places as far away as Red Bank, New Jersey, and if another smelly greaseball with a walrus mustache pressed his sweaty cheek to hers, she would scream. She had been told that maybe Uncle Joe would be coming in from Arizona for the party, but at the last minute, he couldn't make it. Her sister had boasted that her fiancé Matt had connections, and would be able to supply beer for the party (prohibition having been in full force for almost two years now), but as usual Matt had failed to make good on his promise. The only beverages were soda pop, and some hooch certain to cause blindness or baldness, plus the ever-present dago red, still being fermented in basements all over Harlem, just as though the Volstead Act hadn't been passed at all. Her father was ossified by eight o'clock. It was the first time she'd ever seen him that way. He kept telling everyone what a pity it was, *che peccato,* that Umberto, Tess's father and Cristina's grandfather, the man who had taught him his trade, had passed away two years ago and could not be here to enjoy the joyous occasion of Cristina's engagement to this fine young man, Matteo Diamante (already known as Matty Diamond in the streets, years before Legs Diamond achieved renown as a gangster). And then he said it was also a shame that none of the family back in Fiormonte could be here, either, and seemed to recall quite suddenly that a great many members of the Di Lorenzo family were now dead, his father having passed away in 1916, and his mother the following year, and then his youngest sister, Maria, who had asked him why there were no gifts on Christmas morning in the year 1900, and he had promised her there would be gifts the following year, but had never returned,

119

and now she was dead of malaria, none of them here to share this festive occasion—and he began to cry, which Stella thought extremely sloppy and very old-fashioned.

Her sister's fiancé was a darkly handsome young man who affected the speech and mannerisms of some of the gangster types he knew only casually, and who was enormously flattered to have been dubbed Matty Diamond, which seemed to have class and swagger and a touch of notoriety besides. Actually, he was an honest cab driver, who went to confession every week, and he'd probably have fainted dead away if anyone so much as suggested that he assist in the commission of a crime. But it was hinted in Harlem nonetheless that he had "connections," and these mysterious connections were supposed to be capable of performing services such as providing beer for his engagement party, which they hadn't. He was crazy about Cristina, and insanely jealous as well. He was drinking the bathtub gin, and was almost as drunk as Francesco.

Stella, at twenty, loved her sister dearly and wished her nothing but the best of luck, but she did think seventeen was a little young to be getting engaged, especially when the man in question was six years Cristie's senior, and reputed to have lost two toes to frostbite during the war. (He certainly *danced* as though he had two missing toes.) She herself had been offered proposals of marriage by two different men in the past year, one of whom was a second cousin, naturally turned down since she didn't want to have idiot children. The other was a rookie policeman named Artie Regan, whom she'd met at her father's tailor shop, where he always seemed to be dropping in to pass the time of day with Pino and Papa until she got wise to the fact that he was really coming by to catch a glimpse of her. She had dated him on and off for more than six months until she realized he was serious. Her father had never shown anything but the coldest courtesy to Regan, and she knew that if she even mentioned that Regan "wanted her," her father would take to the streets with a meat cleaver. An Irishman? The memory of the southern Italian is long, long, long. So she'd said so long to Artie, who really was a very nice and gentle sort of person for an Irish cop, and had decided she'd take her time finding the right man, even if Cristie *was* in such a hurry to get herself engaged to a fellow with only eight toes.

On the night of her sister's engagement party, Stella was wearing a red-beaded dress with black fringe and plunging V neck, breasts bound in the flapper style, stockings rolled below her rouged knees, red satin slippers. She had had her hair shingle-bobbed two months before, in the current vogue, and she was wearing golden hoop earrings and carrying a black-beaded bag with red fringe. A package of Sweet Caporal cigarettes was inside the bag. She wouldn't have dreamt of smoking in her father's presence, or even in public, but whenever she was in the bathroom alone, she puffed away like a steam engine. (She once caught Cristie smoking, and swatted her, telling her she was too young.) Dancing with her brother Luke to the miserable music Mr. Jimmy Palmer and his five specters were making, she felt sophisticated and chic and svelte and gorgeous and desirable, and she had no idea that Jimmy Palmer himself, watching her through the holes in his hood while banging away at his drums, was thinking the exact same thing. Her chubby brother Dominick came waltzing out onto the floor in a wise-aleck, fifteen-year-old solo imitation of his older sister and brother, and Luke kicked out at him playfully with one long leg, and Jimmy Palmer watched Stella's backside as she bumped it in disdain at the younger boy, and saw, as Luke turned her in his direction, the creamy white expanse of throat above the V-necked yoke of the red dress, and not bad gams either, altogether a very spiffy dish.

God knows what music he was playing in those days, or how he could possibly concentrate on it while simultaneously watching Stella through the holes in his hood. He was not to form his own Dixieland band until 1924, following an already well-established

121

trend. But jazz had found its way from New Orleans to Chicago in 1917, and men like King Oliver, Louis Armstrong, and Jelly Roll Morton were beginning to be imitated in black Harlem and elsewhere in New York as well. Chances are, though, that my father's band was more influenced by Paul Whiteman, who called himself the King of Jazz, but who played the sort of music I don't even like to think about, much less dwell upon. The Phantom Five undoubtedly played a great many fox trots, tangos, and two-steps, the craze for such lunatic dances as the bunny hug, the turkey trot, the kangaroo, the snake, the grizzly bear, the crab, and a veritable zooful of others having all but vanished during the war. And possibly, just possibly, one or another of his musicians might occasionally have tried a lick in emulation of what they considered to be real nigger funk, but their stuff was mired, man, it had to be. I heard many of my father's subsequent bands when I was growing up, and I would say that Stella's assessment of the Phantom Five in 1922 was probably accurate: they were lousy. (My father claims, however, that Mike Riley, the trumpet player who coauthored "The Music Goes 'Round and 'Round," a resounding hit that all but smothered the airwaves in 1935, had played in one of his early bands. I guess it's true. My father has a way of hitching his wagon to any passing star. He claims, for example, that James Cagney grew up in his neighborhood. "Oh sure, I knew Jimmy when we were kids." I am his most recently passing star.) *Whatever* he was playing in that hot and smelly hall on 116th Street, he played it without benefit of sheet music; my father never learned to read a note of music, and could not tell a single paradiddle from a double.

He made his move during a ten-minute break. Munching a ham and cheese sandwich on a soggy roll, his hood tucked into the white cord sash at his waist, he two-stepped over to Matty Diamond, who was said to have connections and who had recommended the Phantom Five to the girl's father. Matty was standing at the makeshift bar, wooden planks set up on horses and covered with a long white tablecloth, in deep and serious conversation with his future father-in-law. Both men were pissed to the gills. Francesco had a glass of red wine in his hand. Through a pair of twisted straws, Matty was sipping homemade gin from a soda pop bottle.

"How's it going, Matt?" Jimmy asked.

"Fine, who's that?" Matty said, and turned away from the bar.

"Me. Jimmy Palmer. Music okay?"

"Beautiful," Matty said, and put his arm around Jimmy. "That is some beautiful music you fellows are making. Where'd you learn to play that way, huh?"

"Oh, I been playing drums a long time now."

"Well, it certainly shows, the way you play them things," Matty said. "Papa," he said, and turned to Francesco, "I want you to meet Jimmy Palmer, he's the leader of the band there."

"*Piacere*," Francesco said, and held out his hand. The ensuing handshake was a bit awkward in that the hand Francesco extended was the one holding the glass of wine.

"Nice to meet you," Jimmy said.

"*Conosce 'La Tarantella'?*" Francesco asked.

"Oh, sure, would you like to hear that?" Jimmy said.

"He likes all that greaseball music," Matty whispered.

"Well, we like to play to suit everybody," Jimmy said. "Say, who's the . . . ?"

"Why do you fellows wear them things, them costumes?" Matty asked.

"Just an idea," Jimmy said, and smiled.

"It's a good idea," Matty said. "It makes you look very good, them costumes."

"Thank you. Matty, I was wondering if you knew . . ."

"Listen, I think maybe you ought to figure on overtime," Matty said. "Papa, I think maybe the band ought to stay past twelve, don't you think?"

"*Cosa?*" Francesco said, and belched.

123

"How much you fellows charge for overtime?" Matty said.

"Well, overtime's more expensive," Jimmy said.

"Sure, how much, don't worry about it."

"We get six dollars a man for overtime."

"That's an hour? Six dollars an hour?"

"That's right."

"What does that come to for all of you fellows?"

"Thirty dollars. It'd cost you more with a union band."

"Oh, sure. Papa, they want thirty dollars more if they play after midnight."

"*Cosa?*" Francesco said.

"It's okay," Matty said. "Don't worry about it, Jimmy."

"Who's the girl in the red dress, would you know?" Jimmy asked.

"Who?"

"Over there."

"What girl?"

"In the red dress."

"The girl in the red dress?"

"Over there. The beaded dress."

"Oh, yes," Matty said.

"Who is she, would you know?"

"Oh, yes."

"Well, who?"

"That's my sister-in-law. My future sister-in-law. Stella."

"What'sa matta my Stella?" Francesco asked.

"Nothing, Papa. This man here wanted to know her name."

"Stella," Francesco said, and nodded in agreement. Stella was most certainly his daughter's name.

"Well, I'll see you around, huh?" Jimmy said, and put on his hood, and walked over to where Stella was talking to her sister. "Hi, Stella," he said. "How do you like the music?"

Stella turned to look at him. She had green eyes. He did not know any girls with green eyes.

"The music is absolutely the cat's meow," she said sarcastically, but her tone was lost on him. He was drowning in her eyes.

"Glad you like it," he said. "I'm Jimmy Palmer. It's my band."

"You've got *some* band there, Jimmy Palmer," Stella said. "All you need now is some horses, and you could go out burning crosses on niggers' lawns."

"Oh, yeah," Jimmy said, missing the allusion to *Birth of a Nation*, which Stella had seen four times. "You know any horses can play saxophone?"

Stella laughed and looked at him more closely. Or rather, looked at this hooded and sheeted person, brown eyes showing in the holes of the hood, some two or three inches taller than she was, a nice voice, he seemed to speak English very good. "Jimmy Palmer," she said. "Is that an Italian name?"

"That's the name I use," he said.

"Use for what?"

"For when I'm playing. We play all over the city," he said.

"What's your real name?"

"Jimmy Di Palermo."

"Are you from the other side, or were you born here?"

"Here," he said. "On a Hun' Third Street."

"I was born here, too," Stella said, and smiled.

"You got any requests or anything?" Jimmy said.

"Yeah, I got one request," Stella said.

"What's that? We'll play it in the next set."

"It's not a song," Stella said.

"What is it, then?"

"Why'n't you take off that thing on your head and let a person see what you look like? That's my request."

"Sure," he said, and took off the hood.

He was not a bad-looking fellow. His eyes, as she already knew, were brown. He had a longish, thin nose, not unlike her father's, black hair combed back straight from his forehead sort of like Valentino's, though of course he wasn't half so handsome. He

125

had a nice smile and good teeth. She wondered what he was wearing under that sheet. He probably dressed like a greenhorn.

"*Il fait très chaud aujourd'hui,*" she remarked, and much to her surprise, he answered, "Oh, *beaucoup, beaucoup, mam'selle,*" and she said craftily, "Do you know what that means?"

"Oh, yes, I picked up a little French when I was over there."

"In the war, do you mean?"

"Yes, I was with the 107th Infantry Regiment, 27th Division, and I picked up a little French."

"We must have a talk sometime," Stella said.

"*Comme vous voulez,*" Jimmy said, which he had picked up from a little French hooker he had picked up. "Are you sure there's no request you'd like to hear? We can play almost anything."

"I don't suppose you would know my favorite song," Stella said.

"What song is that, Stella?"

"It's 'The Sheik of Araby.'"

"Oh, yes," Jimmy said, "we can play that. My piano player has the sheet music. Lots of people think that that particular song was written for Valentino, for the piano players to play in the movie houses, you know, when they're showing the picture. But that's not true, Stella. Actually, it's from a Broadway show. There was a show last year called *Make It Snappy*. That's what 'The Sheik of Araby' is from. It's printed right on the sheet music."

"I didn't know that," Stella said.

"Yes, it's true."

"I do love the song, though."

"We'll play it for you in the next set."

"That'll be the berries," she said.

"I do a lot of cymbal work in it, makes it sound more like the desert. Stella?" he said.

"Yes?"

126

"I don't know whether we'll be playing overtime or not, that hasn't been worked out yet, Matty's still talking it over with your father. But even if we do play overtime, we'll probably be finished along around one o'clock, maybe one-fifteen by the time I get the drums packed and pay the guys. . . ."

"Yes?"

"I was wondering, I know it'll be kind of late, but I thought you might like to take a ride over to the West Side, there's some nice jazz clubs there with nigger musicians, it's a lot of fun and perfectly safe, otherwise I wouldn't even be asking you."

"Oh, do you have a car?" she asked casually.

"No, but my trumpet player has one, and him and his girl'll be running over there afterwards—she's the little blond girl sitting there near the bandstand, the one with the green beaded dress, do you see her?"

"Yes, she seems very nice," Stella said.

"Oh, she is, a very nice girl, they're keeping steady company, they expect to get married sometime next year. We made that dress for her."

"What do you mean? Who did?"

"Me and my mother. We have this crochet beading and embroidery business, I make all the designs, and we've got these girls for us who do the work. That's a very spiffy dress you're wearing yourself, Stella, I meant to compliment you on it."

"It was in *Vanity Fair*."

"I'm sure of that, it's very swanky."

"Though it's just a copy."

"It's a very good copy, though. And the color is beautiful with your eyes and hair. You have very pretty eyes, Stella."

"And you've got a very pretty line," she said, and smiled.

"No, that's no line. I saw those eyes and I couldn't believe you were an Italian girl, I've never seen eyes like that on any Italian girl I know."

127

"Well, I'm American, don't forget," Stella said, bridling for just an instant.

"Oh, naturally, can't I tell that? I'm only saying those are really beautiful eyes, and I'm not trying to be fresh, I honestly mean it."

"Well, thank you," Stella said, and didn't know what to do with her suddenly really beautiful eyes, so she lowered them.

"So what do you think? Would you like to come along with us when we go over there?"

"Well, I would have to ask my father," Stella said, and glanced at Francesco, who was sitting at a table with Pino, his head on his folded arms. Pino was singing *"Pesce Fritt' e Baccalà"* at the top of his lungs. His eight-year-old son, Tommy, sat stiffly beside his father, looking terribly embarrassed. "Or my *mother*," Stella amended.

"Well, *could* you ask her? We'll only stay an hour or so. You could ask your sister and Matty to come along, too, if you like. There's plenty of room in the car, it's a Pierce-Arrow."

"A Pierce-Arrow," Stella said, "I'm *sure* my mother will say okay."

"*Au 'voir*, then," Jimmy said, and went back to the bandstand.

As the Phantom Five played "The Sheik of Araby," which had not been written for Rudolph Valentino, but instead for a Broadway show called *Make It Snappy*, and as Pino Battatore sang another chorus of the song they had learned together in Fiormonte, Francesco sat at the table with his head on his folded arms and tried to understand why he'd been crying just a short while ago. He had cried when news of his father's death first reached him, and he had cried again when his mother died, and again when his sister Emilia had written to tell him of Maria's illness and subsequent death; he had thought he'd cried for all of them when it was necessary to cry, and appropriate to cry, and timely to cry. But tonight, at his daughter's engagement party, his darling angel Cristina, who was to marry a fine and handsome boy, he had cried again, and he could not understand why. And so he listened to

128

Pino's rasping off-key voice beside him, and heard Tommy pleading with his father to be still, and off at the other end of the room the Phantom Five went into another chorus of "The Sheik of Araby," with Jimmy Palmer doing a lot of cymbal work to simulate the mood of the desert—and suddenly Francesco knew.

"But my family will be *here*," Pino had said to him long ago, and he remembered those words now, and realized that *his* family, the family of Francesco Di Lorenzo, *was* here. There was no family in Fiormonte; his mother and father were dead, Maria was dead, Emilia had left for Torino with her husband, who hoped to find work in the steel mills. The family was here. He had a beautiful, gentle wife whom he loved and cherished, and for whom he would work hard all the days of his life; he had a seventeen-year-old daughter who was engaged to be married; and a twenty-year-old daughter who was sure to marry soon herself, once she found the right boy, she was fussy, Stella, he liked that about her, she was not easy to please, his Stella, his star; and Domenico, such a smart boy, studying so hard at a very difficult high school in the Bronx, a ninety average, that was very good, they said, a ninety; and Luca, so tall, so gentle, who played the violin and piano beautifully, just like his cousin Rodolfo in Fiormonte. . . . But no, Rodolfo had been killed in the war, Rodolfo was dead. The family was here.

Fiormonte had been the family, but now the family was here.

He sat up and looked at Pino, and Pino abruptly stopped singing.

"*È qui*," he said to his friend. "*La famiglia è qui.*"

"*Cosa?*" Pino asked.

Francesco watched his daughter as she went to the bandstand and began talking to the drummer, who kept playing all the while she chatted and smiled at him. On the dance floor, his other daughter, his angel Cristina, danced in the arms of a man who not ten minutes before had called him "Papa." Francesco was forty-two years old. For the longest time he had been twenty-four,

129

and had dreamed of going home. He was now forty-two, and knew he would never go home again, never return to Italy, never.

The family was here. He was the head of the family, and the family was here. *Home* was here.

He suddenly covered Pino's hand with his own and squeezed it very hard.

2

They stood on line outside the free employment agency, four thousand men every day of the week, six thousand on Mondays, when presumably the chances of finding work were higher. There was not much talking on the line. Most of the men knew they would not get a job, but they were still trying, their hopelessness was not yet total. They waited in the bitter cold for two hours, sometimes three, and then a thousand of them were led inside, following each other up the long flight of steps to the huge open room with desks and telephones and men with megaphones. They filled out forms—name, address, age, education, religion, color. And then they waited for the phones to ring. A ringing phone meant a job offer. One of the megaphone men would answer a phone, and then call out a job—"Man needed to shovel snow, forty cents an hour"—and there would be a rush to the desk, and the job-seekers would be warned again to stay in line behind the rope, and another phone would ring, and a megaphone man would announce, "Skilled mechanic, seventy-five cents an hour, might be a full day's work," and another rush to the desk, and another warning. Each of the men knew if he didn't get a job in the hour allotted to him upstairs, he would have to leave and come back the next day, and fill out the form again, and wait another sixty minutes for that phone to ring. If nothing came during that length of time, they would all be herded out of the big room again, and another thousand men who'd been waiting on line outside the building would be led upstairs to listen for those ringing telephones that meant someone had a job offer for them. Two hundred, three hundred men found temporary work each day. Most found nothing. They would wander over to the park afterward, and sit on benches and stare at their shoes. It was better than going home.

I was blind, and I did not see those long lines outside the employment bureaus and the soup kitchens. I did not know that men in shabby overcoats and caps stood on street corners selling apples for five cents apiece. I did not see the mob of depositors outside the bank on 116th Street, clamoring to withdraw lifelong savings, storming the big brass doors after they were closed. My grandmother Tess lost three thousand dollars when they shut down that bank. The Hooverville shacks that sprang up overnight along the shores of the Hudson were described to me by my mother, but I never saw them. Dust storms and floods, natural disasters that perversely aggravated the nation's miseries, were something I heard about only on the radio or in the Movietone newsreels whenever my mother took me to the pictures, but I could neither see nor visualize events of such enormity. An angry mob of unemployed veterans marching on Washington and demanding World War I bonuses was a spectacle I could not have conjured in my wildest imaginings.

This was the winter of our despair, but I did not realize it. I was part of something far more exciting.

I was in on the creation of a myth.

❖

In 1932, a month short of my sixth birthday, I began attending the Blind School, as it was called by fourteen of its pupils, including me. Actually, it was a standard New York City elementary school, except that it also had a class of fourteen blind kids. The school I should have gone to, had I been able to see, was P.S. 80 on 120th Street near First Avenue. But P.S. 80, like most of the other schools in the city, simply wasn't equipped to teach the sightless, and so we were bused from surrounding neighborhoods to 104th Street and Third Avenue, where a classroom with a specially trained teacher and suitable equipment had been set up in the old brick building there (since torn down, I understand). We rarely had contact with the sighted kids in the school, except for joint activities like assembly programs and school plays. For the most part, the fourteen of us were isolated in a virtual one-room schoolhouse, with the ages of the pupils ranging from five to eleven. Miss Goodbody taught all our subjects, and referred to us aloud all the time as "My dear little darlings." This was not condescending; she adored children, and all the kids at the school, sighted *or* blind, were her dear little darlings. But *we* referred to ourselves as "little blind bastards." Some of us were less blind than others, of course, but none of us could see worth a damn, and the appellation seemed appropriate—even if it *did* try to disguise self-pity with arrogance.

We were cruel to each other sometimes.

We were blind, but we were children.

Despite the loving care of Miss Goodbody, we remained convinced that we were misfits, a freakish band of outsiders isolated in a classroom at the end of the hall, or being marched to assembly or play in a chattering sightless unit, the corridors around us going mysteriously still as we passed through. Unlike Orphan Annie's countless legions, we wore the badges of *our* secret society without pride or passion. Little blind bastards, we were . . . and ashamed of it, I suppose. Ashamed because we felt if only we'd been *better* (Christ knows where; in the womb?), we wouldn't have been born blind. We could not accept the possibility that our parents, those sources of sustenance, comfort, and support, had done anything to deserve the likes of us, and so we figured we ourselves were somehow to blame. And no matter how hard Miss Goodbody tried to engender a feeling of self-worth in us, we always came away with a single inescapable fact: we were blind. We were not as good as other people. We were inferior products. Why was anyone bothering with us at all? Why didn't they simply throw us into the nearest incinerator?

When I began taking piano lessons from Miss Goodbody, I told all the kids in class that I was *better* than they were. *They* were the little blind bastards; *I* was musical—Miss Goodbody had said so. Whenever I wore a new suit to school, even though I couldn't see what the hell it looked like, I boasted about my grandfather the tailor, and told all the other kids he made clothes for very rich people, a lie no one ever believed. And even though I recognized this same cruelty in the other blind kids whenever it was directed at me, I turned insight into sight and told myself that only *I* was smart enough to see through the ploy (to *see* through it, mind you), and understand that a bragging little blind bastard was nonetheless blind, a part of the club, a freak, an outcast—a *nothing*.

The thing I liked most about the Blind School was those piano lessons with Miss Goodbody, who had discovered during our Bluebird-Blackbird sessions in the school auditorium that I could accurately reproduce by voice any note she struck on the keyboard. This must have astonished her. I was officially a Blackbird with a terrible singing voice, but I never sang off key, and she was beginning to find out I had perfect pitch. Today, I can identify as many as five notes being struck simultaneously on the keyboard, even if they're cacophonous. That's not an extraordinary feat; you're either born with a good ear or you're not. But Miss Goodbody took it as a sign from above that I was destined to study the piano. Since the lessons were free, they were encouraged by my mother—even though I hated them at first. In defiance and frustration, I would sometimes get up from the piano and, groping for the nearest wall, place my hands on it, palms flat, and repeatedly bang it with my head. The white keys were impossible. The black notes stood out from the keyboard, and I could feel them and distinguish them from the whites. But that endless row of seemingly identical keys stretching from Mongolia to the Cape of Good Hope? Impossible. There are blind pianists (not very good ones) who play only in F sharp, B, and D flat because there are five black keyboard notes in each of those tonalities. A showboat blind pianist like George Shearing can reach out suddenly with his right hand and plink a G above high C, unerringly true and clean and hard, but that's a very difficult thing to do, believe me, even for men who can see.

I worked like a dog memorizing that keyboard and the major scales, Miss Goodbody drumming intervals into my head and teaching me to play simple five-note pieces in different keys, accompanying them with basic chords, identifying the chords for me. My repertoire of chords was limited in the beginning to the tonic, the dominant seventh, and the subdominant, but I learned to identify and to play these in all the keys. (Miss Goodbody, I've since learned, was somewhat advanced for her time, in that she believed a person could not play intelligently or feelingly unless he knew what was happening harmonically.) Rhythm was a serious problem. I could *hear* the rhythm as well as any sighted person, but conceptualizing a "quarter note" or "four eighth notes" without being able to *see* those notes was enormously difficult. Miss Goodbody helped me with this by singing out the values of the notes, "Quarter, quarter, eighth, eighth, eighth, eighth," simultaneously claping her hands in tempo. By the time I was ready to begin reading Braille music, Miss Goodbody had acquainted me with the entire keyboard, encouraging me to play with "big" motions, forcing me to move out of a habit I'd had in the beginning (clinging to that middle C for dear life, my thumb firmly rooted on it), and teaching me to identify the major, minor, diminished, and augmented triads in all twelve keys.

I should explain that Braille musical notation is rather complicated, and involves a great deal more than simply embossing or

137

raising a *sighted* person's music so that it can be felt by the blind.
To begin with, the bass clef and the treble clef are not normally
indicated in Braille music. Instead, the keyboard is divided into
seven octaves starting with the lowest C on the piano, and using
each successive C as a reference point. When Miss Goodbody was
identifying a specific note, she would say, "That's a second-octave
D," or "No, Iggie, you're looking for a sixth-octave G." I'd been
having enough trouble learning to read *regular* Braille, and now I
was presented with an entirely *new* language—just as music for
the sighted is a language quite different from English or Bantu.
To give you some idea, this is what a simple exercise would look
like in European notation:

I've been told by sighted people who are not musicians that those sixteenth notes in the bass clef of the first and second measures look forbidding, as do the triplets in the treble clef of the last two measures. But believe me, this is a *very* simple exercise. Well, here's that same passage as it would look (or, more correctly, *feel*) in Braille:

Try, then, to imagine the Braille notation for a beast like the "Hammerklavier." The mind boggles. And mine *did*. In fact, I *still* find Braille music confusing at times, even though I studied it for the better part of ten years. Space is a problem in music for the blind, and very often the same symbols are used to mean different things. Imagine being a blind musician for a moment (thanks God, you don't *have* to) and running across a symbol that stands for a whole note as well as an eighth note. Rampant bewilderment? *I* tell *you*. Or stumble across a shorthand musical direction that says, "Count back twelve measures and repeat the first four of them." Dandy, huh?

Patiently, Miss Goodbody taught me to read. I memorized the keyboard, I memorized the chords, I memorized pieces in Braille, feeling the raised dots with one hand while I played the notes with the other, and then reversing the process with the other hand. By the end of my first year of study with her, I was reading and playing simple pieces like Schumann's "The Merry Farmer" (which I heard sung as a bawdy tune years later, the lyrics proclaiming: "There once was an Indian maid/who always was afraid/some young buckaroo/would slip her a screw/while she lay in the shade") and Tchaikovsky's "Doll's Burial," which I hated, and was struggling with more complicated stuff like Beethoven's Sonatina in G and his "Écossaise."

And meanwhile, the myth was taking shape around me.

❖

The apartment we lived in was a fourth-floor walk-up, consisting of a kitchen, a dining room that doubled as a living room because that's where the radio was, and two bedrooms next door to each other—one shared by my mother and father, the other by Tony and me. The apartment was not a railroad flat in the strictest sense. That is, the rooms were not stretched out in a single straight line, like train tracks. But it *was* a railroad flat in that there were no interior corridors, and to get to one room you had to pass through another. My parents must have made love very tiptoe carefully, lest Tony or I, on the way to the bathroom in the dead

140

of night, stumble upon their ecstasy. The kitchen was tiny, with the icebox, the gas range, and the sink lined up against one wall, a wooden table with an oilcloth cover (I *loved* the feel and the smell of that oilcloth) against the opposite wall. A window opened onto the backyard clotheslines, and also onto the windows of countless neighbors with whom, like an Italian (excuse me—American) Molly Goldberg, my mother held many shouted conversations as she hung out the laundry.

Molly Goldberg was part of the growing myth.

We needed that myth in the thirties. We needed it because we were desperate. I used to think my mother was a lousy cook. I used to think her menus were unimaginative. I can still recite the entire menu for any given week from 1933 through 1937, because they didn't change an iota until my father was appointed a regular and we moved to the Bronx. We began eating a little better then. But in those years when he was bringing home his twelve dollars a week from the post office (plus eight cents a letter for special delivery mail), the menus were unvaried. I knew, for example, that Monday night meant soup. The soup was made with what my mother called "soup meat," and which I now realize was the cheapest cut of beef available, stringy and tasteless, and boiled in a big pot with soup greens and carrots. On Tuesday and Thursday nights, pasta was served with a meatless sauce, spiced and herbed, accompanied by salad and bread. On Wednesday night, we ate scrambled eggs with bacon. Eggs cost twenty-nine cents a dozen in those days, but my mother used only eight of them with a pound of bacon (at twenty-two cents a pound) and could serve a dinner for four, including Italian bread and an oil-and-vinegar salad, for about fifty-two cents. Friday night was fish, of course. On Saturday night, we ate breaded veal cutlets. Veal cost sixteen cents a pound as opposed to twenty cents a pound for pork or twenty-six cents a pound for round steak. On Sunday, we went to my grandfather's house for the weekly feast. We were not starving. I don't mean to suggest we were even hungry. I'm only saying that we (not me,

141

not Tony, but certainly my parents) were aware of our plight, and further aware that millions of other Americans *were* hungry and *were* starving.

In 1932, the wife of President Hoover had said, "If all who just happened not to suffer this year would just be friendly and neighborly with all those who just happened to have bad luck, we'd all get along better." Maybe *she* started the myth, who the hell knows? Or maybe it was Hoover's Secretary of Labor who, again in 1932, while people were aimlessly wandering the nation in boxcars and eating roots in barren fields, said, "The worst is over without a doubt, and it has been a disciplinary, and in some ways, a constructive experience." Well, by 1933, the worst was still far from being over without a doubt, and everyone in the country knew that whereas some people had it slightly better than *other* people, *everybody* had it bad. We'd been riding high on those fat years following World War I, and suddenly, literally overnight, we'd fallen into an abyss so deep it appeared bottomless. We rushed to elect Roosevelt in 1932, not because we thought he'd miraculously pull us up into the clear blue yonder, but only because we thought he might somehow arrest our downward plunge before we hit the jagged rocks below. And now it was 1933, and FDR and the NRA and the CCC and the PWA and the WPA and the AAA had given us a whole lot of alphabets, but still not much soup to put them in. "Hard times" was *still* the common denominator; without that specter of hunger constantly leering in the background, the myth would never have come into being.

If Hoover's woman had naïvely stated one element essential to the creation of any myth in any time (a cultural ideal), and if Hoover's man had optimistically stated another (a commonly felt emotion or experience), it was Franklin Delano Roosevelt who became the first of literally thousands of thirties' heroes (or villains) without which the myth could not have functioned. Everybody either hated him or loved him. There was no in between. You never heard anyone saying, "I can take the man or leave him alone." He was *"That* Man," and there was no possible way of remaining indifferent to him or his programs. But if love and hate are opposite sides of the same coin, and you spin the coin often enough and fast enough, the emotions become blurred and all you know is that something's spinning on the table there, and it's got two sides to it, and you can't remember anymore which side was love and which was hate. Hating Roosevelt or loving Roosevelt became almost identical emotions. But more important, in terms of the myth, they became commonly *shared* emotions. Love him or hate him, he was ours. Deliverer or nemesis, he was ours. Thinking about him one way or the other, or both ways, or now one way and then the other, became part of what it meant to be American. We were becoming American, you see. Not the way my grandfather had (he still *wasn't* in 1933, as a matter of fact) or the way my mother had, but in a way that was entirely new and unexpected and naïve and exciting and sometimes deliriously exhilarating. We were beginning to claim people and things as our *own*, establishing tradition where earlier there had been only history to hold us together. The building blocks of the burgeoning myth were Buck Rogers guns and Charlie McCarthy insults, Busby Berkeley spectaculars and John Dillinger stickups, "Life Is Just a Bowl of Cherries," Shirley Temple dolls, "Happy Days Are Here Again." They *were* here again. For the first time. Because however superficial it may seem now, the myth had been conceived innocently and in desperation, and it is no accident that people today look back upon those terrible years of the 1930s with a sense of keen nostalgia. It was then that we became a family.

"I think *we're* gonna have to march, too," my father said. "If we can't get a decent living wage, Stella, we have to march."

"How can government employees march?" my mother asked.

"It won't be the same as a strike. It's just a way of letting them know we're alive."

"You know what Grandpa told me this afternoon?" I said.

"What did Grandpa tell you?"

"That Mussolini is right about Ethiopia. It *does* belong to the Italian people."

"Sure, your grandfather's a greaseball," my mother said. "What do you expect him to say?"

"He's not a greaseball no more," Tony said. "He's been here more than thirty years already."

"Can he run for president?" my mother asked.

"No, but . . ."

"Then he's still a greaseball," she said flatly.

"*I* can run for president," I said. "And Tony can, too."

"Why don't you run together?" my mother said, not without a touch of sarcasm. "President and vice-president."

"Would it be any worse than Roosevelt and Garner?" my father asked, and then said, "How come fish again?"

"It's Friday," my mother said.

"I hate fish," my father said.

"So do I," Tony said.

"Me, too," I said.

"That's right, teach them to be heathens," my mother said.

"Miss Goodbody says Mussolini is a bad man," I said.

"Is she a Jew?" my father asked.

"I don't know. Why?"

"Because the Jews are for Ethiopia."

"Grandpa says Roosevelt is a Jew," Tony said.

"Another one of his greaseball ideas," my mother said. "I get sick and tired of hearing him talk about the other side all the time. If he likes it so much there, why the hell doesn't he go back?"

"He *is* going back," I said. "And I'm going with him."

"Here's your hat, what's your hurry?" my mother said.

"The streets are so clean in Fiormonte, you could eat right off them," Tony said.

"Try eating off your plate right here, why don't you?"

"In Fiormonte, everybody's poor but happy," I said.

144

"Sure, that's why your grandfather came here. Because everybody was so happy in Fiormonte."

"He came here to make his fortune," Tony said.

"So he made it. So tell him to shut up about the other side."

"Vinny the Mutt hit the numbers for five hundred bucks the other day," my father said. "Now *that's* a fortune."

"Miss Goodbody says the numbers is a racket," I said. "What time is it?"

"Seven o'clock."

" 'Amos 'n' Andy'!" I yelled, and shoved back my chair, and ran into the dining room. "She says it supports prostitution."

Radio was the best entertainment medium ever devised for humanity. I am one day going to form a blind men's marching society, and we are going to begin screaming at the tops of our lungs outside movie theaters and television studios, demanding the abolition of any form of entertainment that requires the use of eyes. If you yourself are blind and reading this in Braille (fat chance) or having it read aloud to you by someone who will undoubtedly distort its tonal quality, please consider seriously the possibility of joining this lonely voice, and forming (in the tried-and-true American way) a group that will demand something vitally important in its own tiny, selfish way—the return of the radio as something more than a conduit for bad music and bad news. We will be the only *true* minority group on these shores; the *smallest* one, anyway.

Calling ourselves the Consolidated Organization to Correct Kinescopic Excesses, Yelling to Eliminate Discrimination to the Sightless, we will become known in brief (and again in keeping with the American way of reducing long titles to acronyms) as the COCKEYEDS. And having a title, and a shorthand word representing that title, we will then be able to take our place alongside all those other organizations shouting for separateness and apartness instead of solidarity—proud, worthy, and righteous conclaves

145

like the Brotherhood of Abortion Banners Insisting on Egg Survival; or the Regional Independent Federation of Lovers of Egret Shooting; or the American Readiness Association Clamoring to Halt the Nasty and Intolerable Destruction of Spiders; or, finally, the Committee Against Virtually Everything Stalagmitic. And one day, all of us will happen to meet in the middle of Fifth Avenue, marching in all directions, and we will shout, "Brother!" together at the same instant, mistaking this for a cry of unity instead of an echo in a closed, locked, windowless room. On that day, we will finally discover we'd all been blind. I should only live to see it.

The radio was a blessing, and whereas in those days I felt it had been invented exclusively for the sake of the blind, I now realize it was a necessary ingredient in the mortar that held the myth together—one part radio, one part movies, and equal parts of ballyhoo and hullabaloo. Being the cheapest form of entertainment around, the radio was perfectly suited to the times. But more important, it provided us with hundreds of fictitious families who in turn were incorporated into the larger American family, the myth endlessly reflecting itself in a series of mirrors that threw back images of images. The Goldbergs, the Barbours, Easy Aces, Vic and Sade were all families in the strictest sense of the word, but if a family consists of *any* group of people whose idiosyncrasies, affectations, speech patterns, and personalities are intimately known, why then Jack Benny's gang was a family, and the Lone Ranger and Tonto were a family, and so were The Green Hornet and Kato, and Major Bowes and all his amateurs, and the super-intellects on "Information, Please," and the nuts in Allen's Alley— Senator Claghorn and Mrs. Nussbaum, and boisterous Ajax Cassidy, and Titus Moody saying, 'Howdy, bub," each and every time. We were surrounded by families within families, and not all of them were suffering like the people who came to Mr. Anthony for radio advice each week. ("No names, please," he always cautioned, and this was picked up at once and made an inside family joke on *other* radio shows, and then it filtered its way into the

146

streets so that whenever anyone said, "Hello, Louie," or "Hello, Jim," the response was invariably, "No names, please.")

Each week, we waited breathlessly for that Monday-night radio voice to tell us, "This is Cecil B. De Mille coming to you from Hollllllywood." We wondered along with Bob Hope just *who* Yehudi was, and fell off our chairs when Jerry Colonna replied, "Ask Yehudi's cutie." And when Hope said, "Who's Yehudi's cutie?" Colonna answered, "Ask Yehudi," bringing the expected, "Yes, but who's Yehudi?"—the whole hilarious nonsensical round delighting us. We knew George Burns would end his show with, "Say good night, Gracie," and we knew Baron Munchausen would say, "Vas you dere, Sharlie?" and yes, I *vas* dere, Sharlie, and I loved every minute of it. I had relatives all over Harlem, and all over the airwaves, and by extension all over the United States, because I knew we were all listening to that little box and, somehow, the sound waves miraculously being carried into all our homes were transforming the entire nation into a single giant living room.

In 1933, at seven o'clock every weekday night, the family thirty million Americans listened to was "Amos 'n' Andy." During the ensuing fifteen minutes of air time, telephone traffic dropped by fifty percent, movie theaters called off their scheduled performances and tuned their loudspeaker systems into NBC's Red Network, and the nation's more urgent business stopped dead while a pair of white men named Freeman Gosden and Charles Correll portrayed a gallery of Negro characters they themselves had invented—Amos, Andy, the Kingfish, Lightnin', Brother Crawford, and the whole marvelous crowd at the Fresh Air Taxicab Company. "Those niggers are hot stuff," my mother would say, and indeed they were. I would go around the house after each show, quoting dialogue I had just heard and partially memorized, causing Tony to roll on the floor in laughter all over again.

"Say, s'cuse me for protrudin', stranger," I would say in Andy's voice, "but ain't you got a hold of my watch chain?"

147

"Your watch chain?" I would answer as the Kingfish. "Well, so I does. How you like dat? One of dese solid gold cuff links of mine musta hooked on your watch chain dere."

Ah, yes.

In the thirties, we were well on the way to becoming one big happy family.

❖

On the day they stole Dominick's college ring and Luke's watch (not to mention their trousers), I was in the tailor shop on First Avenue with my grandfather and Pino. It was November, and the streets outside were cold and deserted. The shop, as my grandfather described it to me, had a plate-glass window fronting on First Avenue, the legend *F. Di Lorenzo, Tailor* lettered on it in curving gold leaf. The wooden flooring of the shop window served as a seat for visitors to the shop (seven-year-old me, on this occasion), as well as a repository for a clutter of badly designed and poorly colored posters of men and women wearing the fashionable clothes of 1933, advertising "Dry Cleaning" and "Custom Tailoring" and "Expert Alterations." There were also cardboard movie posters for most of the theaters in the neighborhood, the Cosmo, the Grand, the RKO Proctor's, and even the Palace—familiarly called the Dump by everyone in the ghetto. And, in one corner of the window, the NRA-member poster, with its blue eagle clutching lightning bolts in one claw, and a gear wheel in the other, and the red-lettered legend WE DO OUR PART.

There was a bell over the door of the shop, and it tinkled whenever anyone came in. The numerals 2319 were lettered onto the glass of the entrance door in the same gold leaf that spelled out my grandfather's name and occupation. A sewing machine was just inside this front door, to the left as you came in, facing the long counter upon which my grandfather cut cloth and behind

148

which he did most of his hand stitching. Running at a right angle to the counter was a double tier of clothing rods upon which were hung suits, trousers, dresses, skirts, overcoats, sweaters, all the garments left to be repaired or cleaned or pressed, each bearing a paper ticket pinned to the sleeve or the hem. A flowered curtain behind the counter covered the doorway to the back room, where my Uncle Luke ran the pressing machine. Whenever he was pressing, great billowing clouds of steam poured from between the padded jaws of the machine and seeped into the front of the shop. There was always the smell of steam in that shop. In the wintertime, it was particularly reassuring.

My mother has told me that my grandfather's hair was already white in 1933, entirely white, giving him an older look than his fifty-three years. He was undoubtedly wearing thick-lensed eyeglasses with black frames, and his customary work costume— black trousers and white shirt, over which he wore an unbuttoned, chalk-dusted, black cardigan sweater, a tape measure draped over his shoulders. The big cutting shears that were almost an extension of his right hand were surely on the countertop within easy reach. Pino was sitting at the sewing machine, putting buttons on Salvation Army uniforms. He had lost his job shortly after the Crash, and now worked alongside my grandfather in the shop which was largely sustained by the Salvation Army uniform orders he himself had first brought to his friend. In 1933, he was described to me as a dapper little man with a neatly cropped black mustache, customarily and meticulously dressed in a pinstriped suit, an anachronistic celluloid collar on his shirt, an emerald stickpin holding his tie to his shirt.

The only sounds in the shop were the ticking of the big, brass-pendulumed clock on the wall opposite the clothing racks, and the clanging of the radiators, and the incessant clicking of Pino's thimble and needle. The smells were those of the twisted De Nobili cigars both men were smoking, and the individual human scents (which I knew by heart) of my grandfather and Pino, and

149

a subtler aroma that is difficult to describe unless you have spent a considerable amount of time in a tailor shop. It is the elusive aroma of clothes. A lot of clothes. Clothes of different fabrics and different textures and different weights, but nonetheless giving off a different collective aroma at different times of the year. In November, with the wind rattling the plate-glass window of the shop, the clothes gave off the scent of hidden corners. I sniffed in the aromas, I listened to the sounds.

"Grandpa," I said, because this had become a running gag between us, and I never tired of it, "why do you smoke those guinea stinkers?"

"Who says they're guinea stinkers?" my grandfather said.

"Everybody."

"*Che ha detto?*" Pino asked.

My grandfather said, "*Ha chiamato questi* 'guinea stinkers.'"

"*Ma perchè?*"

"Why do you call them guinea stinkers?" my grandfather asked me.

"Because they stink."

"What?" Pino said. "You're wrong, Ignazio. It doesn't stink. It smells nice."

"That's no guinea stinker," my grandfather said expectedly, delighting me. "That's a *good* see-gah." He puffed on it deliberately and ceremoniously, raising a giant smelly cloud of smoke. "This suit is for you," he said, and rustled a paper pattern. "On Christmas Day, you'll be the best-dressed kid in Harlem."

"I know," I said, and grinned.

"In Fiormonte, on Christmas . . . Pino, do you remember *il Natale a Fiormonte?*"

"*Sì, certo,*" Pino said.

"Some one of these days, Ignazio," my grandfather said, "I'm gonna take you home to the other side. I'll show you my home, okay? You want to come to Fiormonte with Grandpa?"

"Sure."

150

"*È vero, Pino? Non è bella, Fiormonte?*"

"*È veramente bellissima.*"

"From where I lived, Ignazio, you could see the river, no? And before *la fillossera* . . ."

The front door of the shop flew open, the bell tinkled. I smelled my Uncle Luke's aftershave and my Uncle Dominick's b.o.

"What's the matter?" my grandfather said immediately.

"They took our pants!" Luke shouted.

"What?"

"Our pants!" Dominick said.

"*Who* took your pants?"

"They came in the club, Pop," Luke said in a rush, "and they took all our rings and watches, and then they made us take off our pants so we couldn't chase them."

"*Who* took your pants?" my grandfather said patiently.

"They took my class *ring*," Dominick said. "Why are you so worried about my *pants*?"

"*Who?*"

"Some gangsters."

"What gangsters?"

"We don't know. They had guns."

"From *la vicinanza?*"

"I don't know," Luke said. "I never seen them before, did you, Doc?" he asked his brother.

He had begun calling him "Doc" as soon as Dominick entered Fordham University, from which he'd been graduated in June of 1929, shortly before the Crash. In 1933, when I was seven years old, Dominick had just begun his third year of law school. Years later, when my parents first took Tony and me to the World's Fair, my mother spotted the trylon and perisphere and immediately said, "There's Luke and Dominick." She never called him "Doc." In fact, no one in the family ever did, except Luke.

"You got some pants for us, Pop?" he asked.

"Where am I going to get pants for you?"

151

"This is a *tailor* shop," Luke said. "You mean to tell me you ain't got pants for us?"

"In the back," my grandfather said. "The ones near the sink. The ones I use for patches. Don't touch no customer's clothes!" he shouted to them as they went through the curtain. "*Che pensa?*" he asked Pino.

"*Non è buono,*" Pino replied. "*È quasi come Sicilia.*"

"*Sì,*" my grandfather said, and then suddenly turned to the curtain and shouted, "What is this, *Sicily?* Where some bums come in the club and steal from you?"

"What are you hollering at *us* for, Pop?" Luke yelled back.

"Because you let it happen."

"They had guns," Dominick said.

"Hurry up, put on your pants," my grandfather said.

"What's the hurry? They got away already."

"I want you to get your brother-in-law."

Luke came out of the back room. "You mean Matty?" he asked.

"At the taxi stand. Go."

"What for, Pop?" Dominick asked, coming out of the back room.

"He plays cards with thieves," my grandfather said.

The bell over the door tinkled. The scent of soap and lilac pierced the stench of cigar smoke—my Aunt Bianca.

"Good evening, Frank," she said.

"Hello, Bianca," my grandfather said wearily.

"Their pants were robbed, Aunt Bianca," I said.

"Hello, Iggie," she said, and kissed me on the cheek. "Where's your Grandma?"

"Home," my grandfather said. "Cooking."

Luke opened the door and was starting out of the shop when Aunt Bianca said, "What do you mean, your pants were robbed?"

"That's right, Aunt Bianca," he said, and ran out of the shop.

"You, too?" she asked Dominick.

"Yeah," Dominick said.

"A college boy like you?"

Dominick shrugged. "They had guns," he said.

"The broken record," my grandfather said.

"They *did*, Pop."

"What kind of guns?" I asked.

"Big ones, Iggie."

"Did they have masks on?"

"No, no masks."

"Then why don't you know who they are?" my grandfather asked.

"I never saw them before," Dominick answered. "I don't know if you ever noticed, Pop, but I don't usually hang around with crooks."

"I have to see Tessie about doing the table," Bianca said.

"No more table," my grandfather said flatly.

"I have a widow who wants to talk to her husband."

"Not in my kitchen!"

"Then where?"

"Do it in your corset shop."

"My shop doesn't have a three-legged table. I'll talk to Tessie about it. Good evening, Frank." She opened the door, the bell tinkled. She turned back, and said, "You look very handsome today, Iggie."

"Thank you, Aunt Bianca."

"Don't take him by eyes," my grandfather said.

"Come give your aunt a big kiss."

I found her immediately. She pulled me into her arms and into her bosom, and bent to kiss me on the cheek, and then patted me on the head, and I suffocated ecstatically on lilac and soap. "Tell your mother to come to the shop once in a while, it won't kill her," she said.

"I'll tell her, Aunt Bianca."

"Close the door," my grandfather said. "We're not partners with a coal man."

"I was just leaving," Bianca answered, and went out.

"No three-legged table!" my grandfather shouted after her.

"She smells nice," I said.

"The butcher thinks so, too," Dominick said.

"*Sta zitto*," my grandfather warned.

"What for?" Dominick said. "Everybody knows about Aunt Bianca."

"You mean about her sleeping with the butcher?" I said.

"Who told you that?" my grandfather asked.

"She's a widow," Dominick said. "There's nothing wrong with it."

"Is that what they teach you in law school?" my grandfather asked. "That there's nothing wrong with your mother's sister sleeping with the butcher?"

"Well, *what's* wrong with it, Pop, would you tell me?"

"Why doesn't he marry her?" my grandfather asked.

"Maybe he doesn't like her," Dominick said.

"Then why's he sleeping with her?" I said.

"You hear what this child hears?" my grandfather said.

The bell over the door tinkled again, and Luke and Matty came rushing into the shop, out of breath. Matty always smelled of Camel cigarettes.

"What took so long?" my grandfather asked.

"We ran all the way over," Matty said. "Hi, Iggie, how's the kid?"

"Fine, Uncle Matt."

"You love my daughter?" my grandfather asked him.

"What?"

"Your wife, my daughter."

"What is he crazy?" Matty said. "*È pazzo questo?*" he asked Pino. "We been married eleven years, she's gonna have another baby any day, what are you asking me *now* if I love her?"

"Then get back their pants."

154

"What?"

"*And* my ring," Dominick said.

"*And* my watch," Luke said.

"They're crazy, right, Iggie?" Matty said. "How do I know who stole your stuff?"

"Ask who you play cards with," my grandfather said.

The shop fell silent. They were waiting for Matty to say something. I turned to where I figured he was standing. The clock ticked noisily on the wall. Matty sighed.

"What kind of watch, Luke?"

"A Bulova. Seventeen jewel."

"And the ring, Dom?"

"From Fordham. Gold, with a red stone."

"I'll see what I can do."

"*Ma subito,*" my grandfather said. "Quick, you hear?"

"Pop, I *ain't* Al Capone," Matty said, and went out.

"There much pressing back there?" Luke asked.

"There's always pressing back there," my grandfather said. "Thank God."

"Who wants some hot chocolate?" Luke asked. "You want some hot chocolate, Iggie?"

"Don't get chocolate on the clothes!" my grandfather said. Dominick had opened the door and was starting out of the shop. "Where are you going?" he asked.

"Home," Dominick said. "I got torts."

"You got torts, I got clothes," my grandfather said. "Help your brother sort them, then you can go."

"I can do it alone," Luke said. "Go on, Doc."

"Okay?"

"Go, go," my grandfather said.

"Buy me a charlotte russe and stick it in the icebox for when I get home, okay, Doc?"

"Right," Dominick said, and started out again.

155

"Watch when you cross!" my grandfather said.

"Pop, I'm twenty-six years old," Dominick said, and closed the door behind him.

"Well, back to the eighth circle," Luke said, and went through the curtained doorway, and started the pressing machine. I don't know where he picked up that reference to Dante. He had dropped out of high school in his sophomore year, going to work first for my Uncle Marco in Brooklyn, and then later helping out part time in the tailor shop. He was now my grandfather's full-time presser, and he earned a good salary, more than my grandfather would have paid an outsider. He rarely played violin anymore, but he banged the piano obsessively, and I think he dreamed of starting his own band one day, I don't know. He once approached my father about joining *his* band, and my father (hypocrite who couldn't read a fucking note) said, "Can you read music, Luke?"

"Sure I can read music," Luke said. "I studied violin for four years, didn't I?"

"I mean *piano* music," my father said.

"Well, no, I can't read piano music, no. I mean, I can read the *notes*, but no, I couldn't play from no sheet music, if that's what you mean."

"Well, suppose somebody should come up to the piano with her own music, like, you know, to sing a song at one of these affairs? Could you play it for her?"

"If I knew the song, I could play it by ear."

"But suppose you didn't know the song?"

"Then I guess I couldn't play it," Luke said. "But I know almost every song ever written."

"Sure, but suppose the sax player or the trumpet man know it only from the sheet music, you understand me? Only in the key it's written. Then what?"

"Well, then I don't know what," Luke said.

I overheard that conversation when I was supposed to be asleep, the way Luke had overheard my mother's story about the Chinese rape artist. Luke was the one who later repeated the Charlie Shoe story to me. He told me he thought *maybe* it was true, but why anyone, even a Chink, would have wanted to touch Stella when she was eleven and ugly as sin (according to Luke) was beyond him. "Your mother puts on airs," he said to me. "She always did."

My Uncle Matt got back the ring and the watch, but not the pants. It was not to be the last of *our* family's encounters with that *other* family—the Murdering And Filching Italian-Americans.

❖

I knew my way around the neighborhood by heart, and was allowed almost complete freedom in moving from the house of one aunt or goomah or cousin to that of another; the only restriction was that I ask someone to cross me whenever I came to a curb. On Easter Sunday in the year 1934, we were still living on 120th Street between First and Second Avenues, and my Aunt Bianca was living above her corset shop on 116th Street, also between First and Second. The route to her building was a simple one.

I came down four flights of steps to the ground floor of our own building, and then across the wide top step of the stoop, and down four narrower steps to the sidewalk. Then I turned right and walked down to First Avenue and made another right at the corner. I always walked close to the buildings, rather than the curb, and I knew each of the tenements on the block, knew where two iron posts with a chain hanging between them indicated there were steps leading down to a basement (careful!), knew where a wrought-iron fence separated Dr. Mastroiani's sandstone building (the only two-story building on the street) from the pavement, knew the pillars on either side of the wide stoops of the three buildings after the doctor's, and the open court in the big apartment building close to the corner, and then the barber pole (which I'd walked into two or three times before I firmly located its exact distance from the barbershop door), and then the

157

plate-glass window of the *pasticceria* on the corner, and then the right turn onto First Avenue. I carried a bamboo cane in those days; it was the cane my father once used in his Charlie Chaplin imitation.

From the corner of First Avenue and 120th Street, there were four streets to cross before I got to my Aunt Bianca's house. In musical terms, and in descending diatonic order, these were 119th Street, 118th Street, 117th Street, and last but not least, since it was a very wide street, a street held for a full four beats, rather than a single beat like the streets before it, the concourse or boulevard or esplanade or simply big mother of a street that was 116th. The musical reference above is no accident, I'm sure. I made the mistake that day *because* of a difficult (for me) waltz, which I was playing in my head as I carried an Easter plant to my Aunt Bianca. The plant was a gift from my mother. She did not particularly like Aunt Bianca, but Aunt Bianca had made her six brassieres free of charge two weeks before, and this was my mother's obligatory payoff, and thank God Aunt Bianca hadn't made the bras two weeks before *Christmas* because that would have required a grander gift, and I'd have been carrying an entire forest down First Avenue.

Visualize Blind Iggie Di Palermo, beribboned aspidistra in a red clay pot clutched in my left hand and pressed against my scrawny, almost eight-year-old chest, Daddy's discarded Charlie-Chaplin-imitation bamboo cane in my right hand, blue eyes open wide and naked, Grandpa's new Easter jacket on my back, brand-new knickers covering my skinny legs, tap-tap-tapping down the avenue with that waltz in my head. What happened was that I made it to the curb at 119th Street and then, perhaps because at that moment I was five bars into the coda, just after the trills, and the piece called for a seven-bar run of eighth-note triplets in the right hand—I turned right with my *feet* also, instead of waiting for someone to cross me to the other side. I tapped blithely up 119th Street, mentally playing that piece for all it was worth, the

158

bamboo cane rapping out the three/four beat while the melody soared in my head, and when I got to the corner of Second Avenue, I asked someone to cross me, thinking this was the corner of 119th Street and *First* Avenue, believing I was heading south instead of west, and knowing I still had three streets to cross before turning right again toward my Aunt Bianca's shop in the middle of the block. Those streets were, in my busy, busy head, 118th Street, 117th Street, and then 116th Street. Instead, I crossed in succession and with the kindly help of pitying parading pedestrians, Third Avenue, and then Lexington Avenue, and then Park Avenue, and made a right turn on Park Avenue, heading uptown, heading *north* again instead of *west*, in which direction I *should* have been heading had I been on 116th Street, where I was *supposed* to be. . . . Are you hopelessly confused? So was I.

I heard voices.

The voices belonged to black people.

I knew those voices well. I imitated them every day of the week. But it was rare for any black people to wander down to 116th Street between First and Second Avenues, which is where I believed I was at the moment. I suddenly began to wonder exactly *where* I was. Vague memories began to filter back. Hadn't I heard the sound of an elevated train roaring overhead as I replayed the first section of the piece, and while I thought I was being helped across 119th Street? When had they built a crosstown elevated structure on 119th Street, and how come nobody had told me about it? And hadn't I heard *another* elevated train when I thought I was being led across 118th Street? I was suddenly frightened. I stopped stock still in the middle of the sidewalk.

"Buck, buck, how many fingers're up?"

They were playing Johnny-on-a-Pony.

"Three!"

"Wrong, man, *two*."

"How come when you on *our* backs, we can never guess the 'mount of fingers?"

159

"You think I'm lyin'?" I heard the sound of sneakers slapping against the sidewalk; the person talking had leaped off the backs of the "pony" team. "How many fingers did I had up, kid?" There was a sudden silence. I could hear the shuffling of more feet on the sidewalk now. "You there with the flower pot," he said. "How many fingers was I holin' up?"

"Me?" I said.

"Tell 'em how many fingers they was."

"I didn't see," I said. He was much closer to me now. They were all moving close to me. I didn't know how many there were. I began listening for separate voices.

"Why wuhn't you payin' 'tention?"

"Whut you doin' on this block, man, you can't pay 'tention?"

"Where you goin' with that plant?"

"To . . . to my aunt's."

"Who your aunt?"

"Aunt Bianca?"

"*Who*? Talk *English*, man."

"Aunt Bianca."

"*Look* at me when you talkin'. Whutchoo lookin' ever' which way for?"

"He blind."

"That ain' no reason for him not to be payin' 'tention when we got a serious prolum to solve. How many fingers was I holin' up there?"

"I . . . I couldn't see the fingers," I said.

"Where'd you get that horse blanket?"

"What?"

"*This* thing." A hand flipped at the lapel of my jacket. I backed away a pace.

"It ain't a horse blanket," I said.

"Where'd you buy that thing? Over to the horse stables?"

"I didn't buy it. My grandfather made it."

160

"What's he do, sell horses?" somebody asked, and they all laughed.

"He's a tailor."

"What kind of tailor? A horse tailor?"

"He's a real tailor," I said. "He's got a shop on First Avenue."

"Oh, on First Avenue?" somebody said. "Whut's he, a *wop* tailor?"

"Are *you* a wop, too?"

"I'm an American," I said.

"Americans doan go roun' wearin' horse blankets."

"On'y wops 'n' horses do."

"Le's see that horse blanket, anyway," someone said, and I felt hands tugging at the jacket.

"Leave it alone," I said, and backed away again.

"Whut you doin' comin' roun' here in that shitty horse blanket, carryin' that pot full o' shit?"

"Get away from me," I said, and raised my father's bamboo cane.

"Well, now, lookee here," somebody said.

"He a *real* fierce li'l bastard, now ain' he?"

"Le's see that cane."

"Le's see that flower pot."

"Where you get that horse blanket?"

"Please, I want to go to my Aunt Bianca's."

They were all around me now. They were poking me. Somebody reached for my cane. Somebody else yanked at the sleeve of my jacket, and I pulled my arm away. Someone tapped me on the shoulder, and giggled and danced away when I whirled on him.

"Please," I said. "I'm blind."

"Please," someone mimicked. "He blind."

I felt someone tugging at the potted plant, heard a tearing sound, realized a leaf had been pulled from the aspidistra, and then felt it striking my face. I backed away and collided with

161

someone who pushed me forward against someone else. They began shoving me back and forth then, spinning me around in the circle they had formed, tossing me from one to the other as I flailed at them with my father's bamboo cane, the cane whistling on the air and never striking home. Neighing like horses, they snatched leaves from the plant as I spun dizzily in the circle, tossed the leaves into my face, laughed as I tried to protect the plant, the cane always moving but never connecting, until someone snatched it from my hands, and I heard a sudden loud cracking sound, and realized it had been snapped in two. I held the potted aspidistra in two hands, using it as a weapon, swinging it back and forth in front of me, but someone knocked it to the pavement, and I heard the pot smashing into a hundred pieces, and then someone tore at my right sleeve, loosening my grandfather's careful stitches, and then ripped it all the way, pulling it free of the shoulder, and someone ripped the other sleeve loose, and someone else tore the jacket up the back. One of them shoved at me from behind, and I fell to the sidewalk, trying to cushion the blow with my hands, and my hands hit some of the broken pieces from the aspidistra pot, and I pulled them back in pain and hoped they were not bleeding. On my knees, I crouched on the sidewalk, and somebody laughed, and then they all laughed, and then they left.

I don't know how long I crouched on that sidewalk, listening for sounds, turning my head sharply from right to left, uncertain whether they were really gone or were silently preparing another attack. No one came to my assistance. (Many years later, when I asked Biff Anderson why no one had come to my assistance, he laughed heartily and said, "Man, you was *white*. This whole fuck-up didn't just happen yesterday, you know.") I got to my feet. I did not know where I was. My cane was gone. Flailing the air with both hands, I groped for a building that would define the inner limits of the sidewalk. Instead, I fell off the curb, and scrambled back onto the sidewalk, and got to my feet again, rush-

162

ing forward in panic, hands outstretched, palms open, and slammed into a solid brick wall. Hand over hand, I felt my way along the side of the building, and came at last to the corner. If I had made a right turn when stumbling into this street, then I would have to make a left turn to get back home.

My grandfather found me wandering along First Avenue. He must have been dressed in his own Easter finery, black suit, white shirt, black tie, a straw boater on his head. He was carrying a white cardboard carton of pastries in his hand, I later learned. He was not out looking for me, he had merely gone to the *pasticceria* on the corner to buy some pastry for the holiday, and was undoubtedly walking back to the apartment with a jaunty spring in his step on this beautiful clear bright sunny Easter morning, and had seen his grandson in tears and in tatters, and perhaps even then did not rush to me at once, but approached me slowly and cautiously, as though unwilling to believe his own eyes.

"Ignazio!" he shouted, and I rushed to him, rushed to his voice, rushed sightlessly into his outstretched arms, and he clutched me to his chest, and said, "*Madonna mia! Ma, che successe? Oh, Madonna. Ignazio, Ignazio, chi ha fatto questo?*" and stroked my face with his hands, brushing at the tears, and said, "*No, no, non piangere, caro, caro, non piangere,*" and then angrily shouted, perhaps to the heavens, "What kind of place is this, what kind of country?" and hugged me to him again, and said, "*No, no, carissimo, non ti preoccupare,*" and then said, "What happened? Tell Grandpa."

Sobbing, I said, "They didn't like my . . ." and then stopped short of saying the word "jacket" because my grandfather had made the jacket for me, and I did not want to hurt him. "My haircut," I said.

"Your haircut?" he said, puzzled. "What's the matter with your haircut? Oh, *Madonna*, look what they did, your jacket is ruined. Who did this?"

163

"Some boys," I said. "Five or six boys."

"Were they Irish?" he asked immediately and suspiciously.

"No."

"Then what? Colored?"

I nodded.

"*Bastardi*," he said.

"Grandpa?" I said, and began to weep again.

"Yes, yes. Ignazio. Come now, no more tears."

"Grandpa . . . why do I have to be blind?"

"Ah, ah," he said, and hugged me and rocked me. "Ah, Ignazio, dear baby, dear child, I would give you my own eyes if that would make you see. Come, you must not cry. Here, here," drying my eyes and my cheeks with his handkerchief, and then abruptly and surprisingly saying, "Do you want a *cannolo*? See? Here's the pastry box. Do you feel the string? Give me your hand. Here. Do you see the string?"

"Yes, Grandpa."

"Ooooo, I can't break the string," he said. "It's too strong for me. Help me break the string, Ignazio."

"You can break the string, Grandpa."

"No, I can't, I can't. Look! Do you see? I can't do it. Oh, what a strong piece of string. Help me, Ignazio."

I felt along the string with both hands, and took it in my fingers, and broke it. Then, sobbing, I threw myself into my grandfather's arms again.

"Don't you want a *cannolo*?" he said gently. "Tch. No more crying, please. We'll go to the tailor shop and wash your face before your mother sees you. Do you know what Grandma made for us? Rigatoni! That's your favorite, no? And antipasto, and meatballs, and roast beef, and potatoes, and salad, and nuts, and I'll slice a peach in wine and let you have some of that. We'll get you drunk, eh, Ignazio, we'll make a regular *ubriacone* out of you, eh? Tch, look at your jacket. Never mind, I'll make a new one for you. Come. Take my hand."

164

He was standing opposite me. I knew he was holding out his hand, but he did not reach for my own hand. He simply stood there, waiting.

And I reached. I touched air. I groped.

And finally, I found his hand and took it in my own.

❖

"Well, there are good and bad in every kind."

My mother used to repeat this maxim on the average of twice weekly. I don't think she meant it to apply to black people; it didn't apply to them that Easter morning. It occurs to me that she repeated those identical words to me years later, when I told her I was going to marry a Jewish girl. "Well, there are good and bad in every kind." Then she went to stick her head in the oven. (Just a joke, Mom, full of little jokes.) Actually, she was very tolerant about the entire matter, which was more than could be said for Rebecca's father, the Mad Oldsmobile Dealer.

In 1934, though, when my mother viewed her demolished little boy, she was not quite so tolerant. Immediately, she challenged the manhood of all the assembled wops in my grandfather's apartment and demanded a Sicilian vendetta in the grand old style of the one that had been visited upon poor Charlie Shoe way back there during the Perils of Pauline. It was my father who reasoned that we would never be able to find a half-dozen anonymous niggers on Park Avenue, and even if we *did* find them, what were we supposed to do? Beat them up? In their own territory? The "in their own territory" was an afterthought. My father had no stomach for violence, even if his own darling little blind bastard had just been the victim of violence. In that respect, my father was distinctly anti-American. He managed to convince the others that discretion was the better part of valor, and we all sat down to enjoy my grandmother's rigatoni.

I kept thinking about those kids who'd beat me up.
I kept wondering why they'd done it.

❖

I don't wish to nag a theme the way I would a note in a blues chorus, but when I first began playing jazz, there were no factions, no divisions, you either knew how to blow or you didn't. Jazz was the true melting pot, the full realization of the American myth I'd learned as a kid. I can honestly say I never got any draft about being a white man playing black music until 1950. I'd been married to Rebecca for almost two years by then. We had one child and another on the way, and times were not precisely rosy. I was still playing here and there in some of New York City's lesser-known toilets, and when I got a shot at cutting a record with some fairly well-known musicians, I thought success was just around the corner. I met the leader of the band and his trumpet player in front of the Brill Building. Both men were black. The leader, a bassist named Rex Butler, took one look at me and (just as my mother had said, "Mama, it's the Jew," in the presence of the dry-goods salesman) said to his trumpet player, "This white cat won't swing, man." The worst thing you can say about any jazz musician is that he doesn't "swing." He can have great chops, he can be inventive as hell, but if he doesn't swing, forget him. The trumpet player remained silent. I didn't know whether he was nodding his head in agreement or picking his nose non-committally. "Sorry, man," Butler said, and that was that; they cut the record with a black piano player.

That was in 1950.

Sixteen years before that, I was still trying to reconcile what had happened to me on Park Avenue with what was happening everywhere around me. I was almost eight years old and beginning to make some value judgments of my own, and it seemed to me that whereas my grandfather's concept of family was a limited one,

166

including as it did only half the wops in Harlem, Fiormonte, and the suburbs of Naples, it nonetheless was not in conflict with the larger concept of family being developed in the American myth. I did not yet know it was a myth; that realization would come later, much later. For me, at eight, it was a glowing dream which had as its basis an impossible and unlikely collection of people from different nations who, united by a common ideal and a rapidly growing common tradition, and working together to achieve that ideal, could make this the strongest, most prosperous, most enlightened country on the face of the earth, with liberty and justice for all whether they were Irish, Italian, Negro, German, English, Czech, or double-check American.

In 1934, I thought I knew what being American meant, even though my concept seemed to clash violently with my mother's. To her, Fiorello La Guardia, the goddamn *mayor* of New York, was "just another greaseball," whereas Father Coughlin was an "American," and she wouldn't have missed his radio broadcast every Sunday night if you'd offered her "all the tea in China." I *still* don't understand that woman, and I've known her for forty-eight years. I was thirty-seven before I discovered she'd always hated fish and therefore cooked it in the most impossibly inedible manner every Friday night of my childhood merely because she considered herself a good Catholic. But she had quit going to confession when she was sixteen, and I don't think she's stepped inside a church since the day she got married, and I *know* she practiced birth control because when I was a kid I found a small box in the top drawer of the dresser, on the side belonging to my father, and my brother Tony said, "Iggie, those are nothing but scum bags." I listened to my mother when I was young, but I couldn't decipher what she meant by "I'm *American*, don't forget," because it didn't jibe with the larger concept of the American family as it was being taught everywhere around me—and especially by Miss Goodbody.

Miss Goodbody told me that the proper descriptive term for a

167

colored person was neither nigger nor boogie, but instead Negro. She told me that calling a Negro a nigger was tantamount to calling an Italian a wop. Since I hadn't ever been called a wop except by the six niggers on Park Avenue, I wasn't even aware that the term was derogatory. The only other place I'd heard the expression was in my own kitchen, from the lips of Stella the All-American Girl, who used it interchangeably with "greaseball," "ginzo," "guinea," and sometimes "greenhorn" (though this last term of affection was usually reserved for the Irish). But I began thinking about it. And I decided I would be very careful about using the word "nigger" so casually, and that I would not refer to Jews as "Jews," which somehow also sounded derogatory, but instead say "Jewish people." Similarly, Miss Goodbody taught me to say Pole for Polack and Spanish for Spic—which I'd never said, anyway, since the massive Puerto Rican influx hadn't yet begun in New York, and the slur was alien to us wops in the ghetto. In fact, the first time I ever heard the word was when Miss Goodbody warned me against using it.

Well, once you've revised your vocabulary, you've come a long way toward revising your thinking. I find it ironic that after all those years of training myself to say "Negro," I then had to learn to say "black," which in my youth was only *half* a word, the unvoiced expletive "bastard" being clearly understood, as in the black expression "mother," where the "fucker" is as silent as the X in "fish." Do I sound bitter? The hell with you; I'm blind. And besides, I know something now that I did not know then, and there is almost as much exhilaration in recognizing the lie as there was in living it. It's the *truth* that keeps eluding me; it's the truth that's so difficult to find. The lies are always there, you see, and just when you think you've cornered one with the broom, another one pops out of a tinned-up hole on the other side of the room, and you've got to start all over again. There are times, admittedly, when you think you'll never be able to cope with this place that's overrun with scampering lies, times when you wonder why in Christ's name you bother searching for the truth at all; who the hell are you—Diogenes? Wouldn't it be easier to just lie down and relax somewhere under a shade tree, with clouds drifting through an azure sky you've never seen and can never hope to see, and just allow the lies to run free over your body, to lick your face into final submission and pick the flesh from your bones, revealing at last the stark white truth of your skeleton? Or is there perhaps a sweeter form of surrender? Might you not put a bullet in your brain, or a knife in your heart, could you not slit your wrists in the bathtub, or jump off the Brooklyn Bridge, or onto the tracks of the subway your grandfather or mine built, and end it, shit, just *end* it? Yes, I suppose you could. But then you'd never have known, isn't that so? And how can you hope to learn anything, sonny, if you don't ask questions?

❖

My Aunt Bianca's corset shop on a Saturday afternoon in September, shortly before my eighth birthday. I am curled up in a floppy armchair draped with brassieres. My aunt is working at one of her dress dummies, fashioning a corset for a lady of gigantic proportions. There are pins sticking in her mouth, and when she answers my questions, she mumbles around the pins. A soft, slow, gentle autumn rain nuzzles the plate-glass window of the shop. Somewhere far in the distance, there is the lingering intermittent rumble of thunder.

"Are brassieres sexy?" I ask.

"What?" she says.

"Tony says they are."

"Well . . ."

"Are they?"

"Not to me," Aunt Bianca says.

"What does that *mean*, anyway?"

"What does what mean?"

169

"Sexy."

"Go ask Tony."

"Do you think he knows?"

"Maybe," Aunt Bianca says. "He's advanced for his age."

"Yeah." Silence. Distant thunder. "Aunt Bianca?"

"Mmmm?"

"Why do ladies wear them, anyway?"

"You ask too many questions," she says.

❖

My grandfather first took me to meet Federico Passaro on a bit-terly cold day in January of 1935. Showing the proper deference to an educated man (and especially a man educated in *music!*), he alternately addressed Passaro as either *Dottore* or *Professore*, tell-ing him how long I'd been studying, and how beautifully I could play, and then explaining that I had perfect pitch, which phenomenon he demonstrated by striking three random notes simultaneously on the keyboard, and asking me to identify them —which of course I did. Passaro seemed singularly unimpressed by my feat. At least, he made no comment about it. I later learned that he, too, had perfect pitch, so what was the big deal? All he wanted was to hear me play, but I was shivering (literally and figuratively) at the electric heater in the corner of the room, and beginning to think my hands would never get warm.

I liked his voice. His English was tinged with a faint accent, and when he spoke to my grandfather in the Neapolitan dialect, even this sounded less harsh than it did in the streets of Harlem. He was described to me later by my grandfather as a short, squat man in his early sixties, with a wild thatch of black hair, a hooked nose ("like a Jew's, Ignazio"), and lips perpetually pursed as though in displeasure. When I finally sat down to play a piece I knew cold—C. P. E. Bach's "Solfegietto"—he stood by my side at the piano and listened attentively, his even breathing interrupted only

170

once, when I fluffed a passage I'd played without error perhaps a hundred times before.

I wish I could say that something startling happened the first time I played for Passaro. I couldn't see his reactions, of course, but I can guarantee there was no dramatic B-movie-type revelation, with Passaro shouting *"Madonna mia!"* in discovery of a remarkable child prodigy in his living room. I simply played the piece through, cursing myself for the fluff (but blaming it on my cold chops), and when I'd struck the final chords, I sat at the piano in silence, my hands in my lap, and waited.

"Well," my grandfather said in Italian, "what do you think?"

"Who has been teaching you?" Passaro asked.

"Miss Goodbody. At school."

"And you've been playing for how long?"

"I started when I was six."

"How old are you now?"

"I was eight in October."

"So that's more than two years."

"Yes."

"Has your teacher given you any Chopin?"

"Just the A-Major Prelude."

"Bach, of course."

"Yes."

"Mendelssohn?"

"The 'Six Pieces for Children.'"

"No Brahms, eh?"

"No."

"How does she teach you? Does she play the piece for you, or what? I've never taught a blind person."

"The pieces are in Braille," I said. "She usually plays them through first, and then I read the notes. In Braille."

"Ah," Passaro said.

"So what do you think?" my grandfather asked in Italian.

"I've never taught a blind person," Passaro answered in Italian.

"How long do you practice every day?" he asked me.

"Two hours."

"If I teach you, I want you to practice not only during the hours you've set aside for practice, but also when you simply *feel* like playing. That is important to me."

"Okay," I said.

"How will I know what compositions are available in Braille?" Passaro asked.

"I can get a list from Miss Goodbody," I said.

"Why do you want to leave her?" Passaro asked.

I hesitated. Then, looking up from the keyboard for the first time, I turned in the direction of Passaro's voice, and said, "I can play better than she can."

"I see," Passaro said. "Will you expect to play better than I can?"

"Yes," I said.

"I've played at Carnegie Hall," Passaro said. "I gave a recital at Carnegie Hall fourteen years ago."

"Okay," I said, and nodded.

"Okay? What does that mean, okay?"

"If you want me to play at . . . whatever you said, I'll do it."

"What do you want?"

"I just want to learn how to play better."

"For what? To amuse your friends?"

"Just to be real good," I said.

"Do you think you're good now?"

"Yes."

"You're very sloppy," Passaro said. "If a student of mine had been studying with me for two and a half years . . ."

"It's not that long," I said.

"Then what? Two years and two months? Even so. I would stop giving lessons to someone who was still so sloppy after all that time."

"Well," I said, "I don't think I'm so sloppy. Just because I made a dumb mistake . . ."

"I'm not talking about the mistake. I've heard *giants* make mistakes, though rarely. I am talking about your fingering. I am talking about *this*," he said, and his right hand must have darted out because the next thing I heard was a descending arpeggio, "instead of *this*," he said, and the identical arpeggio sprang clean and crisp and true from the instrument. "Do you hear a difference?"

"Yes."

"Can you play what I just played?"

"Maybe."

"Try it."

"Was that an F sharp?" I asked. "The first note?"

"Was it?"

"Yes." I found F sharp above high C, positioned my right hand over the keys, and played the arpeggio slowly and carefully, F sharp, C sharp, A, and then to F sharp again, repeating the notes until I reached the center of the keyboard. I took my hand off the keys.

"That was sloppy," Passaro said.

"Well, it was the first time I played it."

"I've never taught a blind person," Passaro said. "I don't like students who whine or complain or who don't do the work. If I have to worry about hurting your feelings because you're blind, then I don't want to teach you."

"Well, how would you hurt my feelings?" I asked.

"Doesn't it hurt your feelings to know you're sloppy?"

"No."

"It should," Passaro said.

"Miss Goodbody doesn't think I'm sloppy."

"If you can play better than she can, how would she *know* if you're sloppy?"

173

I burst out laughing.

"You think that's funny?" Passaro said.

"Yeah," I said, still laughing.

"Don't laugh when the *professore* is talking," my grandfather said.

"When can you get me this Braille list?" Passaro asked.

"Will you teach him?"

"First I want to see the list. If there are enough compositions on it, compositions I *want* to teach . . ."

"There are millions of pieces in Braille," I said.

"Including Chopin's C-Minor Polonaise?"

"I don't know."

"What if I told you you'll be playing it in three months' time?"

"I don't even know what it sounds like."

"It sounds like *this*," he said, and he reached across me with his left hand, and began playing simultaneously with his right hand, and what I heard was impossibly intricate.

His hands stopped abruptly. "Well?" he said.

"It took me three months to learn the 'Solfegietto,' " I said.

"And you *still* play it badly," he said. "What do you think of what I just played?"

"It sounded hard."

"It *is* hard."

"I don't know if I could play it in three months."

"You're right. You probably won't be playing it for three years."

"*Allora, dottore*," my grandfather said. "*Sì o no?* Will you teach him or not?"

"Get me the list," Passaro said.

❖

It is my brother who takes me to my weekly piano lesson in the Bronx. My mother says we resemble each other. "Ike and Mike, they look alike," she says, making reference to the Rube Goldberg cartoon creations, and not to what my name will become one day in the distant future. Tony has blond hair, like mine, but it is curly. His eyes are blue, too. His chin has a cleft in it. I have explored it with my hands; I know his face as well as I know my own. We board the Third Avenue El on 125th at eleven o'clock each Saturday morning. We sit side by side on the caned seats, and exchange dreams while we ride up to Tremont Avenue. I am going to play at Carnegie Hall one day. (I know what Carnegie Hall is now; Passaro has told me. He has also promised me I will play there.) My brother is going to be a famous ballplayer. Winter or summer, he wears a leather mitt on his left hand and repeatedly socks a baseball into the pocket as we ride uptown, the steady rhythm counterpointed by the clacking of the wheels along the track.

He reels off batting averages, and lifetime records, and describes a game my Uncle Dominick took him to see in Yankee Stadium. Lou Gehrig is his hero. He tells me he is going to marry Letitia. (They are both eleven years old.) He says he is going to become rich and famous and then he and Letitia will move to Mamaroneck, in a private house where he'll live all the time except when he has to go on the road with the team. When he was in the third grade, his teacher invited him and three other kids to her house in Mamaroneck for a Saturday outing. Tony says the house was like in the movies. That's the kind of house he wants to live in someday. He tells me I'll come visit him. He says I'll play a concert someplace, and come to his house afterward in a big black Cadillac limousine driven by a chauffeur, I'll still be wearing my black tuxedo from the concert, and he and Letitia will be having a big party for me with champagne and everything in their private house in Mamaroneck. And when he plays at Yankee Stadium, he'll get Uncle Dominick or Uncle Luke to take me to the game, and they'll describe the action to me, and when he comes to the plate he'll point his bat at the left-field bleachers and that'll mean he's going to put one away for me.

He says he will ask Letitia if she has a friend for me. He promises that when I'm a big concert player and rich and famous, I'll have beautiful girls hanging all over me, rich girls in long satin dresses, wearing pearls at their throats, draped on the piano, and never mind that I'm blind, that won't matter to them, Iggie. He doesn't want no rich girls in satin, my brother Tony. All he wants is Letitia, who's the most beautiful girl in the world. He tells me he wishes I could see her, she's so *nice*, Iggie, I mean it, I love her so much. And then he describes her for me again, and I try to conjure Letitia, try to create an image that will match the voice I have heard so many times. We will both be rich and famous, my brother and I.

This is America.

It is entirely possible.

On my ninth birthday, he gives me a dog. The dog is a mutt he paid three dollars for in the pet shop on Third Avenue. With a little help from my grandfather, I name the dog Vesuvio. Vesuvio is a good dog with but a single failing: he refuses to be housebroken. My mother is a compulsive housekeeper, then *and* now, and does not need a half collie–half spitz (imagine *that* mating scene!) messing up her nice linoleums. In a desperate attempt to keep Vesuvio out of the dining room and bedrooms, thereby encouraging him to go on the paper we have put under the kitchen sink, she removes two leaves from the dining room table and stretches them across the doorway to the kitchen at night, one on top of the other, constructing a barrier she hopes will keep him out of the rest of the apartment. But one night, getting out of bed and walking toward the kitchen for a glass of water, she forgets about those two dining room leaves and bangs her shins against them and, according to her, almost breaks both her legs. That does it. I come home from school one day to discover that Vesuvio has been taken away by the ASPCA. Naturally, I decide to leave home. The first person I complain and confide to is my grandfather.

176

"She gave Vesuvio away."

"Who?"

"Mama."

"*Ma perchè?*"

"He was making in the house."

"Sit down, stop crying. Now stop. You're a man, no? Men don't cry all the time. Who took him?"

"The ASPCA."

"Who's that?"

"It's a place that takes dogs. Grandpa, I'll bet they're gonna kill him."

"No, no."

"Yes, Grandpa. They'll put him in a room with gas."

"Why would they do that? No. They'll find a home for him in the country, where he can run free. That's what a big dog like Vesuvio needs, a lot of room. Don't worry, they'll take good care of him."

"Are you sure?"

"Yes, Ignazio, I'm sure."

"Grandpa, let's go to Fiormonte."

"Right this minute?"

"Yes. I never want to see her again, Grandpa, I mean it. I *hate* her."

"So you'll go to Fiormonte in hatred? To such a beautiful village? No, Ignazio, that would be wrong."

"Then I'll go to Newark, New Jersey."

"Newark? Why Newark?"

"Goomah Katie lives there."

"Goomah Katie has five sons of her own."

"She'd take me in."

"Maybe. But even so, I don't think you'd like Newark."

"You know why this happened?"

"Why?"

"Because somebody put the Evil Eye on me."

"Who told you that?"

"Aunt Victoria."

"Aunt Victoria is a fool. There's no such thing as the Evil Eye."

"Mama sent me there because I was coughing, and she wanted to find out if somebody'd taken me by eyes, and Aunt Victoria dropped the oil in the water, and held the plate under my chin, and it made eyes."

"That's because oil and water don't mix."

"It don't *always* make eyes, Grandpa."

"No, only half the time."

"Well, that's what it was, anyway, Grandpa. The Evil Eye."

"Ignazio, don't talk like a greaseball, eh?"

"Miss Goodbody says 'greaseball' is a bad word."

"Miss Goodbody is a Jew like Roosevelt. What does she know?"

"Are Jews bad, Grandpa?"

"Roosevelt is bad."

"But I *like* Miss Goodbody."

"That's right, you *should* like your teacher."

"Even if she's a Jew?"

"There are good Jews and bad Jews. Roosevelt is a bad Jew."

"Why?"

"Because he says bad things about Mussolini."

"Is Mussolini good?"

"Mussolini is very good."

"Then why does Miss Goodbody say bad things about him, too?"

"Because she's a Jew."

"Grandpa . . . was Jesus a Jew?"

"No."

"Miss Goodbody says he was a Jew."

"She's lying."

"He wasn't?"

"He was Italian."

That afternoon, I tried everything I knew on my grandfather.

First I agreed with him that the only good people in the world were Italians, hoping this would soften him up enough to take me to Italy. I reminded him that in Fiormonte you could eat off the streets, whereas in Harlem you lived in peril of your very life, witness the brutal beating I had suffered at the hands of six hundred Ethiopian savages on Park Avenue that time, remember? My grandfather said that October was not a good time to be going to Fiormonte, and when I asked him why not October, he said, "April is better." So I asked him to call Goomah Katie in Newark, New Jersey, and tell her he was bringing me there to stay with her, and explain to her that I was no trouble at all even though I was blind, I was just a quiet little kid who played nice piano, and I would be a definite asset to her household, and my grandfather said, "Goomah Katie doesn't have a piano."

I then suggested that he could perhaps talk to my mother and convince her either to get Vesuvio back from the ASPCA or else buy me another dog, and I even offered a sort of bribe by promising I'd go to the opera with him sometime if only he would talk to my mother. My grandfather said, "I don't like to interfere in your mother's house." So I said it might be a good idea if he told my mother she was no longer welcome in *his* house if she didn't get my dog back or get me another dog, and he said, "She's always welcome in my house, Ignazio, the same as you." I told him I was a poor little blind kid who needed something furry and loyal to love me, and he said, "You're not poor and you're not little, and your mother loves you more than Vesuvio ever could." So then I hinted that my piano lessons might suffer if I didn't have man's best friend around to stroke and pet while I ran over the pieces in my head, and he said, "Professor Passaro doesn't have a dog," and finally I said, "Gee, Grandpa, I thought you loved me," which was my last desperate stab at getting that damn dog back, or getting another dog, or getting out of the city, and my grandfather said, "I do love you, Ignazio. But a dog is a dog, and a family is a family." I'm surprised he didn't add, "And a good

179

cigar is a smoke," because he lit up one of his guinea stinkers at that point, perhaps to signal that the debate was over, and then he said, "Stay home, have a cup of hot chocolate, okay?"

So I decided to stay.

❖

I used to hide a lot. Under the dining room table, or under the bed, or in the closet—I think it made me feel less blind. I'm not sure why that was true. I think an enclosed space, a tight small space, was somehow less threatening to me. I was hiding under my Uncle Luke's bed on Christmas Day. In the kitchen, the women were doing the dishes, except for my Aunt Victoria, who was playing cards with the men in the dining room. I could hear their voices and the sound of Pino tuning his mandolin, and in the kitchen the rattle of dishes and the metallic clatter of utensils. I lay flat on my back under Luke's bed, and listened.

"Does anybody want more coffee?" my grandmother asked.

"No, thank you, Mom," Matty said.

"You deal," my father said.

"Somebody's light," Dominick said.

"Me," Luke said.

"Aunt Victoria? You in?"

"I'm in."

Aunt Victoria was a chord I would not learn till years later, a D-flat dominant, augmented nine, augmented eleven—shrill, dissonant, sharp, and irritating. She was my grandmother's other sister, a spinster, as hard and ungiving as Bianca was soft and generous. I didn't like her. Nobody liked her. My mother said Aunt Victoria was the way she was because she was constipated. When Tony heard this, he suggested that we buy her a tin of Ex-Lax for Christmas. Tony and I both hated Ex-Lax. As a weekly routine in our house, we were given one laxative or another

180

each Saturday night before we went to bed. Ex-Lax or milk of magnesia or citrate of magnesia. They were all terrible. But being an American meant being regular.

"What do you say, Aunt Victoria? Can you open or not?"

"I pass."

"I'll open for a penny," Luke said.

"Without me."

"Cristie, are you bringing in that pastry?"

"Hold your horses."

"Raise it a penny."

"Out."

"I'll see you."

"Cards."

Pino began playing an Italian song. His son Tommy, who was twenty-one years old and reportedly as handsome as his mother had been beautiful, immediately began singing along with his father, and then my grandfather joined in, and the three of them together sang at the tops of their voices while the poker game continued around them. In the kitchen, the women talked above the noise of the game and the doubtful harmony of the singers. For Christmas, my brother Tony had given me a pair of woolen gloves to keep my hands warm when I went up to Passaro's with him each Saturday, and my Uncle Luke had given me a black leather fleece-lined aviator's helmet with goggles on it, and my grandfather had made me a brand-new mackinaw, and my parents had bought me electric trains with an engine that whistled, and I was thinking maybe I should get out from under the bed and go play with the trains my father had set up for me in the front room of Grandpa's house, when all of a sudden I heard the sound of cards being slapped onto the tabletop, and my Uncle Luke yelled, "Son of a *bitch!*"

My grandfather and Pino stopped singing. Tommy's voice hung in the silence for just an instant longer.

181

"Hey!" my grandfather said.

"She stays in the game when she hasn't got anything, and ruins my draw!" Luke said.

"Hey, what's the matter with you?"

"I hate to play with goddamn women in the game."

"I put in my money, didn't I?" Aunt Victoria said, and then very calmly added, "I deal, I believe. If you don't like playing with women, just drop out, sonny boy."

"That's right, I *don't*."

"*That's* obvious."

"What's that supposed to mean?"

"Take it how you want it."

"What'd she mean by that crack?"

"Play cards, play cards," my grandfather said.

"No, what'd she mean?"

"I meant that someone who's thirty-two years of age should at least be engaged by now."

"What business is it of yours?"

"Luke!" my grandmother called from the kitchen. "That's your aunt you're talking to."

"What do I care who she is? Tell her to mind her own business."

"Hey, come on, Luke . . ."

"You keep out of this, Doc!"

"Ah, *now* we're getting to it!" Aunt Victoria said. "Do you hear how he talks to his own brother?"

"He's *my* brother, I can talk to him any way I . . ."

"Certainly. You think I don't know *why?*"

"Are we playing cards here, or what?" my father asked.

"It's because you're jealous of him," Aunt Victoria said. "*He's* the one who went to college, *he's* the one who's engaged already. . . ."

"Come on, who's dealing?" Matty said.

"You're not fooling me, sonny boy," Aunt Victoria said. "You think I don't know what's eating you? You think I was born yesterday?"

"Why the hell don't you go home?" Luke said.

"Tessie, are you listening to this?" Aunt Victoria said.

"Luke, that's your aunt!"

"So who asked her to come here?"

"*I* did!" my grandfather said, and suddenly everyone fell silent. "Is this a family?" he asked. "Is this a family on Christmas?" No one answered. "Victoria, you talk too much, you always did. Luke, apologize to your aunt."

"What for?"

"Because she's your aunt."

"She can go straight to hell!" Luke said, and stormed out of the room and into his bedroom, where I was hiding under the bed. He slammed the door, went directly to the piano, and began playing loudly and angrily. In a moment, my grandfather came into the room and closed the door again behind him.

"Hey," he said. "Stop the piano a minute. Listen to me."

"Leave me alone, Pop."

"Come on, what's the matter with you?"

"Nothing. Just leave me alone, Pop, okay?"

"You want to go to college?" my grandfather said.

"No," Luke answered. His hands stopped, the sound of the piano stopped.

"If you want to go to college, I'll send you to college."

"I'm thirty-two years old, Pop," Luke said. His voice was very low. From where I lay under the bed, I could barely hear him.

"So? Your brother is twenty-five."

"He's a lawyer already. Anyway, that ain't it."

"Then what?" my grandfather asked. "Tell me."

"The hell with it."

"Tell me."

"It's just . . ." Luke said, and hesitated. I held my breath in

183

the silence. "Pop," he said at last, "I don't know where I'm going."

"Where do you want to go?"

"I don't want to be a presser, that's for sure. I'm sorry, Pop, but . . ."

"All right. What do you *want* to be?"

"I don't know."

"You can be anything you like. In this country, you can be anything."

"Sure," Luke said. "Do *you* believe that, Pop?"

My grandfather did not answer. There was another long silence. Then my grandfather said, "What is it, *figlio mio*, what?"

"You think I don't *try* to get girls?" Luke said suddenly and passionately. "Look at me, Pop. I'm a skinny marink, I'm cock-eyed without my glasses; you think I don't try?"

"You're a very handsome boy," my grandfather said. "You take after my cousin Rodolfo in Fiormonte, may he rest in peace. He was very tall like you, and very handsome."

"Yeah."

"In Fiormonte, the girls would go crazy for you."

"This ain't Fiormonte, it's Harlem. You know what they call me?"

"What?"

"Stretch. They call me Stretch."

"So?"

"So how would you like to be called Stretch?"

"What does that mean, Stretch?"

"Well . . . skinny, I guess."

"You know what they called *me* when I was young?"

"What?" Luke said.

"*Ciuco.* That means donkey. It means jackass."

"Why'd they call you that?"

"I have big ears. Listen, you see your mother? She was a beauty, even more beautiful than Angelina, may she rest in peace, who was Pino's wife. Do you think your mother cared about my ears?" My grandfather paused, and then said, "You want to go to college?"

"It's too late, Pop," Luke said.

"If you don't want to work in the tailor shop, you don't have to."

"What would I do, Pop?"

"What do you *want* to do?"

"I don't know," Luke said.

From under the bed, I wanted to shout, "Tell him, Uncle Luke! Tell him you want to have a band! Tell him you asked my father for a job in his band! Please, Uncle Luke, tell him!"

Luke did not tell him. He simply said, again, "I don't know."

"All right, don't worry," my grandfather said. "You'll find something. Something will please you. And you'll find a woman, too, and she'll love you, don't worry. Now come in the other room. Make up with your aunt. She doesn't realize."

"Do *you* realize, Pop?"

"Maybe," my grandfather answered. "Come," he said. "It's your family in there."

They went out of the room, and I lay still and thoughtful under the bed. Pino began playing his mandolin again, and soon there was laughter.

❖

There are many different ways of approaching the same tune. I usually play it the way I *feel* it, but I try nonetheless to keep in mind the composer's intent. I would never, for example, take the outrageous liberties Barbra Streisand took with "Happy Days Are Here Again," however spectacular the result may have been. Nor would I rob any tune of its emotional content by imposing upon it a technical virtuosity that might be dazzling but essentially false to the mood. It's one thing to know your tools; it's quite another to use those tools so cold-bloodedly that they render the

185

tune meaningless. There are thousands of tunes in my head, a veritable catalog of chord charts and melodies. Pick a tune, any tune (almost), and I will sit down at the piano and play it for you in all twelve keys. In fact, I don't feel I really *know* a song unless I can play it in all twelve keys. To a jazz musician, that's not a particularly impressive accomplishment. Once he knows the chart, he can transpose it to any key and tack on the melody in that new key. The melody is unimportant to the jazz musician. When you hear him say, "Oh, that's a great tune," he's not referring to the melody. He is referring to the chord progression. He will, in fact, play the melody in the so-called head chorus only to orient the audience, and then will improvise entirely *new* melodies in the second chorus and each succeeding chorus. But I'll immediately turn a deaf ear to those musicians who try to transmogrify a keyboard or a horn into a laboratory. At the piano, I could give you (though it would pain me) a fair demonstration of a coldly antiseptic atonal style, and you might even enjoy it, who knows? But music to me is something quite more than a sterile unraveling. For example, I would never play "Tina in the Closet" in the following manner:

TINA IN THE CLOSET

© November 17, 1936

by

Ignazio Di Palermo and Tina Carobbi

The purpose of this brief experiment was to test the application to human sexual response of the James-Lange Theory, specifically and primarily inquiring into the involuntary visceral and/or skeletal response of a ten-year-old male subject in close proximity with and to a nine-year-old female subject in a controlled space. Toward that end, a voluntarily induced, emotion-provoking situation was created spontaneously. A secondary objective was to have been an exploration of the responses of the nine-year-old female subject. Since the female, however, was unavailable for post-laboratory evaluation, data supplied by the male alone was deemed insufficient basis for objective conclusions.

Both subjects were fully clothed and selected at random. Both were in excellent physical and mental health, the male measuring 142.24 centimeters and weighing 33.11 kilograms, the female measuring 134.62 centimeters and weighing 31.20 kilograms. Neither had previous medical histories of male-aggressive/female-passive frotterism, and exhibited no overt tendencies toward neurotically motivated behavior in these areas, though this was not the concern of the experiment and did not enter formally into either laboratory considerations or post-lab evaluations. Similarly, an inquiry into the nature of prepubescent incestuous exploration seemed inappropriate since male and female subjects were not genetically related, although "family ties" could easily have been presumed (with resultant erroneous conclusions) in that female was the younger sister of the recently acquired bride of male's uncle. For purposes of the experiment, a game of "hide-and-seek" was proposed, in which male subject's older sibling was declared "It." While he counted aloud from one to ten, male and female enclosed themselves in the control space, a recess measuring 182.88 by 213.36 centimeters, adjacent to the entrance door of the externally circumscribing space, and normally utilized for the storage of wearing apparel. Male subject's mother and her sister-in-law were in the kitchen eating cakes and honey.

Though insufficient data exists to support this premise, it is reasonable to posit that male's sibling soon tired of the game, his blind brother being expert at it, and abandoned the externally circumscribing space in favor of the outdoors. Male and female remained hidden in the spontaneously created control space, waiting for the absentee sibling to discover them. By all accounts (the male's), he was standing directly to the rear of and adjacent to the female. Female, it should be noted, was wearing a thin cotton dress and cotton panties. After fifteen minutes and thirty-two seconds of anterior-posterior proximity, male discovered, much to his surprise and amazement, an unaccustomed and totally unexpected engorgement of erectile tissue, producing a state of rigidity normally associated with arousal of the male organ of copulation in higher vertebrates. Simultaneously (and on the basis

187

of unsubstantiated data supplied by male), female demonstrated involuntary skeletal activity of the dorsally located area of juxtaposition, experienced as "wiggling" and "rubbing" motor responses accompanied by seemingly unrelated verbalizations and frequent eruptions of muted laughter. Postulating on the James-Lange Theory, it would appear that sensory fibers in the aroused structures of male and female alike had been activated, causing visceral and skeletal contributions as the impulses passed back to the cortex. What had previously been non-emotional perceptions were augmented by "feelings," which (as described by the male in post-laboratory discussions) were multi-leveled and altogether discombobulated.

As previously stated, female subject did not contribute data, but when male subject reported to his mother the visceral/skeletal responses and the "feelings" accompanying them, she said, "You didn't *touch* her, did you?" When subject responded in the negative, she then said, "Your father will tell you all about these things when he gets home."

Subject's sibling explained the phenomenon thusly: "Iggie, that was nothing but a Russian hot iron."

Subject's father chose not to comment later that night. Or any other night, for that matter.

It had been a sin to develop a hard-on while standing behind Tina, who was after all my Uncle Dominick's sister-in-law. (I learned to call it a hard-on and not a hot iron at about the same time I learned it was a sin to have one.) It was a sin to throw away bread, according to my mother. She always kissed a crust of stale bread before throwing it into the garbage can. She still does. It was a sin not to eat what was on my plate while people in China were starving. It was a sin to make fun of anybody.

"Then why do they make fun of me in the street," I asked, "and call me blind names and make believe they pinned something on my back, when they didn't?"

"What blind names?" she asked.

"They call me Orbo the Kid."

"What?" my mother asked. "What's that supposed to mean? Who's Orbo the Kid?"

"Orbo means blind."

"Who told you that?"

"Grandpa."

"What does he know, he's a greaseball," my mother said.

"Mama, *orbo* is an Italian word. *Orbo*. It means blind."

"So what?" she said. "What's wrong with being called Orbo the Kid? It's like Vinny the Mutt."

"It's different," I said.

"How is it different?"

"Vinny works for Western Union, don't he? And a guy who delivers telegrams is called a mutt, and *that's* why he's Vinny the Mutt."

"So you're blind, and *orbo* means blind, and you're Orbo the Kid. I don't see any difference at all."

"You know who picks on me the most?"

"Who?"

"Rocco, who's crippled."

"Well," my mother said.

"You know what *I'm* gonna do? I'm gonna call *him* Gimpy."

"What for?"

"That means when you limp."

"No," my mother said, "don't do that. That's a sin, Iggie."

My brother had started a collection of records he jealously guarded, running over to my grandfather's house to play them in private on the big wind-up Victrola in the front room. I think if my mother knew Tony took Letitia up there with him every Friday afternoon, she would have considered *that* a sin, too. I kept bothering him to let me hear his records, and finally he told me why he couldn't.

"Letitia says I shouldn't let you hear them."

"Why not?" I asked.

"Because it's personal."

189

"What is?"

"Hearing the records."

"Well, you let *her* hear the records, don't you?"

"That's right, that's what's personal."

"Well, I'm your own brother," I said.

"That's right."

"Blood is thicker than water," I said, quoting my mother.

"Yeah, but this is different, Igg."

If truth be known, I was more interested in hearing about all the things Tony and Letitia *did* together than I was in hearing his latest Count Basie single. Tony rarely talked about her anymore, though, and I could only imagine what was going on in my grandfather's front room each Friday while the curved speaker blared Glen Gray and the Casa Loma. My fantasies were invariably the same. In them, Tony was standing behind Letitia and rubbing up against her while he reached around with both hands and unbuttoned her blouse button by button and then unclasped her brassiere, which I already knew how to do with brassieres that didn't have girls inside them because I handled a lot of brassieres in my Aunt Bianca's shop. Since his records were intimately linked with those Friday-afternoon sessions, Tony must have feared that if he let me listen to them I might catch a whiff of early-adolescent musk mixed in with the sound of Duke Ellington's "In a Sentimental Mood."

Or maybe he was afraid I'd disparage the music he loved so much. It occurs to me that this was a real danger at the time. Only once had I asked Passaro to get me the sheet music for a song I'd heard on the radio, during one of Benny Goodman's Saturday-night broadcasts. The tune was "You Turned the Tables on Me." Helen Ward sang it, and I'll never forget it as long as I live, not because it's a great tune, but because of the storm it fomented. Passaro dismissed it as inconsequential, and in fact went so far as to say it was not music at all.

"It makes me sad," he said, "to think you would even *consider* suggesting to me that I get a piece for you that could be played not only by an organ grinder, but possibly by his monkey as well."

"Okay, Mr. Passaro," I said.

"It makes me *more* than sad," he said. "It *grieves* me, it hurts me *here*," he said, and realized I couldn't see what he was doing, and quickly added, "It pains me in my *heart*," and struck his chest with his closed fist so that I could hear the grieving, painful, hollow thump, "to think that perhaps I'm wrong about you, Ignazio, perhaps you are *not* serious about the piano after all, perhaps you are *not* willing to sacrifice yourself to your destiny."

"All right, Mr. Passaro," I said.

"No, it's *not* all right," he said, his voice rising. He was pacing, his heels clicking along the parquet floor; I sat at the piano with my hands in my lap, and wished I'd never heard of Benny Goodman. "*Not* all right at *all*, Ignazio! For *what* have we been studying and practicing these past two years, *more* than two years? For *what?* So you can come to me with a request for trash, ask me to procure for you a piece of junk I would not allow in my house except to start a fire in the stove with! Am I a procurer of trash for you, of *junk*, am I a man who would insult my own integrity and be unfaithful to your promise as a musician by allowing you to . . ."

"All right, all right," I said. "I'm sorry."

"*More* than sorry is what you must be!" Passaro shouted. "I hear that *junk*, that trash, and it gives me pains in the chest," he said. "The drums, ba-*dohm*, ba-*dohm*, ba-*dohm*, and the cornets making noise, and the saxophones, ah-waah, waah, waah! Never!" he shouted. "*Giammai!*" reverting to Italian, which he rarely did. "And the piano? Is that how to treat a piano? A *piano?* What is it they *do* with the piano? Is *that* what you wish to do with the piano, Ignazio? Do you wish to tinkle? Then go tinkle in the bathroom, not here, not where we study *music!* Do you want to play in Carnegie Hall, or do you want to play in the Paramount

191

movie house downtown? Decide. Decide now. I have no time to waste with ungrateful people to whom I am devoting *all* of my energy and *all* of my years of musical experience. *Decide*, Ignazio!"

"I already decided," I said.

"And what is your decision?"

"I want to play in Carnegie Hall."

"Then never again ask me to . . ."

"I won't, I promise."

"*Never*."

"I promise, really."

"All right," he said. He cleared his throat. "Did you practice this week? Or were you too busy listening to Benny Goodmans?"

"I practiced a lot."

"How long?"

"Three hours every day."

"Did you learn the Mozart?"

"Yes, Mr. Passaro."

"All *ten* variations?"

"Yes, Mr. Passaro."

"Clean? Or sloppy as usual?"

"Clean," I said.

"Play them."

The swing bands were, of course, as binding an ingredient in the mortar of the myth as were the radio and the movies and the comic strips and the jive talk already filtering its way into the streets ("That's *icky*, Iggie"), all of them reinforcing the sense of unity of a nation that was coping with the more serious business of pulling itself slowly out of the pit. I might have been as captured by the new sound as my brother Tony, had it not been for Passaro. Nor am I talking about his aversion to swing. Any classical musician might have been put off by swing. I am talking about an idea he implanted in my head, an idea intricately bound up with a myth entirely alien to him, and in keeping with everything I believed to be American.

192

Passaro thought I was a musical genius.

It's a common failing for blind musicians to believe they're more talented than musicians who can see, but when this fallacy is reinforced by a teacher who's beginning to believe you're Busoni reincarnated, and telling your mother you're going to burst upon the performing world in ten years (make it eight, make it *six!*) with such dynamic force that the reverberations will be felt and heard all over the world; and when you couple this with the only proposition in the American Dream that is *still* valid (but only if you're free, white, and thirty-five), phrased for simplicity's sake as "*Anyone* can become President of these United States!"—why, man, you have *got* to begin believing you are some-thing special.

I was something special.

Me.

Ignazio Silvio Di Palermo.

I was already into stuff like Bach's French and English Suites (not *all* the movements, but *some* of them), and his two-part inventions, and able to analyze them harmonically as I played them. I knew every chord on that keyboard (or thought I did until I began playing jazz), knew their primary, secondary, and tertiary functions, knew their patterns of progression and their categories of motion, knew modulation and transposition, and was improvising my own little tunes, upon which I was already writing variations. I was playing movements from Beethoven sonatas while working simultaneously on Chopin's Opus 72, Number 1 in E Minor, and I was pounding my Czerny and my Hanon like crazy, and I was going to prove that in America all men are created equal, and even the blind grandson of a poor but humble tailor could rise to spectacular heights and achieve fame and fortune if only I ate my Wheaties and faithfully decoded Little Orphan Annie's messages, and didn't rub up against plump little girls in coat closets, which was a sin, and didn't say "nigger" or "Jew," which was un-American and probably also a sin, and practiced the piano hard, and stopped bringing Passaro requests for trash and junk, and just stuck to being what I was and what I was destined to become—a goddamn musical *genius!*

I'm now forty-eight years old, and I know I'm not a genius. I also know that even *shleppers* and *shmucks* are rewarded in this great land of ours. But then? Ah, then.

Where else but in America? I thought.

Where else.

❖

When the Muscular Action Federation to Intensify Anxiety came around to see my grandfather, I was in the shop telling him and my grandmother about two new pieces Passaro had given me. I was sitting in the window seat, as usual. The bell over the door tinkled, and a man said, "Mr. Di Lorenzo?"

"Yes?" my grandfather answered.

I turned toward the door. Whoever the man was, he had not closed the door behind him. He was standing just inside it, and a cold February wind was swirling into the shop.

"We'd like to talk to you, Mr. Di Lorenzo," another man said.

"Close the door," my grandfather said.

The men did not close the door. The one who had spoken first now said, "Mr. Di Lorenzo, we'll make this short and sweet, okay? Your son-in-law tells us you ain't interested in our proposition."

"That's right," my grandfather said.

"What proposition?" my grandmother asked.

"Mr. Di Lorenzo, you'd *better* get interested, okay?"

"Why? So I can give you fifty percent of what I . . ."

"We'll take forty."

"No. I give you nothing."

"Mr. Di Lorenzo, you wouldn't believe the things that could happen to a tailor shop."

194

"Are you Italian?" my grandfather asked.

"I was born right here in Harlem," the man answered.

"You didn't answer my question."

"I'm Italian, yeah."

"Then leave me alone."

"This is nothing personal, Mr. Di Lorenzo."

"To me, it's personal," my grandfather answered.

"It can get a lot more personal, believe me," the other man said. "What do you say?"

"I say no."

"We'll be back, Mr. Di Lorenzo, okay?" the first one said.

"You can expect us," the other one said, and they went out of the shop and closed the door.

"Tell me," my grandmother said.

So he told her.

My Uncle Matt had come to him two weeks back and said he wanted to discuss a private matter. The way my grandfather reported the conversation, it had gone something like this:

"These guys I play cards with . . . you know the guys?"

"The crooks," my grandfather said.

"Well, they ain't bad guys, Pop. They gave back the stuff that time, didn't they?"

"If they hadn't taken it in the first place," my grandfather said, "they wouldn't have had to give it back."

"Well, they didn't know it was Luke and Dom, you know how it is. Anyway, we were playing the other night, and . . . they had a sort of idea."

"What idea?"

"They were thinking they might want to get in the dry-cleaning business, you know what I mean?"

"What for?"

"It's a good business," Matty said.

"Who says?"

"Well, you ain't exactly starving, are you, Pop?"

"I'm a *tailor*, that's why I'm not starving."

"Yeah, Pop, I know, but . . ."

"Tell them dry cleaning is a lousy business."

"Well, they don't think so, Pop. They really want to get in it, Pop."

"So let them get in it," my grandfather said.

"These guys, Pop, they had *your* business in mind."

"They want to buy my business? *Ma perchè? Sono pazzi questi tuoi amici?*"

"Not buy."

"Then what?"

"They want to come in with you, Pop."

"Come in?"

"In the business. They want to be your partners."

"I don't need partners. I got a partner already. Tessie's my partner. I don't need no more partners."

"Well, they think you do, Pop. Need some partners."

"Tell them I don't."

"They want fifty percent."

"I'll give them fifty percent of *shit*," my grandfather said.

"Pop . . . they could make trouble."

"Let them make it."

"You don't know these guys."

"No, only *you* know them, Matty."

"Look, they might be willing to talk, you know? Settle maybe for forty percent, or even thirty."

"Of what?" my grandfather asked. "My life? This shop is my life. Tell them to go to hell, all of them."

"Pop, you're making a mistake."

"*They're* making the mistake," my grandfather said.

"These guys don't fool around. They want something . . ."

"I came from the other side with nothing thirty-six years ago," my grandfather said. "*Senti?* Nothing. I was twenty years old; I

196

came with nothing, I found nothing. Now I have something. And I'm not giving fifty percent of it to anybody—or forty percent, or thirty percent, or anything. Tell them no. You hear me. Tell these *cafoni* that Di Lorenzo the tailor said no."

My grandmother listened, and then said, "Give them what they want, Frank."

"I'll give them nothing," he said.

"Frank . . ."

"Nothing."

They came back the very next morning, a Sunday, and smashed the plate-glass window of the shop. When they called my grandfather on the telephone Monday morning, he told them the answer was still no. So on Monday night, they pried loose the boards my grandfather had nailed across the broken window, and they went into the shop with cans of paint, and spilled the paint all over the clothes hanging on the racks, and all over the Salvation Army uniforms he'd been cutting in the back of the shop, paint as red as blood. He told them no again. On Saturday night, a week after they had first visited his shop, they broke in again and slashed the pads on the pressing machine, and broke the treadle on the sewing machine, and put the blades of his big cutting shears between the floorboards and snapped them off, and shattered the face of the hanging wall clock, and ripped down the flowered curtain dividing the front of the shop from the back, and pinned a Salvation Army jacket to the counter with a knife sticking up just below the left breast pocket, where the heart was. When they called my grandfather again on Monday morning, he told them the answer was still no. He told them there was nothing left for them to do but cripple him or kill him, and if they did that there would be no more tailor. And if there was no more tailor, there was no more business. And forty percent of nothing was nothing. They left him alone after that. I guess they considered him small potatoes, a waste of their valuable time. In frustration, they beat up my Uncle

197

Matt, and stopped playing cards with him, and made it impossible for him to get a medallion for his own cab, even though he'd been saving for one and had been assured a fix was in.

I tell this story not to illustrate the wisdom of my mother's "There are good and bad in every kind." I am not a press agent for the good wops in America, who know as well as I that most of the men in organized crime are *bad* wops. Nor do I have any desire to disprove the specious reasoning in the syllogism (1) All men are crooks; (2) Most crooks are Italians; (3) Therefore all Italians are crooks. I'll leave that to the politicians massaging the voters in Italian ghettos. I'll leave that to the men who compile the long lists of marvelous contributions Italians have made to American life, starting all the way back with Amerigo Vespucci, and continuing on upward through Cristoforo Colombo, and Frank Sinatra and Mario Puzo and, according to my father, Burt Lancaster. ("Burt Lancaster is Italian, did you know that, Ike?") Dwight *Jamison* is Italian, did you know *that*, Pop? Who the hell cares *what* they are?

Nor does this anecdote have much to do with the care and feeding of the myth, except perhaps tangentially, since the myth was nurtured by the Eighteenth Amendment, which made it a crime for Americans to manufacture or to consume alcoholic beverages, thereby creating a nation of lawbreakers dedicated to the pursuit of booze and unifying us on a level somewhat removed from Ken Maynard's horse. A side effect of prohibition was the emergence and spectacular rise of a gangster elite who supplied the booze drunk by the *honest* lawbreakers in the speaks. Those men went out of the whiskey and beer business in December of 1933, when the amendment was repealed. This was February of 1937, and that was all water under the bridge (so to speak), and who could blame those erstwhile distillers and distributors for seeking other business opportunities like the one my grandfather's shop seemed to offer, and besides, that's not the point at all, not *even* tangentially.

Well, then, Ike, *you're* the one with the selective memory, you're the one differentiating between the strong left-hand chords and the wispy sprinklings in the right hand. Why does this particular event (which happens to be true, but no matter) seem overwhelmingly important to the development of your theme, whereas Aunt Bianca's corset shop got the ethereal "September in the Rain" treatment? Are you trying to demonstrate that your grandfather was a courageous man, which undoubtedly he was? Are you trying to indicate that his act of defiance was uncommonly risky in that it might just as easily have led to his untimely demise, causing him to wake up one dismal February morning with an ice-pick sticking out of his ear? What *are* your motives, Ike baby?

Ulterior, I'm sure.

Jane Austen is reputed to have said, "I write about love and money. What else is there to write about?" Maybe that's all there is to write about in England, lady. This is America. I played the head chorus back there in 1901, when my grandfather came to these shores, but that was only to identify the tune. This is the second chorus, this is where you have to start paying attention. I'm transposing and improvising at the same time. And in America, we have transposed the word love to mean sex, we have transposed the word money to mean power, and power means violence, and sex and violence often mean the same damn thing. Those nice guys who smashed my grandfather's window and spilled paint on the clothes and ripped up the pressing machine and broke the sewing machine (and later Matty's head) were just learning to be American, that's all, and were perhaps more foresighted than all the rest of us who were learning to be American at the same time. If they had been true forerunners, of course, true innovators, true seminal figures, they'd have taken the next logical step, thereby distilling sex and violence into its purest native essence. For reasons known only to themselves, however, they stopped short of buggery.

Richard Palumbo didn't.

❖

We moved to the Bronx in April of 1937, three weeks after Richard Palumbo buggered Basilio Silese in the locker room of the Boys' Club on 110th Street.

Coincidentally, my father was appointed a regular at about the same time Richard decided to broaden the scope of his sexual activity; I'm not sure which of the two events motivated the move to the Bronx. I rather suspect it was the buggery, which my brother Tony was obliged to report in detail to my mother when we got back to the apartment on 120th Street. I did not know until then that my brother's nose was bleeding, or that his left eye was swollen and partially closed. I had sat on a bench in the locker room throughout the entire terrifying experience, still dripping wet from the swimming pool, a towel draped over my lap, listening to sounds, jerking my head from left to right, trying to understand what was happening, knowing only that it was something unspeakably horrible, and realizing suddenly that my brother Tony had become involved. Now, in the kitchen of our apartment on 120th Street, I listened to my mother's terse interrogation and Tony's reluctant responses, and began to piece together the story and became frightened all over again.

"What happened?" my mother said.

"Nothing," Tony answered.

"Nothing? Your nose is bleeding, look at your eye, what happened?"

"I had a fight."

"Where?"

"At the Boys' Club."

"Who with?"

"Richard Palumbo."

"Why?"

"Forget it, Mom," Tony said.

"What happened, Iggie?"

"I don't know," I said.

"Somebody better *start* knowing," my mother said. "What happened, Tony?"

"I told you. I had a fight. Now that's it, Mom, so let's forget it, okay?"

"Why'd you have a fight?"

"How do I know why?"

"Iggie?"

"I don't know, Mom."

"Where at the Boys' Club?"

"In the locker room," Tony said.

"I thought you and Richard Palumbo were friends."

"We are."

"Then why'd you have a fight with him?"

"I don't know why. We just had a fight, that's all."

"When was this?"

"After we came out of the water."

We have been swimming for close to an hour. We come to the club every Saturday, carrying woolen swim trunks and towels with us. We change in the locker room and then spend an hour in the pool, after which we dry ourselves and dress again and go home. Even in the summer months, my brother takes me to the Boys' Club to swim because the public pool in Jefferson Park is too crowded. A man blows a whistle at the deep end of the pool, near the diving board, when it is time for us to come out of the water. That means our hour is up, and they'll now let another batch of kids into the pool. In the summer months, they let us swim as long as we want because not so many kids are there. But this is April.

"You came out of the water . . ."

"We came out of the water, and we went into the locker room, and a fight started, and that's it. I got homework to do, Mom. If you don't mind . . ."

"Your homework can wait. You went in the locker room, and then what?"

"I told you."

"You *didn't* tell me!"

"We went in the locker room, and the guys started fooling around, and a fight started between me and Richard. That's what happened. Okay? Can I go do my homework now?"

"Fooling around *how?*" my mother asked.

"Just fooling around. The way we always do."

"*How?*"

I can hear the slap of wet feet against the tiled floor of the locker room. My brother, who always dresses much faster than I, has gone to the office to find out when we have to renew our membership cards. My locker door is open, the smell of contained sweat assails my nostrils a foot from the bench upon which I sit drying myself. There is laughter in the echoing room, and shouted obscenities, and bellowed lines from popular songs. Someone yells, "Hey, Basilio, watch your ass!"

"Look, Mom, there's a lot of fooling around goes on in a locker room."

"This is the first I'm hearing about it," my mother said. "What kind of fooling around?"

"Like they hide your clothes sometimes, or they tie your shoelaces in knots, or rub chewing gum in your hair . . . like that."

"Very nice," my mother said. "Is that what Richard did?"

"No."

"Then what did he do?"

"Nothing."

"Then why did you have a fight?"

I know the sound of a wet towel being snapped, and I also know the feel of that fiery lash against my backside. Being blind saves me from most childhood cruelties, but occasionally someone will whip his towel at me from behind, without realizing I am his target, and then immediately apologize—"Gee, Iggie, I'm sorry, I didn't know it was you."

Basilio Silese is the target today.

"He was giving Basilio the towel."

"What do you mean?"

"Richard. He was hitting Basilio with the wet towel."

"Hitting him?"

"His ass."

"His *what?*"

"His behind, I'm sorry."

"I still don't understand you."

"Mom, he was snapping the towel at him. Like a whip, like cracking a whip at his behind. And I came in, I was up in the office, and I told him to stop, and he wouldn't, so I hit him."

"Why did you butt in?"

"He was . . . hurting Basilio."

I hear only the snap of the towel each time it connects with Basilio's flesh. He screams and tries to run away but Richard, whose voice I now recognize, keeps crooning, "Watch your ass, Basilio," and whick, the towel snaps out yet another time, and Basilio shrieks again, and there is the sound of bare feet slapping on the tiles as he tries to escape. There are more boys after him now, I hear towels snapping at him wherever I turn my head. I am becoming frightened. "Watch your ass, Basilio!" and whick, and another shriek of pain, and the sound of running feet, someone slipping to the tile floor, "Watch your ass, Basilio!" and someone shouting, "Richard has a hard-on!" and then all of them chanting the words into the echoing room, "Richard has a hard-on, Richard has a hard-on," and then sudden silence.

"He was hurting him with the towel?" my mother said.

"Yes."

"So you hit him, is that right?"

"Yes, Mom."

"You're lying, Tony."

"I'm telling you the God's honest truth, may I drop dead on the floor if I'm lying."

Basilio is struggling. The locker room is ominously still except for the grunts that come from the floor not six feet from where I am sitting. "Hold still, you fuckin' pansy!" Richard says, and Basilio murmurs, "Please, please don't," and someone says, "Give it to him, Richie." Silence. A single sharp penetrating scream shatters the brittle stillness, and then there is the sound of labored breathing and another sound like the whimper of a wounded animal. From the far end of the room my brother Tony yells, "Hey, what are you doing there?" No one answers. I hear Basilio sobbing. I hear Richard's harsh rhythmic breathing. "Get off him," Tony says. His sneakers are hitting the tiled floor as he runs toward the bench. "Get off him!" he shrieks.

"How was he hurting him?" my mother asked.

"I told you. With the towel."

"What was he doing to Basilio?"

"He was hitting him with the towel."

"And that's why you butt in?"

"Yes."

"Tony, why are you lying to me?"

"I'm not," Tony said, and began crying. "I'm not, Mom, I swear."

"What happened? Tell me everything that happened."

"He was giving it to Basilio in the ass," Tony said in a rush, and then he must have thrown himself into my mother's arms because his next words were muffled.

❖

My manager, a man named Mark Aronowitz (who doesn't call too often these days), is fond of describing business deals in sexual terms.

204

"Look, Ike, the offer is fifteen hundred a week, and that's it. I can tell you they'll go to three grand, but what's the sense of jerking ourselves off?"

Or: "I know the Cleveland gig is a drag, you think I don't know it? But it's only for a week; am I asking you to *marry* the fucking joint?"

Or: "Don't tell him it's firm yet. Drummers are a dime a dozen. Feel around a little, decide whether you want to get in bed with him."

Or (most frequently): "We've been screwed, Ike. Here's the story. . . ."

I sometimes try to imagine where Basilio Silese went from that day in the Boys' Club locker room. Is he now a hopeless faggot wearing lavender satin gowns and mincing about in high-heeled slippers? Or has he gone the opposite route, screwing every female he can get his hands on in order to prove his own asshole is inviolate? It's tough enough being a "man" in this country; Basilio certainly didn't need a snotnosed thirteen-year-old locker-room stud seeding premature doubts before an audience of two dozen sighted kids and one blind bastard breathlessly listening to every grunt and moan. And what of Richard Palumbo? Did he ever consider his assault homosexual? Probably not. He was the *man*, you see, the bold attacker, the conquering hero till my brother Tony declared him villain of the piece. He was Richard Palumbo of the Mount-*ees* rather than Basilio Silese of the Mount-ed. He had cautioned, "Watch your ass, Basilio," and in America that's fair enough warning because if you *don't* watch your ass, someone's going to lay claim to it. "We've been screwed, Ike. Here's the story. . . ."

I still think back with horror upon what happened in that locker room thirty-seven years ago—thirty-seven *years!* And I know that Richard Palumbo's assault upon Basilio Silese's backside is linked in memory to my own innocent (Stop claiming it was so innocent! You got a hot iron, didn't you? And a *Russian* one at that!) rubbing up against Tina, my aunt's plump little sister. I don't know much about writing, but I *do* know how to play the piano, and there are some tunes I won't touch. Come to me with a request for "I Don't Know Why," and I'll turn you down cold, and not only because it's a lousy tune. For me it conjures Poe Park in the Bronx, where Tony took me just before he got sent overseas, telling me he'd fix me up with a girl, and indeed finding a big-breasted sixteen-year-old for me, who kept saying over and over again, "It's amazing, it's truly amazing, I never before realized a blind person could dance," while leading me around the packed dance floor girdling the band shell, her guiding hand firm in the small of my back as we avoided collision after collision, Bobby Sherwood blowing the tune on his horn, and singing the lyrics in a lulling monotone. I sat on a bench with her later, and she said, "Take off your glasses, I want to see what a blind person's eyes look like." I got off the bench, and stumbled through the crowd, groping, until I reached the Grand Concourse and found the lamppost Tony had told me to wait by, in case we got separated.

Don't ask me to play "I Don't Know Why." My fingers lock on the keyboard, and I can't get through the first bar. And I guess if you ask me to play "Tina in the Closet," another old favorite, I won't play it as the passionate, enclosed, excruciatingly ecstatic awakening it was, but will play it *exactly* as I did earlier—as a takeoff on a tune, a facetiously scientific, emotionless rendering. Why? I don't know why, but I *do* know why: because of what Richard Palumbo did.

If you're still alive, Richard, and if by now you realize you're dealing with Ignazio Silvio Di Palermo, and *not* Dwight Jamison, and if you further realize that it was my dear dead brother Tony who punched you in the mouth that day, I'm going to tell you that I also link his death to you and what you did. You're a time machine, Richard. I climb into you climbing into Basilio, and I'm transported backward to my own excitement that day with Tina and am embarrassed by it, and then somebody wrenches the control switch and I'm propelled forward to the year 1943, and my

206

brother Tony is now a full-fledged hero in the greatest homosexual enterprise ever invented, and he is killed, he is screwed, he is fucked in the ass at the age of nineteen years, six months, and six days.

Thanks for the memories, Richard.

❖

The woman downstairs is named Stella Locchi. To differentiate her from Stella Di Palermo, who is my mother, the women on 217th Street call her Stella the Baker, which is her husband's occupation. My mother becomes Stella the Mailman. I don't think she likes this too much. In Harlem, where the name Mary was as common as the name Sarah on the Lower East Side, there had been a Mary the Street Cleaner, and a Mary the Barber, and a Mary the Electric Company, and a Mary the Mutt (who had married Vinny the Mutt), and a plethora of other Marys, including Mary the Virgin, who was not *la Madonna* but instead a spinster lady of eighty-seven, who lived alone in a room behind Carlo Fiaci's candy store, and who was labeled with her own occupation rather than that of any kin, all of whom had predeceased her. But Stella was a very special name; there had not been a single other Stella in all the streets of the *vicinanza*, none that my mother knew, at least, and it irks her now to have to share her stardom with a Stella who owns the building we are living in, and from whose husband we buy our daily bread on White Plains Avenue. If my mother had known her prospective landlady would be a Stella, she would not have taken the apartment, even though it was close to the Santa Lucia School for the Blind.

Mrs. Locchi pointed this out to my mother the Saturday we went to see the apartment.

"I notice the little boy is blind," she said. "There's a blind school on Paulding Avenue, you know. It's very good. He could walk there. Can he walk places by himself?"

"Yes, he can walk places by himself," my mother said. I think her tone was lost on Stella the Baker, whose name and husband's occupation we did not yet know; my mother can be as subtle as a pit viper when she so chooses. "He can also play the piano very nicely, and is being trained for Carnegie Hall," she added, putting away the stiletto and bringing out the machete.

"My, my," Mrs. Locchi said.

"I hope you don't mind hearing the piano," my mother said. "He practices sometimes three, four hours a day."

"I *love* the piano," Mrs. Locchi said. "My own son, Gerardo, plays the clarinet, and he's only seven. He's not blind, of course."

"So few people are," my mother answered.

"Your hubby is a mailman, is that right, Mrs. Di Palermo?"

"He's a letter carrier," my mother said, which probably sounded more American to her.

"There's a post office on Gun Hill Road," Mrs. Locchi said. "I'm not trying to push you into taking the apartment, but he could walk to work every morning. The Williamsbridge post office. Right on Gun Hill Road."

"Well, right now, my husband is working as a regular at the Tremont station," my mother said.

"But he could get a transfer, couldn't he?" Mrs. Locchi asked.

"Yes, maybe."

"How old are you, young man?" Mrs. Locchi said.

"Me?" I said.

"No, your brother here."

"I'll be thirteen in June," Tony said.

"My, my, you're big for your age," Mrs. Locchi said. "What grade are you in?"

"I'll be starting high school in September."

"Oh, that's too bad, because there's a junior high right across the street. You could have walked right across the street to school each morning. Not that the *high* school is very far, either. Evander Childs. That's on Gun Hill Road, a few blocks from the post office. Most of the kids on the block walk there, too."

"How much *is* the apartment?" my mother asked.

"We're asking thirty-five a month."

"We're paying twenty-six now."

"Yes, but that's Harlem," Mrs. Locchi said. "Up the street, they're asking forty dollars for only *three* rooms. This is five rooms when you count the sun porch, which you could use as a bedroom for one of the boys. Thirty-five a month isn't a lot for this apartment. You go ask around, you'll see."

"It *is* convenient, I suppose," my mother said.

"And there are plenty of kids on the block," Mrs. Locchi said. "All ages. Your sons will have plenty of kids to play with. It's a nice neighborhood."

"It seems very nice," my mother said.

"Very quiet," Mrs. Locchi said.

"Yes."

"And no niggers," she said.

"Negroes," I said.

"That's right," she said, and patted me on the head, startling me half out of my wits because I hadn't sensed her hand coming at me. "So you're going to play at Carnegie Hall when you grow up. Isn't that nice," she said.

"Well, let me talk it over with my husband," my mother said.

"I don't want to rush you," Mrs. Locchi said, "but a woman was here looking at the apartment just before you, and she said she'd call me back at seven tonight."

"My husband works half a day Saturday," my mother said. "I'll call you early this afternoon."

"If you'd like to leave a small deposit with me now, you can talk it over with your hubby, and then if you decide against it, I'll return the money."

"How much of a deposit?" my mother asked.

"Whatever you like," Mrs. Locchi said. "Five dollars? I'll tell you the truth, the woman who wants the apartment is German. I prefer an Italian family. You're Italian, aren't you?"

"I was born here," my mother said, bridling.

"Oh, me, *too*," Mrs. Locchi said, never once realizing how close she had come to blowing the deal.

❖

Santa Lucia's was indeed within walking distance, and after Tony had taken me there once or twice, I learned the route by heart, and got there and back without mishap every weekday morning. There was one wide avenue, and also three side streets to cross before I got to the school. I sometimes had to wait a long time, especially in the winter, for someone to help me across the streets, but that didn't bother me. I just busied myself playing piano inside my head, my books and my cane tucked under my arms, my hands nestled in the pockets of my mackinaw, my fingers moving against the felt linings. There were lots of pieces to play in my pockets. I had been playing piano for five years by then, the last almost-three of them under Passaro's tutelage, and I was firmly convinced that I was a prodigy for whom nothing was too difficult. Preludes and fugues from *The Well-Tempered Clavier?* Duck soup for eleven-year-old Ignazio Di Palermo. A Chopin etude, a Mozart sonata, a Debussy prelude, a Ravel pavanne, I had them all in my pockets and under my fingers. I was hot stuff.

Santa Lucia's was a lot different from the Blind School in New York. At Santa Lucia's, *all* the kids were either blind or only partially sighted, and this created a sense of unity that had been totally lacking in Manhattan, where fourteen of us were isolated from the sighted community and made to feel (though not through any fault of Miss Goodbody, bless her heart) like outcasts. There's a certain similarity between being blind and being black, and I first felt its full impact in the forties, when I began playing jazz. It was then that I realized how dumb those kids on Park Avenue had been. They'd once understood they were only beating up another nigger. My thinking has changed since the forties. Forget

210

being blind; I now realize we're *all* niggers. But back in 1937, during my first week at Santa Lucia's, conditioned as I was by the Blind School, I tried some of the boastful cruelty that had proved so effective against the little blind bastards in Manhattan.

Fortified by Passaro's promises, I immediately told my classmates that I was studying to be a concert pianist, and that pretty soon I'd be playing at Carnegie Hall. (You think I'm blind, don't you? Heh-heh. *You're* the ones who are blind. *I'm* going to play at Carnegie Hall.) The kids told me they thought that was great. Puzzled, I told them I was a musical *genius*, for Christ's sake! So the kids asked our teacher if they could hear me play sometime, and Sister Margarita arranged for me to give a recital in the school auditorium. After the recital, all the kids came up and told me I was marvelous, and asked how long it had taken to learn to play that way, and one kid—a girl named Susan Koenig, who had the voice of an angel—held my hand in her own and gently patted it, and said she had never heard anything so beautiful in her life. I had played Beethoven's "Moonlight" Sonata (which I announced as "*Sonata Quasi Una Fantasia*," to make it sound even more impressive), and I was about to tell her that whereas perhaps I had made a few errors in the exceedingly difficult (in fact, ball-breaking, even to pianists who've been playing for half a lifetime) *presto agitato* movement, I *had* nonetheless tried it in public, even though I was still working on it—when one of the nuns came over. She introduced herself as Sister Monique and said she had never been able to overcome the first movement's doubling effect in the right-hand octave, and that somehow the triplets always overwhelmed the melody, and she would be grateful to me if one day I showed her how I'd managed to achieve just the proper touch. I was a trifle flabbergasted. What *was* this place, anyway—a family?

Well, not quite. But pretty close to one. Santa Lucia's had been started in 1906 in a four-room apartment in the West Farms section of the Bronx. The man who'd founded it had been blind himself, a devout Catholic who chose to name it after Santa Lucia of Syracuse, the patron saint of anyone afflicted with ophthalmia and other diseases of the eye. There are patron saints for everything and everyone, of course, but Lucy's story is sort of interesting, if you've got a minute. Apparently some young swain was so stricken by her gorgeous peepers that he told her he was unable to sleep at night, and unable to concentrate on what he was doing during the day. Taking her cue from Christ himself ("If thine eye offend thee, pluck it out"), Lucy did just that, and sent both beautiful orbs to the young man, together with a message that read (according to usually well-informed sources), "Now you have what you desired, so leave me in peace!" The man became a Christian on the spot; Lord knows what he'd been before. And God, ever merciful, later returned Lucy's eyes and her vision to her while she was at prayer.

In the early days, Santa Lucia's had accepted only "legally blind children of the Catholic faith," and had taught them through the sixth grade. But after the death of the founder in 1928, the trustees moved the school to its present location and expanded not only its physical plant but its restrictive entrance requirements as well. When I started there, it was still being administered by nuns, but it was fully accredited by the Regents of the State of New York, and it accepted any legally blind boy or girl over three years of age, regardless of race, creed, or color. That was nice. It fit perfectly into what I thought America was supposed to be. Santa Lucia's, too, had recently become a six-six school, which meant that once I had completed my elementary-school education (I entered the sixth grade in September of 1937), I could continue my secondary education there for the *next* six years, without having to look around for another school. I loved Santa Lucia's, but it took me four months to get my father to come to school and meet the nuns who were teaching me. When he finally did come, he stood silently by my side, and held my hand, and let them do all the talking. His hand was sweating.

212

For me, everything was beginning to fall into place, and every-thing seemed right. "If you think *this* is something, you shoulda seen *Mamaroneck*," Tony said, but to me the Bronx was perfect. I loved the school, I loved the new neighborhood, and I especially loved a little girl across the street, with whom I went to the movies every Saturday, after my piano lesson. Her name was Michelle Dulac, and her father taught French at the junior high school. Tony would take me to my piano lesson, the ride to Passaro's consuming a half hour of my brother's burning time, and then he would wait impatiently in the other room while I played Chopin for the next hour, and then he would hurry me home again on the Third Avenue El, impatiently tapping his feet, scarcely able to speak. When we got back to the house at one or a little bit after, he would bolt down a sandwich and swallow a glass of milk in a long single gulp and dash out of the house again, running for the elevated station on 219th Street and White Plains Avenue. His destination? The fair Letitia, whose loss he mourned for a full eight months, his record collection growing in direct proportion to his grief. He never got to play his records for her anymore, because my grandmother took Saturdays off from the tailor shop, and the front room of her house was no longer as sacrosanct as it had been on those long Friday afternoons of yore. But neither did he play them for *me*. (To an Italian, even a third-generation *American* Italian, a vow is a vow.) My parents had given him a record player for his birthday in June, and now that he had his own room, he would go in there and lock the door, and all I heard through the thick wooden panels were the forbidden muffled sounds of the pounding drums and the screaming trumpets and the moaning saxophones, and occasionally the sound of a thirteen-year-old cry-ing.

My mother adored Michelle Dulac—naturally.

"*Bonjour, Michelle,*" she would say. "*Comment allez-vous aujourd'hui?*"

"*Très bien, merci, et vous, Madame Di Palermo?*"

"*Comme ci, comme ça,*" my mother would reply, beaming, and then, because Michelle and I were on our way to the movies, she would add, "*Vite, vite, nous manquerons le match de football!*"

At the movies, Michelle and I sat in the children's section and watched (*she* watched, *I* listened to) six cartoons, two chapters, a newsreel, and two feature films starring the motion picture families of the various studios, and these blended in my mind to become one big movie family which in turn became a part of *our* family, the great *American* family that seemed to be proliferating wildly and uncontrollably and excitingly, the democratic experiment on the very edge of proving itself valid and enduring, the impurities burning off in the crucible of hard times easing, the residual mettle hardening into something glowing and impervious.

In the evenings, or on long summer afternoons when I'd finished my practicing or my homework, I went over to Michelle's and she read to me aloud from her vast collection of comic books, introducing a whole new batch of families to add to those already surrounding me, comforting me, nourishing me. None of the neighborhood kids considered our relationship serious, possibly because a blind person isn't expected to have a "girl friend" in the accepted sense, especially when he's only eleven and the girl is three months younger. (Tony knew better.) Too, since I couldn't play football or baseball or handball except with the kids at Santa Lucia's (and *those* athletic contests were full-scale riots, believe me), the other kids on the block thought it perfectly reasonable for me to have a girl for a fast friend, and readily accepted the fact that blind Iggie spent a lot of time on the floppy old couch in the Dulac living room, the windows behind us open to the sounds of the street and the shouts of the other children, Michelle reading aloud the ballooned dialogue of the comic book heroes and heroines, and describing the action in the drawings.

Outside, we heard the bells of the Good Humor truck, and the voices of the women calling to each other in English or Italian.

The first girl I ever kissed was Michelle Dulac.

I kissed her on a January day in 1940, after two years and nine months of movies and comic books. She had a collection as high as the ceiling. It occurs to me that if she still owns it, it must be worth a fortune. But why would she still own it? Superman and the brood he spawned died with the rest of the family, even though their mummified corpses are still around.

The first breast I ever touched was Michelle Dulac's.

I touched it in the back seat of her father's Pontiac coming home from Orchard Beach on the Fourth of July that same year. We were both thirteen, we were both wearing damp bathing suits. Michelle said she was a little chilly, and draped a blanket over us, covering us to our chins. In the front seat, Mr. and Mrs. Dulac were talking to each other in French. The rain that had forced us to leave the beach was drumming on the roof of the automobile. The blanket was sandy. My hand hovered an inch above Michelle's right breast for perhaps twenty minutes, the fingers spread and suspended between the blanket and the top of her bathing suit, the entire hand paralyzed. When I finally mustered the courage to touch her (would she scream?), I attacked her hapless budding tit with a ferocity I normally reserved for the third movement of Bach's *Italian* Concerto. Mixing styles and techniques, I played arpeggios up and down that tiny perfect slope, tapped two-fingered trills on the scant nipple, shifted to the bass clef and executed a pianistically perfect series of descending triplets from her left collarbone to her left breast, and then attempted a swift, smooth glissando to her belly button. She grabbed my wrist.

"Careful," she murmured, and her father up front said, "What, Michelle?" and she said, "Truck up ahead," and he said, "I see it," and still clutching my wrist, she brought my hand back up to her

215

breasts again. We were both panting when we pulled up in front of her house on 217th Street.

"Are we here already?" Michelle asked breathlessly.

"Home sweet home," her father said.

Under the blanket, Michelle was frantically retying the straps of her bathing suit, which she had loosened to allow me greater finger dexterity, musical genius that I was. I was meanwhile trying to figure how I could get out of the automobile without exposing the grotesque bulge in my trunks.

"It's still raining," her mother said. "Why don't you kids stay in the car till it stops? Or shall I get you an umbrella?"

"No, we'll stay in the car," Michelle said.

We stayed in the car, or the equivalent of the car, for the next thirteen months. I felt her up constantly. Every chance I got, I felt her up. I felt her up in her living room and in her kitchen and once in her bedroom when her parents were away for the evening. I felt her up riding behind her on the rack of her bicycle, and I felt her up in Bronx Park under the trees and sitting on benches and lying on the grass; I felt her up incessantly. I felt her up in the Loews Post and the Laconia and the Melba and the Wakefield, and I felt her up on the Grand Concourse in the Loews Paradise, and in Mount Vernon at both the Embassy and the Biltmore, while the voices of my vast American family flooded warmly and approvingly from the theater speakers. I felt her up against the schoolyard fence and against the clapboard shingles of Mr. Locchi's house while my mother entertained the ladies of her sewing club upstairs, and I felt her up in more driveways and behind more hedges than anyone on the block or in the entire Bronx even knew existed. From July of 1940, when I was still thirteen, to the day she moved away in the fall of 1941, when I was almost fifteen, I deliriously stroked, squeezed, kneaded, patted, probed, and poked those perfect pubescent peaks as they metamorphosed with her own advancing adolescence into beautiful, bountiful, bouncing, bursting . . . I get carried away even now.

216

"Je t'aime, je t'adore, qu'est-ce que tu veux encore?" Michelle would ask in metered breathlessness, but each time I demonstrated what more I desired, each time my hand wandered down to the hem of her skirt, her own hand would dart out with all the terrible swiftness of The Flash, and her fingers would grip my wrist with the viselike strength of Sheena of the Jungle. "No, baby," she would say, "not now." Not now meant never. Only once did I manage to steal my hand onto the soft silken secret of her panties, and then for just an electric instant before those swift descending fingers closed again upon my wrist and snatched my hand away.

In August of 1941, her father took a job teaching at a Queens high school. We said our good-byes one early September midnight, locked in embrace on the lawn behind the house of an old ginzo we called "The Paintbrush" because of his walrus mustache, the crickets and katydids racketing in the bushes, my hands desperately clutching those prized departing possessions.

"I love you," she whispered. "I'll always love you, Iggie."

"Oh, and I love you, Michelle. Oh, *God*, how I love you."

She moved out of my life forever the very next day.

She remains the most beautiful woman I have ever known.

❖

My brother Tony was seventeen years old when the Japanese bombed Pearl Harbor. He immediately asked my mother for permission to enlist in the Air Corps. My mother talked it over with my father, and then my grandfather, and then got back to Tony with an unequivocal "No."

"I'll enlist, anyway," Tony said. "I'll lie about my age."

"And I'll call the Air Corps and tell them you're a liar," my mother said. "And a little snotnose besides."

"You're making a mistake," Tony said. "I could be a good flier. I could be a goddamn *ace!*"

217

"Don't use that kind of language around your mother," my father said.

"You want Hitler to take over the world?"

"Hitler won't take over the world, don't worry," my mother said.

"How do *you* know? What does he do, call you on the telephone every day? 'Ja, hello, Shtella?'" Tony said, falling into an imitation of all the Germans he'd ever seen on the motion picture screen. "'Das iss Adolf here. I haff decided not to take over d'vorld. Votchoo tink of dat, Shtella?' For Christ's *sake* Mom!"

"The matter is settled."

"And don't talk like that."

"Who told you to say no? Grandpa?"

"The matter is settled."

"Was it him?"

"Grandpa had nothing to do with it. I'd have to be out of my mind to let you go fly an airplane. That's *that*, Tony."

"And we don't want to hear no more about it," my father said.

"Wait'll some Jap comes marching in here with a bayonet," Tony said.

"Sure," my mother said.

"It could happen," Tony said.

"Sure," my mother said. "It could also rain elephants."

"*Damn* it, Mom . . ."

"Tony," my father said, "I'm not going to warn . . ."

"This is *important* to me, Pop!"

"I thought baseball was important to you," my mother said.

"*Baseball?* The whole fu . . . the whole *world* is at war, and you expect me to think about baseball?"

"No, *you* want to think about flying airplanes," my mother said.

"Yes, that's right."

"Sure," my mother said.

"Right," Tony said.

"The matter is settled."

Tony went down to see my grandfather the very next day. He

got back to the house at about six o'clock. I was in my room, practicing. When I heard his knock on my door, I immediately pulled my hands from the piano.

"Igg?" he said. "Okay to come in?"

"Sure, Tony."

He walked in, shut the door behind him, and sat on the bed. I turned from the piano.

"What'd he say?" I asked.

"Argh," Tony said.

"Did you tell him?"

"Yeah."

"What'd you tell him?"

"I told him I wanted to join the Air Corps."

"What'd he say?"

"He said he knew. He's a fuckin' old *greaseball*, Iggie. He asked me if I wanted to go bomb Italy. He asked me what I'd do if they told me to go bomb Fiormonte. I said Who the hell is going to ask me to bomb Fiormonte, Grandpa? What the hell is in Fiormonte to *bomb?* So he tells me it's a beautiful village. So I said Grandpa, the generals aren't interested in bombing beautiful villages; what they want to do is bomb *military* targets, not beautiful villages. So he says there's a bridge in Fiormonte, across the river there, and maybe the generals'll tell me to bomb the bridge so supplies won't be able to go to Bari or wherever, because Bari is a seaport. So I said Grandpa, the generals aren't going to be interested in a shitty little bridge in Fiormonte, and he said It's a *nice* bridge, Antonio. So I said Look, Grandpa, I'm not trying to take away from the goddamn bridge, I'm just trying to tell you nobody's going to send me to bomb Fiormonte, and anyway, I don't *want* to fly a bomber, I want to fly a *fighter* plane, I want to be a *fighter* pilot."

"That's right," I said.

"*Sure*, that's right. You know what he said? He said Then what'll you do, machine-gun innocent women and children from your airplane? I said Grandpa, why would I do something like that? And he said Because it's war."

"You should've told him you wouldn't do nothing like that, Tony. You wouldn't, would you?"

"Of course not, what the hell do you think I am? I thought you knew me better than that, Iggie."

"But suppose they *ordered* you to do it?"

"Who?"

"The generals."

"Do what?"

"Machine-gun women and children."

"I wouldn't do it," Tony said. "I just *told* you I wouldn't do it, didn't I?"

"Then they'd court-martial you."

"No, they wouldn't."

"Sure, they would. If you don't obey orders . . ."

"Iggie, we're getting off the goddamn track! Here's what I want to do. After your piano lesson Saturday, I want to take you to the tailor shop."

"What for?"

"To talk to him."

"To Grandpa?"

"Well, now, who the hell do you *think* I mean? Pino? Of *course* to Grandpa."

"Well . . ."

"He'll listen to you," Tony said. He hesitated, and then said, "He likes you better than me."

"No, he don't Tony. He likes us the same."

"Listen, I don't care about that, I swear to God. I just want you to convince him, okay? If he says I can enlist, then he'll tell Mom, and she'll sign the papers. Will you do it, Igg?"

"Sure, Tony, but I don't know. If *you* couldn't convince him . . ."

"Just say you'll try, okay? This means a lot to me, Igg."

"Sure, Tony."

"Okay?"

"Sure."

"Don't tell Mom."

"I won't."

"We'll say we went to a movie on Tremont Avenue."

I knew it wouldn't work even before I went to talk to him. I had tried something like this with him a long time ago, when my mother had given away Vesuvio. If he wouldn't let *me* go to Goomah Katie's in Newark, he sure as hell wasn't going to let *Tony* drop bombs on Fiormonte.

I talked to him for three hours.

He refused to change his mind. In June of 1942, Tony turned eighteen and registered for the draft. A month later he received his greetings from Uncle Sam, and left to begin his training as an infantryman in the United States Army.

❖

I immersed myself in music.

I realize now that Passaro was an extraordinary teacher, who encouraged me to take reckless musical chances, allowing me to swim out as far as I dared, but always ready to dive in and pull me back to shore if and when I got into serious trouble. Shortly after Tony was drafted, for example, he started me on Beethoven's C-Minor Concerto, which, as I'm sure you know, is not exactly "Twinkle, Twinkle, Little Star." (*That* tune, as I'm sure you also know, is the theme for the Mozart K. 265 variations, sometimes known as "Ah, *vous dirai-je, maman,*" especially to French scholars like my *own* dear maman, Stella Di Palermo.) Passaro probably knew the Beethoven was beyond my depth, but he also knew I was a gifted musician, and when you've got a truly talented student—or so the theory goes—you push him relentlessly, you give him tremendously difficult compositions, you keep after him day

221

and night because if he's going to be a concert pianist, he's got one hell of a large repertoire to learn, and he isn't going to learn it by playing the "Mikrokosmos" over and over again.

Well, hell, Passaro had me playing the Grieg Concerto when I was *twelve*, though he'd prepared me beforehand with a series of little exercises he himself invented. He had decided that Czerny and Hanon were not helping me build my repertoire— my repertoire, my sacred, spiring repertoire. "You must build a repertoire, Iggie, there are *thousands* of compositions to master!" And so he would teach me a single precise exercise, and I would discover to my surprise that it miniaturized a very tricky technical passage in a piece he was about to present. When he sprang the Grieg Concerto on me, I realized I'd been practicing (as an exercise!) the descending double thirds in the first movement, and when I got to them in the actual piece, they seemed relatively easy.

Inspiring me with tales of Great Musicians He Had Known, firing my ambition ("You will win all the prizes, you will perform in Carnegie Hall!"), he pushed me into the Beethoven C-Minor because he honestly believed I *would* win all the awards. Then, as now, there were prestigious young musicians' prizes being offered all over the country—Eastern Seaboard, West Coast, and points between. Like a farmer who had fattened a hog, Passaro was anxious to exhibit his livestock and cop a blue ribbon, and push he did, oh, how he pushed! And I, in turn, missing my brother tremendously, fearful he would be sent overseas at any moment, accepted each new Passaro prod gratefully, and stilled my anxieties by spending hours at the keyboard. "That's nice, Iggie," my mother would say. "Play that part again." I played that part again. And again. And again, and again, and again. And the months passed painlessly.

I can never truly understand motivation. Cause and effect have always been mysteries to me, except at the piano. I still don't know whether the Rachmaninoff concert had anything at all to do with

222

my later decision to move into jazz. Passaro obtained the tickets three months in advance, and had shpieled nothing but Rachmaninoff, Rachmaninoff, Rachmaninoff all through August, September, and October. I don't know whether it rained for twelve days and twelve nights in June of 1901, when my grandfather was digging his subway, but I *do* know what the weather was like on November 7, 1942, because I vas dere, Sharlie. It was cloudy but mild most of the day. In fact, the temperature was hovering in the low fifties when we entered the concert hall which (Passaro kept telling me) would one day resound with cheers for *me*, Ignazio Di Palermo, supreme virtuoso. The hall was packed. I am blind, and I do not like crowds. Passaro guided me through the throng, his hand firm on my elbow. This annoyed me. He should have known better than to be *shoving* me through the goddamn crowd. Our seats were in the balcony, we took the elevator up, there were excited voices everywhere around me, people bumping into me. Passaro's guiding fingers pushed at my elbow, we found our row, "Excuse me, excuse me," Passaro said, pulling me behind him now as we moved past knees and more knees, searching for our seats.

"There are chairs on the stage," Passaro whispered to me. "Wooden chairs. There must be most than a hundred of them. Folding chairs, Iggie. Every seat in the house is filled. Oh, Iggie, can you *feel* this? Can you feel the excitement?"

There was indeed a hum in the air, an almost tangible sense of expectation, tinglingly electric. Passaro read to me from the program. Rachmaninoff was to play his own transcriptions of the Prelude, Gavotte, and Gigue from Bach's Partita in G Major, followed by Beethoven's Opus 31, Number 2, and then a Chopin program, including the C-Minor Polonaise (I remembered the first time I had ever heard it, when Passaro reached across me on that January day in 1935, and I remembered him asking if I thought I could play it in three months' time), and then Rachmaninoff's own *Études Tableau* ("You yourself will compose

223

one day," Passaro whispered to me), and finally a selection of Liszt pieces. The audience fell silent all at once, the absence of sound shocking after the incessant hum that had preceded it. "Here he comes," Passaro whispered into my ear, and then, with the precision of a single pistol shot, the audience broke into applause. "He's crossing to the piano," Passaro whispered. "He's sitting," and the applause stopped as abruptly as it had begun, its brief thunder replaced by a stillness now laden with the agony of anticipation.

Rachmaninoff began playing.

❖

The concert was disappointing for both of us, on different levels and in different ways. All the way back to Tremont Avenue, Passaro could not stop talking about how badly Rachmaninoff had played.

"Ah, yes, it is all there still, of course, he is a master, he is a giant, there is no one today who understands the mechanics of the keyboard the way he does, *nessuno*, and he is sixty-nine years old, remember! Did you hear the way he handled the pianissimi— a whisper, a caress, a touch of balmy air. And the fortissimi! Did you hear, Iggie? He does not pound, he is strong, there is force and power, but he does not pound, do you understand now why I tell you 'Don't pound,' eh?

"But what? Is that Bach he played, or is it Rachmaninoff? How dare he add counterpoint to the Prelude? A giant, yes, but what was Bach, a midget? There is a style to Bach that cannot be tampered with, I don't *care* about pianistic effectiveness, is this a circus sideshow? This is *Bach*, and he does not need contrapuntal embroidery, nor does he need what Rachmaninoff did with the Gavotte, those harmonies and figurations, what were those? Those were unforgivable lapses of taste. Beethoven, all right, I can understand. He has *never* played a Beethoven sonata well in his life. Good phrasing, enormous charm, but no *feeling*, and what is Beethoven if not feeling? The Adagio movement, especially, did you hear it? Why, why, *why* did he play it allegretto? He made it sound like a Field nocturne; what is the *matter* with that man?

"Speed, speed, all was speed, he was running a foot race. Even the Chopin was played too rapidly, although, yes, I hope you noticed the way he played the F-Sharp Nocturne, did you hear those lovely, lovely details, yes, that was good, that was magnificent, that is the Rachmaninoff I took you to hear. But the Polonaise? Too fast. And the F-Minor Ballade? Why did he choose to turn its beautiful theme into a sickening little waltz, and then accentuate it on the off beat when it entered again later, in the bass? The Scherzo? Too fast. Chopin did not intend it to be played so fast, that was not his meaning. The Liszt, of course, well, what can one say about Rachmaninoff's Liszt? His Liszt has always been magic, and today, yes, I suppose, yes, perhaps. Perhaps *there* and in the Chopin nocturne, you heard the real Rachmaninoff. But the rest? Ah, forgive me, Iggie, eh? I wanted more for you. I wanted you to hear more."

As for me, I'd heard more than enough.

In fact, I didn't know what Passaro was talking about. I had been overwhelmed by Rachmaninoff's mastery of the instrument, his dazzling speed, the brilliance of the tones he coaxed, whipped, snapped, teased, demanded from the piano, the soaring giddiness of his invention, the breadth and depth of his interpretations. Stunned and speechless, I'd sat through the entire performance scarcely breathing for fear he would somehow miss the trapeze, falter in the midst of his aerial keyboard acrobatics and tumble to the sawdust below.

When we left Carnegie Hall, I was crushed.

For despite Passaro's wild promises of prizes to be won and accolades to follow, I knew for certain on that dismal November day that I would never in a million years be able to play the way that man up there on the concert stage had played.

❖

On the sixth day of July in the year 1943, four days before General Patton's Seventh Army invaded the island of Sicily, my brother Tony wrote a letter to my grandfather. It was a very brief letter, and it was written entirely in Italian, which Tony had tried to learn at Evander Childs High School.

Caro Nonno,
Non posso rivelare esattamente dove son'io adesso, ma basta il dire che in breve tempo io vedero tutt'i posti che tu hai avuto descrivuto quand'ero piccolo. Non poss' aspettare! Scusi, per piacere, il mio Italiano misero! Ti voglio bene.

Il suo nipote,
Antonio

Roughly translated, my brother had written:

Dear Grandpa,
I can't reveal exactly where I am at the moment, but suffice it to say that in a short while I'll be seeing all the places you described when I was little. I can't wait! Please excuse my miserable Italian. I love you.

Your grandson,
Tony

My grandmother called the day they received the letter. I answered the telephone, and she told me first that they'd heard from Tony, and then she read the letter to me in Italian, and then translated it. She told me his Italian wasn't really too bad, and she wondered why he had apologized for it. Then she asked me how the piano was coming along, and finally told me to put my mother on. That was on July 12, six days after my brother had mailed the letter. We later figured it had been posted from North Africa, where Patton's invasion force was massed for the strike at what Winston Churchill called the "soft underbelly" of Europe.

Eight days later, on the twentieth, my brother was killed in the vicinity of Porto Empedocle, on the western coast of Sicily. The War Department telegram arrived on the twenty-first, and a letter from Tony's lieutenant, a man named Arthur G. Rowles, arrived two weeks later. There wasn't much Rowles could say. He wrote that my brother had fought bravely and well. He reported that he had been killed by an Italian soldier who, in the midst of what appeared to be a headlong, disorganized retreat, had suddenly whirled, raised his rifle, and fired blindly and erratically at the advancing squad. Only one of his bullets struck home, the one that killed Tony—"instantly and mercifully, he did not suffer," the lieutenant wrote. Why the Italian had not surrendered, as his comrades were doing everywhere around him, was a mystery to the lieutenant. He wrote, too, that a heavy artillery attack, German or American, began almost the moment my brother fell to the ground. The man who had slain him threw his rifle down and began running up the road to Porto Empedocle as it erupted in blossoms of earth and boulders and hot flying shrapnel. He was still running, still on his feet, apparently unscathed, as he disappeared into the dust.

We did not tell my grandfather that an Italian had killed Tony.

❖

I went into his room.

It was raining. The rain lashed the room's single window, which opened on a potholed driveway that ran steeply from the street to the small porch outside the kitchen. We usually came in through the kitchen door, Tony and I.

I sat on his bed.

I listened to the rain in the gutters and the drainpipes and against the windowpanes. There was undirected anger in my grief. I was angry at General Patton, who had sent my brother into combat. I was angry at my grandfather, who had refused to let Tony fly, and angry at my mother, who had steadfastly upheld his greaseball decision. And I was angry at Tony, for letting himself get killed. What the hell was the matter with him, getting killed like that? And I began to cry again.

I played his records because I was angry and grief-stricken, I played them in defiance of his privacy and his secrecy, played them in a futile attempt to find him again, to share with him something he had loved, to make his records and therefore himself an ineradicable part of *me*. I found them on the shelves above the record player my parents had given him for his thirteenth birthday. I selected one at random, put it on the turntable, and turned the volume control up full. When my mother heard the music blaring, she came into the room.

"Iggie?" she said. Her voice was tremulous. She had not stopped crying since the telegram arrived. "What are you doing, baby?" she asked, and sat beside me, and gently passed her hand over my forehead, brushing back my hair.

"Listening," I said.

❖

I listened all that night. There were 347 records in his collection. He had taken very good care of them, but he had also played them often and they were badly worn. The sound sputtered and crackled from the speaker, the needle caught in tired grooves and endlessly repeated notes or full measures, skipped over hairline cracks, skimmed the shellacked surfaces of the 78s. I had heard some of the tunes before, on the radio. But the others, the ones I had *not* heard . . .

You can believe this or not. I have known jazz musicians for the better part of my life, I have played with them and rapped with them, and suffered with them, and I can tell you that my experience was not unique. Anyway, I don't care what you think;

this is the way it happened. I could not read the labels on the records, and to me the ten-inch disks all felt the same. I recognized some of the tunes, but I did not know who was playing them. I kept pulling the records from the shelves and removing them from their protective sleeves and putting them on the turntable haphazardly, mixing swing with ragtime with boogie-woogie with Dixieland with barrelhouse with stride with blues, big bands and small ensembles, vocalists and soloists, a hopeless mélange of chronology and style.

I called my mother into the room. It was three o'clock in the morning. She had been lying awake, I realized, because she came to me instantly.

"Who's this?" I asked, and handed her the record I had just heard.

"Just a minute," she said. "Let me put on a light."

I heard the click of the floor lamp alongside Tony's bed.

"Let me see," my mother said, and took the record from my hand. "Art Tatum," she said. She pronounced his name "Tatt-um."

"Are there any more of his?" I asked.

"What?"

"On the shelf."

"Iggie, it's late. Can't you . . . ?"

"Mom, *please*. Are there any more records by him?"

"Just a minute," she said. I heard her rummaging around. "Iggie, I need my glasses," she said.

I waited. When she came back, she said, "Tony loved these records."

"Yes," I said.

"Do you like them, Iggie?"

"Yes," I said.

"Tch," she said, and in that single meeting of tongue with gum ridge, she came to terms with my brother's death. The click that resonated into the silence of Tony's room was desolate and forlorn; it echoed a Neapolitan acceptance of the inevitability of fate.

229

As she looked through the records on his shelves, she spoke to me and to herself in disconnected phrases and sentences separated by long silences and the crackle of the stiff paper sleeves on my brother's records. "Uncle Dominick used to take him to Yankee Stadium," or "Seven pounds, six ounces; a very big baby," or "Always good to you," or "Do you remember when he sat on Pino's cigar?" or "Loved that girl so much," or "Lou Gehrig, it was," or, as she searched, "Tattum, Tattum," and finally, "He died for America, Igg."

She handed me the records she had found.

"Can you listen to them in the morning?" she asked. "Your father has to go to work. You're keeping him up, Iggie."

"I'll play them very low," I said.

"Did you love him, Igg?"

"I loved him," I said.

"He's dead."

"Yes, Mama."

"He's dead," she said, and went out of the room.

I listened to Tatum.

And first I thought That's *it*. That's how I want to play.

And then I thought *I* can do that. *I* can play that.

I listened again. I played the records again and again. And I became more and more convinced that I could do it, I could actually *do* it. I sat trembling with discovery, each brimming chord, each gliding arpeggio absorbed by my very skin, penetrating, vibrating within me as though some secret unborn self were augmenting the sound, the music threatening to explode from my dead eyes and my shaking hands, lift off the top of my skull, flow ceilingward in a dizzying fireworks display of sharps and flats and triplets and thirty-second notes. I must have made my decision at once, long before I'd heard all the Tatum records, long before I'd run them through the machine a second, third, and fourth time; I probably had made the decision even before I'd called my mother into the room to identify this man who was playing piano as I'd never heard it played before. It was that sudden, it was that simple, I make no apologies. It happened that way. I heard jazz for the first time in my life, played by a giant, on *my* instrument, and I knew at once that this was the way the piano was meant to be played, and this was the way I was going to play it from that moment on.

Stultifyingly ignorant—I could read in Braille only the language of classical music, and had no concept of this new language—blissfully naïve as to its complexity, desperately hungry to get to the piano and *try* it, try to *play* it, waiting for my father's alarm to go off at a quarter to five, soaringly optimistic, knowing that once I got my hands on the keyboard, the music would leap magically from my fingers, I lay on my brother's bed and stared sightlessly at the ceiling and contemplated a journey to a land more alien than any I might have imagined in my most fantastic dreams.

As my grandfather had done in 1900, I decided firmly and irrevocably to chance the voyage.

It remained only to discuss the matter with Federico Passaro.

❖

He listened in silence to the records I had brought with me.

He listened while Tatum played "Rosetta" and "St. Louis Blues" and "Moonglow" and part of "Begin the Beguine," and then he abruptly lifted the needle from the player.

"Yes?" he said. "You wanted me to listen. I listened."

I took a deep breath. "I want to play like that," I said.

"Like what?"

"Like what you just heard."

"What *is* that?" he said.

"Jazz."

"Ah, yes. Jazz."

"It's what I want to play."

"What do you mean?" he said. "For fun? For amusement?"

"Mr. Passaro . . ."

"Well, I can see no real harm in it," he said, surprising me; I had expected a tantrum similar to the one I'd provoked with my request for "You Turned the Tables on Me." But Passaro actually chuckled, and then said, "In fact, the man has good technique. Has he had classical training?"

"I don't know anything about him."

"What is he playing in the bass clef? Tenths? They sound like tenths to me. And not *open* tenths, either. You may find the stretch difficult. Well, try it, I don't think it can hurt you."

"I've already tried it," I said.

"Ah? And can you reach those chords?"

"I have to stretch for them, you're right."

"Well, that won't hurt you. His arpeggios are very clean, too; he *must* have had classical training. I'm not familiar with all the chords he played in the twelve-bar piece. What were those chords?"

"I don't know."

"They seem to utilize many notes outside the mode. Well, no matter. If you want to fool around with this for your own amusement, I have no . . ."

"*All* the time, Mr. Passaro."

"Eh?"

"I want to play it *all* the time."

"What do you mean, *all* the time?"

"That's what I want to play."

The room went silent.

"Let me understand you," Passaro said.

"I want you to teach me to play the way he plays," I said. "Art Tattum. That's his name. That's how I want to play."

"Iggie, this is a bad joke," Passaro said, and chuckled again. "I'm a very patient man, you know that by now, we've been together for more than seven years, very patient. But this is a bad joke. Are you finished with it? If so, I'd like to . . ."

232

"Mr. Passaro, can you teach me to play what he's playing?"

"No," Passaro said, his voice suddenly sharp. "Of *course* not! What are you saying?"

"I don't want to play this way anymore."

"What way?"

"This way," I said, and my hands moved out to the keyboard, and I ran through the first four bars of a Chopin scherzo, and then abruptly pulled back my hands and quietly said, "That way, Mr. Passaro."

"*That* way," he said, "is the only way I teach."

"Well," I said.

His voice softened again. "What is it?" he asked gently, and sat beside me on the piano bench. "Ah, Iggie, I've been stupid. Forgive me. Your recent loss, your brother, I know the grief you must . . . forgive me, please. Go home. Please. I'll see you next Saturday, do the exercises I gave you, get your hands back in shape, have you practiced much, I'm sure you haven't. Come back next week. Forgive me for being inconsiderate. I get so involved sometimes, I . . . forgive me."

"Mr. Passaro," I said, "I don't want to come back next week unless you can teach me to play like Tattum."

I felt Passaro stiffen beside me. He was silent for several moments, and then he rose, and moved away from the bench and the piano, and began pacing the floor.

"No," he said. "I won't allow this to happen. No. No, Iggie, I'm sorry. No. You can't do this. I will not permit it. It's been too long. No. I've given you . . . I've invested . . . I've . . . no. Enough! You'll go home, you'll do your exercises, and next week we'll pick up again on the Moussorgsky. There's a lot to be done. They are already holding auditions for many of the prizes. If we . . ."

"Mr. Passaro, I don't . . ."

"Stop it!" he shouted. "Do you want to kill me? Stop it, *please*, stop saying this . . . these . . . please, Iggie."

233

"I don't care about prizes, Mr. Passaro. I don't want any prizes. I want to play like Tattum."

"Tattum, Tattum, *quello sfaccime, che c'importa* Tattum? He's a piano player; you're an *artist!* I've made you an *artist!* You came to me with talent, and I took it, and shaped it, and put in your hands what's in my *own* hands. You're destroying me. Do you want to destroy me, Iggie?"

"No, Mr. Passaro, but . . ."

"I thought you loved music. I thought my own love for music . . ."

"I *do* love music!"

"Then stop talking about trash!"

"I'm sorry, Mr. Passaro."

He fell silent. When he spoke again, he had controlled his anger, and his voice was intimately low.

"Iggie," he said, "how many pupils do you think . . . how many do I have like you? How many do you think?"

"Mr. Passaro . . ."

"One. In twenty years, *one.* I have no others like you. I've *never* had another like you, I may never have another as long as I live. I've never lied to you, Iggie. Never. I said you'd win prizes, and you will. I said you'd play in Carnegie Hall . . ."

"I don't want to play in Carnegie Hall."

And then he exploded.

He called me an ingrate, he called me a fool, he called me an immature child, he told me I was *truly* blind if I was ready to throw away a brilliant career as a concert pianist. He told me he was not mistaken about my future, he would not have lavished such attention on me if for a moment, for a *single* moment, he had thought he was mistaken. And for *what?* Were all those hours of patient instruction to be wasted? Did I think it was a simple matter to teach a blind person? He had given me more time and more energy than he'd given all his other pupils together, and now *this.* He reviled my decision, he spit upon my decision, he told

234

me I would come to regret it, he promised I would be back on my knees begging him to teach me again, and he told me by then it would be too late, my repertoire would be gone, I would have squandered precious hours on the playing of trash, my opportunity will have vanished, my promise will have corroded, my future will have been flushed down the toilet like shit.

"So go!" he shouted. "Leave me! And good luck to you!"

It was a curse.

❖

In the back room of my grandfather's tailor shop, I told him of my decision. He listened carefully. He was sixty-three years old, and he had been in this country for forty-two years, and I think he still found many of its ways baffling and incomprehensible.

He was pensively silent for a long time.

Perhaps he was thinking if only he had sent Luke to college, perhaps he was thinking if only he had allowed Tony to join the Air Corps, perhaps he was thinking that here in this America you could not expect the young to follow in the footsteps of their elders, you had to let them go, you had to let them run, you had to set them free.

In his broken English, he said, "Go play you jazza. And *buona fortuna*, Ignazio."

It was a blessing.

3

Oscar Peterson once said: "First you learn to play piano, then you learn to play jazz"—or words to that effect. I once heard him play eighteen straight choruses of "Sweet Georgia Brown," and while he was on the sixth chorus, I thought He'll never top that one, but he topped it in the seventh, and then again in the tenth, and he kept topping himself as he went along, utilizing a personal retrieval system to yank idiomatic ideas out of his mind and push them into his hands, shaping those ideas into an entirely fresh improvisational line, each chorus having no intrinsic relationship to the one preceding it or the one following it, except as part of an original, imaginative, and (to me) inspirational flow. But he had paid his dues, he had the technical knowledge stored in the computer bank of his memory, all of it was under his hands; those years of learning Bach and Chopin from one of the best classical teachers in Canada finally paid off when he came down to New York and promptly knocked off everybody's hat.

In 1943, I knew how to play piano, but I didn't know how to play jazz, and if there was anyone teaching it, I couldn't find him. It's a different tune today, when jazz has been elevated to the stature of an art form. (I *still* think it's only folk music, and I've been playing it for thirty-one years now, but I suppose mine is a minority opinion.) Today you can find jazz departments at Indiana U. and the New England Conservatory and several other revered institutions across the length and breadth of this great creative nation. And even those schools without departments per se are offering courses in jazz. It wasn't that way in 1943. In 1943, there was nobody. I had only my brother's records.

His collection of piano stylists was fairly comprehensive, I now realize, including such early ragtime players as Scott Joplin and James P. Johnson, and some good representative barrelhouse piano playing by Jelly Roll Morton and Frank Melrose, and stuff by old jazzmen whose names alone seemed to promise strange and exotic keyboard happenings—Pine Top, and Cripple Clarence, and Speckled Red; Cow Cow, Papa Jimmy Yancey, Willie the Lion—and then moving up through men like Meade Lux Lewis, Albert Ammons, and Biff Anderson. Most of the records, though, were by Fats Waller, Earl Hines, Teddy Wilson, and Art Tatum. I liked these best, possibly because there were more of them than any of the others. I've since learned that there was a direct line of succession from Waller to Tatum and from Hines to Wilson, but I didn't know it then. I only knew that I liked the way these men played jazz.

I once sat in with Dizzy Gillespie, and he jokingly (I think) said, "I sure wish you cats would give us back our rhythm," and I jokingly (I think) replied, "Okay by me, Diz. Just give *us* back our harmony." Well, harmony and rhythm were jogging along there simultaneously in the left hand of every piano player I listened to, and it was the left hand that delineated the various styles I learned to identify. But even though I was no stranger to counterpoint (who *could* be after all those years of Bach?), and even though I had no difficulty recognizing that the chords in any jazz chorus were held for either two beats or four beats, and the rhythm was a steady four/four, and the melody was built on eighth notes, I nonetheless had difficulty understanding how all

240

of these units were put together to get that distinctive . . . I'm sorry, but "swing" is the only word that describes it. Jazz is by definition a duple musical system. Everything in it is based on equivalents and multiples of two; that's part of its symmetry. But those three levels of duo-divisible rhythm moving in counterpoint were pressed into a *larger* rhythmic context that seemed like . . .

Well, magic.

I'm blind. To me, there's no such thing as sleight of hand. I figured it was simply a matter of sitting down and learning a new system. There was no one to teach me, and so I had to teach myself. If Tatum had learned it, *I* could learn it. I now know that Tatum was perhaps the greatest keyboard virtuoso since Franz Liszt. But ignorance is bliss, and I figured if I had once mastered the "Hungarian Rhapsody," I could now master this thing called jazz.

❖

Back in 1937, Susan Koenig had gently patted my hand and told me my "Moonlight" Sonata was the most beautiful thing she'd heard in her life. In December of 1943, we were both seventeen years old, and I was itching to get into her pants (or *anybody's*, for that matter). I had no real idea what she looked like, but I had formed some tactile, olfactory, and auditory impressions—I had touched her a little, smelled her a lot, and hardly listened to her at all.

Every Friday afternoon, Santa Lucia's held a social for its juniors and seniors, and I had been dogging Susan's tracks for the better part of a year now, seeking her out in the school gymnasium while the record player oozed Harry James's "I Had the Craziest Dream," Dinah Shore's "You'd Be So Nice to Come Home To," or Freddy Martin's "I Look at Heaven," a popularization of the Grieg Concerto upon which I'd worked so long and hard. I was working equally long and hard on Susan, who—unless my senses

241

were sending absolutely haywire messages to my brain—looked something like this:

1. She was approximately five feet four inches tall. I reckoned this by deducting from my own height the distance between the top of my head and the tip of my nose, which, according to my Braille ruler, was six inches. The top of Susan's head came to just under my nose. Subtracting six inches from my own height, which was five feet ten in 1943, I got a girl who measured five-four.

2. Her eyes were brown. She told me this. She wore shades all the time. So did I.

3. She wore her hair very long, almost to the middle of her back. It would brush the top of my hand as we danced. The style was unusual for 1943, when girls were wearing shoulder-length pageboys, with or without high pompadours. But Susan later told me it was simpler and neater for a blind girl to wear it long and straight.

4. Her brassiere size was 36B. I pressed against her chest a lot and based my estimate on empirical knowledge, having handled many such garments in my Aunt Bianca's corset shop, and having been intimately involved with Michelle's bras during the thirteen-month period of her extraordinary growth. Michelle's bra size, when she moved away in 1941, was a 34C.

5. The top of Susan's head smelled of Ivory soap. Her ear lobes smelled of Worth's *Je Reviens*. She later identified this brand name for me while my nose was nestled between her naked breasts, where she also dabbed a bit of that intoxicating scent.

6. Her voice, angelic back there in 1937 when she'd praised me for my performance, had lowered in pitch to a G above middle C, somewhat husky, always breathless, even when she wasn't whispering in my ear as we endlessly circled that gymnasium floor and tried to avoid collisions.

Did you know that blind people can detect the presence of an object by the echoes or warmth it gives off, and even by changes it causes in the air pressure, which are felt on the face? A little-

242

known fact, but scientifically authenticated. I once detected the presence of a short, fat lady standing on the corner of White Plains Avenue and 217th Street, and asked her if the approaching trolley went to Fordham Road. When she did not reply, I asked the question again and discovered I was talking to a mailbox. The mailbox did not answer me. But then again, neither did it answer the Martians when they insisted it take them to its leader. Which reminds me of what Django Reinhardt, the gypsy jazz guitarist, said when he first came to America in 1946: "Take me to Dizzy."

Susan Koenig made me dizzy.

We did not talk very much as we danced our way around the world, preferring to sniff each other and rub against each other, and derive whatever small erotic pleasures we could while the eagle-eyed nuns watched our every fumbling move. But in our brief, breathless conversations over the course of countless Fridays spent in that room lingeringly reeking of dirty socks and jockey shorts, I learned that Susan's father had been born in Munich, and that he'd gone back there in the fall of 1934 because he wanted to be in on the big resurrection Mr. Hitler was promising. Mrs. Koenig, an Irish-American lady born and raised in Brooklyn, chose not to accompany her brown-shirted mate on his return to the fatherland, and so the two were separated when Susan was eight and her older brother was ten. Her parents were legally divorced in 1938, by which time Herr Koenig was probably smashing the plate-glass windows of Jewish merchants— "Good *riddance* to him!" Susan said. She had no idea where he was now, and no desire to find out. Her fear, before her brother was drafted, was that he might be sent to Europe, where he would meet his own father on a battlefield and put a bullet between his eyes. Not that she cared about her father. But suppose the reverse happened? The thought had been too dreadful to contemplate, and she'd been enormously relieved when her brother was sent to the Pacific, even though she was terribly afraid of all the awful things the Japs did, like burying prisoners up to their necks in ant hills, and then covering their faces with honey and letting the ants eat them to death—*urggh*, it was disgusting. She could not wait for her brother to get home from the war. They had had such good times together.

The thing that interested me most about Susan's autobiographical meanderings as we meandered the length of the gymnasium and back again in time to Ellington's "Don't Get Around Much Anymore" (which I'd heard on one of my brother's Duke records as "Never No Lament," before lyrics were added to it) was the incidental information it provided on her mother's occupation and hours of employment. Her mother had never remarried, and she now worked as a saleslady at Macy's downtown. Normally, she worked only five days a week, Monday to Friday, from 9:30 A.M. to 5:30 P.M., except on Thursdays, when the store was open till 9:00 P.M. But Thanksgiving had come and gone, and the annual Christmas rush was on, despite the fact that a war was raging in Europe and the Pacific, and her mother had been asked to work a full day on Saturdays as well, until the holidays were over. Counting off a steady four/four beat, shuffling around the gym floor, sniffing in Susan's *Je Reviens* and pressing against her as discreetly as I knew how, I made a lightning calculation: on Saturdays her father was in Germany, her mother was in Macy's, and her brother was on a censored atoll. This meant that Susan would be alone in the Koenig apartment any Saturday I decided to drop by to discuss jazz and the weather while inadvertently and accidentally taking off her pants. This was a discovery of no small importance to a seventeen-year-old blind boy. For whereas normally sighted youngsters of my age were being granted licenses to drive in 1943, and thereby had access to mobile bedrooms, we underprivileged blind adolescents, possessed of the same over-riding sex drives, could find no appropriate spaces for the un-leashing of those furious urges, it being December and quite cold

244

in Bronx Park, where if you took down a girl's drawers, she might suffer frostbite rather than defloration.

Two weeks after the Friday dance at which I'd learned that Susan was alone in the apartment virtually all day every Saturday, I found my way to White Plains Avenue and asked a mailbox whether the approaching trolley went all the way to Mount Vernon or stopped at the Bronx border, as many of them did; Susan lived just a block over the city line. The mailbox turned out to be a short, fat lady, who told me it did indeed go all the way. Determined to do the same, I hopped onto the trolley and rode it uptown, and then walked down the short street to Susan's block, and found Susan's address with a little help from a kindly neighborhood yenteh who led me into the lobby of the building, and summoned the elevator for me, and told me it was the fourth floor, and wanted to know if she should come up with me and show me the exact door; little did *she* know what was on the mind of the Mad Blind Rapist, Ignazio Silvio Di Palermo!

"Who is it?" Susan asked when I knocked on the door.

"Me," I said.

"Iggie?" she asked, recognizing my voice at once.

It was exactly twelve noon.

I lost my virginity an hour later.

❖

I started by telling Susan I just happened to be in the neighborhood and thought I'd drop in. This was an outrageous lie that might have been swallowed had Susan herself not been blind. Being blind, she knew that none of us just *happened* to be *anyplace*. We took ourselves where we wanted to go, and normally we prepared ourselves in advance with detailed mental maps of the exact transportation systems we would use, and the exact number of streets we would traverse after we got off a trolley,

245

train, or bus, and the exact number of doorways to the dentist's or the fishmonger's. (Actually, we could *smell* the fish store and didn't have to count doorways.)

But she let the lie pass, which I thought was an encouraging sign, and she told me she was delighted I'd dropped in, or stopped by, or whatever it was she said, because she found it terribly lonely sitting here all alone in the apartment from eight in the morning when her mother left to sometimes nine or ten at night when her mother got home. It was so cold this month that she hardly went outdoors anymore, and just sitting here listening to the radio or reading Braille got terribly boring, though now that her brother was gone and there was no one to help her with the selection of her clothes, she had begun occupying herself by marking them according to color and style, using little French knots on the red dresses and sweaters, or cross stitches on the blue ones, or a single bead sewn into a green skirt, where it wouldn't show when she was wearing it, and hanging color-coordinated belts with their proper skirts, and making little Braille labels for drawers containing different shades of nylon stockings or different-colored panties and brassieres. I cleared my throat at the very mention of these unmentionables, and said that I myself paid little attention to my appearance, sometimes going to school wearing different-colored socks, or a green tie with a blue suit, or black shoes with tan trousers. My mother kept telling me I looked like Coxey's army, whatever that was. Susan giggled. She didn't know what Coxey's army was, either, but it sounded very funny. She told me it was different for a girl, a girl had to look attractive even if she *was* blind, and I told her I thought she looked very attractive, and she said Why, thank you Iggie.

Blind people, if you haven't realized it by now, accept the words "see" and "look" without any feelings of self-consciousness or embarrassment except when some well-meaning dope says, "Just *look* at that rain, will you?" and then immediately and fumblingly

246

adds, "Oh, for*give* me, please, I should have realized you can't . . . I mean, I *know* I shouldn't have . . . that is, I meant . . ." as if we hadn't heard the rain, and smelled the sudden scent of dust riddled on a summer street, as if we hadn't *seen* the goddamn rain. Susan said if I was truly serious about becoming a jazz piano player (and I assured her I was), well, then, wouldn't that mean I'd have to perform before audiences? Sighted audiences? So maybe I *should* begin paying a little attention to the way I dressed, because whereas a suit with an egg stain on it didn't mean very much to *us*, it did offend people who could see, and evoked the sort of pity none of us encouraged and all of us resented.

I told her maybe she was right (actually I did nothing at all about the way I dressed until Rebecca made it a real issue years later), and since Susan had provided the perfect opportunity for further conversation, having mentioned jazz, I told her about all the exciting discoveries I'd been making, all of which I'm sure thrilled her to the marrow. I had figured out all by myself, for example, that a great many of the songs I was listening to and trying to learn had the identical sequence of chords in the first two bars and that the progression, in the key of C at least, was C six, A minor, D minor, and G seven. Susan would probably recognize these as the underlying chords of "We Want Cantor"—if she tried it she'd see what I meant. Susan tried "We Want Cantor" in her husky, breathless voice, and admitted she'd never realized such an amazing thing about that particular tune. Well, it's not only *that* tune, I said. Songs like "I Got Rhythm" and "These Foolish Things" (Oh, I *love* that song, Susan said), yes, I said, and "Ain't Misbehavin'" and dozens of other songs I'd been learning, *all* started with those same chords in the first two bars.

That's really interesting, Susan said, would you like to see how I've arranged my things?

She led me into her bedroom, and told me that because all her bobbysocks were white, she had them all in this drawer here, but

247

when it came to stockings, they were difficult to tell apart because there were her *best* ones, for example, which she wore to the socials on Friday, and her everyday ones for less special occasions like when somebody was coming to the house to visit, and also they came in so many different shades (though she tried to buy neutral shades that went with any color), and she usually identified the pairs by tying them together after she'd rinsed them out and let them dry, and immediately putting them into drawers marked with Braille labels—here, Iggie, these are my good stockings, feel them, they're much better than the ones in the other drawer.

When it came to garter belts, she had only two of them, a white one and a black one, and she identified the white one with a tiny button sewn here near the catch, can you feel it, Iggie? The brassieres were another problem, because if she wore a dark brassiere under a white blouse, it showed through the fabric, and if she wore a white brassiere with a black dress, say, and one of the straps showed, it looked positively horrible. She'd never had any trouble with her clothes when her brother was home because he'd helped her choose colors and styles and was kind enough and honest enough to tell her when something looked dowdy or shabby. Well, as a matter of fact, he'd begun helping her dress when she was eight years old and her father left the family and her mother had to take a job and left for work early each morning. Here's one of my drawers for panties, she said. These are my favorite ones, they're a pale blue with lace around the leg holes, can you feel the lace, Iggie? They're rayon, I don't usually wear rayon panties for every day, I've got a drawer full of cotton panties, those are here, Iggie. Like, for example, when I'm just wearing an old skirt and a blouse, like today, I'll just wear a half-slip and cotton panties under it, that's what I'm wearing today. My brother used to kid me a lot about wearing cotton panties, he said only snotnosed little kids wore cotton panties, if I was as grownup as I *thought* I was, I'd be wearing rayon, he always used to kid me that way. Well, I'm sure you're not interested in my underthings.

248

We sat on the edge of her bed, and I told Susan I'd known her for, gosh, how many years was it now?

Six, Susan said.

Yeah, six years, I said, *wow*, that's a long time to know somebody. And whereas I had *some* idea of what she looked like because, you know, we'd talked a lot and all, and naturally I knew a lot of things about her . . . I'd never in all that time explored her face with my hands, which was possibly the only way I'd ever *really* get to know what she really looked like, ever get to form a mental image to augment the other impressions I'd . . .

You can touch my face if you like, she said, and very softly added, Iggie.

I touched her face. Gently, lingeringly, with both hands, I touched the wide brow below the delicate hairline, and then gingerly explored the arched eyebrows, and then lifted the dark glasses onto her forehead, away from her sightless eyes, and touched the lids and the lashes, and while the glasses were still raised I touched the bridge of her nose and felt along it to the delicately curved tip, a fine film of perspiration on it, and then moved my hands outward toward her cheekbones, I have freckles, she said, and I answered You never mentioned that, and she murmured Yes. And then I gently lowered the glasses over her eyes again, and ran my hands lightly over her cheeks and the line of her jaw and her chin, and explored her mouth, touched the bow of her upper lip where it curved away from her teeth, and the fleshy lower lip, and then the moist inner membrane as she parted her lips and I said You're beautiful, Susan.

Sitting on her bed, my hands in my lap again, we began talking about the nuns at school, the ones we particularly loved or despised, and about kids we'd known for God knew how long, and how we would miss them after we graduated next June, though I said it wasn't necessary to lose track of people you really liked or admired, it would be a shame, for example, if she and *I* lost contact after we'd known each other such a long time. Susan

249

quickly said Oh, *no*, we mustn't let *that* happen, and I agreed No, we certainly mustn't, not now that we were really getting to know each other even better. Susan said there were some kids, though, she wouldn't *mind* seeing the last of. Kids like Donald Hagstrom, who was always using being blind as an excuse to go feeling around, did I know what she meant? No, I said, and Susan said You know, he puts his hands out in front of him and goes feeling around, you know, hoping he'll, you know, bump up against someone, you know, like in the coat closet or someplace, just feeling *around*, do you understand what I mean, Iggie?

Oh, I said.

He's done that to me a few times, Susan said. I slapped his face for him one time. I *know* he can tell I'm there, and it's not only me, it's lots of the other girls, too, he knows we're there, he just makes believe he's groping around, it's really humiliating and embarrassing. Girls don't like to be *grabbed* that way, Iggie. I mean, if they're going to be touched at all, especially there where it's so personal and private, they want to be touched gently. The way you touched my face. That way.

This way? I asked, and I reached out and touched the soft skin of her neck, and she said Yes, that way, but of course *he* touches lower. Donald, I mean. When he touches. And not as gentle as that. A little lower, though.

Here? I said.

Yes, she said, but you'd better stop, Iggie, because we're all alone here and my mother won't be home till very late tonight, so I don't think you should be doing that, do you?

I guess not, I said.

Though it feels very nice, she said, you have nice hands.

Thank you, I said.

You're welcome, she said, but please stop, okay? My brother has very gentle hands, too, did I tell you he used to dress me when I was very small? Well, actually, he used to help me dress right until the time he left for the Army. He'd sit here right on the edge of the bed, right where we're sitting, and I'd be putting on a pair of stockings and fumbling with the damn garters, Iggie, I really don't think you should be doing that, do you? and he'd say he hoped I wasn't planning on wearing *those* stockings with the red dress or the green one or whatever it was, he was really very helpful, I miss him a lot.

The buttons are different, you know, she said. On a girl's blouse. They're the reverse. I mean, from a boy's. Lots of boys have trouble unbuttoning a girl's blouse because the buttons are turned around. I remember once, will you promise not to tell this to anyone, I was fifteen, I guess, and I'd gone to a party at a girl's house up the street, she can see and everything, she's not blind, and they had a keg of beer there, I think it was a party for some boy who was going in the Army, I'm not sure, it was right after Pearl Harbor. And I drank a lot of beer, and I got very, well, not drunk, but sort of tipsy, you know, and when I came home my brother was lying here on my bed, reading, my mother was out someplace, he took one look at me and said, Oh-oh. I couldn't even unbutton my own *blouse*, would you believe it, he had to unbutton it for me. And even though he'd had lots of practice dressing me when I was small, he still had trouble getting my blouse off that night, I guess because I was weaving all over the room, oh, God, it was so silly. I finally passed out cold and didn't remember a thing the next morning, my clothes were on the chair there, Iggie, you're getting me very hot.

I am now going to attempt something that might frighten even the likes of Oscar Peterson. I am going to demonstrate what it is like to play a jazz solo, and I am going to do so in terms of what happened with Susan Koenig in her bedroom that day after we got through the basics of taking off her blouse and her bra and her skirt and her half-slip and finally her cotton panties (but not her dark glasses), and after she unbuttoned my fly and helped me off with my undershorts and fell upon me with blind expertise and unbridled passion. I am going to prove to you not only what a great piano player I am, but also what a unique and marvelous writer I *could* be (if only I had the time), and I am going to do so by demonstrating what jazz would *look* like if you were reading it in the English language instead of hearing it in a smoky night-club. An impossible feat, you say? Stick around, you ain't seen nothing yet.

To keep this simple (look, he's already copping out!), I'm going to use a twelve-bar blues chart with only twenty-one chords in it, as opposed to a more complex thirty-two-bar chart with as many as sixty-four chords in it. If I were playing a *real* blues chorus, the chords I'd use most frequently in the key of A flat, let's say, would be A-flat seven, D-flat seven, and E-flat seven. But we're not concerning ourselves with chords in what follows; we're substituting *words* for chords.

This, then, would be the chord chart for "Jazzing in A Flat," as it is known in England (a pun, Mom), or, as it is known to American blues buffs, simply "Up in Susan's Womb." (Another one; sorry, Mom.)

BAR 1: SUSAN
BAR 2: ME
BAR 3: SUSAN
BAR 4: BED
BAR 5: ME
BAR 6: ME
BAR 7: DECEMBER and AFTERNOON
BAR 8: HOT and COLD
BAR 9: AFTERNOON and EVENING
BAR 10: AFTERNOON and EVENING
BAR 11: SUSAN and BEDDED and I and MYSELF
BAR 12: LIMP and DUSK and BED

252

There are four beats in each bar, but the last two bars combined have only seven beats in them and are called, traditionally and unimaginatively, "a seven-beater," the last beat understood but not played. If you count all the capitalized words in all the bars above, you'll discover there are exactly twenty-one of them, just as promised. Their selection was determined by the actual incidence of a conventional set of chords in a typical blues chorus, with which I've taken no liberties. For example, the word "bed" in the chart represents an A-flat dominant chord, whereas the word "bedded" represents an A-flat dominant inversion—"bed," therefore, becomes "bedded," a different but similar chord.

The first chorus of the tune will consist of these chords being played in the left hand and the composer's melody being played in the right hand almost exactly as he wrote it. I'll add a swing to it that did not exist in the original sheet music, but for the most part I'll play it almost straight, in order to identify it (solely as a courtesy) for my audience. The choruses following the head chorus will be improvised, invented on the spot, and will bear no resemblance to the original tune, unless I choose to refer back to it occasionally, again solely as a courtesy. I am interested only in the chord chart. And the chart consists of those twenty-one words listed above. The rest is all melody—*my* melody, not the composer's. In fact, the melodies I improvise in each succeeding chorus may have nothing whatever to do with sex per se, except as sex defines the overall "mood" of the tune. In short, the blowing line I invent to go with the chord progression doesn't *need* to make an emotional or philosophic commitment to the composer's melody. I can use all sorts of musical punctuation in my running line—eighth notes, eighth-note triplets, thirty-second notes, sixty-fourth notes, runs—the way I would use commas, semicolons, periods, or exclamation points. I can repeat sequential figures, augmenting or diminishing licks as I see fit, or I can utilize silences if I choose. (A jazzman listening to J. J. Johnson once said, "I

253

sure like those notes he's playing," and another cat replied, "I like the ones he *isn't* playing.") I can do whatever I want with whatever melody I invent. I am entirely free to create.

But I cannot deviate from the chart. Once the chart is set in motion, it is inviolable, it is inexorable, it is inevitable. I am locked into it tonally and rhythmically, I cannot change SUSAN to ALICE, nor can I hold that chord for longer than the four beats prescribed in Bar 1, though I can of course repeat it four times in that measure, if I like. At the end of those four beats, ME must come in for another four beats; the chart so dictates. When it comes time for me to play AFTERNOON for two beats in Bar 7, I'd better not be lingering on DECEMBER. I can use substitute chords, or passing chords, or what are known as appoggiatura chords—SHOT to HOT or BLIMP to LIMP—but only to get me *where* I have to be when I have to be there. Jazz is a moving, volatile, energetic force that is constantly *going* someplace. Each chord exists only because it is in motion *toward* the next chord and *from* the chord preceding it. It's pure Marxist music, in a sense, utilizing the dialectic process throughout. I can take the chord EVENING and break it into an arpeggio if I choose, transforming it into a linear EVE, EN, ING, or I can play it diatonically E,V,E,N,I,N,G, as a mode, or I can play it as a shell, EVNG, but I *have* to play it; it is part of the chart, and the chart is the track upon which the express train of my improvisation runs.

So—in the first twelve bars, I'll play "Jazzing in A Flat" as the composer wrote it, mingling and mixing right-hand melody with left-hand harmony because we're doing prose here and not musical notation, and anyway, that's exactly as you'd hear it. In the next twelve bars, I'll improvise a jazz solo with a blowing line unrelated to the original melody except where brief reference may be made to it, the entire improvisation based on those twenty-one chords in the relentless chord chart. Then, utilizing whatever bag of tricks I possess, I'll take us into the final twelve bars, where I'll play the head again almost as straight as I did at the top, and then go home

254

("head and out," as it's called). All of this will be enormously abbreviated, you understand. A jazz solo, especially on a blues chart, can go on and on all night. *This* solo will consist of only three choruses.

Ready?

Ah-*one*twothreefour . . .

SUSAN spent six hours with/ME, who soon learned that/SUSAN was not a virgin, that her/BED had been shared with her brother, who, like/ME, had desired her, but, unlike/ME, had been humping her for years./DECEMBER was *my* turn, that AFTERNOON apartment/ . . . HOT radiators clanging, COLD wind rattling the windows,/ AFTERNOON waning, EVENING on the way. Oh, that/AFTERNOON! Coming four times and, in the EVENING, once again in/SUSAN's mouth. BEDDED still, she asked that I let MYSELF out, lying there/ LIMP, still wearing dark glasses, as DUSK shadowed the rumpled BED.

SUSIphANY SU SU whispering/ME, and oh, andering, MEandering, black-eyed/SUSAN *flam*-boy-ant, optimum/BED! a dead hollow vesper, a con-spir-a-see/ME-eyed poinciana, ME-eyed,/*o sole* ME-eyed poin-/DEE-CEM-BER, all white, and A-F-T-ERNOON all all all unending./HOT musky HOT mustard, COLD stinking COLD thurible,/ AFTER-sun and NOON sinking, E,V,E,NING fuck and tongue, an/ AFTERtaste, but NOON gone, AFTER-NOON screaming, screening EVEN-ING/SUSAN, SUSANitary seas, BEDAzzled by moonlight and I . . . I . . . coconut-fronded, MYcamelsELFconsciousness slinkily slumbering/LIMPingly stuttering, DUSKily darkening, deepening daisies and violets in BEDS.

SUSAN six hours with/ME all astonished, for/SUSAN's no virgin, her/BED was her brother's!/ME she fucked royally,/ME she taught brotherwise, all through/DECEMBER, or all AFTERNOON at least./ HOT dizzy licks, COLD chops but warm cockles,/AFTERNOON heat begat cool EVENING's expertise./AFTERNOON practice for EVENING's fel-ay-she oh/SUSAN! oh Christ! how she BEDDED and wedded and urged that I be MYSELF,/LIMPly suggested she'd best be alone now,

255

DUSK softly shrugging and hugging her naked and leaving her lying in shades on her BED.

❖

The bar was on Fordham Road, just off Jerome Avenue.

"It's full of niggers," my Uncle Luke said. "Let's get out of here."

This was February of 1944, and you could hardly walk through any street in New York without stumbling upon a place offering live jazz. I had asked Luke to take me to this particular bar because Biff Anderson was playing here this weekend. There were eight Biff Anderson records in my brother's collection, two of them with him backing the blues singers Viola McCoy and Clara Smith, four of them made when he'd been playing with Lionel Howard's Musical Aces, the remaining two featuring him on solo piano. His early style seemed to be premised on those of James P. Johnson and Fats Waller. Waller, I had already learned, was the man who had most influenced Tatum. And Tatum was where I wanted to be.

I was not surprised that the place was full of black people. I had begun subscribing to *Down Beat* and *Metronome*, which my father read aloud to me, and I knew what color most of the musicians were; not because they were identified by race, but only because there were pictures of them in those jazz journals. My father would say, "This Tatum is a nigger, did you know that?" (He also told me Tatum was blind, which was of far greater interest to me, and which confirmed my belief that I could one day play like him.) Or "Look at this Jimmie Lunceford," he would say. "I *hate* nigger bands. They repeat themselves all the time." I knew Biff Anderson was black, and I expected him to have a large black audience. But my Uncle Luke must have been shaken by it; he immediately asked the bartender for a double gin on the rocks.

256

"How about your friend here?" the bartender asked. He was white.

"I'll have a beer," I said.

"Let me see your draft card," he said, and then realized I was blind, and silently considered whether or not blind people were supposed to register for the draft, and then decided to skip the whole baffling question, and simply repeated, "Double gin on the rocks, one beer." We had to register for the draft the same as anyone else, of course, and—at least according to a joke then current—even blind people were being called up, so long as their Seeing Eye dogs had twenty-twenty vision. I didn't have a draft card because I wasn't yet eighteen. I'd have skipped the beer if the bartender had raised the slightest fuss; I was there to hear Biff Anderson play, and that was all.

The bar was a toilet. I've played many of them. It did not occur to me at the time that if someone of Biff's stature was playing a toilet in the Bronx, he must have fallen upon hard times. Nor did I even recognize the place as a toilet. I had never been inside a bar before, and the sounds and the smells were creating the surroundings for me. Biff must have been taking a break when we came in. The jukebox was on, and Bing Crosby was singing "Sunday, Monday, or Always." Behind the bar, the grain of which was raised and then worn smooth again, I could hear the clink of ice and glasses, whiskey being poured, the faint hiss of draft beer being drawn. There was a lot of echoing laughter in the room, mingled with the sound of voices I'd heard for years on "Amos 'n' Andy." The smells were beer and booze and perfume, the occasional whiff of someone who'd forgotten to bathe that month, the overpowering stench of urine from the men's room near the far end of the bar—though that was not what identified this particular dump as a toilet. To jazz musicians, a toilet is a place you play when you're coming up or heading down. I played a lot of them coming up, and I played a few of them on the way down, too. That's America. Easy come, easy go.

257

"Lots of dinges here tonight," the bartender whispered as he put down our glasses "What're *you* guys doin' here?"

"My nephew's a piano player," Luke said. "He wants to hear this guy."

"*He's* a dinge, too," the bartender said. "That's why we got so many of them here tonight. I never seen so many dinges in my life. I used to tenn bar in a dump on Lenox Avenue, and even *there* I never seen so many dinges. You hole a spot check right this minute, you gonna find six hundred switchblades here. Don't look crooked at nobody's girl, you lend up with a slit throat. Not you, kid," he said to me. "You're blind, you got nothin' to worry about. You play the piano, huh?"

"Yeah," I said.

"So whattya wanna lissen to *this* guy for? He stinks, you ask my opinion. I requested him last night for 'Deep Inna Hearta Texas,' he tells me he don't know the song. 'Deep Inna Hearta Texas,' huh? *Anybody* knows that song."

"It's not the kind of song he'd play," I said.

"You're tellin *me*?" the bartender said. "He don't *know* it, how could he play it? I don't recognize half the things he plays, any-way. I think he makes 'em up, whattya think of that?"

"He probably does," I said, and smiled.

"He sings when he plays," the bartender said. "Not the words, you unnerstan' me? He goes like uh-uh-uh under his breath. I think he's got a screw loose, whattya think of that?"

"He's humming the chord chart," I said. "He does that on his records, too."

"He makes records, this bum?"

"He made a lot of them," I said. "He's one of the best jazz pianists in the world."

"Sure, and he don't know 'Deep Inna Hearta Texas,'" the bartender said.

"There's got to be four hundred niggers in this place," Luke said.

258

"You better lower your voice, pal," the bartender advised. "Less you want all four hunnerd of 'em cuttin' off your balls and hangin' 'em from the chandelier."

"There ain't no chandelier," Luke said.

"Be a wise guy," the bartender said. "I tole the boss why did he hire a dinge to come play here? He said it was good for business. Sure. So next week *this* bum goes back to Harlem and *we're* stuck with a nigger trade. And he can't even play 'Deep Inna Hearta Texas.' Can *you* play 'Deep Inna Hearta Texas'?" he asked me.

"I've never tried it."

The bartender sang a little of the song, and then said, "*That* one. You know it?"

"I've heard the song, but I've never played it."

"You must be as great a piano player as him," the bartender said.

"How about another double?" Luke asked.

"Fuckin' piano players today don't know how to play *nothin'*," the bartender said, and walked off to pour my uncle's drink.

"*I* know 'Deep in the Heart of Texas,'" Luke said.

"Whyn't you go play it for him?" I said.

"Nah," Luke said.

"Go on, he'd get a kick out of it."

"Nah, nah, c'mon," Luke said, "Anyway, here he comes."

"Who?"

"The guy you came to hear. I *guess* it's him. He's sittin' down at the piano."

"What does he look like?"

"He's as black as the ace of spades," Luke whispered.

"Is he fat or skinny or what?"

"Kind of heavy."

"How old is he?"

"Who can tell with a nigger? Forty? Fifty? He's got fat fingers, Igg. You sure he's a good piano player?"

259

"One of the best, Uncle Luke."

"Here's your gin," the bartender said. "You want to pay me now, or you gonna be drinkin'?"

"I'll be drinking," Luke said.

From the moment Biff began playing, his heritage was completely evident. Johnson had taught Waller, and Biff had learned by imitating both, and when Tatum took Waller a giant step further, Biff again revised his style. He played a five-tune set consisting of "Don't Blame Me," "Body and Soul," "Birth of the Blues," "Sweet Lorraine," and "Star Eyes." This last was a hit recorded by Jimmy Dorsey, with Kitty Kallen doing the vocal. It was, and *is*, a perfect illustration of a great tune for a jazz improvisation. The melody is totally dumb, but the chord chart is unpredictable and exciting, with no less than nine key changes in a thirty-two-bar chorus. I still use it as a check-out tune. Whenever I want to know how well someone plays, I'll say, "Okay, 'Star Eyes.'" If he comes up with some fumbling excuse like "Oh, man, I don't like that tune so much," or "Yeah, yeah, like I haven't played that one in a long time," I've got him pegged immediately. It's a supreme test tune for a jazz musician, and Biff played it beautifully that night.

He played it beautifully because he played it *exactly* like Tatum. A tribute, a copy, call it what you will, but there it was, those sonorous tenths, those pentatonic runs, the whole harmonic edifice played without Tatum's speed or dexterity, of course, but letter perfect stylistically. I was sitting not fifty feet from a man who could play piano like Tatum, and I had been breaking my balls *and* my chops for the past seven months trying to learn Tatum by listening to his records.

"Let me have another one of these, huh?" Luke said.

"Hey, Uncle Luke," I said. "Go easy, huh?"

"Huh? Go easy?"

"On the gin."

"Oh. Sure, Iggie, don't worry."

The music had stopped; I could hear laughter and voices from the bandstand.

"What's he doing up there?" I asked Luke.

"He's standing near the piano, talking to a girl."

"Can you take me up there?"

"Sure, Iggie. What're you gonna do? Play a little?"

"I just want to meet him. Hurry up. *Please*. Before he leaves."

"He's lookin' down her dress, he ain't about to leave," Luke said, and he offered me his elbow, and I took it and got off the bar stool, and followed him across the room, moving through a rolling crest of conversation and then onto a slippery, smooth surface I assumed was the dance floor, and heard just beyond earshot a deep Negro voice muttering something unintelligible, and then caught the tail end of a sentence, ". . . around two in the mornin', you care to hang aroun' that long," and the voice stopped as we approached, and my Uncle Luke said, "Mr. Anderson?"

"Yeah?" Biff said.

"This is my nephew," Luke said. "He plays piano."

"Cool," Biff said.

"He wanted to meet you."

"How you doin', man?" Biff said, and he must have extended his hand in greeting because there was a brief expectant silence, and then Luke quickly said, "Shake the man's hand, Iggie."

I extended my hand. Biff's hand was thick and fleshy and sweating. On my right, there was the overpowering, almost nauseating smell of something that was definitely not *Je Reviens*.

"You play piano, huh?" Biff said.

"Yes."

"How long you been playin'?"

"Twelve years."

"Yeah? Cool. Hey, Poots, where you *goin'*?" he said, his voice turning away from me. There was no answer. I heard the click of high-heeled shoes in rapid tattoo on the hardwood floor, disappearing into the larger sound of voices and laughter. Somewhere behind me, the jukebox went on again—David Rose's "Holiday for Strings."

"Dumb *cunt*," Biff said, and turned back to me again. "So you been playin' twelve years," he said without interest.

"I've been trying to learn jazz," I said.

"Mmm," he said, his voice turning away. I heard the sound of ice against the sides of a glass. He had picked up a drink from the piano top.

"He's real good," Luke said. "He studied classical a long time."

"Yeah, mmm," Biff said, and drank and put down the glass again with a small final click.

"Why'n't you play something for him, Iggie?"

"That's okay, I'll take your word for it," Biff said. "Nice meetin' you both, enjoy yourselves, huh?"

"Hey, *wait* a minute!" Luke said.

"There's somethin' I got to see about," Biff said. "You'll excuse me, huh?"

"The kid came all the way here to listen to you," Luke said, his voice rising. "I went all the way uptown to get him, and then we had to come all the way down here again."

"So what?" Biff said.

"*That's* what!" Luke said. His voice was louder now. "He's been talkin' about nothin' but you ever since he found out you were gonna be playing in this dump."

"Yeah?" Biff said. "That right?"

"*Yeah!*" Luke said, his voice strident and belligerent now. It was the gin talking, I realized. I had never heard my uncle raise his voice except while playing poker, and nobody was playing poker right that minute. Or maybe they were. "So let him play piano for you," Luke said. "It won't kill you."

"You think I got nothin' better to do than . . . ?"

"What the hell *else* you got to do?" Luke asked.

"That's okay, Uncle Luke," I said.

"No, it *ain't* okay. Why the hell can't he listen to you?"

"I just wanted to meet him, that's all," I said. "Come on."

"Just a minute, you," Biff said.

"Me?"

"You're the piano player, ain't you?"

"Yes."

"Then that's who. What can you play?"

"Lots of things."

"Like what?"

"Tatum's 'Moonglow' and 'St. Louis Blues,' and . . ."

"That's plenty. Just them two, okay? If you're lousy, you get one chorus and out. Now if your uncle here don't mind, I'm goin' to the *pissoir* over there while you start playin', because I got to take a leak, if that's all right with your uncle here. I can listen fine from in there, and soon's I'm finished I'll come right back. If that's all right with your uncle here."

"That's fine," Luke said.

"Show him the piano," Biff said. "I'll cut off the juke on my way." He climbed down from the bandstand and walked ponderously past me toward the men's room.

"Black bastard," Luke muttered under his breath, and then said, "Give me your hand, Iggie," and led me up the steps and to the piano.

I played. I wish I could report that all conversation stopped dead the moment I began, that Biff came running out of the men's room hastily buttoning his fly and peeing all over himself in excitement, that a scout for a record company rushed over and slapped a contract on the piano top. No such thing. I played the two Tatum solos exactly as I'd lifted them from his record, and then I stopped, and conversation was still going on, laughter still shrilled into the smoky room, the bartender's voice said, "Scotch and soda, comin' up," and I put my hands back in my lap.

"Yeah, okay," Biff said. I had not realized he was standing beside the piano, and I did not know how long he'd been there. I waited for him to say more. The silence lengthened.

263

"Some of the runs were off, I know," I said.

"Yeah, those runs are killers," Biff said.

"They're hard to pick up off the records," I said.

"That where you got this stuff? From Art's records?"

"Yes."

"Well, that's not a bad way. What else do you know?"

"A lot of Wilson, and some Waller and Hines . . ."

"Waller, huh?"

"Yes."

"Takin' it off note by note from the records, huh?"

"Yeah."

"Mmm," Biff said. "Well, that's okay. What've you got down of Fats?"

" 'Thief in the Night' and 'If This Isn't Love' and . . ."

"Oh, yeah, the sides he cut with Honey Bear and Autrey, ain't they?"

"I don't know who's on them."

"That's all shit, anyway," Biff said. "That stuff he done with 'Fats Waller and his Rhythm.' 'Cept for maybe 'Dinah' and 'Blue Because of You.' "

"I can play those, too."

"Can you do any of his early stuff?"

"Like what?"

"Like the stuff he cut in the twenties. 'Sweet Savannah Sue' and . . . I don't know, man. . . . 'Love Me or Leave Me.' That stuff."

"No, I don't know those."

"Yeah, well," Biff said. "Well, that wasn't half bad, what you played. You dig Tatum, huh?"

"Yes. That's how I want to play."

"Like Tatum, huh?"

"Yes."

"Well, you doin' fine," Biff said. "Jus' keep on goin' the way you are. Fine," he said. "Fine."

"I need help," I said.

"Yeah, man, don't we all?" Biff said, and chuckled.

"A lot of Tatum's chords are hard to take off the records."

"Jus' break 'em up, that's all. Play 'em note by note. That's what I used to do when I was comin' along."

"I've tried that. I still can't get them all."

"Well, kid, what can I tell you? You wanna play Tatum piano, then you gotta listen to him and do what he does, that's all. Why'n't you run on down to the Street; I think he's playin' in one of the clubs down there right now. With Slam, I think."

"What street?" I said.

"*What* street? *The* Street."

"I don't know what you mean."

"Well, kid, what can I tell you?" Biff said, and sighed. "While you're down there, you might listen to what Diz is doin'. Dizzy Gillespie. Him an' Bird are shakin' things up, man, you might want to change your mind. Hey, now, looka here," he said.

"Hello, mothah-fugger," someone said cheerfully.

"Get up there an' start blowin'," someone else said. "We heah to help you."

"Don't need no help, man," Biff said, and chuckled.

"Whutchoo doin' in this toilet, anyhow?" the first man said. "*Dis*graceful!"

Biff chuckled again, and then said, "Kid, these're two of the worl's *worse* jazz musicians. . . ."

"*Sheeee*-it," one of them said, and laughed.

"Been thrown off ever' band in the country 'cause they shoot dope an' fuck chickens."

All three of them laughed. One of them said, "We brung Dickie with us, he gettin' his drums from the car."

"The shades is he's blind," Biff said, and I realized one of the other men must have been staring at me. "Plays piano."

"Hope he's better'n you," one of them said, and all of them laughed again.

265

"What's your name, man?" Biff said. "I forget."

"Iggie."

"This's Sam an' Jerry. You sit in with 'em, Iggie, while I go dazzle that chick. I'm afraid she goan git away."

"Hey, come down, man," one of them said. "We here in this shithole to blow with *you*, not some fuckin' F-sharp piano player."

"I'm not an F-sharp piano player," I said.

"Hey, man, gimme a hand with this, somebody said. I figured that was Dickie, who'd been getting his drums from the car. "Come on, Jerr, move yo' black ass."

"Any blind piano player I *know*'s a F-sharp piano player," the other man insisted.

"*Tatum's* blind," Biff said, "and he can cut your ass thu Sunday."

"He only *half* blind," Sam said.

"I can play in any key on the board," I said.

"There now, you see? Sit down with Iggie here, an' work out a nice set, huh? And lemme go see 'bout my social life. Play nice, Iggie. Maybe you can cover up all they *mis*takes."

"*Sheeee*-it," Sam said, and then laughed.

I listened as the drummer set up his equipment and the trumpet player started running up and down chromatics, warming up. Sam asked me to tune him up, and when I asked him what notes he wanted me to hit, he said, "Jus' an A, man," sounding very surprised. I gave Jerry a B flat when he asked for it, and he tuned his horn, and meanwhile Dickie was warming up on his cymbals, playing fast little brush rolls, and pretty soon we were ready to start the set. I'd never played with a band before, but I wasn't particularly scared. I'd listened to enough jazz records to know what the format was. The piano player or the horn man usually started with the head chorus (I didn't yet know it was called the head), and then the band took solos in turn, and then everybody went into the final chorus and ended the tune. I figured all I had to do was play the way I'd been playing for the past seven months, play all those tunes I'd either lifted from my brother's record collection or figured out on my own. Biff, after all, was a well-known and respected jazz musician, and he had told me that what I'd played wasn't half bad, which I figured meant at *least* half good. Besides, *he* was the one who'd asked me to sit in.

"You *sure* you ain't a F-sharp piano player?" Sam asked behind me.

"I'm sure," I said.

"'Cause, man, I don't dig them wild stretches in F sharp," he said. "You got some other keys in your head, cool. Otherwise, it's been graaaand knowin' you."

"Well, *start* it, man," Jerry said to me. He was standing to my right. The drummer was diagonally behind me, sitting beside Sam. I took a four-bar intro, and we began playing "Fools Rush In," a nice Johnny Mercer–Rube Bloom ballad, which I'd never heard Tatum do, but which I played in the Tatum style, or what I considered to be the Tatum style. We were moving into the bridge when Sam said, "Chop it off, kid." I didn't know what he meant. I assumed he wanted me to play a bit more staccato, so I began chopping the chords, so to speak, giving a good crisp, clean touch to those full tenths as I walked them with my left hand or used them in a swing bass, pounding out that steady four/four rhythm, and hearing the satisfying (to me) echo of Sam behind me walking the identical chords in arpeggios on his bass fiddle. As I went into the second chorus, I heard Jerry come in behind me on the horn, and I did what I'd heard the piano players doing on the records, I started feeding him chords, keeping that full left hand going in time with what Sam and the drummer were laying down, though to tell the truth I couldn't quite understand *what* the drummer was doing, and wasn't even sure he was actually keeping the beat. It was the drummer who said, "Take it home," and I said, "What?" and he said, "Last eight," and the horn man came out of the bridge and into the final eight bars, and we ended the tune. Everybody was quiet.

267

"Well, you ain't a F-sharp piano player, that's for sure," Sam said. "But you know what you can do with that left hand of yours, don't you?"

"You can chop it off and shove it clean up your ass," the trumpet player said. "Let's get Biff."

They were moving off the bandstand. In a moment, and without another word to me, they were gone. I sat at the piano alone, baffled.

"What's going on here?" a voice asked. "Who the hell are you? Who's that band? Where's my piano player?"

The voice belonged to a fat man. I could tell. I could also tell he was Jewish. I know it's un-American to identify ethnic groups by vocal inflection or intonation, but I can tell if a man's black, Italian, Irish, Jewish, or whatever simply by hearing his voice. And so can you. And if you tell me otherwise, I'll call you a liar. (And besides, what the hell's so un-American about it?) I was stunned. Some black bastard horn player had just told me to shove my precious left hand up my ass, and I didn't know why.

"You!" the fat man said. "Get away from that piano. Where's Biff?"

"Cool it, Mr. Gottlieb," Biff's voice said. "I'm right here; the boy's a friend of mine."

"Do you know 'Deep in the Heart of Texas'?" Gottlieb said. "The bartender wants 'Deep in the Heart of Texas.'"

"Beyond my ken," Biff said, in what sounded like an English accent.

"What?" Gottlieb said, startled.

"The tune. Unknown to me," Biff said.

"What?"

"Advise your barkeep to compile a more serious list of requests," Biff said in the same stuffy English cadences, and then immediately and surprisingly fell into an aggravated black dialect, dripping watermelon, pone, and chitlings. "You jes' ast you man to keep de booze comin', an' let *me*—an' mah frens who was kine

268

enough to come see me heah—worry 'bout de music, huh? Kid, you want to git off dat stool so's we kin lay some jazz on dese mothahs?"

"What?" Gottlieb said.

"I'll talk to *you* later," Biff said as I climbed off the stool and off the bandstand.

❖

My uncle Luke had drunk too much. His head was on the table, touching my elbow, and I could hear him snoring loudly as Biff talked to me. On my right, the girl with the five-and-dime perfume sat silent and motionless, her presence detectable only by her scent and the sound of her breathing. The trumpet player had left around midnight. The bass player and the drummer had followed him at about one. We were alone in the place now, except for the bartender, who was washing glasses and lining them up on the shelves, and Gottlieb, who had tallied his register and was putting chairs up on tables, preparatory to sweeping out the joint. As he passed our table, he said, "This ain't a hotel, Mr. Jazz," and then moved on, muttering.

"Cheap sheenie bastard," Biff said. "He's got his bartender watering my drinks. You okay, Poots?" he asked the girl. The girl did not answer. She must have nodded assent, though, the motion of her head and neck unleashing a fresh wave of scent. Biff said, "Fine, that's fine, you jus' stick aroun' a short while longer. Now, you," he said. "You want to know what's wrong with how you play piano?"

"Yes," I said.

"You're lucky Dickie's a gentle soul. Dickie. The drummer. Otherwise he'da done what Jo Jones done to Bird in Kansas City when he got the band all turned around. He throwed his cymbal on the floor, and that was that, man, end of the whole fuckin' set. 'Scuse me, Poots."

269

"Well, *they* ended the set, too," I said. I still didn't know that Bird was someone's name. This was the second time Biff had used it tonight, and each time I'd thought he meant bird with a lower-case *b*; the reference was mystifying. For that matter, I didn't know who Jo Jones was, either. But I figured if he'd thrown a cymbal on the floor, he had to be a drummer, whereas all I could think about the use of the word "bird" was that it was a black jazz expression. (Come to think of it, it *was*.) "And I'll tell you something, Mr. Anderson, your bass player pissed me off right from the start. Excuse me, miss. Making cracks about F-sharp piano players."

"Well, le's say he ain' 'zackly de mos' tac'ful of souls," Biff said in his watermelon accent, and then immediately added in his normal speaking voice, "But he's a damn fine musician, and he knows where jazz *is* today, and *that's* what he was trying to convey to you."

"I'm no damn F-sharp piano player," I said.

"He didn't know that. Anyway, that ain't what got him or the other boys riled."

"Then what?"

"Your left hand."

"I've got a good left hand," I said.

"Sure," Biff said. "If you want to play alone, you've got a good left hand, and I'm speakin' comparative. You still need lots of work, even if all you want to play is solo piano."

"That's what I want to play."

"Then don't go sittin' in with no groups. Because if you play that way with a group, you're lucky they don't throw the *piano* at you, no less the cymbals."

"Mr. Anderson," I said, "I don't know what you're talking about."

"I'm talking about that bass," he said.

"That's a Tatum bass," I said. "That's what you your*self* played. That was Tatum right down the line."

270

"Correct," Biff said.

"So?"

"Maybe you didn't notice, but I was playin' *alone*. Kid, a rhythm section won't tolerate that bass nowadays. Not after Bird."

"What do you mean, *bird*? What's that?"

"Parker. Charlie Parker. Bird."

"Is he a piano player?"

"He plays alto saxophone."

"Well . . . what *about* him?" I said. "What's *he* got to do with playing piano?"

"He's got everything to do with everything," Biff said. "You tell me you want to play Tatum piano, I tell you Tatum's on the way out, if not already dead and gone. You tell me you want to learn all those Tatum runs, I tell you there's no room for that kind of bullshit in bop. You know why Sam . . ."

"In *what*, did you say?"

"Bop, that's the stuff Parker's laying down. And Fats Navarro. And Bud Powell. Now *there's* the piano player you ought to be listening to, Powell; he's the one you ought to be pickin' up on, *not* Art Tatum. You want to know why the boys shot you down, it's 'cause you put them in prison, man, you put them in that old-style bass prison, and they can't play that way no more. These guys're cuttin' their chops on bop. Even *I'm* too old-fashioned for them, but we're good friends, and they allow me to get by with open tenths and some shells. Sam wants to walk the bass line himself, he don't want to be trapped by no rhythm the *piano* player's layin' down, he don't even want to be trapped by the *drummer* no more. Didn't you hear what Dickie was doing behind you? You didn't hear no four/four on the bass drum, did you? That was on the cymbals; he saved the big drum for klook-mop, dropping them bombs every now and then, but none of that heavy one, two, three, four, no, *man*. Which is why they told you to stick your left hand up your ass, 'scuse me, Poots, to *lose* it, man.

271

They wanted you to play shells in the left hand, that's all, and not that pounding Tatum rhythm, uh-uh. You dig what I'm saying?"

"What's a shell? What do you mean, they wanted me to play shells?"

"Shells, man. You know what a C-minor chord is?"

"C, E flat, G, and B flat," I said.

"Right. But when Powell plays a C-minor, all he hits are the C and the B flat. With his pinkie and his thumb, you dig? He leaves out the insides, he just gives you the shell. He feeds those shells to the horn players, and they blow pure and fast and hard, without that fuckin' pounding rhythm and those ornate chords and runs going on behind them all the time, and lockin' them in, 'scuse me, Poots. Piano players just can't *play* that way no more."

"*Tatum* does," I said. "And so does Wilson."

"A dying breed," Biff said in his English accent, "virtually obsolete. *Look*, man, I was with Marian McPartland the first time she heard Bud play, and she said to me, 'Man, that is *some* spooky right hand there,' and she wasn't shittin'. That right hand *is* spooky, the things he does with that right hand. He plays those fuckin' shells with his left—the root and seventh, or the root and third—because he's got tiny hands, you see, he couldn't reach those Tatum tenths if he stood on his fuckin' head, 'scuse me, Poots. Some of the time he augments the shell by pickin' up a ninth with the right hand, but mostly the right is playin' a *horn* solo, you dig? He's doin' Charlie Parker on the piano. There are three voices dig? Two notes in the shell, and the running line in the right hand, and that's it. Tatum runs? Forget 'em, man! They're what a piano player does when he can't think of nothin' new, he just throws in all those rehearsed runs that're already in his fingers. That ain't jazz, man. That's I don't know what it is, but it ain't jazz no more."

"You people going to pay rent on that table?" Gottlieb said.

"What're you thinking, kid?" Biff asked. "I can't tell what you're thinking behind them shades."

"I just don't understand what you're saying."

"You don't, huh? Well, here it is in a nutshell, kid. The rhythm ain't in the left hand no more—it's passed over to the right. The left hand is almost standin' still these days. And if you want to keep on playin' all that frantic shit, then you better play it all by yourself, 'cause there ain't no band gonna tolerate it. That's it in a nutshell."

"I still want to play like Tatum," I said.

"You'll be followin' a coffin up Bourbon Street," Biff said. "Look, what the hell do I care *what* you play? I'm just tryin' to tell you if you're startin' *now*, for Christ's sake, don't start with somethin, already *dead*. Go to the Street, man, Fifty-second Street, dig what the cats are doin. If you don't like it, then, man, that's up to you. But I'm tellin' you, sure as this sweet li'l thing is sittin' here beside me, Tatum and Wilson are dead and the Bird is king, and jazz ain't never gonna be the same again." He suddenly burst out laughing. "Man, the cats goan drum me clear out of the tribe. They got strong hostility, them boppers."

"I want to hear them play," I said.

"Get your uncle to take you down the Street. Diz an' Oscar—Pettiford, Oscar Pettiford—got a fine group at the Onyx, George Wallington on piano. Go listen to them."

"Will *you* take me there, Mr. Anderson?"

"Me? I don't know you from a hole in the wall," Biff said.

"Oh, *take* the fuckin' kid," Poots said.

❖

Well, he didn't take me. He didn't take me because, as it happened, he was leaving for California in a week to play a gig out there, and if things went well for him, he would stay there through the winter and spring, and probably wouldn't be back in New York till June or July. When I asked him if he'd take me to the Street when he got back, he told me again that he didn't know me from a hole in the wall, and said I should get my uncle to take me. Uncle Luke was still asleep, and snoring very loudly at that point. I told Biff my uncle had other things to do, and besides, he couldn't teach me to play the kind of piano I wanted to play. Biff said Now hold it *just* one minute, kid, who said anything about *teaching* you piano? I never taught anybody in my life, and I ain't about to start now. I don't know you from a hole in the wall, go down the Street, get yourself some bop records, it's been nice talkin' to you.

My mother would not allow me to go down to Fifty-second Street, either alone *or* accompanied by Luke. She said she wanted me to maintain my good grades at Santa Lucia's, especially since I'd be graduating in June, and besides, I was doing *enough* gallivanting, what with running off on mysterious errands every time the phone rang. The telephone calls were from Susan Koenig, of course, and they would notify me that her mother would be gone for the evening or the afternoon, whereupon I would hop the trolley to Mount Vernon and spend a few blissful hours in bed with her. Or up against the sink. Or on the kitchen table. All that ended in April when her brother—whose obnoxious name was Franklin—was inconsiderate enough to get himself shot in the foot by a Japanese sniper, thereby earning himself a Purple Heart and managing somehow to finagle a boat ticket to the States at a time when nobody, but *nobody*, was being sent home for minor wounds. In April, too, a week or so before Easter, the Virgin Mary came down to visit my mother and precipitated a family crisis that was more immediate to me than jazz, or the war, or the fact that Susan seemed to prefer her brother's brand of houghmagandy to mine.

She appeared to my mother on 218th Street and White Plains Avenue at three o'clock in the afternoon. There is nothing particu-

274

larly noteworthy about that corner, and God alone knows why Mary chose it for her return to Earth. My mother had been out marketing, and was loaded down with shopping bags as she wended her gentle way homeward that afternoon. The Virgin was wearing black. Black topcoat and black stockings, black shoes, and a small black hat. She approached my mother and said, "Stella Di Palermo?"

"Yes?" my mother answered, puzzled. She had never seen this woman before. We had been living in the Bronx for seven years, and my mother knew most of the neighborhood ladies, but this woman was a stranger to her.

"I'm telling you this for your own good," the woman said. "Your husband Jimmy is in love with a woman on Pelham Parkway. He goes to see her almost every day, after work."

"Who are you?" my mother asked.

"Never mind," the woman said. "God bless you, Stella," and walked off.

My mother stood there watching her as she disappeared. She was forty-one years old, young Stella, and a strange lady in black had just told her that her beloved husband was enamored of a woman on Pelham Parkway, which was exactly where my father delivered mail. My mother immediately concluded that the woman in black was the Virgin Mary. Why this association should even have occurred to a person who hadn't been inside a church for twenty-one years is beyond me, but again, I have no desire to probe the convoluted mental processes of anyone who happens to be my mother. Maybe Easter had something to do with it. Maybe the religious identification was triggered by the fact that my mother had seen a miniature replica of the crucifixion in the window of the butcher shop an instant before she was confronted by the lady in black. It doesn't matter. My mother gets these fixed ideas. If Charlie Shoe was a hophead rape artist, then the lady in black was the Virgin Mary, and that was that. And *that*, believe me, was more than enough. As fate would have it, my father was late getting home from work that afternoon, and this naturally confirmed everything the Virgin Mary had whispered to my mother in the street. I was not as fortunate as my father; I got home from school at my usual time and found a raving lunatic in the kitchen.

"I thought it was the bum," my mother said. "I'll kill him. I'll kill him the minute he comes through the door."

"What?" I said.

"Him and his whore," she said, pronouncing the last word "hooer."

"What do you mean? What . . . ?"

"You think I'm stupid?" she said. "Where is he, it's four o'clock, he's supposed to be here at three, where is he, the bum? He's with that whore, that's where he is. We've been married twenty-one years, the dirty bastard, he's rotten through and through, *la Madonna* opened my eyes, she told me what your father's been doing, oh, and I *believed* him, I *believed* him when he told me he was lining up wedding jobs after work, sure, *some* wedding jobs, I'll kill him when he gets home, don't you say a word, Iggie, I'm going to kill that rotten son of a bitch."

"Mom, sit down, will you? Mom, please . . ."

"What am I stupid?" she said. "I *must* be stupid to let this happen. I called my father, I called him the minute I came in the door, I put down my bundles and I called him at the tailor shop. I told him *la Madonna* stopped me on White Plains Avenue and told me what a bum my husband was, told me he's been seeing this whore from Pelham Parkway every day, every *day*, I told him, who knows where they do it, she must have an apartment there, he probably delivers mail to her, or else he met her at one of those beer parties he plays, of *course*, why *else* does he go all over the Bronx playing those jobs, to meet whores, I told my father, I told him. And he said What *madonna*, what are you talking about, my own *father*, would you believe it, he sticks up for that rotten son of a bitch, I saw her with my own eyes, all in black, she had this sad face, there were tears in her eyes when she told

276

me, and she said God bless you, Stella, and then she vanished, my own father didn't believe me. He told me to calm down, he told me to wait till Jimmy comes home, talk to him, find out what it's all about, my own father, what's there to find out about when *la Madonna* comes to me and *tells* me, what's there to find out, Iggie, oh, Iggie, what's there to find out?"

"Mom," I said, "Grandpa was right. When Pop gets here . . ."

"I'll *kill* him!" she said.

"Mom, *please*," I said, and burst into tears.

She came to me, she clutched my head against her bosom. Frantically she stroked my hair, and the hysterical monologue went on, and I half listened, and prayed her rage would run its course before my father stepped through that kitchen door, because I knew for certain she would stab him with a bread knife if she did not calm down before then. "How could he do this to us? To *me*, sure, he doesn't love *me*, he *never* loved me, but to *you*? Iggie, how could he do this to *you*, doesn't he know you're his son, doesn't he have no respect for the family, you're blind, doesn't he know that, isn't that enough for you to bear, do you have to be ashamed of a bum for a father? Oh, no wonder, oh *now* it makes sense, oh yes *now* I understand, I thank you sweet *Madonna*, I get on my knees to thank you, I've been stupid, so stupid, I'll take care of you Iggie don't worry your mother loves you she'll always love you no matter what that bum does I don't care if he *ever* comes back I'll kill him when he comes in this house that dirty bastard twenty-one years I've been good to him twenty-one years and he finds himself a cheap rotten whore a blond woman *la Madonna* said an Irish whore with blond hair she lives on Pelham Parkway he goes up there all the time when he's delivering mail he met her at one of the beer parties he plays *la Madonna* said it's been going on for years now she said she told me everything Iggie and she said God bless you Stella oh Iggie what am I going to do how are we going to manage my own father won't believe me."

277

In my mother's temporary insanity there was irrefutable logic. If the woman in black had not been the Virgin Mary, then how did she know who my mother was? My mother, after all, had never seen her before, so how could this woman, unless she was the Virgin Mary, immediately identify her as Stella Di Palermo? And similarly, if the woman had not been the Virgin Mary, how could she have known what my father was up to on Pelham Parkway almost every day after work, how could she possibly have known that he was in love with another woman? My father maintained that the lady in black was a troublemaker, that my mother was a fool to believe a stranger who had stopped her on the street and told her such a lie, how did my mother know the woman wasn't some kind of nut? "Then how did she *know* me?" my mother screamed. "Why did she pick *me* out of the crowd, the avenue was crowded, everybody was out shopping, she came up to me and said right off Stella Di Palermo, she *knew* me, you son of a bitch!" My father told my mother (this was all in my presence) that she was as crazy as the lady who'd stopped her, if she believed such a thing. My mother said, "Oh, no, *I'm* not crazy, *you're* the one who's crazy if you think I'm going to live under the same roof for another minute with a bum who's running around with some cheap Irish whore on Pelham Parkway," and my father said, "For Christ's sake, Stella, will you please shut up, you're giving me a headache," and she said, "*I'll* give you a headache, you rotten son of a bitch," and my father left the house.

My mother immediately went through all the drawers on his side of the dresser, searching for evidence that would link him incontrovertibly to the mysterious blond Irish whore on Pelham Parkway. She found a bill from a jewelry shop, and she read it off to me triumphantly—"One pair gold earrings, sapphire chip, forty-seven dollars and twenty-two cents, where are those earrings, Iggie? Did *you* ever see those earrings, this bill is dated January twenty-eighth, did he give those earrings to *me*, did you ever *see* those earrings in this house? He gave them to his whore, he spent

278

our good money on an Irish whore!" My father told her on the telephone that he had picked up the earrings for a friend in the post office, my mother could go check with the jeweler if she wanted to, but she said, "Sure, the jeweler'll lie, too, you think I'm stupid?" He had gone to stay at my Uncle Nick's house in Corona, and on Good Friday, Nick came to my mother as an emissary. Nick told her she was foolish to believe a strange woman who'd come up to her on the street. . . .

"*What* strange woman?" my mother shouted. "*La Madonna,* do you understand me, Nick? *La Madonna,* all in black!"

"Sure, but after all, Stella, are you going to believe some crazy person or your own husband?"

"I'm not crazy, don't worry," my mother said.

"Who said *you* were crazy, Stella? I'm telling you this person, this woman who came up to you . . ."

"*La Madonna!*" my mother said.

"Now come on, Stella," Nick said, "make sense, will you? What the hell is *la Madonna* gonna be bothering coming here to the Bronx to tell you about Jimmy, huh?"

"He's a no-good bastard," my mother said.

"All right, so what do you wanna do? I'm wastin' time here. You want me to tell him to come home, or you want me to tell him to go drop dead? Which is it, Stella?"

"Why won't he tell me the truth?"

"He swore to me on the Bible he ain't got no other woman; now what more do you want, Stella?"

"He's a liar," my mother said.

"So okay, I'll tell him to go drop dead, okay? What do you want me to tell him, Stella?"

"Who cares *what* you tell him? Who *cares* about him or what he does with his whore?"

"The kid's sittin' right here," my Uncle Nick said. "You shouldn't talk that way in front of the kid."

"Why not? He *should* know what kind of bum his father is."

279

"Okay, so I'll tell Jimmy not to come home, okay? Is that what you want me to tell him? I'll tell him whatever you want, Stella. I ain't gonna buck the system, that's for sure. You buck the system, you wind up with a busted head."

"Tell him what you like."

"Well, what kind of answer is that, Stella? Now listen to me, I'm gonna talk to you like you was my own sister, all right? He's been at my house since last Wednesday, he goes to work in the morning, drives all the way here to the Bronx, and comes home for supper every night when Connie's puttin' the macaroni on the table. Now if he's foolin' around with a woman here in the Bronx, why's he comin' back to *my* house in Corona every night, would you please tell me that?"

"Because she's *married*, why do you think?" my mother said. "*Married*, you understand, Nick, or are you thickheaded like your brother? If I knew who she was, if *la Madonna* had only told me who she was, I'd go see her husband, *he'd* fix Jimmy's onions, you can bet on that."

"Stella, if you don't know who this woman is supposed to be, how do you know she's married?"

"You think I'm stupid?" my mother said.

"Stella, I think you ain't listening to me," Nick said. "Look, it's two days till Easter, where you gonna be spending Easter Sunday?"

"At my father's house."

"Okay. You want me to tell Jimmy to come here Easter morning, pick up you and the kid and take you to Harlem? How's that, Stella?"

"Who cares?" my mother said. "Tell him what you like."

"Okay, I'll tell him to pick you up Easter, okay?"

"Tell him what you like. Who cares?" my mother said.

My father came back to the house at ten o'clock on Easter morning. Nick had neglected to mention that the day after my father had left home, he'd withdrawn most of the money in my mother's and his joint savings account. He was driving a new Dodge, and carrying armloads of gifts for my mother and me. (I forget what my presents were.) The trip to my grandfather's house in Harlem was frosty with silence. When we got to the apartment on First Avenue, my grandfather clasped my father in his arms and said, "Jimmy, *Buona Pasqua!* Come! You have to help me bring some wine from the cellar."

"I'll help," Pino said from the other room.

"No, Pino, *sta qui*," my grandfather said. "Jimmy and I can manage alone."

I do not to this day know whether or not my father had an Irish whore on Pelham Parkway. I did not believe the Virgin Mary had accosted my mother on White Plains Avenue, of course, but I could find no reasonable explanation for a strange woman coming up to her with such information. I thought of a great many possibilities, but none of them made much sense. Was it conceivable, for example, that the woman in black had *herself* been my father's doxy, and that she'd gone to my mother seeking revenge after a lovers' quarrel? Or was she the sister of my father's whore? Or her mother? Or was it all simply a case of mistaken identity? My father's partner on the Pelham Parkway route was named Jimmy, too, and he also wore a mustache, and was about my father's size, though a bit heftier. Was it *he* who'd been *shtupping* the lady every afternoon? Had the informer in black fingered the wrong fornicating mailman?

I began to check up on my father. I became the first blind detective in history. I would drop in unexpectedly whenever he was playing a wedding or a dance, using the excuse that I wanted to sit in and get some practice playing with bands. My father's band— he then called it James Palmer's Rhythm Kings—was square to the toes, and sitting in with them was total torment. But I wasn't there to advance my musical career. I was Ignazio Di Palermo, Private Eye. Blind in both, I wouldn't have recognized an Irish whore if I'd tripped over her vagina and stumbled into County

Killarney. (Remind me to tell you the joke about George Washington's horse sometime.) I never did get the goods on my father, nor did he ever once deviate from his story: The lady in the street was crazy, he did not know a whore on Pelham Parkway or anyplace else in the world, the receipt for the gold earrings with the sapphire chips had been given to him by the jeweler when he went to pick them up for a friend. Eventually, my mother forgave him. But to keep the matter in perspective, and to correct any misconceptions about the extent of her willingness to forget, she promptly stopped talking to my Uncle Nick, who had served as nothing more than an innocent go-between in the entire affair. Nick was a house painter. He died in 1953, when he suffered a cerebral hemorrhage after a fall from a ladder. My mother had not spoken to him since that Good Friday in 1944, and she did not go to his funeral.

❖

Who says there never *were* any streets of gold in America? In 1944, I found one. I had learned from an issue of *Down Beat* that Biff Anderson was back in New York. I sought him out again. I told him I'd been trying to understand bop, and was hopelessly confused. He told me that was tough shit. I told him he was the one who'd advised me not to even *try* playing Tatum piano, that bop was the new thing, and that was what I should be learning. He said That's right. So where am I supposed to learn it? I asked. Nobody's teaching it, Biff, there aren't any bop solos in Braille, there aren't even any *Tatum* solos in Braille, what am I supposed to do? (I was using the little-blind-bastard ploy that hadn't worked on my grandfather with Vesuvio; it didn't work on Biff, either.)

"Look," he said, "I don't know you from a hole in the wall, I got enough problems of my own, I don't need a blind man hanging around me all the time asking questions."

"Biff," I persisted, "if you saw me walking down Broadway with a cup full of pencils, you'd take pity on me, wouldn't you?"

"Oh, sheeee-it," he said.

"Biff, all I'm asking you to do is take me around a little, help me to understand the styles, okay? And then if I decide I want to play bop . . . which is what *you* advised me to do, right? am I right?"

"Yeah, yeah," he said.

"Then all I want you to do is give me a lesson every now and then. Or even if I decide to play Tatum, okay? I just need some help, that's all. I can't take it off the records anymore, I'm not getting anywhere."

"Where in hell you want to *go*, man?" he asked.

"I want to be the best jazz piano player who ever lived."

"Oh, sheeee-it," he said again.

"I can't pay you much for the lessons, Biff. . . ."

"Ain't gonna *be* no lessons," he said.

"Fifteen, twenty dollars a week maybe, that's what I was paying the man who taught me classical music. . . ."

"Man, you one hell of a pushy blind person, you know that?"

"I've got to be," I said.

He was quiet for a long time.

Then he said, "I must be outa my fuckin' mind."

Fifty-second Street was pure gold. I very nearly suffered a cardiac seizure the first time Biff took me downtown and I learned (he had saved it as a surprise) that Tatum was playing at the Famous Door, with a bassist and a guitarist as his sidemen. We got there at ten, and I sat there in ecstasy till two in the morning, when Biff took me up to meet Tatum. The next night we went to hear Sidney Bechet, an old-time New Orleans soprano sax player, and the night after that Biff took me to hear Coleman Hawkins at the Onyx. Biff had played with Hawkins many years back, and he told me this man could shake down the Empire

283

State Building with his horn. Man, he shook me to the roots. He was playing with two young musicians who had cut their chops on bop, a drummer named Max Roach, and a trumpet player named Howard McGhee. Biff asked me to pay particular attention to the drummer, who had learned from Klook Clarke (another new name to me), and I listened to him very carefully and did not like what I heard. The next night we went to the Downbeat and listened to Red Norvo on the vibraphone, and the night after that we caught Eddie Condon playing Chicago-style jazz, and Biff introduced me to him, and later told me he was the one who'd said, "The boppers *flat* their fifths; we *drink* ours." For the next six months, or seven, or eight, Biff and I walked from door to door on the Street, and then taxied downtown or crosstown to every jazz joint he could find, listening to the main attractions and the intermission bands. For me, it was like rushing through an encapsulated chronology of jazz from its earliest beginnings to its then current form, all the giants and near-giants assembled, blowing for all they were worth in cabarets stinking of booze and smoke— Bobby Hackett, Don Byas, John Kirby, Pee Wee Russell and Bud Freeman and Zutty Singleton and, of course, the Bird—who was playing at the Three Deuces with a band that spelled Erroll Garner, who was the feature attraction.

I hated what the boppers were doing. I'd hated their music on the few records I'd heard, and I hated it all over again hearing them in person. I cursed Kenny Clarke, who, Biff told me, was the first drummer to stop playing time, hated the klook-a-mop explosions that erupted unexpectedly from bass drum or snare like mortar shells in an undeclared war. I hated those flatted fifths the horn men were playing, though Biff told me he'd first heard them played on a *piano* as far back as 1940 (while I was still laboring over Chopin) by a man named Tadd Dameron, who was also one of the first to play in what Biff described as "the legato manner," using his English accent, which I learned was both defensive *and* derisive. I think he hated bop as much as I did, but he was stuck

284

with it, he recognized it as the wave of the future, and like my Uncle Nick, he wasn't about to buck the system. I hated Gillespie and I hated Parker and I hated Powell and Wallington, Pettiford and Monk, and the whole damn gallery of men who were, it seemed to me, forcing me to change my path even before I'd firmly placed a foot upon it.

To me—I was eighteen and eager and excited and ambitious—these men were doing this deliberately, were trying to screw up my life, were out to get *me* personally. I wasn't far from wrong. They were out to get Whitey, though he was known as Charley in those days. They were playing music they thought the white man could not steal, changing the names of songs so that when they played them with strangely revised charts, they would be unrecognizable to square Charley—"Ornithology" was "How High the Moon"; "A Dizzy Atmosphere" was "I Got Rhythm"; "Hot House" was "What Is This Thing Called Love?"; "Donna Lee" was "Back Home in Indiana." The machine-gun chatter in the early stages of this war was an idiomatic cliché vocalized as "Bu-REE-bop," or "Du-BEE-bop," and probably deriving from Gillespie's "Salt Peanuts," a tune with a I, VI, II, V chord pattern and a Sears Roebuck bridge. Salt-PEA-nuts—the tonic, the octave, and the tonic again. The "Salt" was an eighth note on the second beat of the bar, followed by an eighth-note rest. The "PEA" was an eighth note on the upper tonic, and the "nuts" was an eighth note on the tonic below; beamed together they comprised the third beat of the bar. And there you were—"Ru-BEE-bop" or "Bu-REE-bop," later shortened to "bebop" or "rebop," and finally to "bop" as the definitive label for the new jazz.

Freed from the need to express themselves in an archaic musical tongue, the boppers invented a shorthand verbal language as well, and this became the coinage of everyday communication. A word like "ax" was first used to describe a horn of any kind, but its scope rapidly expanded to include *any* instrument, even the guitar and piano, which are about as far removed from an actual ax as

285

a giraffe is from a water buffalo. The word "gone" was initially an abbreviation of the expression "out of this world." If you are out of this world, why, then you are literally gone, no? But it was also used in brief exchanges such as this:

"So I'll see you Tuesday, man."

"Gone."

The "gone" meant "okay," or "all right," or "agreed," and was frequently used interchangeably with the word "crazy," which also expressed approval, and which was sometimes linked with the word "like."

"Like three bills for the gig, cool?"

"Like crazy."

"Like" was probably the most overworked word in the new jazz vocabulary. If, on the battlefield, soldiers (black *and* white) were using "fuck" in its numberless variations—"Pass the fuckin' ammunition, you fuck, or fuck if I give a fuck what fuckin' happens" —so were black musicians at home using "like" with every fucking breath.

"I was like walking along, when I dug this wigged-out chick, she like gassed me."

"Like I'm short of gold, you got like a pad for me tonight?"

"Like, dig, man, you puttin' me on?"

"Like I got eyes for like retiring like in Paris."

"Like gone, man."

"Like I like *love* you like."

Like *I* like *hated* it, man.

I hated the music, which I thought was simplistic, crude, mysterious, irritating, architecturally inept, and utterly without warmth or feeling. I figured the only reason Bud Powell was playing such primitive stuff was because he had tiny hands, as Biff had pointed out, and couldn't reach those resounding Tatum chords. Tatum had riches to squander; he threw gold coins into the air, rubies poured from his ears, he swallowed emeralds and belched black pearls. Bop seemed impoverished to me, and the boppers—

for all their dexterity—made music I considered emotionless and cold. I know a lot of jazz players who assign colors to keys. B flat will become brown, F will be green, E pink—meaningless references for me. I think instead in terms of warmth or lack of it. D is my favorite key, but only because it represents the *feel* of sunshine, and not because I think of it as saffron or burnt umber. Keys, as a matter of fact, have never meant very much to me. The problem confronting me each time I sit at the piano is not what *key* I'm going to play in, but only what I'm going to *do* with the tune. If I'm going to bomb out in E flat, I'll bomb out in G as well. As far as I was concerned, the boppers were bombing out in all twelve keys, and if they were playing in *any* color at all, it was the opposite of black, which most of them were; the music they made was cold and white. Dead white. I listened to it, and I thought This can't be it, this can't be where it's going, this has got to be a fad.

I hated them for systematically and maliciously (I thought) destroying a sound I had loved instantly and without reservation from the first minute I'd heard it; I hated them for their exclusivity, which I did not recognize as naked hostility until that day years later when Rex Butler put me down on Broadway; I hated them because they caused me to long for acceptance into their inner circle, where they spoke a childlike code, easily cracked and therefore no code at all, and yet impossible to imitate without incurring derision from them. Actually, I was missing the point, and it took me a long time to realize that Charlie Parker had been right. He understood, intuitively, that jazz as it was being played had come as far as it could ever go. There was no longer any way to modify or refine the existing system; it had to be completely demolished. He had reevaluated the entire harmonic and rhythmic structure and decided—not consciously; none of these decisions are ever conscious—to return jazz to its purest form.

I did not know what to do. I had given up classical piano in favor of jazz, and had hardly registered as an alien before my adopted country exploded in revolution. I now had the choice of sticking with the Tatum style and perfecting it (eating cake, so to speak, while the rabble was clamoring at the palace gates), or learning to play a music I did not like or even understand. I could either go it alone, play solo piano if I chose—solo piano *already* had its head on the chopping block, and George Shearing would lop it off forever in 1947—or I could learn to play with other musicians in small ensembles where the piano player was a part of the rhythm section and, except when taking a chorus, was expected to feed chords to horn players. I had no idea that running down a chart for a horn player could be excitingly heady stuff when the horn players were inventive geniuses like Parker or Gillespie. I did not realize that the bass line of the thirties had indeed been a prison, or that Powell and Wallington and many, many others were freeing the right hand from those cop-out pentatonic runs, more suited to the playing of bagpipes than the playing of piano. In bop, the concentration on the right-hand blowing line—the truly creative line, the invented melody line— was intense. The very system of using hollow shells in the bass demanded that the right hand be innovatively restless at all times, free to express ideas and feelings. And the left hand was no longer rigidly playing the rhythm, but was playing *against* the rhythm—and that was freedom, too. I didn't realize this when I first told Biff I'd made up my mind. I only knew that I could either go it alone, or I could learn to play music with other men in . . . well, a family. If it happened that the family was black, and perhaps angry, that was something I would have to cope with. This was America.

I made the American choice.

❖

Rebecca.
I suppose we have to get to Rebecca sooner or later.

The last time I saw her was when I went back to the Talmadge house to pick up the personal belongings I'd left behind, all of which had been clearly detailed in our separation agreement. When I wrote Rebecca trying to set a time and a date, she wrote back saying she didn't know why I felt I still needed all that "small assorted junk." The small assorted junk included two pieces of sculpture we'd bought in Venice, and a complete set of the *Encyclopaedia Britannica*. Rebecca would not let me take the *Britannica*. She said I'd given it to the family as a gift, and she intended to keep it. I did not argue the point. When I left the house in Connecticut for the last time, I took with me the sculpture and the outdoor furniture and my own extensive record collection, including the jazz I'd first listened to in my brother's room—small assorted junk. I also took with me a Braille edition of *The Well-Tempered Clavier*, which Rebecca had bought for me in London and given to me as a birthday present years ago.

That was the last time I saw Rebecca.

The first time I saw her was in July of 1945. Franklin Roosevelt was dead, and the war in Europe was over, but everyone was saying that the end was still nowhere in sight. An invasion of Japan was expected, and we all knew it would be bloody and costly, but by God we would finish the job in the Pacific the way we had in Europe, all of us out there doing our part—the tobacco-spitting kid from the Ozarks alongside the wisecracking kid from the Bronx and the snooty rich kid from Boston and the divinity student from Duluth and even the handsome sun-bronzed kid who'd tried to dodge the draft because he was making it with four blond starlets in a Malibu beach house, but who'd ended up realizing the fight was *his*, too, he was part of the family, and the family was out there struggling for survival. For me, the war had ended the day they killed Tony. I still believed in the myth, of course; I *had* to if I was to make any sense at all of my brother's death. But victory was a foregone conclusion; America always emerged triumphantly. Even when Roosevelt died, I knew we would pull ourselves together and get on with this distasteful job that needed finishing. In those days, Americans were good workers, possibly because we'd come through the Depression years *longing* for work, and were now grateful for any job that came our way, even if it happened to be war. Today . . . don't ask. If I played piano the way the man who installed our Talmadge kitchen cabinets did his job, people would throw rotten eggs and tomatoes at me. Rebecca later said that the man who'd installed our cabinets was to blame for the divorce, since his shabby work caused a connubial fight that lasted for a week. Rebecca dear, men who install kitchen cabinets, however shoddily, are not responsible for divorce actions.

Biff had been busy teaching me every chart he knew, which he said I had to learn—"That's the nexus, man, the nexus." His method of teaching was . . . well . . . not quite the same as Passaro's. Very often, Biff would give me the chart for a tune, and I would discover that some of the chords were different from the ones on the sheet music. He would tell me to never mind the sheet music, *this* is the right chord. And when I complained that it *couldn't* be the right chord, he would say, "This's the chord we *play*, man. This's the chord that *sounds* right."

A great many jazz musicians are very superstitious people, and Biff was one of them. Erroll Garner, for example, refuses to learn to read music because he thinks it'll fuck up the way he's playing. (Mary Lou Williams told me he *can* read, but Erroll insists he can't and won't learn, besides.) I once got into a discussion with George Shearing about his sound, and the "locked hands" or "block chord" architecture of it, which had as its forerunner the Glenn Miller saxophone section—a clarinet on top of the four saxophones normally found in a big band. I was telling George this meant that the melody could be played in two separate voices an octave apart, and I was about to go into a further technical exploration of it, when I detected (we're both blind, and such detection wasn't easy) that he was becoming a bit agitated, and

290

finally slightly angry, or maybe just frightened. He didn't want to know about it. His block system had only been one of the major shaping forces in the history of jazz piano, emulated by every young piano player in the country (including *me* at one time), but he didn't want his style dissected. He was an articulate man, and he didn't quite put it in these words, but what he was saying was, "Man, don't bug me. I just blow, that's all."

Biff just blew, that was all. He had his own Rube Goldberg system of working with harmony and rhythm, and he explained chords to me the way he'd learned them. "Play me a C-diminished ninth," he'd say, and I'd play it, and he'd say, "That ain't no C-diminished ninth, I don't know *what* that is, man." I'd *played* a C-diminished ninth, all right, but what Biff had *wanted* me to play was a C-dominant chord with a flatted ninth. (Similarly, in Biff's argot, a half-diminished became "a minor flat five.") He taught me all the things he knew, hundreds of charts and tricks, milking the minor, moving voices; he gave me gratuitous advice: "Don't play in B for no horn players, that's a bum key for them, five sharps in it"; he told me stories about jazz men; "There was this one night with Philly Joe Jones, he turned the whole band around with his drumming. Did it as a joke. Got them so fucked up, they lost the meter"; he laid down the law: "Don't you *never* lose the meter, man. You play them chords in their proper order, and you hold them for how long you're supposed to, and that's *it*, man"; issued warnings and proclamations: "Don't you never mess with dope, you hear me? Lots of cats, they go listen to Bird, they go home and try to play like him, and they can't do it, and they figure they got to go shoot dope the way he does. That ain't the answer, dope ain't what makes Bird play like he does. I don't mind drinkin', that goes together, booze and piano does. But you ever shoot a needle in your arm, I'll personally come bust your ass, Iggie, you hear me? Blind or not, I'll kick your ass all over the block I ever hear you're messin' with dope."

The week before I met Rebecca, Biff had taken me up to

291

Harlem with him. He didn't live in Harlem anymore, but he went up there for a haircut every Wednesday. I don't want to get into a dissection of that. All I know is that Biff lived on Canal Street, in a big loft that used to be a hat factory, and there were hundreds of barbershops in the area, including some barber colleges on the Bowery, but Biff went uptown to Harlem for his haircut every Wednesday. I was with him that Wednesday because he wanted me to meet a drummer who was putting together a trio and looking for a piano player. Biff figured I was about ready to get out there on my own; the only way I'd ever *really* learn to play ensemble piano was to start playing with a band. The guy he introduced me to must have been under a hot towel when we came into the barbershop. Biff told him I was a good man, told him I'd been getting down all the bop shit, knew hundreds of charts, and if he hadn't yet hired a piano man for the gig on Staten Island, I was the man Biff was recommending for the job. The guy's name was Herbie Cooper. He kept mumbling all the while Biff talked. Finally, Biff said, "So what do you say, man?"

"This's a union club," Herbie mumbled. "You union?"

"No," I said. "But I can join."

"Costs more'n a bill to join," Herbie said. The barber must've taken off the towel; I could suddenly understand him. "Gig don't pay but seventy-five a week."

"How long you booked for?" Biff asked.

"Just a week. Hardly be worth the kid makin' that kind of investment."

"He got to join the union sooner or later," Biff said. "Might's well be now."

"How old're you?" Herbie asked.

"I'll be nineteen in October."

"Your folks goan fuss 'bout you playin' a club way out on Staten Island?"

"Don't worry about that," I said.

"How you goan *git* there, man?" Cooper said.

"I don't know," I said. "How're *you* gonna get there?"

"I got a car," Herbie said. "Where you live, man?"

"In the Bronx."

"I ain't goan way to the Bronx to pick up no piano player. I can git me a piano man lives right aroun' the corner here, an' he damn good, too, used to play with Lunceford."

"If he used to play with Lunceford," Biff said, "he ain't goan take no fuckin' job in a Staten Island toilet for seventy-five a week. How much *you* gettin' as leader, Herb?"

"I don't see as that's rightly your business," Herbie said.

"Give the kid a break," Biff said. "You got my word he's a good man. What the hell more you need?"

"*You* goan pick him up in the Bronx, man? I need a blind piano player like I need a fuckin' hole in the head."

"I'll come to Harlem," I said. "If you'll give me a ride from here, that'll be fine."

"Gig starts this Saturday. You goan be able to join the union an' all by then?"

"I'll do it tomorrow," I said.

"We all colored in this band," Herbie said as his final defense.

"I'm blind," I said, as mine.

"Well, you go join the fuckin' union, an' git back to me by Friday. I ain't heard from you by then, I git me another piano man."

"I'll call you soon as everything's set," I told him.

"Fuckin' kid better be good," Herbie said to Biff.

Which is how I happened to be playing piano in a bar on Staten Island on the night of July 18, 1945, when a girl standing near the piano said, "That's a nice Erroll Garner imitation."

This was my first paying job. I had started on Saturday night, and this was Wednesday, and whereas no bedazzled teen-ager had yet come up to the bandstand and requested a plaster cast of my cock, I was nonetheless learning that simply being up there, and visible, and making music was somehow attractive to certain types of girls. There are, I'm sure, countless theories to explain why some girls will go to bed with musicians after no more formal an introduction than a single chorus of "Stardust." ("Stardust," by the way, is a joke tune to jazz musicians. Whenever anyone says, "Let's play 'Stardust,'" the whole band breaks up. It has a good melody, but a totally dumb white chart.) I have never been able to understand the groupie phenomenon. I have never been able to understand the telephone, either, but that hasn't prevented me from using it over the years. After I hit it big in 1955, it was not uncommon for girls to come to the piano, and, without preamble, whisper, "Let's ball, Ike."

This girl standing at the piano was Jewish. I knew that voice. For those of you who are not familiar with it, I refer you to the *other* Barbra Streisand. There are *two* Barbra Streisands. One of them sings. The other one talks. The singer enunciates each and every word clearly and meticulously; you cannot find a vocalist anywhere in the world who has more respect for lyrics. The talker is a Jewish girl from the Bronx (or Brooklyn—the difference is slight). I am not for one moment suggesting that Barbra Streisand goes to bed with blind jazz musicians; I have certainly never had the pleasure myself. (Please don't call me, Barbra, I've got enough problems right now.) But you don't grow up in Harlem and later an Italian section of the Bronx without learning that *all* Jewish girls put out. The girl at the piano was Jewish, and she had just delivered a perfectly acceptable opening line—"That's a nice Erroll Garner imitation"—and just as my grandfather had entertained high hopes of 'na bella chiavata the night he and Pino dated those two "American" girls back in 1901, I now assumed I was on the verge of terminating the celibacy imposed by the return of Susan Koenig's brother. I waited till we finished the set. The girl was still standing there. I turned to her and smiled.

"How do you know *he* isn't imitating *me?*" I said.

"I meant it as a compliment," she said.

"Well, thanks," I said. "I like him a lot."

"So do I. Marvin took me to hear him a few weeks ago."

"Marvin?" (Mild foreboding.)

"My boyfriend."

"Oh. I take it he likes jazz."

"Oh, yeah, he digs it even more than I do."

"He *digs* it, huh?" (Defensive sarcasm.) "Well, well, well."

"Yes. He was the one who suggested we come all the way out here tonight. We came over on the ferry."

"That's nice," I said. (What does she want? Why'd she come up here to the piano?)

"Well," she said, "I've got to go now."

"Is that *it?*" I asked.

"Huh?"

"I mean, is *that* why you came up here? To tell me it was a nice Garner imitation, and your boyfriend is Marvin, and you came over on the ferry?"

"Yeah. What'd you think?"

"Well . . ." (Desperate fumbling.) "Some people come up with requests or . . ."

"No."

"Okay."

"It *was* a nice Garner imitation."

"Thank you." (Hope springs eternal.) "What's your name?"

"Rebecca. What's yours?"

"Iggie."

"*Iggie?*"

"That's short for Ignazio."

"Oh. Well, Iggie, thanks again. Marvin and I really enjoyed . . ."

"You're not leaving right this minute, are you?"

"Yes, it's late. We've got a long ride back to the Bronx."

"What's your phone number?"

"Why?"

295

"I'd like to call you."

"Why?"

"Well . . ." (To *fuck* you, why do you think? You're Jewish, aren't you?) "To talk about . . . uh . . . jazz and . . . uh . . . Garner and . . . uh . . ." (Uh, *shit!*)

"We don't have a phone."

"Well, how does Marvin get in touch with you? Like when he wants to go 'dig' jazz someplace, how does he let you know? Does he send a carrier pigeon?"

"He calls Shirley."

"And takes *her* instead?"

"No." (A suppressed laugh at my devastating wit?) "We don't have a phone yet because we just moved into a new apartment. Shirley lives across the hall."

"What's her last name?"

"Ackerman. But don't call her."

"Why not?"

"Well, what's the sense?" she said.

"Why'd you come up here?" I asked.

"I wanted to see what you looked like up close."

"What did I look like far away?"

"Okay." (A shrug in her voice?)

"What do I look like up close?"

"Okay." (Another shrug?)

"So?" I said.

"So?"

"Let me call you."

"I'd rather you didn't."

"Is the phone listed in Shirley's name?"

"No."

"What's her father's name?"

"Don't call, okay? I mean it."

"Okay," I said.

"I mean it."

296

"I said okay. What color are your eyes, Rebecca?"

"Green," she said.

"My mother's eyes are green."

"What color are yours?"

"Blue."

"Blue," she said. "Well, good night," she said.

"Good night," I said.

❖

I called the following night, a Thursday. I started calling at six o'clock, before heading crosstown to Harlem where Herbie was waiting to take me to Staten Island again. I knew Rebecca lived in the Bronx, and I knew that her friend, Shirley Ackerman, lived across the hall. I did not know Shirley Ackerman's father's first name (nor even the name of Lincoln's mother's doctor's dog). I asked my mother to read me all the Ackerman phone numbers listed in the Bronx directory. There were two columns of them. Patiently, she recited the numbers as I punched them out with my stylus. Then I carried the phone and the list into the bathroom, and closed the door on the telephone cord, and began dialing. Blind people, if you are interested, invented the digital system of dialing long before the telephone company did. That's because we count the holes in the dial when we're telephoning anyone. The first hole is just the number 1, but the second hole is the number 2 and also the letters ABC. The third hole is 3 and DEF and the fourth hole is 4 and GHI and a partridge in a pear tree. When dialing the prefix OL 4, therefore, I automatically translated it to 654. That was the prefix for the twelfth number I dialed. There was a Shirley Ackerman at only one of the numbers I'd dialed previously, but she did not know a Rebecca across the hall. My second Shirley Ackerman answered the telephone, and when I asked if she would run across the hall to get Rebecca for me, she said, "Who's this?"

"A friend from school," I said.

"From Barnard?" she asked, surprised. Barnard was an all-girls' school.

"Columbia," I said, recovering quite nimbly, I thought.

"What's your name?" she asked.

"Just tell her it's the guy who helped her with her English homework that time."

"Well, don't you have a name?" Shirley asked.

"Yes, but she doesn't know it, it wouldn't mean anything to her. Just tell her what I said."

"Well," Shirley said dubiously, but she put down the phone and went to call Rebecca across the hall. I thought I'd been pretty clever. It seemed to me that at one time or another Rebecca *must* have accepted English-homework assistance from one male student or another.

The first thing she said when she picked up the phone was, "I told you not to call."

"What are you doing tonight?" I asked.

"I'm seeing Marvin."

"How about tomorrow night?"

"I'm seeing Marvin tomorrow night, too, and every night till we get married."

"What are you doing the night *after* you get married?" I said.

"What do you want, Iggie?" she asked.

"I want to see you."

"Why?"

"Why the hell not?" I said.

"I love Marvin."

"That's a good reason," I said.

"Okay?"

"I didn't realize it was that serious."

"It is," she said.

"Okay. Look, lots of luck, huh? Forgive me for calling. I honestly didn't realize . . ."

298

"That's all right," she said.

"Well, so long then."

"So long," she said.

I hung up, and immediately dialed Susan Koenig's number. Her brother answered the phone.

"Who's this?" he said, before even saying "Hello."

"Iggie," I said. "Who's *this*?"

"Franklin," he said.

"Benjamin or Roosevelt?" I asked.

"What are you, a wise guy?" he asked, and hung up.

I tried again just before I left for Harlem, and this time I was lucky enough to avoid his surveillance system. I told Susan I still thought of her fiercely and passionately (this was already more than a year after Fodderwing had returned from the Pacific), and I suggested in the most delicate language I could muster that it was neither psychologically sound nor genetically safe for a girl to be fucking her own brother.

Susan said, "I don't know what you're talking about," and hung up.

On Saturday night, the band concluded its Staten Island engagement. I told Herbie how happy I'd been, and expressed the hope that I'd fulfilled his expectations.

"You was adequate, man," he said magnanimously.

❖

The meeting between Biff and my grandfather takes place in a club in Greenwich Village, where Biff is playing a one-night stand. He is late arriving, and the owner of the place is in an uproar. Biff placates the boss, stops briefly at our table to be introduced, and then excuses himself, saying he has to go to the men's room. The moment he is gone, my grandfather whispers, "Ignazio?"

"Yes, Grandpa?"

"This man is a *nigger*, did you know that?"

"Yes, Grandpa."

"*Eh!*" he says, or something that sounds like "*Eh!*" an explosion of breath that translates into English as "Okay, you know it; I just wanted to make sure you knew it."

As sidemen that night, Biff is using a drummer, a bass player, and two horn men—one on trumpet, the other on sax—the usual instrumentation for a bop combo. The set they play is strictly Parker-Gillespie, all the stuff those two have been laying down, some of the tunes not even named yet, the charts picked up by emulating musicians who put them into the jazz lexicon and only later identify them as "Epistrophy" or "Swingmatism" or "A Night in Tunisia." Biff is in trouble almost from go. He tries desperately to control his trained left hand, but it keeps trying to play time—fleshed-out tenths leap unexpectedly from his fingers, a brief swing bass oom-pahs over the riding ching-ching-ching-ching of the drummer's top cymbals, tenths walk precisely in meter with the bass fiddle. He pulls himself back suddenly, you can feel the effort, and he begins playing shells again, using only two fingers of his left hand, and he tries to get a rhythmic line into his right hand, but the right is trained as well, it responds automatically, filling spaces where he feels *something* is needed, a florid little run sprinkling into that arid bop desert like an impossible rain squall. There is something hysterical about the way he plays, and something bitter, too. The marvelous counterpoint I'd listened to on my brother's records is all but gone. Biff keeps squelching his left and forcing his right into strange new patterns, and it is like listening to half a piano player. The people are responding strangely, I can hear their constant chatter all through the set. They are there to hear Biff Anderson, yes, but in their minds jazz is jazz and they expect Biff to play the jazz they are starting to hear everywhere around them, even though they know this is *not* the kind of jazz upon which he built his reputation. It is quite an odd demand—somewhat like going to see a Clark Gable movie and expecting him to play Andy Hardy.

Biff comes over to the table after the set, and sits down on my right, so that I am between him and my grandfather. He asks my grandfather if he'd care for something to drink, and my grandfather orders a glass of red wine, and Biff tells the waiter he'd like a bourbon and water, and I fill in the lag before the drinks come by asking Biff a lot of questions about the sidemen. When the drinks arrive, my grandfather says, "*Salute,*" and drinks, and makes an odd sound that tells me this is not the sort of red wine *he* is used to making and drinking. Abruptly, he says, "So what about my grandson?"

"You got some grandson here, Mr. Di Lorenzo," Biff says.

"Is he a good piano player?"

"Very good. An' gettin' better all the time."

"What you played," he says. "That was jazz?"

"That was jazz," Biff says.

"I don't like it," my grandfather says.

Biff begins laughing. "You ain't alone."

"Do *you* like it?"

"Well, that's a difficult question to answer," Biff says. "It's changin' right now. It's in the mist of change, you dig? If you mean do I like playin' piano, yes, I love it. It's what I've been doin' all my life, and I guess it's what I'll keep *on* doin'." Biff laughs again. "That is, if they *let* me."

"Who?" my grandfather says.

"The people who're changin' it all."

"What people?"

"Mainly Parker, Powell, and Gillespie. Klook. Them."

"Why don't you go see them?" my grandfather asks. I think he feels these men are politicians like Marcantonio, people you can go to with complaints or requests for favors. I don't think he quite understands that they are musicians, and that the revolution in jazz is not being legislated.

"I've seen them," Biff says.

"You told them?"

301

"Told them what?"

"That you don't like it?"

"No. No, I didn't tell 'em that, Mr. Di Lorenzo."

"Why not?"

"Well, it don't matter to them what *I* like or don't like. They're playin' what *they* feel."

"Do you play what *you* feel?"

"I try. It's . . . well, it's like learning a new language, that's all. You got to put your feelings into new words."

"Ah," my grandfather says. This he understands. He has been trying to learn a new language for forty-four years now. "Are you teaching this language to Ignazio?"

"Yes, sir."

"How can you teach it if you don't understand it?"

"Oh, I *understand* it, all right. I just don't quite *feel* it yet."

"Ah," my grandfather says, and strikes a match. "You want a see-gah?" he asks Biff.

"I don't smoke," Biff says.

"Tell me some more things."

"What do you want to know?"

"Is this where you play jazz? In bars?"

"Mostly."

"This is where Ignazio will play jazz?"

"In better places than this, I hope. This is a toilet, Mr. Di Lorenzo."

"Yes," my grandfather agrees. "But even in better places, they'll still be bars, eh?"

"Bars, clubs, cabarets, yes. That's mostly where jazz is played."

"Mm," my grandfather says. "You drink a lot?"

"Enough."

"Mm," my grandfather says.

"Booze and piano go together," Biff says.

"Mm," my grandfather says. "Why?"

302

"Because there's always a drink on top of the piano."

"The girls here," my grandfather says, and pauses. "*Mi sembrano puttane*, you understand me?"

"No."

"He says the girls look like prostitutes."

"Some of them are," Biff says.

"Mm," my grandfather says. "Where do you play in these bars? In New York?"

"All over. All over the country. Or at least I used to. I even played in Paris and Stockholm."

"Paris, eh? Paris."

"France," Biff says.

"But now you play only in New York, eh?"

"I can't get many gigs other places."

"Jobs," I explain to my grandfather.

"Mm, jobs. Why not?"

"Because it doesn't last that long."

"What doesn't?"

"A career in jazz."

"*How* long?"

"Five, six years. Seven the most. I'm just hangin' on now, Mr. Di Lorenzo. I was on the way down long before this new stuff came in. I'm talkin' about big money. I can still earn a living, more or less, but I don't make big money no more."

"What do you call big money? If you play jazz, what's big money?"

"Well, I was pullin' down three, four bills a week in the thirties, an' that's when people were starvin', and I'm not nowhere near the piano player Tatum or Wilson is. I guess Art is still makin' . . . what? a thousand a week? But I ain't sure how long that's gonna last for him, not with this new jazz we've been tellin' you about. An' that's just playin' club dates; he makes money on his records, too, and other stuff." I hear Biff lifting his glass. He drinks, I hear him swallow, he puts the glass back on the table and says, "Mr. Di Lorenzo, I get the feeling you don' want no bullshit where it concerns your grandson's prospects. . . ."

"That's right, no bullshit."

"So, okay, I'll lay it right on the line. I already told you he's a good musician. I don't know where he's goin' yet, but lots of young kids comin' up today don't know where they're at, either; this bop ain't so easy as you think. You hear Bird play, you want to go out an' hang yourself, I'm not kiddin'. He's that good, he's that brilliant, you just want to go kill yourself. Instead, you try to do on *your* instrument whatever he's doin' on his saxophone, an' that's where it is today, and Iggie—if he keeps up with this—will have to do Parker on the piano, I s'pose, same way everybody *else* is doin' Parker on whatever instrument they play. That's where it's at now; I can't tell you how long it'll last, but even when it's gone, I know for sure it'll have changed everything for keeps. What I'm sayin' is I think Iggie's got the chops, the hands, Mr. Di Lorenzo, and he's got real feeling for what he plays, and I think he's got a good head, too, but that don't mean it'll be easy for him.

"It won't be easy 'cause first of all he's blind. I know Iggie good enough to talk about his bein' blind without fear of offendin' him; I wouldn't hurt him for anything in the world. But he's blind, Mr. Di Lorenzo, and he's gonna run into a lot of the same things colored musicians are up against. Not 'cause he's colored, but 'cause he's blind. He can't read regular music, he can only read Braille, and that means he won't be able to get jobs that are bread-an'-butter jobs to good paper men—men who can read music good. I mean, even if by some miracle some Broadway producer decided to hire Iggie to play for a big musical, and wanted to have Iggie's part written out in Braille, even if that happened, why, Mr. Di Lorenzo, it would just be too much *trouble* for everyone concerned, they just wouldn't be able to *cope* with a blind man in an orchestra pit, you understand me?"

"I understand you," my grandfather says, and quickly covers my hand with his own.

"So let's count that out as a possibility. Iggie ain't gonna be called in by no contractor who needs a piano player to fill a chair on a big-band record date, and ain't no radio station gonna call him up to do studio work, an' he's not about to get a rush call from the guy runnin' *Carousel*, just forget them as possibilities, okay? That means he'll have to make it either as a solo piano player or with a small group, and I think he already knows solo piano is on its last legs; where jazz is at today is in the small group. He's got to work hard, and get his bag of tricks together, and start himself a group makin' the right sound in the right time and in the right place. An' he'll start makin' some records with that group, and if they catch on, he'll have it made. He gets a couple of hit records, he can count on some good club dates followin' them, and some real gold playin' and makin' more records that'll bring in royalties, and so on, it'll keep mushroomin' for maybe five or six years, he can be pullin' down, oh, say fifty thousand, seventy-five thousand a year while he's on top. If he doesn't just blow that gold, he can make himself some good investments so that when things begin to taper, when the records stop sellin' because maybe another sound has come in, or another style, or another piano player comes up with the right thing in the right time an' place, why, then Iggie'll have enough to tide him over while he ain't makin' as *much* gold but is still playin' here and there because people still know his name. He's got to *make* it first, you understand. Lots of guys *never* make it.

"There's things he's gonna have to deal with whether he makes it or not. They're all part of jazz, and you might as well know the whole story, you said you didn't want no bullshit. He's gonna be playin' mostly in clubs. And there're gonna be whores in lots of those clubs, because that's where whores hang out. Even if he don't run with whores, there are gonna be *other* women, they dig musicians, I don't know what it is. And he's gonna be traveling

305

around a lot playing these clubs, and I got to tell you marriage and music don't go together, I been married and divorced twice myself, though I ain't even sure the last divorce is legal. And there's gonna be gangsters in lots of them clubs because gangsters *own* most of them. And there's gonna be booze, because like I told you before, booze and the piano *do* go together. There's also gonna be dope, because lots of these new musicians comin' up think dope's gonna help them play like Bird, an' even if they *didn't* believe that, there's always been dope around jazz music, I know guys who were usin' cocaine when I was still playin' in Kansas City, that's just the way it is. I already told Iggie I'd break his arm if he ever went near no narcotics, and I think he knows I'm not kiddin' him.

"But all these bad things in jazz ain't what should be concernin' you, Mr. Di Lorenzo. What you should be thinkin' about are the *good* things. And they got nothin' to do with makin' a lot of gold, or becomin' famous, or whatever. They got to do with the way playin' jazz makes you *feel*. Pee Wee Russell once told somebody—he's a clarinet player, Mr. Di Lorenzo—he once told somebody the moment of truth comes for him each time he stands up to take his chorus, that's the most important thing in his life. Well, it *is*, Mr. Di Lorenzo. It's jumpin' in the middle of the ocean. It ain't swimmin' out gradually, it's jumpin' right out to where you can't see no land no more, it's usin' everything you know to stay afloat and to swim however far out you think you can, and then like magic you get whisked right back there to shore again, and you wrap it all up with a big yellow ribbon, and there you are, and you feel good and clean and happy all over, and there ain't many things I know that can make you feel that way in life, Mr. Di Lorenzo, there just ain't many I know of."

My grandfather has been silent through all this, and he is silent now for several more minutes. Biff lifts his glass again. I sense he is a bit uneasy; perhaps he thinks he's gone too far. He is not at the piano where he can jump into the middle of that ocean

306

he described, and swim out as far as he dares. My grandfather is, to him, an unknown quantity. He waits.

My grandfather says, "I never talked to a colored man before. I don't understand why you should care about Ignazio."

"Why shouldn't I?" Biff answers. "Used to be a nice, friendly feeling in jazz, Mr. Di Lorenzo. Used to be you *played*. That's changin'. And maybe I got to change my *style* to keep up with what's comin' in, but, man, I don't have to change the way I *feel*. I got to get back on the stand," he says. "You goan stay for another set?"

"Yes," my grandfather says.

He orders another glass of wine and listens while the band plays a set that includes "A Dizzy Atmosphere," "Anthropology," and "Keen and Peachy." As they play, I think Yes, I will make between fifty and seventy-five thousand dollars a year, and yes, I will cut records and I will make sound investments so that when another piano player comes up with the right sound in the right time and place I'll have enough to tide me over and I'll still be playing because people will remember my name.

Iggie Di Palermo, I think.

They will know my name, and they will remember it.

I will *make* it.

I will not be one of those guys who never make it.

"Pffffff," my grandfather says. "What *noise*."

❖

By Christmas of 1945:

1. My mother had been visited on earth by the Virgin Mary, who displayed a worldly wisdom unbecoming to the Mother of God, almost destroying a happy family in the Bronx, and causing an innocent house painter to suffer the lifelong torments of Stella's silent treatment.

2. My Aunt Victoria, at the age of sixty-four, had finally found

307

herself a husband, a widowed Sicilian pig farmer who lived in New Jersey with five hulking sons, spoke barely a word of English, and reputedly beat her regularly with a sawed-off rake handle.

3. Pino Battatore's son, Tommy, had either jumped or been pushed to his death on the elevated tracks of the Third Avenue El one black September midnight. The police found four thousand dollars in cash in the inside pocket of his jacket, together with a large collection of policy slips. When the cops told Pino his son had probably been involved in the numbers racket, Pino told them they were lying bastards.

4. My Aunt Bianca's boyfriend, Rafaelo the butcher, had dashed into her corset shop one bright October day shouting, "Bianca, he caught me, he caught me!" scaring her half out of her wits till she realized he was making reference to the man upstairs, who had just stumbled upon the butcher in bed with his wife. My Aunt Bianca, who'd been working on a brassiere, belatedly stuck her sewing needle into Rafaelo's left buttock, thereby effectively ending their relationship.

5. My Uncle Dominick's unmarried, sixteen-year-old daughter had got herself pregnant by a detective in Brooklyn, where Dominick now lived next door to his wife's parents, who ran a pizzeria on Coney Island Avenue.

Now *that*, my friends, is the stuff upon which soap operas are built. I made it all up. But only because I wanted to prove I could easily find a job writing for CBS if ever I became arthritic and couldn't play piano anymore. I'm also about to make up what happened on that Christmas Day in 1945. You'll know it's another lie the moment you read it.

My grandfather's house was abnormally cheerless. We had none of us grown accustomed to Tony's death; I doubted if we ever would. My Uncle Dominick was spending Christmas Day with his wife's family in Brooklyn, and Aunt Victoria was in New Jersey with her sadistic pig farmer, and Uncle Joe had canceled (again) his promised trip from Arizona, and Pino was in mourning and would have considered it sacrilege to have played the mandolin. When the telephone rang, my Aunt Bianca rushed to answer it, hoping (I think) that it was the butcher. "Iggie," she said, "it's for you."

I got up from the dining room table. I had been sitting very close to my grandfather, because he'd been oddly silent all through the meal, and I wanted to touch him every so often, just to make sure he was there and all right. I touched him now as I went to the phone, just rested my hand on his shoulder for a moment, and he covered it briefly with his own, and then I went out into the hallway and put one finger in my ear as I picked up the receiver, hoping to drown out the clatter of the women doing dishes in the kitchen.

"Hello?" I said.

"Iggie?" a woman asked. She was black.

"Who's this?" I said.

"You don't know me," she said. "Biff ast me t'call. Said I should try the Bronx first, an' if you wasn't there, I should look up Lorenzo, *Di* Lorenzo in Harlem. Is this Iggie?"

"Yes," I said

"Biff's sick," she said. "Can you come down here right away? I don't know whut t'do."

"What's the matter with him?"

"Well, like you know, man."

"No, I don't know. What is it?"

"Well, like can you jus' come down here right away?"

"Have you called a doctor?"

"No," she said. "Can you get here right away, please?"

"Well, what . . . ?"

"Please, man," she said.

"Where are you? Canal Street?"

"Yes."

"All right," I said. "Tell him I'm on the way."

I put the receiver back on the cradle, and went into the bedroom for my coat.

"Who was that?" my mother said.

"Biff's sick. I have to go down to Canal Street."

"Does he know you're blind, your nigger friend?"

"He knows it, Mom."

"So why is he dragging you out of the house on Christmas Day?"

"*Che successe?*" my grandfather asked.

"Biff is sick," I said.

"*Where* did you say you're going?" Aunt Bianca asked.

"*Canal* Street," my mother said.

"I'll take a taxi, don't worry about me."

"I'll go with you," my father said.

"I can get there okay, Pop."

"Let him go, Jimmy," my mother said. "The hell with him *and* his nigger friends."

"I got the cab right downstairs," Matt said. "You want me to drive you down?"

"Thanks, Uncle Matt, I'll be all right."

"Iggie," my grandfather said.

"Yes, Grandpa?"

"*Stat' attento,*" he said. "Be careful."

"I will, Grandpa."

I went downstairs, and stood on the corner outside the *pasticceria,* waiting for a cab heading downtown, raising my cane whenever *any* kind of vehicle approached. I must have been standing in the cold for perhaps ten minutes, regretting having turned down my Uncle Matt's offer, when suddenly an automobile pulled to the curb.

"Where are you going?" a girl's voice asked.

"Canal Street," I said.

"You'll never get a taxi, this is Christmas," she said. "You want to share mine?"

"Thank you," I said.

I heard the door opening. I felt for it, edged my way around it, and using it as a guide and a support, climbed into the taxi. I was reaching over to pull the door shut behind me, when the girl said, "Can you manage?"

"Yes, thank you."

"Okay," she said.

I closed the door, slamming it to prove I was entirely capable of performing such a simple action.

"Don't break the window, huh, Mac?" the cabby said.

"Sorry," I said.

"So what is it now? Houston, then Canal?"

"Yes," the girl said.

The driver put the cab into gear and pulled away from the curb. The girl and I sat side by side in silence.

"This is very kind of you," I said at last, in apology for having slammed the door.

"Listen," she said, "don't I know what it's like trying to get a cab?" Her voice was pure Bronx Jewish. I suddenly thought of Rebecca, the girl with the green eyes. We rode the rest of the way downtown without saying another word to each other. On Houston Street, the girl directed the driver to the building she wanted, and then offered to pay him what was on the meter. I told her that wasn't necessary, I'd take care of it when I got to Canal Street. She then offered to pay at least half, but I refused that as well. Sighing, she got out of the cab, said, "Happy Chanukah," and slammed the door behind her.

"*Everybody's* tryin' to bust my windows today," the cabby said, and threw the taxi into gear again, and squealed it away from the curb. He was silent for several moments, and then suddenly and angrily said, "Why'n't you let her pay?"

"What for?" I said. "I'd still be standing on that corner if it hadn't been for her."

"For *her*? For *me*, you mean. By rights, I ain't supposed to

311

pick up no passenger when I already *got* a passenger in the cab. That's ridin' double, an' that ain't allowed. By rights, when I let her out on Houston, I shoulda collected what was on the clock and then thrown the flag again. That's by rights."

"What difference does it make?" I said.

"I work percentage, Mac. Every time I throw the flag, I get a percentage of the first drop, too. What do you think I ony get a percentage of ony the rest, is that what you think? By rights, I'm gettin' gypped out of part of the fare."

"I'll make it up on the tip," I said.

"Sure," the cabby said. "Everybody'll make it up on the tip."

"I can't read the meter, anyway," I said, "so just charge me whatever the fuck you want, and shut up, will you?"

"Nice," he said. "Nice for a blind person."

"Just drive the fuckin' taxi," I said.

"Very nice," he said. "Oh, beautiful."

When we got to Canal Street, I paid him what he said was on the meter, and then added a dollar to it. "Can you make it upstairs?" he asked.

"I can make it."

"I'll help you upstairs, if you like."

"I don't need any help, thanks."

"Fuck *you*, too," he said, and drove off.

There was usually an old black man running the cage elevator in Biff's building. But this was Christmas, and after I'd been ringing the bell for several minutes, I realized he probably had the day off. I felt around in the hallway for a door leading to the steps, found a metal fire door, eased it open, and cautiously began climbing. The iron stairwell stank of urine and booze. I had been coming to this building for more than a year now, but I had always been taken up to the third floor in the elevator run by the old black man, who smelled of whiskey a bit, true, but never of tiger piss. Biff had described him to me as a punch-drunk old club fighter who always wore a brown leather jacket and a woolen watch cap. In all the time I'd been taking lessons from Biff, the old man had never said a word to me. I'd get into the elevator, he'd carry me to the third floor, and then pull open the gate and wait for me to get out. The stench began to dissipate as I climbed higher. I figured the ground-floor landing was a haven for bums who wandered over from the Bowery. I kept climbing, tapping the metal steps. I had counted the steps from the ground floor to the first-floor landing, and knew there were thirty-six of them between floors. When I reached the third floor, I opened another fire door, and then located the elevator door so that I could direct myself from there to Biff's loft. There was a bell set into the metal door-jamb there. I knew exactly where it was. I reached for it, and heard the bell ringing inside the loft. Footsteps approached the door.

"Who is it?" a voice said. It was the voice I'd heard on the telephone.

"Iggie," I said.

I heard the night chain being removed, and then the lock being turned. The door opened.

"You're blind," she said at once.

"Yes."

"He didn't tell me. Whut the fuck help *you* gonna be, man?"

"Where is he?"

She closed and locked the door behind me. I knew my way around the loft by heart; it was as familiar to me as my own home in the Bronx. The grand piano, which Biff had bought in better times and never parted with, sat against the Canal Street wall, huge windows above it opening to the street. There was a battered easy chair near the piano, and a mattress on the floor in the middle of the loft. Biff was lying on that mattress. All I could hear was his tortured breathing.

"Biff?" I said.

He did not answer. I reached out to touch him. He was drenched with perspiration. The sheets under him were wet.

313

"Biff?" I said again. I turned to the girl. "Is he unconscious? What's the matter with him?" I was beginning to panic. I could not see him, and he was trembling under my hand, and I did not know what was wrong with him. "Why didn't you call a doctor?"

"I didn't figure it was nothin' at first," the girl said. "He was ony complainin' his neck felt stiff, tha's all. I figured it was bad shit."

"What? What do you mean?"

"Lots of bad shit runnin' roun' the city." She was silent for a moment. She must have been staring at me, she must have been trying to look through my dark glasses and see into my eyes, read what was in my eyes as though I were sighted, trying to fathom my confusion. "Listen," she said, "I thought you an' Biff was friends."

"We are."

"An' you don't know?"

"Don't know *what*, for Christ's sake?"

"That he's a junkie?"

"No," I said. I was not answering her question. I was denying the information she had just given me. "No," I said again.

"Hooked clear through the bag an' back again," she said.

"I don't believe you."

"Come down, man, he been a addict for ten years now."

"Then . . . then . . . what . . . ?" There was a sudden sharp movement on the mattress; his body lurched under my hand.

"Oh, Jesus!" the girl said.

"Where's the telephone?" I said.

"Ain't none here," she said. "I called fum a booth downstairs."

"We've got to get an ambulance," I said.

"What *for*, man? One thing we don't need on Christmas is any heat about dope."

"Where's that phone booth?" I said. "Don't leave him alone, you hear me? Just stay with him while . . ."

"Cool it, man," she said softly. "I'll go make the call."

He died that night. He died of asphyxia or exhaustion or a

combination of both. Medical bullshit. I listened to medical bullshit from an intern in the charity ward of a hospital built twenty years before my grandfather first came to these shores. Biff died in spasm induced by the tetanus bacillus that had infected a subcutaneous abscess on his left arm, undoubtedly caused by repeated insertions of a hypodermic needle. He'd been a dead man a week or two before I'd arrived at the loft that Christmas Day; that was the incubation period, the intern told me, that was how long it had taken for the exotoxin to launch its fatal attack on the central nervous system. He died with his jaws locked shut. He died in a room as black as the color of his skin. (Light, it had something to do with light, they did not want light in the room.) The nurses tiptoed quietly past the door, not because a man was dying inside, but only because any sudden noise (it had something to do with noise) might set off another racking spasm. The spasms were killing him. He was being shaken to death and choked to death, that poor lovely son of a bitch.

I left the hospital at ten minutes past one on the morning after Christmas. That was five minutes after they'd pronounced Biff dead. A thin drizzle was falling. I stood outside the main entrance with the girl. She didn't say anything for a long time. Then she sighed, and said, "Well, that's that, man," and began to weep. She did not want to go back to the loft. I took her to Harlem in a taxi, and then I found a pay phone in a bar where bad jazz musicians were trying to play Charlie Parker, and I called my grandfather's house. He answered the telephone before it rang twice. I told him not to worry, I was okay. I went to the bar, and sat down, and began drinking, and got drunk for the first time in my life. When the black bartender asked me what I was doing up in Harlem, I said, "I don't know. What are *you* doing up in Harlem?" and he laughed.

That's what happened that Christmas Day.

I made it all up.

I like to think, even now, that I made it all up.

315

In 1946, I began playing at a place called Auntie's on Macdougal Street in New York's Greenwich Village. The "auntie" who ran the joint was a crazy old Frenchwoman named Madeleine. She paid me and my sidemen $350 a week for playing six nights a week, from 10 P.M. to two in the morning. I gave the bass man and the drummer a bill apiece, and kept $150 for myself as leader. My bass player was black, my drummer was white. The odd sets were played by a piano man who was black; his name was Oz Rodriguez. Oz was in his late fifties, a gifted musician steeped in Waller and Hines. He played solo piano the way I'd first heard it on my brother's records, spelling us during our fifteen-minute inter-missions and doubling as an accompanist whenever anybody wanted to sing a song. Madeleine was always wanting to sing a song. I sometimes think she opened the club only so she'd get to do her world-famous imitation of Piaf as often as she liked. She used to bug poor Oz out of his mind. Once she came to me and asked if I'd accompany her on "La Vie en Rose." I told her I wasn't an accompanist, I was leader of the house band. She told me she could get another house band any time she wanted. I said she was free to do so, if that was her desire, but the boys and I had built at least *something* of a following since we'd begun play-ing at Auntie's and I'd hate to have to move over to the new club that had opened two blocks south of Sheridan Square, and take good steady drinking clientele to another place. "Ike," she said, "*tu es vraiment un bâtard aveugle.*"

I had adopted the "Ike" the moment I got the steady gig at Auntie's. The name came to me out of the blue. I went into the kitchen one night, and said to my mother, "How do you like Blind Ike?"

She said, "What?"

"For a name," I said.

316

"What do you mean for a name?"

"For the trio. The Blind Ike Trio."

"*Ike?*" she said. "What's that?"

"Instead of Iggie," I said.

"What's the matter with Iggie?"

"Nothing, I just think Blind Ike sounds better. There are lots of blind piano players, you know. George Shearing is blind, you know."

"Does he call himself Blind Ike?"

"Well, no, but . . ."

"Then why do you want to call yourself Blind Ike? Your name is Iggie. What's the matter with *that* name?"

"Nothing, Mom. I'm thinking of what *sounds* better, that's all."

"Iggie sounds fine to me."

"Well, I'm going to tell Madeleine to put it on the poster outside the club. The Blind Ike Trio. Okay?"

"If you decided already, why are you asking me?"

"Because if you ever come down to Macdougal Street, I want you to know who I am."

"I know who you are," she said. "You're Iggie, that's who you are."

(But today she calls me Ike, the same as everyone else.)

I can't remember what kind of piano I was playing back in 1946. I was searching for a style, and stealing from everything I heard. There was a lot to hear. I'd listen to it, and try it for a while, and then abandon it when I heard something I liked better. Jazz musicians are notorious thieves. I'm not talking about the fact that throughout the history of jazz the white man has packaged and commercialized the innovations of the black man. That's not theft. That's American free enterprise. I'm talking about a lick that'll suddenly pop up in a horn solo, deliberately or unconsciously swiped from something the musician heard the night before at another club, or on a record, or hummed from behind the door of a pay toilet. I listened a lot, and stole a lot. Or, to put it more

317

delicately, I was "influenced" a lot. By Nat Cole, Garner, Powell (reluctantly, because I *still* thought he was a crude pianist), Hampton Hawes, Herbie Hancock, Joe Albany, Lennie Tristano, Mary Lou Williams, Clarence Profit, Monk, Oscar Peterson—the only man, incidentally, who ever had the motor skills to play Charlie Parker on the piano, a consummate musician with more technical facility than any of us. I listened to whoever was making records or appearing in person in New York City, and invariably tried to copy what they were doing. The sidemen in the trio— Stu Holman on bass and Cappy Kaplan on drums—were my accomplices in crime. We stole outrageously, casing joints all over the city, busting open a style the way we might a bank vault, plundering what was inside, throwing away the wrappers around the bills, spending all the loot, and then searching for another safe to crack. We were serving our apprenticeship in the only way we could. None of us, you see, were true innovators. But in America, you don't have to be.

I was sitting at the bar. We had just finished a set, and Madeleine was arguing in French with one of her countrymen who kept insisting it was time we forgave the German people. (This was May of 1946; the war in Germany had ended only a year ago!) The voice on my left said, "Hello, Iggie, long time no see."

There are very few accidental meetings in the city of New York. Yes, sometimes you will run into an old classmate, and you will babble on unenthusiastically about old times long forgotten—do you ever see Charlie Hobbs, who used to throw scum bags filled with water from the elevated IRT, whatever happened to Jennie Whatshername, who used to be so good in math, and golly, you've got fourteen kids now, huh, wow, amazing, yes, I'm with Amalgamated Life over in Newark and gee, great to see you again, give my regards home, huh, got to run. That happens rarely; it's a big city. The girl on my left sounded a lot like Rebecca with the green eyes, and she was in Auntie's on Macdougal Street in Greenwich Village, and I had not spoken to her since that

318

Thursday night in July, ten months ago, and I turned to face her, and I held my breath and thought This can't be an accident; if it's her, it can't be an accident. Aloud, I said, "Is it you?"

"Who?" she asked.

"Rebecca."

"Is it Iggie? Or is it Ike?"

"It's Ike, but it's Iggie. Is it you?"

"It's me," she said.

"Where's Marvin?" I asked quickly.

"Marvin? Who's Marvin? Oh, Marvin. Marvin is married."

"Not to you, I hope."

"Not to me. He married a singer. Would you believe it? I think he kept taking me to all those jazz joints only so he could meet a singer."

"Listen," I said, "you didn't happen to pick me up in a taxicab last Christmas, did you?"

"No," she said. "*What?*"

"Outside a *pasticceria* on First Avenue?"

"No."

"Are you sure?"

"Positive. I was in Miami last Christmas."

"I'm glad you're back."

"So am I."

"What's your last name?"

"Baumgarten. What's yours?"

"Di Palermo. How'd you know I was here?"

"I saw an ad in the paper. I figured Blind Ike? Had to be."

"So here you are."

"Here I am."

"So what are you doing Monday night? I'm off Mondays."

"Take it easy," she said.

"Why?"

"Well . . ."

"What is it?"

319

"Well . . . you see, my father has trouble with Italian names."

"Huh?"

"In fact, he has trouble with *any* names that aren't Jewish."

"Huh?"

"He's what you might call a raging bigot."

"You're kidding," I said. "You're kidding, aren't you?"

"Am I? My father's got two specialties—selling Oldsmobiles and hating the goyim."

"What's that?"

"Goyim? That's you. Do you know what a pogrom is?"

"Yes."

"A pogrom is what'll happen if my father ever finds out I came here to see you. He'll come riding down from the north Bronx with his tallis thrown over his shoulder . . ."

"His *what?*"

"That's a prayer shawl."

"Of course it's a prayer shawl," I said. "But your father's got some tallis, too, if he can throw it over his shoulder."

Rebecca burst out laughing, and then sobered immediately. "Listen," she said, "I'm a nice Jewish girl, and . . . and not whatever you're thinking."

"What am I thinking?"

"I mean . . . you know. I don't make a habit of following piano players all over the city."

"I should hope not."

"In fact, I don't know what I'm doing here," she said.

"Well," I said, "look . . . uh . . . why don't you . . . would you like a drink or something? I mean, Jesus, what*ever* you do, don't go running off again, okay?"

"Why'd you call me that time? You didn't even know what I looked like."

"I still don't. What do you look like, Rebecca?"

"I'm gorgeous, what do you think?"

"That's what I think," I said.

"You don't look Italian at all," she said.

"What do Italians look like?"

"Oh, you know, short and dark and . . . not like you."

"I'm really Jewish," I said. "I got kidnapped from my very religious Jewish parents by a band of Sicilian . . ."

"I only wish," she said.

"Why?"

"Because . . . listen, do you want to know something? I got Marvin to take me back to Staten Island two weeks later. But you were gone. There was another band there. I'll tell you the truth, I was relieved. I once went out with an Irish boy, and my father chased him down the stairs."

"Rebecca, you've got to be . . ."

"Michael, his name was. Michael Sullivan."

"Rebecca, let's worry about your father later, okay?"

"No, let's worry about him now."

"Okay," I said, and fell silent.

"Are you worrying?" she asked.

"I'm worrying," I said.

"Where shall I meet you Monday night?" she asked.

❖

It had been a suffocatingly humid week, and the stifling heat in the Mosholu Parkway apartment staggered me as we came through the front door. (There was a mezuzah on the doorjamb, similar to the one my grandfather's "Kasha" had touched her fingers to in the year 1901. I did not see it.) I had been dating Rebecca for close to three months, but I had not yet met her parents. Rebecca had prepared both of them for our impending visit, and Honest Abe Baumgarten had said, predictably, "If you bring a blind *shaygets* up here, I'll shoot him on the spot." The apartment was strange to me, the lingering cooking smells alien. There were voices, men talking and laughing. Rebecca led me into

321

the kitchen. I recognized the sounds of a poker game in progress and suddenly thought of my Uncle Luke. "Daddy," Rebecca said, and the voices stopped.

"Daddy, I'd like you to meet Ike Di Palermo," she said. Her voice had a frightened quaver in it. She was clinging to my left hand, and her own hand was sweating.

"How do you do?" I said, and extended my right hand.

I stood there for several minutes with my hand extended, and suddenly realized no one was going to take it. I pulled it back.

"Who deals?" somebody asked. I later learned this burning question had been put by none other than the Mad Oldsmobile Dealer.

"Ike is a piano player," Rebecca said.

"Do you know 'Far, Far Away'?" someone at the table asked.

I had been playing piano since the time I was six, but I swear to God I had never heard this old saw before. Innocently, I said, "No, I'm sorry, I don't."

"We don't want you to *play* it," the man said. "We want you to *go* it."

"Far, *far* away," someone else said, and everyone burst out laughing.

"Who's shy in the kitty?" Abe asked.

"I don't want to be in the kitty," someone said.

"The kitty is for Ratner's," Abe said. "September fifth, we're going to Ratner's. Get up a nickel."

"I don't want to go to Ratner's," the man said. "Go without me, I don't want to be in no kitty."

"We need a cup for the *fecahkteh* kitty," someone said.

"Anybody got a tin cup?" Abe said.

"Excuse me," I said, and turned to go, and knocked something off the cabinet close to the table. I stooped to pick it up.

"I'll get it," Rebecca said.

"I can find it," I said, and got down on my knees, and scrambled around on the floor for whatever it was, something metallic, an ashtray, a small pot, something; I didn't know *what* the hell it was, and I couldn't *find* it, either. Rebecca said, "Leave it, Ike. I want you to meet my mother."

She took my hand and led me into what I supposed was the living room. The ladies were seated there silently. They had heard the exchange in the kitchen, and were now awaiting my approach.

"Mom, this is Ike," Rebecca said.

"How do you do?" Sophie Baumgarten said. She had risen from the couch or wherever she'd been sitting, and was approaching, I felt her approach. "Won't you shake hands?" she said, and I realized her hand was extended, and I put out my own hand, and she took it. *Her* hand was trembling. This was costing her a lot. "Sit down, why don't you? We were just talking about how hot it's been this week. A *record*, in fact, I heard on the radio last night. Would you like something cool to drink?"

"No, thank you," I said.

"And this is my sister Davina," Rebecca said.

"How do you do?" I said, and extended my hand again.

"Nice to meet you," Davina said. Her voice was pitched a trifle lower than Rebecca's; her handshake was cool, and dry, and firm.

"Are you sure you wouldn't like something to drink?" Sophie asked.

"Thank you," I said, "but Rebecca and I have to be going. Thank you, Mrs. Baumgarten," I said. "Come on, Rebecca," I said.

As she led me past the kitchen, someone at the table said, "Leaving so soon?"

"Shut *up*, Seymour!" Rebecca snapped. I had recognized the voice. Seymour was the man who'd made the request for "Far, Far Away."

"I like your boyfriend," Seymour said. "He seems like a very *Gentile* fellow." He slurred the word "Gentile" so that it sounded almost like "gentle"—but not quite.

"Let's go, Ike," Rebecca said, and led me out of the apartment, slamming the door behind us.

"The lousy bastard," she said.

To this day, I do not know whether she was referring to Seymour or her father.

❖

Rebecca Baumgarten is four years old when her sister is born. Her mother names the new baby Davina, which in Hebrew means "the loved one." Sophie intends no slight to her first-born daughter, whose name in the ancient tongue means "the captivator." But in Rebecca's four-year-old head, the *new* child is the loved one, isn't that what they named her? She asks her grandfather about this.

"*Zayde*," she says, "why do they love Davina and not me?"

"They love you both together," the old man says.

They are sitting outside his dry-goods store on the lower East Side. It is the summer of 1932. The old man is in a cane rocker he bought from the sidewalk stand of Shmuel two doors down. Rebecca sits at his feet on a stool she has dragged from inside the store. The old man wears a black pair of pants, and a white shirt, and a brown sweater with buttons up the front. He wears a black silk yarmulke. She has never seen him without the yarmulke. He has had a white beard for as long as she can remember, and wireframed eyeglasses perched on his nose. His nose is like the Indian's on the buffalo nickel. He is a very handsome man, her grandfather. His name is Itzik Galdek, and he is her mother's father. He came to this country in 1890, from a city named Bialystok, on the Polish border some twenty-five miles from Russia. He explains now that Rebecca's sister was named Davina not because she is any more loved than Rebecca herself, but only because she came second. They are Ashkenazic Jews, he explains, and the Ashkenazim will not name a child after a living relative. When Rebecca was born, in 1928, her grandmother of the same name was already dead, and so she was named after her, which was a great honor because her *bubbeh* was a fine and wonderful woman.

"Rivke, that is your name in Yiddish," he tells her. "Rebecca is what that means, Rivke. Now . . . if your sister had been born first, she would most likely have been named Rivke, she would have been given *your* name, do you see? But your sister was born only last month, isn't that so, and Rivke was all used up already, they had used up this fine and honorable name on *you*, my *bubeleh*, and so your mother had to search around for another name, and she picked one that had been my beloved sister's, who is now dead, too, may she rest in peace, and that is why *she* is Davina and *you* are Rivke, Rebecca, eh? Now tell me what you are learning in Hebrew school."

In Hebrew school, she is learning Biblical stories, prayers, and a smattering of language. Whenever they have dinner at her grandfather's house, she gives the Hebrew blessing. "*Bo-ruch a-toh a-do-noy, e-lo-hay-noo me-lech ho-o-lom, ha-mo-tzee le-chem meen ho-o-retz,*" and each time she has to try very hard not to say "*ha-mo-tzee le-chem* Minnie Horowitz," the way the boys do when they're joking in the streets. She lives two doors away from the dry-goods store, on the third floor of a five-story tenement. The neighborhood is exclusively Jewish, but occasionally the goyim come in to make trouble; they are always making trouble. Her mother will not wear any jewelry if she is out at night, for fear she will be attacked by goyim and robbed of her treasures. This is what her mother calls her wedding and engagement rings, her pearl earrings, a garnet brooch that was Grandmother Rivke's in the old country: her treasures.

"The goyim make trouble because they drink," old Itzik tells her. He has been in this country for forty-two years now, coming to these shores when he was twenty-four. His name was Yitzchak then, the Hebrew for the Biblical Isaac. He is now known by its Yiddish equivalent, Itzik, and already everywhere around him he hears young men being called Isadore and Irving, anglicizations of the name he had proudly worn in Poland. "In Poland," he tells her, "the goyim would drink all the time, and then they would come into the *shtetl* and do terrible things; I do not wish to befoul your young ears with stories of the terrible things they did. Sometimes, the Cossacks would ride in and take men away for the army, spirit them away from home and loved ones, never to be seen or heard from again. The Russians owned Poland then, *bubeleh*, they would come to take the young men, line them up in the square near the fountain, pick them out, you, you, you, you, *tsssst*, they would disappear from sight.

"I learned a trick," the old man says, and chuckles with the memory, "*such* a trick, Rivke, it fooled those *farshtinkener* Cossacks. There was a man in the ghetto, he knew already about army raids from the Crimean War, when they used to come, the Cossacks, and take away the young men to get killed by the French. So he showed me a thing to do with my leg, do you want to see, Rivke, I can still do it. I paid him plenty; it cost me, don't worry. But when they came the next time, the Cossacks, I did the trick, this is the trick, *bubeleh*, see?" he says, and he rises from his rocker and before Rebecca's astonished eyes he pulls his left leg up into the socket where leg joins hip and makes the leg a full two inches shorter than it normally is. Still chuckling, he grasps the leg between both hands again, and manipulates it, freeing it from the socket. "They thought I was a cripple, those *paskudnyaks*," he says, laughing. "I never went in their army; for what reason should I go?"

Every Wednesday night, when she is old enough, her grandfather Itzik takes her to the Yiddish theater on Second Avenue. She watches with her green eyes wide, catching only some of the dialogue, listening to her grandfather as he patiently explains what is happening on the stage and the people in the rows in front of them and behind hiss "*Shah! Shah!*" When she is eight years old and she catches the whooping cough, it is her grandfather who takes her out to Coney Island every day in the dead of winter, and stands on the boardwalk with her and tells her to breathe deeply of the fresh ocean air, this is the way to get rid of the racking cough. "Breathe, *bubeleh*, in, out, in, out, good, darling, good." Her sister is a beautiful child, with green eyes like Rebecca's, but with blond hair and a pert *shiksa* nose. "She looks like a regular Shirley Temple," everyone says, and Rebecca knows this is because her mother rolls Davina's hair into those long blond curls. One night, when her father comes home from work—he works with her *other* grandfather, who owns a business in the garment center, and whom she does not like—he finds her sitting in the middle of her room with her Shirley Temple doll on the floor, her hand wrapped around its leg, the head caved in. He asks her why she did that. "Why did you *do* that, Rebecca? The doll cost me fourteen *dollars!*" She tells him the doll slipped out of her hands.

She loves her father, but she hardly ever sees him. He comes home late more often than not—her mother explains that he goes to his card games—and then he marches directly into Davina's room and Rebecca can hear him laughing with her, and tickling her; he tickles her under the chin all the time, he never tickles Rebecca. He is a big man, her father, six feet four inches tall and weighing 220 pounds. Everyone is always mistaking him for a detective. He is very tough, her father. She can remember when she was six years old and a black man came in the store, her grandfather's dry-goods store, and tried to steal a bolt of cloth, good cloth, too, not a second or anything. Itzik had his eye on the black man from the minute he walked in the store, he wasn't going to let no *shvartzer* take from him. But the man was fast, he snatched up the bolt and ran for the doorway, and Rebecca's father was just coming in to tell Itzik not to forget supper was six o'clock tonight because Sophie had to go to Screeno. He saw the black man running off with the bolt of cloth, and he picked up a broom that was near the doorway, and chased the man all the way over to Third Avenue. When he caught him, the man pulled a knife from his pocket—"You always have to watch those niggers for knives," her father said later, "they all carry knives"— but he took the knife away from the man and beat him up and told him if he ever came anywhere *near* the store again, he would be one dead nigger.

Sometimes, her father takes her for a walk on Saturday, and these are the times she likes best, when she is alone with him, and he lets her stop outside the open door of the delicatessen, and allows her to sniff the aromas pouring out onto the sidewalk—the sour pickles in the barrels, the corned beef and the pastrami, the knishes, the fresh rye bread, the kosher hot dogs. For the longest time, she thinks delicatessens are only for sniffing. She later learns that whenever her father takes *Davina* for a walk, he buys her a knish, or a piece derma, or a nickel-a-shtickel, or some shoe leather, which is dried apricot and delicious. Her father owns a Studebaker with a rumble seat. When they go for a ride in the country, her father, her mother, and her sister sit up front. Rebecca sits in the rumble seat. She does not mind this because she makes up stories about the clouds, sitting with her head back against the leather cushion and watching the sky as the car heads up toward the Catskills—and besides, Davina is just a baby. They keep telling her Davina is just a baby. In the mountains, they stop for lunch at her Aunt Raizel's *kochalayn*, which is a bungalow she rents near one of the big hotels. It is only three rooms and a kitchen with a big stove. Her Aunt Raizel has a daughter named Hannah. Hannah has black hair and brown eyes, but Aunt Raizel does her daughter's hair in the same long Shirley Temple curls. Once, on the way back from the mountains, it begins to rain, and Rebecca pulls the rumble seat closed above her, and then cannot open it again, and is afraid she will not be able to breathe. Her father does not discover that the seat is closed until they stop for gas. He opens it, looks in at her, and says, "Why did you do that,

Rebecca? You could have suffocated." Her face is streaked with tears, her nose is dripping snot. She answers in a very small voice, "It was raining, Daddy." The only time Davina sits in the rumble seat with her is once coming back from the mountains, when her father stops to help a priest who has a flat tire and no spare. Her mother and Davina get in the rumble seat with Rebecca, and the priest sits up front with her father and the tire. Her father lets the priest out at a filling station near the Washington Bridge. That night, when they are eating supper at home, her father says, "He was an interesting man, the *gaylach*."

She is an enormously bright child; her teachers have told her mother that her IQ is 154. She has skipped from 1A to 2A, and again from 4B to 5B, and at the age of ten, she is the youngest child in the sixth grade. But her sister has moved out of kindergarten into the first grade, and some of the teachers Rebecca once had are now beginning to notice Davina, and stopping Rebecca in the hallways to comment on how beautiful her younger sister is. Sometimes, she tries to look at her sister objectively. She studies the green eyes, so like her own, and the blond hair—well, her own hair had been blond when she was a baby, it did not become red and ugly till she was three; perhaps Davina's hair will change, too. She supposes it is the nose. She stands before the mirror and lifts the end of her nose with her middle finger. Her hand hides her mouth, which she considers her best feature, so she raises her arm above her head, and reaches down for the tip of her nose with her hand upside down. When she exerts the tinest upward pressure, her nose becomes very much Davina's nose. She asks her grandfather one day whether she should have her nose cut off.

"Your *what?*" Itzik says.

"My nose, Grandpa. Should I get a nose job?"

"What is *that*, a nose job?"

"They fix your nose," she says.

329

"There's nothing wrong with your nose. That's your grand-mother Rivke's nose. That's a beautiful nose."

"Mm," Rebecca says, but she does not believe him. If it is such a beautiful nose, why is it that none of the movie stars have it? Or none of the models in the magazines? If it is such a beautiful nose, why does everyone tell Davina she's a regular Shirley Temple? She is getting very tired of Davina and Shirley Temple. Her mother has encouraged Davina to learn the words to "On the Good Ship Lollipop," and whenever there is company, Davina sings the song and tap-dances around the living room, and everyone exclaims how beautiful and talented she is, and Rebecca wants to go into the bathroom to throw up. Whenever no one is watching, she hits Davina, who runs screaming into the kitchen. Rebecca is invariably punished for the attack, but she doesn't care because she would rather be in her own bedroom with her treasured books than in the living room with Davina tap-dancing all over the place. In a book called *Ivanhoe*, she discovers a woman named Rebecca. Rebecca is the heroine. She reads the description of the fictitious Rebecca over and over again, until she has memorized it:

The figure of Rebecca might indeed have compared with the proudest beauties of England, even though it had been judged by as shrewd a connoisseur as Prince John. Her form was exquisitely symmetrical, and was shewn to advantage by a sort of Eastern dress, which she wore according to the fashion of the females of her nation. Her turban of yellow silk suited well with the darkness of her complexion. The brilliancy of her eyes, the superb arch of her eyebrows, her well-formed aquiline nose, her teeth as white as pearl, and the profusion of her sable tresses which, each arranged in its own little spiral of twisted curls, fell down upon as much of a lovely neck and bosom as a simarre of the richest Persian silk, exhibiting flowers in their natural colours embossed upon a purple ground, permitted to be visible—all these constituted a combination of loveliness, which yielded not to the most beautiful of the maidens who surrounded her. It is true that

330

of the golden and pearl-studded clasps, which closed her vest from the throat to the waist, the three uppermost were left unfastened on account of the heat, which something enlarged the prospect to which we allude. A diamond necklace, with pendants of inestimable value, were by this means also made more conspicuous. The feather of an ostrich, fastened in her turban by an agriffe set with brilliants, was another distinction of the beautiful Jewess, scoffed and sneered at by the proud dames who sat above her, but secretly envied by those who affected to deride them.

She does not finish the book, it is much too difficult for her, but she has gathered from it precious ammunition to use against her sister.

"I'm in a book," she tells her.

"So am I," Davina says.

"You *are* not!" Rebecca says.

"I am *so*."

"Where? What book?"

"In a book Mommy has in her room. It's Davina's Baby Book, and it tells all about me. How much I weighed and things I said when I was little, and everything about me."

Rebecca does not have a baby book. She takes *Ivanhoe* back to the library and tells the librarian it was lousy. In 1939, when she is eleven years old and enters junior high school, she is jubilant because it means she can escape little Shirley Temple for at least the length of the school day. In the seventh grade, there is a big fat girl named Rosalie, who becomes fast friends with Rebecca—perhaps because Rebecca is the only one in the class who doesn't call her Fat Stuff, after one of the cartoon characters in *Smilin' Jack*. One day, when Rebecca is telling Rosalie about what a pain her little sister is, Rosalie says, "Why don't you just kill her?"

"Always singing and tap-dancing," Rebecca says.

"Yeah, kill her," Rosalie says. "Drown her in the bathtub."

"You could go to jail for that," Rebecca says.

"No, they don't send little girls to jail," Rosalie assures her.

Rebecca considers the idea. She and Rosalie talk about it often and seriously, concocting new methods of murder each time, some of them quite bizarre. Sitting on the front stoop of their tenement, picking their noses, they talk about hanging little Davina, or poisoning her (Yeah, but where would we get the poison? The man in the drugstore would remember us), or throwing her off the roof, or—and this causes both of them to burst into hysterical laughter—holding her head in the toilet bowl. Sophie Baumgarten heartily disapproves of the relationship with Rosalie, even though she knows nothing of these dire plans for murdering her regular Shirley Temple. She disapproves of Rosalie only because she is fat.

"Fat," she says, "disgusting," she says, and spits on the extended forefinger and middle finger of her right hand. "*Ptoo, ptoo!*"

"What's wrong with fat?" Rebecca says. "And anyway, she isn't fat."

"She's fat as a horse," Sophie says.

"Well," Rebecca says, "she's my friend."

"Some friend."

"She's my *best* friend."

"Better you should find yourself a Goodyear blimp," Sophie says.

In school, whenever the friends are together, the other kids begin to chant, "Fat and Skinny had a race/All around the pillowcase/Fat fell down and broke his face/Skinny won the race."

"Yaaaaaah," Rebecca says, and sticks out her tongue.

In the fall, when her father buys the Oldsmobile agency, they move to the Bronx. She misses Rosalie dreadfully, and at her new school she is very wary of making friends. Around the house, she is quiet and unresponsive. She reads now more than she did in Manhattan. Sometimes she memorizes long passages from the encyclopedia. Her mother tells her she must take piano lessons. She begins these when she is thirteen. She hates the piano, and she plays badly. Once, in the kitchen of their apartment, her father's friend Seymour asks, "How old is she now, Abe?" and her father looks at her as though discovering her for the first time, and is silent for a moment, and then says, "Gee, I don't know. How old *are* you, Becky? Eleven? Twelve?" He knows *exactly* how old Davina is. Davina is nine years, two months, and seven days old. She was born on July 12, 1932. Her father knows the date by heart. "Sunshine was born that day," he says, smiling. "My little sunshine. Sing 'My Little Sunshine' for me, baby." Davina no longer sings "On the Good Ship Lollipop," thank God. Nor, at the age of nine, does she any longer sport those Shirley Temple curls Rebecca once found so distasteful. Instead, she combs her hair the way Veronica Lake does, hanging over one eye. Rebecca thinks her sister is too young to be imitating a sex-pot movie star, and she tells this to her mother. Her mother says, "Look who's talking."

Whenever a Veronica Lake movie is playing at the Tuxedo on Jerome Avenue, Rebecca stays away from it. But she goes to the movies every Saturday, and sometimes on Wednesday nights with her mother. Except for Veronica Lake, she loves the movies. She loves the way people meet in the movies. At the movies, she learns to identify all the families of the various studios; just name the studio and she will reel off the names of the contract players. She tries this phenomenal feat of memory on her father one night. She tells him that MGM, that's Leo the Lion, has the biggest family in the bunch, with grandpas like Lionel Barrymore and Lewis Stone and C. Aubrey Smith and Guy Kibbee and Charles Winninger; and grandmas like Edna May Oliver and Fay Bainter and Marjorie Main; mothers and fathers like Greer Garson and Spencer Tracy and Margaret Sullavan and Herbert Marshall; uncles like William Powell and Robert Taylor and Franchot Tone; aunts like Joan Crawford and Laraine Day and Hedy Lamarr; cousins like Mickey Rooney and Judy Garland and Freddie Bartholomew, and *landsleit* from Far Rockaway, like Ruth Hussey, Nelson Eddy, Gladys George, Ann Sothern, and George Murphy.

The Warner Brothers family (she tells her father) is Humphrey Bogart, George Brent, Bette Davis, Olivia De Havilland, Errol

333

Flynn, Ann Sheridan, Edward G. Robinson, Pat O'Brien, Donald Crisp, Priscilla Lane, Ida Lupino, James Cagney, and Ronald Reagan, whom she adores. And then there's the Twentieth Century–Fox family with Alice Faye and Don Ameche and Linda Darnell and Tyrone Power and Henry Fonda and Cesar Romero and Warner Baxter and Sonja Henie and Shirley Temple (she passes over this name very quickly). The Paramount family is Betty Grable and Gary Cooper and Dorothy Lamour and Fred MacMurray and Claudette Colbert and Bob Hope and Bing Crosby on the road to everywhere, and sometimes people from the Columbia family or the Republic family pop up in a picture with one of the other studio families, and then it's like one *big* family, Daddy, it's really terrific, Daddy, she says, and grins at him.

"Daddy?" she says.

He does not answer.

"Daddy?"

Her father is asleep in his chair.

"Well," she says, and goes to her room.

She is not permitted to date until she is seventeen years old, not that any boys are banging down the door. It is Davina, at thirteen, who is the undisputed beauty of the family, with cupcake breasts almost as large as Rebecca's own, and wide hips, and a smile Rebecca considers suggestive. Whenever a boy comes to the house to pick up Rebecca, her sister magically appears in the living room, and extends her hand, and says in a low and studied voice (she is now imitating Lizabeth Scott), "Nice to meet you." The boys invariably ask Rebecca how old her sister is. When she says "Thirteen," they seem disappointed. It is only when she begins going steady with Marvin Feldman that she feels free enough to ask, "Do you think I'm prettier than Davina?"

"Yes," he says.

"Do you think I have a big nose?"

"No," he says.

"I sometimes think I ought to get my nose fixed."

"What for?" he says. "It's an okay nose," and he kisses the tip of it.

From the bedroom, Sophie Baumgarten calls, "Rebecca?"

"Yes, Mama," Rebecca says. She knows what is coming next.

"What time is it, Rebecca?" Sophie asks.

"A little past one, Mama."

"*Already?*" Sophie says.

In December of 1945, just before Chanukah, her grandfather Itzik dies. The last word he utters is "Rivke." Though Rebecca knows this was also her grandmother's name, she chooses to believe the old man's dying breath was drawn for her alone. They bury him on a bleak gray afternoon, and that night Rebecca walks over to the small park near their apartment. Snow is on the ground. She sits on one of the benches with her hands in her coat pockets. The park is empty. She sits alone on the bench until she is shivering from the cold. Then, slowly, she walks back to the apartment.

Davina is listening to the radio.

"Hi," she says.

Rebecca does not answer. In the hallway, she takes off her coat and her muffler, and hangs them in the closet.

"Where were you?" Davina asks.

"In the park."

"Doing what?"

"Sitting."

"That was something, huh? The funeral?"

On the radio, they are advertising gasoline. Davina sits in the big easy chair that is their father's whenever he is home, her shapely legs tucked under her, her loafers on the floor, and she tells Rebecca what she thought of the funeral, how it was despicable of a rabbi who didn't even *know* Grandpa Itzik to go on and on about him as if they were bosom buddies, and Tante Raizel wailing like a banshee when they lowered the coffin into the earth, Davina had

335

never seen anything so horrible in her life. But her voice trails when the commercial ends and the comic comes on again. He tells a joke, and Davina bursts out laughing.

In her room, Rebecca takes off her clothes and gets into bed. She feels very much alone. Except for Marvin, she feels she is now alone in the world. There is only Marvin now to tell her that her nose is an okay nose. ("What is *that*, a nose job?" her grandfather had said. "There's nothing wrong with your nose. That's your grandmother Rivke's nose. That's a beautiful nose.") It is not such a beautiful nose, she thinks. Grandpa, it really is not such a beautiful nose, Grandpa, I love you, Grandpa. Thank you, Grandpa. Thank you, Grandpa. I love you, Grandpa. She cries herself to sleep that night, and dreams that Marvin is making love to her. She screams in the dream, she tries to scream but no sound comes from her mouth. Stop, Marvin, she tries to scream, but Marvin will not, please, she screams, she tries to scream, Marvin, please, no, please, no, you *promised!*—and she sits up straight in bed, her green eyes wide, breathing heavily as she stares into the blackness of the room.

"You promised," she whispers, but she has already forgotten the dream.

In April, Marvin takes her for a walk in the park and tells her he's met a singer, and tells her he is going to marry the singer, and tells her he is sorry. Jonquils are blooming everywhere around them, the small grassy slopes are running wild with jonquils.

"That's okay, Marvin," Rebecca tells him. "Really, it's okay."

It is Marvin who bursts into tears.

❖

I loved you, Rebecca.

I loved everything about you.

I knew you were beautiful because Cappy Kaplan, my drummer, described you to me in detail, not that I needed any physical description. "She's a very *zaftig* person," Cappy said, "about five-six or seven, I can't say for sure, and very nicely stacked, as if you didn't know. Not melons or cantaloupes, Ike, just very nice, well, grapefruits, I would say, very nice. And wide hips, she's very curvy, she looks like a peasant from the old country, you know, with the wide hips for childbearing. Her hair ain't red exactly, it's sort of rust-colored, I guess you'd call it, though maybe she gives it a little help. Her nose is nothing to write home about, a Jewish nose, it's my cousin Carol's nose exactly. Her mouth is okay, lips a little thin maybe, but she's got good teeth, I'm sure she brushes them regular. She dresses good, too. I got to tell you the truth, Ike: standing next to her, you look like a slob."

That was Cappy's description of Rebecca Baumgarten.

My grandfather said, after their first meeting, "*Ha sembrato una settentrionale,*" meaning he thought she looked like a northern Italian. Years later, in Rome, the city of redheads, Rebecca was always being mistaken for Italian. And, of course, being pinched on the ass by Italian men. That is not a myth. Even Rebecca's green death ray could not dissuade those hot-blooded Mediterraneans from trying to cop a feel. *La mano morta* is not a branch of the Mafia, even though it translates literally as "the dead hand." The expression describes a hand hanging limply at the end of a male Italian wrist, seemingly deceased, most certainly detached from its owner, who claims no responsibility for whatever it might be doing while he stands on a corner reading his copy of the morning paper. What the hand is doing is simply none of his business. If a woman recoils from *la mano morta* with a small surprised gasp, the man to whom the dead hand is attached will look at her (*and* it) in surprise equal to the woman's own. *La mano morta.* "Fucking *sex* fiends is what they are," Rebecca said whenever we were in Rome. She also said that in London.

It was Rebecca's guess that her father the Mad Oldsmobile Dealer was approximately as religious as my mother, and objected to me only because I was blind. I did not believe this for a minute.

Not once had he expressed any concern about how a blind man might support his daughter, or protect her from harm, or keep her happy and secure. I flatly told Rebecca she was wrong. If I'd been a blind *Jew*, Abe would have welcomed me into the family, perhaps not without qualms and doubts, but certainly without enmity. "Well, then," Rebecca said, "he must be doing it for Baumgarten Frocks."

"Baumgarten Frocks" was Abe's father, a dyspeptic old cloakie who lived in the back room of their Mosholu Parkway apartment, and made ugly noises in the bathroom each morning. Rebecca hated him as much as she had loved old Itzik. His real name was Moishe Baumgarten, but Rebecca alternately called him Baumgarten Frocks and Moishe Pipik. When she and I first started getting serious about each other, she sounded Moishe on the remote possibility of marrying an Italian musician. The sly old fox knew all about me by then, of course, had in fact received gleeful reports from Honest Abe on the demolition of the blind goy in his kitchen that hot August afternoon. He listened to Rebecca and then began nodding his head in his best *daven*ing manner, and, as though he were reciting the *shachris,* the *minchah,* and the *mairev* (not to mention the *Nina,* the *Pinta,* and the *Santa Maria*), said to his granddaughter, "Ahhh, Rivke, Rivke, how can you even con*side*h such a peth for yourself? Ah pianeh playeh? Ah *shaygets?* Rivke, Rivke," wagging that fine old prejudice-riddled head, "you could merry vun day ah doctuh," he said, "ah lawyeh," he said, and leaving the finest profession of all for last, triumphantly concluded, "ah *biz*nessmen!" When Rebecca told me this story, I told her old Baumgarten Frocks could go frock himself.

That's the way we felt about *all* of them, in fact.

I think if my own grandfather had raised the slightest objection to my marrying Rebecca, I'd have kissed *him* off, too. I mean that. I loved you, Rebecca, and it had nothing to do with descriptions of you. I knew you were beautiful long before anyone told me. Anyway, you'd told me so yourself, hadn't you? "I'm gorgeous," you said, "what do you think?" You *were* gorgeous, Rebecca. I loved everything about you. It's too easy now to remember only the bad times, of which there were many. But there were good times, too—at least as many, and perhaps more—and I loved you thoroughly and completely for more years than I care to count.

How did I love thee, Becks? Let me count the ways.

I had told my grandfather all about you long before I took you to the tailor shop to meet him. I was taking no chances. I enumerated for him all the things I am about to enumerate now, all the reasons for loving you, and he listened patiently, and sometimes made pleased little sounds, encouraging me to go on. I told him first that you were beautiful, and then I told him you were the smartest person I'd ever met, that you could read through a book in an hour, sometimes two, but never longer than that, and retain what you had read, and reel off to me long passages you had memorized from just that single reading. I told him you knew impossibly ridiculous things, facts no one was expected to know, and which you probably wouldn't have known if it weren't for a memory that was almost photographic. I told him you could recite statistics on the area and population of Chile, for example, or list in order all the rulers of France since Pepin the Short; I told him you knew what to call the male, female, and baby animals in any of the animal families—as for instance, a drake, a duck, and a duckling; or a ram, a ewe, and a lamb; or, more exotically, a cob, a pen, and a cygnet. I told him you could, for God's sake, name the methods of execution in every state of the Union—lethal gas in Arizona, hanging in Montana, electrocution in South Dakota, and so on. I told him (I had not yet told him you were Jewish) that you could even name all the popes in order, starting with Saint Peter and coming all the way up to Pius XII, who was the then-reigning pontiff. I was amazed by your knowledge, I told him, and I bet him that when you finally met, you'd be able to tell him the average yearly rainfall in every province of Italy. ("Even Potenza?" he asked, undoubtedly impressed.)

I told him how kind you were, and how generous, how sometimes we'd be walking along together and a panhandler would approach, and you'd catch your breath and stop in the middle of the sidewalk as though someone had suddenly slapped you, and I would hear you opening your pocketbook, and after you gave the man a coin, you would say to me, "We're so lucky, Ike," even though I was blind. My blindness never mattered to you. I told him how concerned you were about all the people of the world, Rebecca, not just the ones in your own family, and not just your close friends (I told him about your unswerving loyalty to Shirley Ackerman, too), but also people in faraway lands you'd never seen. I told him about the argument we'd had the time I was reminiscing about my boyhood and mentioned that my mother was always telling me to eat what was on my plate because the people in China were starving, and I admitted I didn't *care* if the people in China were starving and you hit the ceiling, Rebecca, and wanted to know how *I*, of *all* people, could be so cruel and callous to those less fortunate. ("Well, Ignazio," my grandfather said, "it *isn't* funny, the people in China starving.") I told him you'd call me sometimes late at night and read poetry to me on the telephone, I told him you'd taken me to the Museum of Modern Art and described your favorite paintings in meticulous detail, I told him you'd begun advising me on how to dress, I told him you played piano very badly (by your own admission, Becks), but that you'd always wanted to marry someone creative, and that you'd said marrying me would be the most important event in your life. I told him how much I loved you, Rebecca. I told him all the things there were to love about you, and they were myriad.

And then I told him you were Jewish.

And I said to him, I said, "Grandpa, *that's* important, too." And I explained what it meant to me to be in love with a Jewish girl, and to want to marry a Jewish girl, and I explained what it meant to you, my being Italian, and I told him we had talked about it in great detail, and that none of it mattered to us. "She's not religious," I said, "and I'm not religious, either, Grandpa. Please don't be hurt by that, but honest, I haven't been anywhere *near* a church for five years now. We love each other, and that's all that matters."

I put it to him that simply, but it was much more complicated.

We were, Rebecca and I, the realization of the American myth, which both of us had been living for as long as we could remember. And in that myth the melting pot existed only so that fresh new alloys could be poured from its crucible. If I was copper, then Rebecca was zinc, and together we would create a brass band that marched noisily down the middle of Fifth Avenue playing "America the Beautiful." Her father's objections to our relationship seemed absurd, reactionary, and frankly unpatriotic. We met in secret, we made love in secret, we formulated our plans for getting married in secret, and secretly and privately and proudly, we each glowed with the knowledge that we were fulfilling our separate destinies and moving in the only direction possible for anyone who considered himself American.

We were wrong, Rebecca darling.

But we were both so young.

❖

We had planned the wedding for months, inviting only my parents and grandparents, Rebecca's mother and sister, and some close friends like Stu Holman, Cappy Kaplan, and Shirley Ackerman. Rebecca's mother declined the invitation for Davina and herself, not because she objected to the marriage (she liked me very much, in fact, and gave us two thousand dollars of her personal savings as a wedding gift), but only because she had to live with Honest Abe for the rest of her life, and knew her attendance at our wedding would be considered rank betrayal. On November 17, 1948, two days before Rebecca and I were to be married, my grandfather went to visit Honest Abe at his Olds-mobile agency in the Bronx—and was somewhat baffled by the reception he received. Nor was Honest Abe any less baffled (or at least he *seemed* to be) by the old man's appearance at his *palais d'auto.*

The first inkling we had of my grandfather's visit came from Honest Abe himself. At the Baumgarten dinner table that Wednesday night, on one of his rare personal appearances with the family (being otherwise and usually occupied with his euphemistic poker games), Abe told the story of the mysterious appearance of an old guinea dressed in black and smoking a foul-smelling cigar. "I never turn any of them away," he said. "*Shvartzers,* wops, Irishers, they're all the same to me. If they got money to buy the car, I'll sell it to them. So when he walks in the showroom, I personally go up to him, and I say, 'Good afternoon, sir, may I help you?' and he sticks out his hand and grins, and says, 'Frank Di Lorenzo,' in an accent you can cut with a butcher knife. Do you know anybody named Frank Di Lorenzo, Becky?"

"No, Daddy," Rebecca said, while her mother and sister busied themselves with the pot roast on their plates.

"You're not still seeing that blind *shaygets,* are you?" her father asked.

"Oh, no, Daddy," Rebecca said. She had been seeing me for the past two and a half years, and after Friday she would be seeing me for the rest of her life—or so we both thought at the time.

"He said he came up to the Bronx to tell me how happy he was."

"Who?" Rebecca asked.

"This old wop, this Di Lorenzo with the cigar clamped in his mouth."

"Well," Rebecca said, very carefully spearing some sliced carrots and boiled potatoes with her fork, "it's very possible that a

342

happy Italian came into your showroom, but that doesn't mean I know him."

"What was that goy's name that time?" Abe asked.

"Ike, do you mean? Ike Di Palermo."

"Um, well this was Di *Lorenzo*. At least, I *think* that's what he said; I could hardly understand him. You get these people, they're here in America for sixty years, they *still* don't know how to talk right."

"Like Grandpa," Rebecca said, trying to change the subject.

"Grandpa talks fine," Abe said. "I understand him fine. Anyway, this old wop is slapping me on the back and grinning from ear to ear and telling me he'll see me Friday, and I have to come to his house sometime, maybe for his name day. . . . I *think* he said his name day; what the hell's a name day? I figured I had myself a prime bedbug right there in the showroom, telling me what a fine man I am, and how happy he is to meet me, a nut plain and simple. You know what *I* think?"

"No, Daddy, what do you think?" Rebecca asked, and held her breath.

Abe thought about what he thought. Then he said, "I'll bet that *shaygets* . . . what was his name?"

"Ike Di Palermo."

"Yeah. I'll bet he's going around telling people he's still dating you."

"Why would he do that, Daddy?"

"Why not? A blind piano player? Nothing he'd like better than to have people think he's dating a Jewish girl."

"What's so special about Jewish girls?" Davina asked.

"You're both my special darlings," Abe said, and smiled at his two darling daughters, but patted only Davina's hand.

"Well, whatever Ike does is his own business," Rebecca said. "I haven't seen him since that day he came up here, and I couldn't care less what he's telling people."

343

"That's a good girl," Abe said. "But still, I'll bet that's it."

"So what did you say to him?"

"Who, the wop? Nothing."

"I mean . . . how did you leave it?"

"Leave what? He said he'd be seeing me Friday, so Friday I'll look for him. Who knows? He'll maybe end up buying a car."

Immediately after dinner, Rebecca ran downstairs to the candy store, and phoned me. I listened breathlessly, and then called my grandfather in an effort to determine exactly how much he had told the Mad Oldsmobile Dealer.

In his broken English, my grandfather said:

"I go in the store, he come up, I know he's the fath, I see in the eyes, the face, the look. I say, 'How you do, I'ma Frank Di Lorenzo.' He saysa, 'How you do?' I looka him, he looka me. I tell him, 'I'm Ignazio's granfath,' and he says, 'Attsa nize.' I tell him I come to meet him so he no be stranger the wedding, so he feelsa home, eh? He saysa, 'What wedding?' I tell him Friday, the wedding, whattsa matta he forgets the wedding? He saysa, 'You wanna buy car, or what?' I say to him, 'What car? I'ma talk about how happ I am to marry with you daughter my granson.' He saysa, 'You craze.' I say 'Hey, you, I'ma Frank Di Lorenzo, capisce? It'sa my granson who'sa marry you daught, whattsa matta you? I'ma come alla way the Bronx to say hello, I make a mistake? You no Abe-a Baumgart?' He saysa, 'I'm Abe-a Baumgart, you wanna buy a car, or no?' Ma, Ignazio, ho veramente creduto ch'era pazzo! I try one more time. I say, 'Look, you gotta nize daught, I gotta nize granson, we be nize-a family, you come have supper, you come my name day, I buy pasticcerie, we drinka wine, it'sa nize, okay?' He says, 'I get somebody to heppa you.' An he goes away, he leaves me standa there like a dope. What I do, Ignazio? I do someting wrong?"

As planned, we were married on the nineteenth of November. All through the brief civil ceremony, I expected Abe to come barging in with a minyan of Jewish hoods, all of them standing

344

six feet four inches tall and weighing 220 pounds, as did my imminent father-in-law. Calling upon Jewish tradition, they would place my head upon the floor, and then all ten of them would smash it under a tented napkin. Not even Uncle Matt would be able to save me. But nobody arrived to interrupt the wedding. Afterward, we herded the small group of somewhat cheerless celebrants to a restaurant in Mount Vernon, where Rebecca and I were wined and dined and toasted (three times by my grandfather alone!). We then took a taxi to Pennsylvania Station, where we sent off a telegram and boarded the train to Mount Pocono. At fifteen minutes past midnight, we found ourselves in a deserted, milk-stop railroad station that had no lights and a single phone booth with a broken door. I located the booth in the familiar dark, and Rebecca struck a match (and then another) and dialed the telephone number on the advertising brochure, and handed the phone to me. I told the owner of the lodge we were Mr. and Mrs. Di Palermo (How strange that sounded! Mr. and Mrs. Di Palermo were my parents!) and we were here, but there weren't any taxis, and could he please send a car for us?

Lying in bed together, we tried again to understand her father's reaction to what had happened that afternoon two days before. Was it possible he really hadn't understood what was being said to him? My grandfather's English was atrocious, true, but he generally managed to make himself at least comprehensible. Could Honest Abe honestly have missed the purpose of the visit? Had he really not understood that a wedding was to take place on Friday afternoon, and that the principals to be united in matrimony were none other than a Blind Shaygets and a Jewish Princess from Mosholu Parkway? We reached the conclusion that Abe had understood perfectly and had decided to look the other way. He must have realized there was nothing he could do to stop the wedding, short of breaking both his daughter's legs and sending her to Paris, France, in plaster casts. She had been seeing me against his explicit wishes for more than two years, and it was too late now. He could either pretend he knew nothing about any of it, or else take a futile last stand that would accomplish nothing anyway. And so he'd professed ignorance and innocence; whatever his daughter chose to do was on her own head. The telegram we'd sent, addressed to Mr. *and* Mrs. Baumgarten, to circumvent any later recriminations hurled at poor, bewildered Sophie, read:

DEAR MOTHER AND DADDY:
WE WERE MARRIED TODAY AT 3 P.M. WE ARE
SORRY YOU CAN'T SEE THIS OUR WAY, BUT WE HOPE
IN TIME TO HAVE YOUR BLESSINGS. ALL OUR LOVE.
                                    REBECCA AND IKE

❖

It is a Saturday afternoon in 1955. Sophie has brought her sister to visit us in our apartment on Ninety-seventh and West End Avenue. Sophie visits often; she has an arrangement with Honest Abe. His eldest daughter is dead, he has turned her pictures to the wall—but his wife may visit the grave whenever she chooses. Today she has brought Tante Raizel to meet the blind shaygets, *and Rebecca is showing snapshots I cannot see.*

My own snapshots are up here, in my head.

September of 1950. A sleazy nightclub in Jersey City. We have been married for almost two years. Rebecca tells a joke to my drummer. "A six-year-old boy is banging pots and pans in the kitchen," she says, "and a five-year-old girl comes in and asks him what he's doing. He answers, 'Shhh, can't you see? I'm a drummer.' The little girl grabs him by the hand, and drags him into the bedroom, and tosses up her skirts, and pulls down her panties, and says, 'If you're a drummer, kiss me on the wee-wee.' And the little boy says, 'Oh, I'm not a *real* drummer.'" My real drummer does not find the joke comical. I suddenly wonder whether Rebecca told it only to annoy him. I am beginning to feel she purposely says the wrong things to my musicians. She does not enjoy nightclubs anymore; it is not the way it was before we got married, when each new gig was a circus. Our son will be a year old at the end of the month. He was conceived in December of 1948, a month after we were married. Rebecca is pregnant again, she bears huge babies, she is already swollen to bursting in her fourth month. I suspect she is angry with me for having knocked her up a second time (though she faithfully wears a diaphragm each and every time we make love), angry with me for not making more money, angry with me, too (may God forgive me), for being blind.

"*This is when we were still living on 174th Street,*" Rebecca *says to her aunt. "I was pregnant with Michael at the time. God, look at me, I'm a horse.*"

"*You look very healthy,*" *Tante Raizel says.*

"*She had a terrible time with Michael,*" *Sophie says. "She went into shock right after the delivery. From losing all that weight so fast. Michael weighed almost ten pounds. Do you remember, Becky?*"

"*I remember,*" *Rebecca says.*

She is nursing the new baby when I come home at three in the morning. She sits in an easy chair near the side of our bed, and I hear Michael's sucking sounds as I undress. We are living on the sixth floor of a housing project two blocks from Westchester Avenue. I commute by subway each night to a club in the Village, where I am the intermission pianist; it is difficult to keep bands together unless you can provide work for them. I am earning eighty dollars a week, and we now have two children, and $340 in the bank. Rebecca carries the baby into the room he shares with his older brother, Andrew. I am in bed when she returns. I hear her snapping out the light. We talk for a while. My hand rests lightly on her hip. When I lapse into silence, Rebecca asks, suddenly and unexpectedly, "Do you plan to make love?"

"Would you like to?"

"Would *you?*"

"Sure."

"Let me get my diaphragm."

She gets out of bed and walks down the hall to the bathroom. I hear a colored woman shouting from an open window to her friends on the street below. "G'night, y'all, g'night," and again, "G'night." Silence. From the bathroom, I hear the sound of running water. I lie back waiting, my hands behind my head. I suddenly remember a night in Stockbridge before we were married, when young Rebecca crossed the room as though traversing the burning sands of the Sahara, to climb into bed beside me, and surrender her virginity to me, and mourn its loss immediately afterward. I wait. She always takes an interminably long time to insert the diaphragm. A year ago, when she'd discovered she was pregnant again, she'd said, "I'll *never* learn to put this fucking thing in!" She uses the word "fuck" a lot, my Rebecca, but never to describe what we do together in bed. In bed, we make love. ("Do you plan to make love?") In bed, Rebecca is a contractor hired to construct an edifice, "make" a building she labels "love," for want of a better word. Blueprints and specifications are tucked into her vagina just behind the diaphragm, while like a common laborer I sweat to bring her to orgasm. I touch her mouth often while we make love, I search her lips with my seeing-eye hands. There is never a smile upon her face, she "makes love" joylessly, straining for orgasm and achieving it soundlessly, with never so much as a grunt of pleasure, a groan of acknowledgment, certainly never a passionate shriek. When I ask her each time if she has come (I am never certain), she snaps impatiently, "Of *course* I came! Will you please shut up?" I always want to talk afterward. She always wants to sink back into the pillows, into silence, perhaps so she can admire from a distance this shining fifty-two-story office building we have built together from plans already dog-eared, this "love" we have "made." The bathroom light clicks off, I hear her walking purposefully toward the bedroom. We are ready for the business of fucking.

"*Who's that man holding the baby?*" *Tante Raizel asks.*

"*That's Ike's grandfather.*"

348

"He's a tailor," Sophie says. "He has his own tailor shop."

"Yes? Avrum was a tailor. Do you remember your Uncle Avrum, Rivke? He was a tailor."

Rebecca does not much care for my family. I do not understand this, but I do not have much time to care about her not caring. I am pursuing the hairy beast of success. She tolerates my grandfather because she knows how deeply I love him, but she describes my grandmother Tess as "a crabby, constipated woman," my Uncle Luke as "Mr. Rumples," my Uncle Matt as "the Mafioso," and my mother as "the paranoid nut." Once, when my Aunt Cristina takes the IRT up to 174th Street and walks to the housing project and knocks on the door, Rebecca seems not to know her at first, and then says, in surprise, "Oh, Cristie. Hi." Cristie has come uptown because she wants to see the new baby. Rebecca has her coat on, and is preparing to do the weekly marketing. Andrew is bundled in his snowsuit. The thirteen-year-old girl from next door is in the living room doing her homework. Rebecca takes Cristie into the room where Michael sleeps. "He's beautiful, God bless him," Cristie says.

"Thank you," Rebecca says. "Cristie, I hope you don't mind, but I was just on the way out."

"That's all right," Cristie says, but later she tells my mother, "She didn't even offer me a cup of coffee." When I confront Rebecca with this, she says, "Well, I was all ready to go out; Andrew was in his snowsuit."

"Honey, that was my *aunt!* She made me lemonade every day of my life!"

"She should have called first," Rebecca says.

We visit Harlem rarely. My grandfather still has the tailor shop on First Avenue, but the neighborhood is rapidly turning Puerto Rican, and Rebecca is fearful of making the trip downtown. Where Sophie had once protected her "treasures" from the goyim who drunkenly invaded the ghetto, Rebecca now refuses to bring *her* treasures—Andrew and little Michael—into another ghetto, where they may be harmed. I tell her the neighborhood is actually safer than the one in which we live, and she says, "You're thinking of when you were a kid. It's changed."

I sometimes wish I could go home.

I sometimes know exactly how my grandfather felt during that decade when he was twenty-four and longing to return to Fiormonte.

"Oh, and these," Rebecca says to her aunt. "Oh, these are my favorite pictures."

"That's when Ike took the whole family to Florida," Sophie says, a note of pride in her voice.

"Where?" Tante Raizel asks. "Miami?"

"Pass-A-Grille," I answer.

"Where's that?" she says.

The job is really in Treasure Island. The man who hires me for it, on recommendation from the leader of the house band where I am playing between sets, is fifty-four years old. His name is Archie Coombes, and he tells me at our first meeting that he is probably the world's lousiest drummer, but his brother-in-law owns this small place on the Gulf, and this is how he gets a winter vacation each year; his brother hires him to come down with a pickup trio. The job doesn't pay much, he says, but what the hell, it's been a miserable winter, and maybe I can use some sunshine for myself and the family, he understands I have two kids. He tells me he is also looking for a good bass player, and when I recommend Stu Holman, he asks immediately if Stu is colored. He does not hire Stu. The bassist we end up with is a sixty-two-year-old white man, who reportedly once played with another Whiteman named Paul. I accept the job, but I have the feeling I will be making music with one of the Jimmy Palmer orchestras.

Rebecca is overjoyed. This is January of 1953, and she is six months pregnant with our third child ("I am going to *burn* that fucking diaphragm!"), and we have just come through a siege of chicken pox with Andrew and Michael. The children, in fact, still have drying scabs on their faces when we move into the rented house in Pass-A-Grille. The house is small—it once was the caretaker's cottage for the sumptuous twelve-room mansion that sits on two acres of oceanfront property. We walk through the house with the real estate agent who found the rental for us. I can sense Rebecca's disappointment. Kitchen, living room, bedroom, one bath. We are paying $750 for the month—which is exactly $250 less than I will be earning with the Archie Coombes trio. We are in the living room, the real estate agent is helpfully explaining that the two little boys can sleep together on the sofa bed. She is rattling a doorknob now, trying to open the glass-louvered doors leading to the rear of the house. She flings the doors wide with a sudden grunt, and I feel a rush of sunshine on my face and smell the heavy moisture-laden aroma of tropical plants. Beside me, Rebecca gasps and takes my hand, and leads me into the garden. I can barely keep up with her. She is ballooning with pregnancy, but she moves about the garden like a ballet dancer in flight, stopping at each bloom to identify it for me. "This is hibiscus, and this is bougainvillaea, and look, Ike, oh my God, it's the most beautiful thing I've ever, oh God, it's an oleander!" In the distance I can hear the sound of the surf, and suddenly I smile.

"That was such a happy time," Rebecca says to her aunt.

"What are you reading to them there?" Tante Raizel asks. "What's that book in the picture?"

"Oh, they loved that book," Rebecca says, and falls silent.

"Peter Pan," I say.

"Yes," Rebecca says, and I wonder if she is looking at me.

In the apartment we move to on Ninety-seventh and West End, Andrew has his own bedroom, and Michael shares a room with his new brother. I have started another band. We rehearse in the

351

huge, sparsely furnished living room because we cannot afford studio space. Rebecca constantly tells me that if I'm trying to break the lease, I'm well on the way to success. She no longer believes the *other* success is possible. She has been married to me for almost six years, this is the fall of 1954, and we are virtually standing still except for our boundless capacity to produce big, beautiful children. She is beginning to have doubts, and so am I. What if I *don't* make it? What if I am one of those who never make it? ("He's got to *make* it first, you understand. Lots of guys *never* make it.") This is America, and I am talented and industrious and ambitious, but even in America two bills a week don't go very far when you're trying to raise a family. That is what I am earning with the quintet. Two hundred dollars a week. More or less. Some weeks. Rebecca counts out the money as grudgingly as a miser, putting aside so much for rent, so much for gas and electricity, so much for food and clothing, so much for entertainment. There is not much for entertainment, but then again there is rarely *time* for entertainment, either. I work six nights a week (when I'm working), and because baby-sitters cost more than we can afford, and because Rebecca has learned to hate sitting around smoky toilets while I play piano, and because some of the jobs are out on the Island or over in New Jersey or, once in a blue moon, up in Schenectady or Newburgh, I rarely see Rebecca on any night of the week but Monday. During the day, I either sleep or rehearse. I am pursuing success, certain I can track and trap that hairy beast. I am American.

My family is a new family. It consists of Rebecca and the children, my parents, and Sophie and Davina. (I do not consider Davina's recently acquired husband a part of the family; I never ask him to pour the wine.) I see my grandfather only on holidays, though I try to call him at least once a week. I beg him to move out of Harlem; he has been having trouble lately with Puerto Rican street gangs who come into the shop demanding protection money. He is seventy-four years old, and though I can remember in exact detail the courageous stand he took in 1937, I am now truly fearful for his life. He belittles my concern. "*È niente*," he tells me. "*Non ti preoccupare, Ignazio.*" The Italian words almost move me to tears. I do not know why. I have begun to learn a great many Yiddish expressions. Rebecca's friends tell me I'm more Jewish than she is. "You're a bigger Jew than any of us," they say, and I take pride in this, certain it means they approve of me. They are calling me a white nigger, but I do not realize it.

In bed, in our spacious bedroom overlooking Ninety-seventh Street, in an apartment we are beginning to think we cannot afford, I sometimes wonder who is under the covers with Rebecca and me. It is surely not the two of us alone, grappling with this sweaty antagonist who yields so grudgingly. Is Tina in the closet wriggling her ass on these rumpled sheets, is Basilio in the locker room squirming against a Palumbo cock now become my own? It cannot be the two of us alone, laboring in tangled enterprise gone stale. I never know when she desires me now; she gives me not the faintest clue. I sometimes lie engorged beside her, certain she can sense my heat, yet reluctant to make an overture that will be either rebuffed or ridiculed. Where once *I* was the Blind Shaygets, all of me, all five feet eleven inches of me (a title I wore proudly because it defined her father's own blind prejudice), the appellation has now been applied by Rebecca to three or four or five or seven inches of me instead—my one-eyed cock rising in blind expectation against her flesh. "Ooops, here comes the Blind Shaygets," she says, and sometimes seizes me in both hands, and shakes me, and says in mock (I think) anger, "Don't you ever sleep, *shaygets*? What do you want to do, knock me up again?" She is terrified of having another baby. She sometimes stands before the mirror examining the stretch marks on her belly, and says (although she knows I cannot see), "Look what you did to me." So I lie beside her waiting for a move that never comes, waiting for her to reach for me and murmur, "Do you want to make love?" Sometimes, she encircles the Blind Shaygets with her hand, and gently teases it till I am quaking with desire, and then her hand stops, and I wait. And wait. And wait. And then realize she has drifted off to sleep with a hard-on in her fist.

When we do make love, she tells me I must learn to control what is surely premature ejaculation. If I complain that Susan Koenig never seemed to find my orgasms too swift for her pleasure, she tells me Susan Koenig was a fucking sex fiend, and besides, she doesn't want to hear about Susan Koenig or Michelle whatever-her-name-was with the big tits. So I learn to control my premature ejaculations. While pumping diligently away, Rebecca supervising the work on our construction site ("That's it, a little faster, *no*, goddamnit, don't stop what you're doing"), I allow my mind to consider the conformation of bicycle wheels or roller skates, lemon peels or stale pizza crusts, anything to keep from spurting too soon into that lubricated vault stuffed with dia- phragm and diagrams. And when at last she grudgingly releases what she has been hoarding, expiring on a single exhalation of breath, tumbling from the spire of the Chrysler Building or the top of the Brooklyn Bridge or whatever architectural wonder we have wrought together, only then do I allow myself to consider Michelle's swollen breasts or Susan's grinding hips or thirsting mouth, and come inside Rebecca.

"Those are very nice snapshots," Tante Raizel says.

4

Would you like to know how I became a big success?

By accident.

And overnight, of course. This is America, and all successes here happen overnight. Ten years of studying classical music, and eleven years of learning to play jazz—the nights are longer here, especially now that we're on daylight-saving time all year round.

My mother still can't believe a grown man can earn a living playing piano. If I were not blind, I'm sure she'd insist I find a good civil service job. Even being blind, I should be able to do something else, no? (Like what, Mom? Watch repairing?) Did I mention that my father collects all sorts of things? Anal, I'm sure. Coins, stamps, first-day covers, matchbooks, cigar bands, and of course clippings about his famous son, Dwight Jamison. Didn't I mention it? Time is running out, this is the last thirty-two bars, and I have the feeling there are many things I haven't mentioned yet. He's a collector, Pop is. He is especially proud of his coin collection; he has left it to my youngest son David in his will. I know because my lawyer prepared the will. First let me tell you about that coin collection, and then I'll tell you about my mother's attitude toward piano players in general and me in particular. If I forget anything, just nudge me.

357

My manager, Mark Aronowitz, also collects coins. With him, it's an investment. (Everything with Mark is an investment, which is why he doesn't call me much anymore.) Well, in 1961, 1962, I'm not sure which, the baker decided to sell the house on 217th Street because "the neighborhood was changing." This meant the neighborhood was becoming black. My parents found a new apartment on the Grand Concourse. Ironically, they chose this location because it was close to where Sophie and Abe were living. By that time, they had become fast friends with the Baumgartens, played poker with them every Sunday night, became members of their Family Circle, went to Broadway musicals and kosher restaurants with them, the whole megillah. Anyway, my mother insisted that my father clear out all that junk on the sun porch before they moved. She was referring to his collection of coins, stamps, matchbooks, and so on. I suggested to my father that if he was thinking of selling the coins, my manager might be happy to take them off his hands. "Well, I don't know if he can afford them," my father said. "They're worth a fortune." (Are you ahead of me? You can never anticipate me at the piano because while *you're* listening to Bar 10, *I'm* already working on Bar 11 in my head—but this ain't a piano, ma'am.) My father lugged his precious coins down to Broadway and Forty-seventh, and Mark looked them over and called me that very afternoon. "Ike," he said, "what am I supposed to *tell* your father? The stuff is worth face value; there isn't a rare or even slightly hard-to-find coin in the lot." I handled it by telling my father a lie. I told him he was right, Mark simply couldn't afford the collection, he'd probably do better taking it to a dealer. My father never took it to a dealer. "The hell with it," he said, "I'll leave it to the kids." So when he dies, David will inherit from him something worth maybe five hundred dollars, if that much. It's the thought that counts.

Which brings us to what my mother thinks about piano players.

It was along about this same time, just before the move to the Grand Concourse, while my mother was still ranting and raving about all that junk on the sun porch, that she made a remark I consider classic. We were lingering over coffee (as they say in novels) at the dinner table in the new house Rebecca and I had built in Talmadge. My mother, in her characteristically compromising fashion, said, "If you don't get somebody to take that stuff away, Jimmy, I'm going to throw it in the garbage."

"Aw, come on, Stella," he said.

"Come on, Mom," I said. "That's his hobby."

"That's right, Stella, it's my hobby."

"Your hobby?" my mother said. "If you need a hobby, why don't you get one that doesn't clutter up the whole house?"

"Like what?" my father asked.

(Are you ready?)

"Like your son's," my mother answered. "Playing piano."

I had earned close to four hundred thousand dollars playing piano that year, what with record albums and sheet music and personal appearances and the lot. I owned a department store in Dallas (for the depreciation value) and interests in oil wells (one of which had actually come in), and my tax lawyer had told me I would become a millionaire within the next three years, provided things continued to go well for me. But to good old Stella, piano playing was a hobby, and my success was a freak.

She was right. It was.

❖

Here's what happened.

In 1955, I changed everybody's name. Rebecca Baumgarten Di Palermo became Rebecca Jamison, and I became Dwight Jamison, and my three sons became, respectively and respectfully, Andrew, Michael, and David Jamison. Actually, when we named the boys, who were separately born in 1949, 1951, and 1953, we were trying to find names that sounded good with Di Palermo. Andrew, Michael, and David sounded fine to us—and American besides.

359

We changed the Di Palermo, finally, because we got tired of people asking us how we were going to raise the children. (That was the *good* reason; I still don't know what the *real* reason was.) When you change your name, the Department of Health will send you, at your request, a pink birth certificate with the new name on it. There is no indication on this certificate that your name once was Merton Luftfenster. It merely states that Lance Wasp was born in the city of New York on such and such a date. It looks exactly like the birth certificate that might have been issued way back then when you first drew breath. Not a soul can tell the difference, and it saves you the trouble of producing your court order every time you apply for a passport or a driver's license or an insurance policy or anything requiring proof of age and birthplace. New York City is very accommodating in this respect. But that is only natural since New York perhaps best represents the spirit of constant change that is America.

Marian McPartland once said to me, "Drummers are always disappearing, Ike, have you ever noticed that? I wonder where they *go* all the time."

Marian . . . *people* are always disappearing.

Ignazio Silvio Di Palermo disappeared in 1955, when my lawyer went before a judge to petition for the name change. He said it was for professional reasons, a blatant lie since by then I was known as Blind Ike, and was in fact playing under that name at a club on the East Side. The judge signed a court order, and told my lawyer that the order had to be published in a newspaper of the court's choice within twenty days, just in case anyone had any objections whatever to my becoming more American than I already was. No one objected, and we all became Jamisons. It only remained to send two bucks to the Board of Health for each of those brand-new pink certificates. How simple it is to disappear from the face of the earth, unless (like me) you are plagued by memories.

Everybody (except my grandfather) continued calling me Ike,

of course—they had, after all, been calling me that for almost a decade. But I was now Dwight Jamison. As a boy at the Blind School, I had learned to write my own name in longhand, using a sheet of raised letters, and a board with sunken letters, and writing paper embossed with guidelines a half inch apart. I would feel the raised letters with my fingertips, touching each until I thought I knew each curlicue, tail, and dot. Then I would fit my pencil into the sunken letters on the board, learning how to manually recreate each letter by tracing it over and over again, the pencil tip caught in the grooves. And finally, I would practice my signature on the paper, feeling the raised lines and knowing the upper and lower limits of the defining space. I did not know what my handwriting looked like. My mother said I wrote like a Chink. She should only have known how long and how hard I practiced my signature.

I had to practice another signature when I became Dwight Jamison.

I changed my name just in the nick, as it turned out, because I was on the verge of becoming a big success, ma'am, and think of what might have happened to Kirk Douglas if he'd still been Issur Danielovitch Demsky when he made *Champion*. Talent notwithstanding, my success was pure unadulterated chance, the result of a series of accidents, cause and effect mating to produce an inescapable conclusion. My quintet consisted of five musicians (what else? eight?). Cappy Kaplan, from the original Auntie's trio, had been killed in the Korean War, but Stu Holman was still with me on bass. As drummer, I was using another black man, a kid named Peter Dodds, who succumbed to drugs before we opened at Birdland the following year; he sent us a congratulatory telegram from Lexington, Kentucky, where he was trying to kick the habit. On trumpet, I had a white man named Hank D'Allessio (who had not changed his name for professional reasons) and on vibes another white man named Larry Kimberly. The quintet was what is known in the trade as a "salt and pepper band." But

361

tell me, does the instrumentation strike a familiar note, ring a reminiscent bell? Here's your clue: the vibraphone. In 1955, before I became a big success by accident, I was mostly being "influenced" by George Shearing, who had begun winning all those *Down Beat* polls back in 1949, and who had singlehandedly buried solo piano in a grave so deep that resurrection was impossible. There are some piano players who instantly generate excitement among other piano players, and Shearing was one of them. I had first heard him on a record he had cut for Savoy, and later caught him at the Three Deuces, where he was busting the joint wide open with what was then a trio. By 1950, every piano player in the country was trying to copy him, and I was no exception. The same thing had happened in the thirties, incidentally, when a then-current musician's accolade—"Tatum, no one can overrate 'im"—was coupled with the warning: "Tatum, no one can imitate 'im." I was unabashedly imitating George Shearing in 1955, right down to the incidental blindness and the almost identical instrumentation—I was using a trumpet in place of the guitar George had in his quintet.

When I accidentally tripped over the hairy unwashed body of success, the quintet (mine, not George's) was playing at a fairly decent club on the East Side, pulling down respectable loot (twelve bills a week) and enjoying some sort of recognition in a profession not noted for its charity. On a Thursday night, Larry Kimberly, my vibes player, got sick. (He *said* he was sick; I think he was on a bender. No matter.) I called Mark Aronowitz, who had begun managing me six months earlier, and who had in fact come up with the East Side gig, and told him I needed a vibes player to fill in for the weekend. Mark said he'd get right to work on it; he called me back late Friday afternoon.

"Well," he said, "I've got a flute player for you."

"A *what?*" I said.

"A flute player."

"What the hell am I going to do with a flute player?"

"This is a very fine flute player. He played with the Boston Symphony."

"Mark," I said, "I need a vibes player."

"No vibes players," he said.

"What do you mean, no vibes players?"

"None. Noplace. I called 802, I called every agent and manager I know, I even called Benny up in Connecticut, and asked him for Hamp's number on the off chance *he* might know somebody. But Hamp's out of town, and there is not a single fucking vibes player in the entire city of New York this weekend, and that is that."

"That's impossible," I said. "There must be *thousands* of vibes players looking for work."

"Yeah?" Mark said. "Where are they?"

"I don't want a flute player," I said.

"What do you want? A tenor sax? A trombone? Name it. The only thing I can't get is a vibes player. I thought a flute sounded a lot like a vibraphone."

"Mark, it doesn't sound *anything* like a vibraphone."

"Silvery, you know? This guy is a fine musician, Ike. Take him, try him out. Just for the weekend. I'm not asking you to marry him."

"What's his name?" I asked.

His name was Orion (I swear to God) Burke, and he was the first link in the chain of events that led to the success of the Dwight Jamison Quintet. The second link was a singer named Gerri Pryce. You've never heard of her; she didn't grow up to be Petula Clark or anybody. She was a girl of nineteen who was also on Mark's list of "artists," as he chose to call us. He had been grooming her (and probably fucking her) since she was seventeen, and he had miraculously arranged a recording date for her on the Thursday following the night Orion Burke joined the band. I did not like the way the band sounded with a flute substituting for the vibes —which shows how much I know. But Orry was indeed a fine musician (who insisted on calling himself a "flautist," by the way, pish-posh) and he got on to what we were laying down after a quick Friday rehearsal, and the weekend went by without incident or fanfare. That is to say, nobody came up to the stand to tell us they missed the vibes, but neither did anyone tell us how extraordinary we sounded with a flute in there. Monday was our night off, and on Tuesday Mark called to say he wanted us to back Gerri Pryce on her record date.

"Who's Gerri Pryce?" I asked.

"Nobody you know yet," he said. "She's going to be a big star."

"How much is the gig paying?" I asked.

"Minimum," he said. "This is a very small record company, an independent, but when Gerri hits it big with this single, I'll be able to go back to them and remind them who was on the gig with her."

"Why do I always end up with all the shit gigs?" I asked Mark.

"Oh?" he said. "Oh? Is the gig you're playing now a shit gig? I didn't realize twelve bills a week was shit. You're taking home more than three hundred for yourself each and every week, Ike, and that puts a lot of meat and potatoes on the table, and that is not *shit*, Ike, that is good hard American currency on my block. Now perhaps you consider it an imposition to be asked by your manager to play for somebody who's going to be a singing sensation as soon as this single is released, and who is giving you his sacred word of honor . . ."

"All right, Mark."

". . . that once this record takes off, I'll go back to the company and be in a position to negotiate a contract for the quintet, on terms more acceptable . . ."

"All right, already."

"Three o'clock Thursday, Nola Studios," Mark said, and hung up.

In 1955, it cost thirty dollars an hour to rent space at Nola Studios, and the company cutting Gerri Pryce's first Big Hit Single (or so Mark hoped) had reserved the facilities for three hours of rehearsal and recording time. In addition, they had paid Gerri a five-hundred-dollar advance against royalties, and they were paying the quintet scale, which came to $41.25 for each sideman and double that for the leader. According to union regulations, this permitted them to utilize our talents for a maximum of three hours, in which time they were entitled to cut four ten-inch masters, each side running no longer than three and a half minutes. The A&R man and the sound technician were the company's own, and on salary. Still, the session was going to cost $837.50, which was a considerable amount for a small independent to be shelling out. There was an air of confidence in the studio when we assembled at 3 P.M. Since we were there to rehearse and record only two sides, the three hours should have been more than enough time to ensure a professional job.

But Gerri Pryce, at the age of nineteen, already considered herself a star, even though she had never cut a record, and even though her singing engagements to date had been exclusively limited to a series of toilets on Long Island's Sunrise Highway. She walked into the studio an hour and twenty minutes late, by which time the A&R man—whose name was Rudy Hirsch—was ready to climb the walls. She was accompanied by an entourage consisting of a weight lifter from San Diego, whom she introduced as her chauffeur (his motorcycle was probably parked illegally downstairs), and who grunted "Groovy" when he shook my hand; a fluttery old woman named Mabel, who knocked over Hank D'Allessio's music stand and tittered endlessly while precious seconds were frittering away (she was Gerri's hairdresser, though Christ alone knew why a hairdresser was necessary on a recording date); and Gerri's uncle, a dyspeptic forty-two-year-old Pole (Gerri had changed her name from Przybora) who was there to make sure his niece's innocence remained unsullied; he had heard a lot about musicians, old Uncle Stanislaw. I later heard from Mark (but this may be gossip) that young Gerri had taken on the entire marching band of a high school in Secaucus when she was but a fourteen-year-old cheerleader. But there she was at nineteen, chauffeured, coiffed, cloistered, and an hour and twenty minutes late. She nonetheless insisted, rightfully, that we rehearse the two tunes she was about to record. She had written one of these tunes herself, and this was to be the Big Hit side of the record. The tune was called "Mooning," and the lyric, if I recall it correctly, went something like this:

> Mooning,
> Mooning for you.
> Tuning my heartstrings,
> Tearing in two
> Love letters written
> When we were a duo.
> Mooning for you.
> Do you, oh, do you, oh,
> Moon for me, too?

The chart was the very one I had tried to explain to Susan Koenig on the day she introduced me to the mysteries and delights of blind passion, with that selfsame overworked I, VI, II, V in the first two bars.

"Terrific, ain't it?" Mark Aronowitz said to me as we ran down the chords.

"Bound to be a smash," I said.

We spent close to forty minutes rehearsing the tune, and we were ready to record the first take when Gerri announced that she had to go to the ladies', and swept out of the studio followed by her tittering hairdresser. The boys and I sat waiting for her to come back. Rudy Hirsch was pacing nervously. Five minutes went by. Ten minutes. Rudy said, "Mark, will you for Christ's sake go find her?" Mark went out of the studio, and Orry began blowing a twelve-bar blues, and we all picked up on him and jammed for the next ten minutes, and still no Gerri, and now no Mark either.

"Shut up, you guys," Rudy said. "Where are they?" he asked Uncle Stanislaw, who replied, *"Kto wie?"*

"Go find them," Rudy said to the chauffeur from San Diego, and the chauffeur said "Groovy" and went out of the studio. We were ten minutes into the third and final hour already, and we still hadn't cut a take, nor had we yet rehearsed the tune that was to be the flip side of the record.

Mark came back into the studio and said, "The lady's gone home."

"What?" Rudy said. "What do you mean, she's gone home? *Home?* Where is she?"

"I told you. She went home."

"Why?"

"Female complaint."

"What?"

"She's menstruating," Mark said. "She has cramps."

"What?"

"Rudy," Mark said, "I can't believe you're as hard of hearing as you pretend to be."

"What?" Rudy said. He was about to have a fit. I have heard many men on the edge of throwing a tantrum, and Rudy was right there, an inch away. "Are you telling me that dumb cunt walked out of here because she . . ."

"Have *you* ever tried singing when you're menstruating?" Mark said.

"I have never," Rudy said, "in my entire experience in the music business had some dumb cunt walk out of a recording session because she got her period. I have had a dumb cunt blow every member of the band, including the drummer, and I have had a dumb cunt threaten to slit her wrists if we didn't fire the trombonist, but never, and this goes back thirty years in this fucking business, never have I had a cunt tell me she couldn't sing because she got her period. What the fuck has anybody's *period* got to do with the music business?"

"We'll try it again tomorrow," Mark said.

"The *fuck* we will!" Rudy exploded. "You think *I'm* going back to Harry and tell him we spent all this money for nothing? He'll throw me out the window."

"*I'll* talk to Harry," Mark said.

"I want the five bills back," Rudy said abruptly. "I want that money back. And you tell that cunt singer of yours if I ever lay eyes on her again, I'll give her such a period she'll never forget it in her life. I'll give her such cramps . . ."

"Rudy, please relax," Mark said calmly. "We'll try again to-morrow."

"We'll try again *never!*" Rudy shouted. "I paid for today, not tomorrow. We got forty-five minutes left I already paid for, who's going to absorb that? You? You'll be lucky if Harry doesn't sue you! You wouldn't pull this if we were Columbia, I can tell you that. You think because we're small . . ."

"Rudy, please, you'll have a heart attack."

"That's better than getting thrown out the window," Rudy shouted, and then he must have pressed the button connecting him to the control booth because he suddenly asked in a much calmer voice, "How much time do we have exactly, Ned?"

"Forty-one seven," a voice said over the loudspeaker.

"I'm getting two sides out of this session," Rudy said. "I *paid* for two sides, and I'm going *back* with two sides. What can these shlocks play?"

I realized he was referring to the Dwight Jamison Quintet.

"How about 'Stardust'?" I said.

"Very funny," Rudy said. "Ned," he said, "take your level, and get ready to roll."

"Right," Ned said over the loudspeaker.

"I want a jump and a ballad," Rudy said to me. "How's the time, Ned?"

"Thirty-nine twenty," Ned answered.

Rudy was standing close to the piano now; his voice was almost confidential. "Start playing," he said. "Ned'll let us know when he's got his level, and then it's for real. If we're lucky, we'll get two takes on each side."

"Just a second here," Mark said.

"What now? If we run into overtime . . ."

"These men were hired to back a vocalist," Mark said. "I accepted scale because . . ."

"And you're *taking* scale, too," Rudy said, "or I'll go to AFTRA and your cunt singer'll never open her mouth again in New York. Ned, you ready?"

"Ready."

"How about you, maestro?"

"Give us a minute to run down the tunes, will you?"

"We ain't *got* a minute," Rudy said. "Ned, where are we?"

"Thirty-seven twelve."

"Play," Rudy said. "Play good."

The jump tune we chose was "A Night in Tunisia," which by 1955 had already become a bop standard. We had no opportunity to rehearse it or time it. We did six bars, and then Ned cut in to say he had his level, and I counted off the beat again, and we took it from the top. Rudy stopped us before we got to the bridge, telling us we were playing too fast. Peter Dodds, my drummer, muttered something under his breath. He had cut his chops playing almost *everything* at breakneck speed, and here was a half-assed A&R man telling us we were playing too fast when maybe we were ambling along at 250 on the metronome. I counted off again, slower this time, and we got through the second take without any interruptions from Rudy. He listened to the playback, checked the time with Ned again, and said he wanted another take, this time with an added unison chorus of flute and piano. (Rudy was later to take credit for the "distinctive sound" of the Dwight Jamison Quintet.) We did the third take, and Rudy said it was "satisfactory." (You was adequate, man.) I hadn't much liked the sound of it at all. Orry and I had not rehearsed any of

369

the riffs we played together, and it seemed to me they were extraordinarily sloppy. For the flip side, we had decided on "The Man I Love." Rudy checked the time again, and Ned informed him we had five minutes and twenty-two seconds left before our studio time ended. By union edict, each side of a single could run no longer than three and a half minutes. This meant we had to get the ballad right on the first take. Either that, or Rudy would have to go back to his boss with only one side of a record, and Harry would throw him out of the window.

"All right, let's go, let's go," he said. "You. You got a mute?"

"Me?" Hank asked.

"No, the flute player, who the fuck you think I mean?"

"Sure, I've got a mute," Hank said.

"Put it in your horn. And *you*, I want brushes on the ride cymbal, and no klook-a-mop shit. I want everybody cooling it but the piano and the flute, that's what I want to hear mostly. Open it with piano and flute in unison, then give me two choruses on piano, one on flute, back to the head again and out. You got me? The rest of you guys play anything louder than a whisper, I'll cut off your balls. Ned, what've we got?"

"Four and twenty," Ned said, and he was not referring to blackbirds baked in a pie.

"Let's go, here's your beat," Rudy said. "One . . . two . . ."

"I'll set the tempo," I said.

"You played too fast on . . ."

"It's *my* band, *I'll* set the tempo," I said.

Rudy might have argued the point further, but time was running out, time was tick-tocking along, and success was waiting in the wings to gather us into his powerful arms, and press us to his barrel chest, and belch into our faces. The contretemps lasted no more than ten seconds.

"Just, for Christ's sake, start *playing!*" Rudy said.

I have listened to that unrehearsed, totally improvised version of "The Man I Love" countless times since 1955, in an attempt to understand why disk jockeys all over the country, including those on the rock stations, suddenly began playing the record incessantly. Payola did not account for it. Rudy's company was small and virtually without funds; we might, in fact, have sold many more copies than we actually did if distribution and promotion had been even slightly better. I am firmly convinced, and Rudy swears to it, that nobody got anything under the table. The record simply took off, and I'll be damned if I know why. In my estimation, it is simply not a very good record. All it did was define a sound, and even the sound was an accident.

I still believe we achieved that smoothly rehearsed ensemble effect only because we were trying to prove to Rudy that a group of highly trained musicians did not have to be told how to blow or at what speed. I think Hank and Peter were angry all through the three minutes and forty-four seconds it took us to cut the side. If you listen closely to the record, you can hear a heated understatement from the trumpet and drums, as though they are trying to push through the imposed restraints—the straight mute in the horn, the brushes on the top cymbals. Listening, you can hear rage seething in the background, vibrating beneath the diamond-hard (also somewhat angry) piano, and the silvery-cool tones of the flute. (Mark was later to take credit for the flute; it had been *his* inspiration, he said.)

But in addition to the anger, and perhaps as a result of it, the sound also has that quality of reckless freedom one usually associates with a jam session. We were all of us quite relaxed, despite Rudy's hysteria. Frankly, none of us gave a good goddamn about his problems, nor did we for a moment believe the record would ever be released. We figured Rudy was simply protecting his job. He must have felt fairly certain that Mark would return the five-hundred-dollar advance paid to Gerri Pryce, the unknown disappearing singing star. But he had agreed to pay us for three hours at scale, and we were still there, we had not walked out, we had not had our periods, we had in fact already done three takes on an undistinguished "Night in Tunisia," and he would have to pay us in full whether we cut the second side of the record or not. The way we figured it, the two sides were Rudy's insurance policy. He could not go back to his boss with nothing to show for the company's cash outlay. If his boss didn't like the sides, well, there was no accounting for taste, right? Into the ashcan, and better luck next time; Rudy had done his job, he had delivered a viable record. Meanwhile, all we were getting was scale, and for scale you do not bust your ass. For scale, you relax— especially when the session is going to be over and done with in less than four minutes. We were all very relaxed.

My piano playing on "Man" is almost a put-on, in fact, a combination of clumpy Dave Brubeck, bluesy-funky Horace Silver, and pyrotechnic Oscar Peterson. Orry, too, is more frivolous on this side than on the "Tunisia" cut, perhaps because he was sensing my own devil-may-care, what-the-hell attitude. Our head chorus, possibly the only display of real musicianship on the record, is a small miracle of precision, considering we'd never rehearsed any of the figures we played spontaneously and in unison. (They may have been bop figures we'd both heard before, I'm sure I don't know; they sound fresh and improvisational to me, even now.) The lead-in Orry gives to my piano solo is a corny, overworked bop riff, a series of eighth-note triplets, which he restates at the end of my two choruses and uses as a springboard for his own thoroughly uninspired solo. Eight bars into Orry's solo, Peter and Hank suddenly stop playing, and Stu Holman begins walking the chart on bass, with me tossing right-hand sprinkles haphazardly into the mix (it sounds a little like a stout man walking ponderously on glass, which shatters with each footfall) until we go into the head and home with the full ensemble. Hank takes out the straight mute before we wrap it up, and Peter drops a bass-drum bomb that comes like an unexpected belch, Orry and I repeating the same figures we played at the top, this time more knowledgeably. That last single-string strum on the bass is because

372

Stu Holman somehow thought we were going into another chorus. It promises something that never comes because that's where the record ends. When I later asked Peter and Hank why they'd stopped playing eight bars into Orry's flute solo, they told me he was boring them out of their minds, and they just quit.

That was the record that ensured almost ten years of popularity.

The quintet has probably played "The Man I Love" twenty thousand times since 1955. The musicians come and go, they are replaced, they leave to form groups of their own (as did Orry), they become hopeless addicts (as did Peter), or they simply quit the music business (as did Hank D'Allessio, who is now a real estate agent in Santa Monica). The only one of the original quintet who is still with me when we play infrequent club dates is Stu Holman. But wherever and whenever we play, "The Man I Love" is always requested, and if we deviate by so much as a thirty-second note from the way we played it on that ancient disk, the crowd begins to grumble. We are supposed to reproduce the record note by note, without variation, a demand anathema to jazz musicians. (I knew exactly how Bobby Darin felt, may God rest his soul, when I caught him in Vegas years after his initial success, and he was singing up a storm, better than he'd ever sung in his life, and all the audience wanted to hear was "Mack the Knife.") I'm a better musician now than I was in 1955. I know for certain that any one of my quintets, on occasions too numerous to recall, has played "The Man I Love" better than the original quintet did on that September Thursday in 1955. In fact, when the original quintet (minus Peter, who was in Lexington) opened at Birdland the next year, we jammed on "Man" for a full twenty minutes, and Christ, we were beautiful that night, we put to shame the record that had launched us into the big time.

But who can argue with success?

As Biff had prophesied, we had somehow made the right music in the right time and the right place. By the beginning of 1956, there was not a jazz buff in the United States of America who did not know of the Dwight Jamison Quintet. Rudy Hirsch was jubilant. His boss, Harry Arnberg, offered us a long-term recording contract. In gratitude for the splendid job Harry had done with our first record, Mark Aronowitz promptly signed the quintet with RCA Victor.

That's show biz.

❖

He had turned her pictures to the wall, he had told everyone his eldest daughter was dead. She had married a blind *shaygets*, a wop entertainer, she was dead. But he comes around in 1956, after eight years of silence. Coincidentally, this is after I've opened at Birdland to resounding critical cheers, and am no longer a blind *shaygets* to Honest Abe; I have become his "son-in-law the jazz artist." He has three grandchildren to discover. They distinguish him from "Papa Jimmy," their other grandfather, by calling him "Papa Abe." There is a lot of catching up to do. To facilitate the osmosis of Papa Abe into the family bloodstream, Rebecca puts the "big one" on the turntable. We are living at the time on Park and Eighty-first, in an apartment we've sublet from a saxophone player who is in Paris. The windows are open, a balmy New York spring flirts with the stench of cigar smoke (my father's and Abe's) in the living room twelve stories above the street.

"This is the one that did it," Rebecca says.

"Daddy got a hit with it," Andrew says proudly.

"Well, well," Abe says. "Well, well. What record *was* that?"

" 'The Man I Love,' " Andrew says. "*Everybody* knows that."

I listen to the record. I have not yet grown weary of listening to it. At Sophie's insistence, Rebecca is breaking out the photo album again. "Show him the pictures of when you were in Florida," Sophie says. "Show him the pictures, darling."

"That's a very nice record," Abe says. "I think I heard it on the radio. Very nice."

Success at last. Approval from the Mad Oldsmobile Dealer.

For our perseverance and our courage, and to prove that only good things come to those of us who have the integrity to stand up for our convictions (ours being that only in America can a Jew and a Gentile, working side by side in the same double bed, construct Rockefeller Center), Rebecca and I have been rewarded with S*U*C*C*E*S*S! We have obediently learned the American myth, and faithfully adhered to its precepts, and we can now live in the luxury of its full realization, while simultaneously serving as prime examples of its validity. "Look at your father," Stella tells my children. "He was raised in Harlem; see what can happen in America?" Stella believes it. Rebecca believes it. I believe it.

"How come you never blow me?" I ask her.

"How would *you* like a prick shoved into *your* mouth?" she answers. She never calls it a "cock," though I have asked her to repeatedly. To her, it is a prick. To a man, a prick is a son-of-a-bitch bastard. When I explain this to her, she says, "Who told you that? Susan Koenig?"

But her tone is bantering now, and not at all malicious. In and out of bed, her mood is playful and assured. She often goes around the apartment humming in her slightly off-key voice, and once—to my great surprise—she sings "On the Good Ship Lollipop" at the top of her lungs, waking David, who is in for his afternoon nap. It is as though the hit record, not the record itself, but what the record *means*—the mink coat in the closet, the leopard beside it for sportier occasions, the forty acres of land we have purchased in Connecticut, the jazz-buff architect who is thrilled that he is designing a residence for *the* Dwight Jamisons, the paintings Rebecca buys at Hammer Galleries in anticipation of the move to the country—all of these have caused her to look at herself in a new and exciting way. So when I remind her again

375

that it is a cock, and not a prick, she seizes it just below the head and says, "A cock, is it? Oh, is *that* what you are? Hello, cock, let me kiss you, cock," and kisses it noisily, and then says, "Oh, that's a nice tasty cock, how would you like me to suck you out of your mind, cock?" and goes down on me with a fervor that knocks all memories of Susan Koenig clear across the room, and out the window, and down to Park Avenue, and perhaps clear across the East River. "Now *that* was a premature ejaculation," she says, and giggles against my wet belly, and then murmurs, "Hurry up and get big again, Ike. I want you to fuck me."

I lie with one hand covering my eyes, grinning foolishly at the ceiling. The construction company of Jamison & Jamison, Inc., has finally come through, we have finally made it; all it took was a little sprinkling of success.

"I'm probably putting you to sleep, Daddy," Rebecca says.

"No, no, the snapshots are really very interesting," Abe says. "Quite interesting, Ike," he says, using my name for the first time that day.

When he leaves the apartment later, he gives each of the boys a five-dollar bill. Penance, Papa Abe? For all those wasted years?

You prick.

❖

Actually, I liked him.

He had style, the prick.

The shark, for example. In the spring of 1957, while the house in Talmadge was being built, the saxophone player came back from Paris, and we took a place on Martha's Vineyard for the summer, rather than go through the hassle of looking for another apartment, which we knew we'd be vacating in the fall. I spent a lot of time on that ferry from Woods Hole to Vineyard Haven because the quintet was playing in Boston, and I was virtually commuting back and forth from the island. But the gig ended the last week in August, and Rebecca invited the entire Baumgarten clan to spend that week with us—which I needed like a *loch in kop*; I was exhausted, and scheduled to leave again for San Francisco just after Labor Day.

Our rented house in Menemsha was set high on a bluff overlooking Vineyard Sound and (I am told) the most beautiful sunset anywhere in the Western Hemisphere. But the Menemsha beach was quite rocky that summer, and Davina's husband, an accountant named Seth Lewis (né Levine), constantly complained about having to drive to a beach on the ocean side.

"Don't be a pain in the ass, Seth," Davina told him.

"I thought there were supposed to be private little beaches here," Seth said in his whining adolescent voice. "I thought people swam in the nude here and everything."

"People *do* swim in the nude here," I said.

"If you haven't seen a bunch of aging publishers and their wives swimming around in the nude," Rebecca said, "you haven't lived, Seth."

"Would you like everybody to see me swimming around in the nude?" Davina asked.

"What's so special about you in the nude?" Seth answered.

According to Rebecca, Seth was either as blind as I, or else totally jaded after four years of marriage. Rebecca told me Davina was quite beautiful, and this was a gracious admission indeed, since there was little love lost between the two sisters. Davina was described to me as a tall blonde, her long hair worn loose and sleek, her green eyes dominating the pale oval of her face. She had a generous bosom for someone so slender, and was blessed with spectacular legs besides, which she showed to best advantage in shorts rolled high on her thighs, or long party skirts slit up each side. She was undeniably the center of attraction at most of the insufferably "in" cocktail parties we attended. There was, in fact, almost as much ooh-ing and aah-ing over Davina as there was over the sunsets, or the sneak previews of scores from Broadway shows in preparation, or the new painting by any one of the island's artists in summer residence, or the current performance by this or that visiting actor; everybody was "somebody" on Martha's Vineyard, and Davina Lewis was "somebody," too, if only because she was so extraordinarily lovely. I am speaking now of her physical appearance. Since I had never seen the lady, I could only judge how lovely she was by what she said and what she did. I did not find her particularly attractive. It seemed to me that she made impossible demands on both Seth *and* her father, requesting, for example, that one or another of them drive her all the way to Oak Bluffs so she could ride the carousel (I mean, for Christ's sake, she was twenty-five years old!), or one day forcing Abe to take her all over the island in search of a lobster roll because the shack up on the hill near the beach was temporarily out of them. She was not pregnant, there was no excuse for satisfying this bizarre and childish urge. (She had, in fact, *never* been pregnant, and professed she would jump off the cliffs at Gay Head if ever she missed her period. She said this in the presence of my three sons.)

At cocktail parties, Davina was quick to announce that she was Dwight Jamison's sister-in-law, and seemed to enjoy whatever cachet this guaranteed. I have never (much) begrudged anyone taking a free ride on my coattails. My father has taken advantage of my fame often enough, as has Honest Abe. Even Rebecca, whenever she signed for anything in a department store, was inordinately delighted if a shopgirl asked, "Are you *the* Mrs. Dwight Jamison?" Come to think of it, the only ones who've *never* used my position to further their own are my sons. I have overheard conversations between them and new acquaintances. When the talk got to music and eventually to jazz, my sons never once revealed that their father was *the* Dwight Jamison. I respect them for that. (Or should I? Is there something darker in their act of omission? Come on, you fucking wop! You're as paranoid as the entire city of Naples!) It rankled (a little) when Abe boasted about me to potential car buyers—did you sell more Oldsmobiles because I was your son-in-law, you prick?—and it annoyed me, too, when Davina, sleekly blond and tanned ("She looks terrific, the bitch!" Rebecca said), whispered to a photographer, or a sculptor, or a writer, musician, or swordsman of renown, "Who, me? I'm nobody but Dwight Jamison's sister-in-law," knowing full well she was dazzling the poor bastard, anyway, with her beauty and her phony Hunter College speech major voice.

It did not hurt to put down poor Seth, either. A woman who puts down her husband sounds available, even if she isn't. In those days, I was never quite sure whether Davina was looking around or just taking jabs at Seth to keep him on his toes. Not that I liked *him* very much, either. He had a high nasal voice, and he was invariably complaining about one thing or another. If it wasn't the drive to the beach, then it was the service in a restaurant. And if it wasn't that, it was the sand in the bedroom. Or up his ass, for all I know. He was a mean little man who kept telling me I should get a new tax lawyer, when the lawyer I already had was well on the way to making me a millionaire. He kept yelling at my kids. Once, when he told Michael to stop making so much noise, I told him, "Michael lives here."

"I am your guest," Seth said.

"You can fucking well take the next ferry back," I said.

"Oh, is *that* it?" Seth said. "Well. I didn't know *that* was it." But he didn't take the next ferry back. Nor the one after that, either. He stayed the whole damn week, while Sophie, who never went to the beach, sat on the back porch and knitted. She was probably knitting a shawl identical to the one she wore around her shoulders on the hottest days. Sophie was always chilly. "It's in my blood," she said. She wore that gray woolen shawl to all the cocktail parties, too, where she chatted nervously with strangers—"How do you do, I'm Rebecca's mother"—and seemed clearly out of her element. Not so with Abe, the prick. Abe would meet a movie star and immediately and familiarly say, "Oh, sure, John [or Frank or Joe or Sam], I saw that picture you made, you were actually very good in it." Or, if introduced to the man who'd written the lyrics for one of Broadway's long-run musicals, Abe would burst into a song from the show, invariably out of tune, and then would slap the man on the back and say, "You wrote that, huh? What do you know? I sell Oldsmobiles."

He had style, the prick.

Of a sort.

On the day Abe took my eldest son fishing, Rebecca and I had a terrible fight. The fight was over a woman. Specifically, it was over a woman who had asked me to play "The Man I Love" at a cocktail party the night before. Rebecca knew I hated requests for "The Man I Love," and she wanted to know why I had so readily succumbed to this particular request from someone she termed "a horsy Wasp cooze from Bedford Village."

"I just felt like playing," I said.

"With whom?" she said. "The cooze?"

"I felt like playing *piano*," I said.

"I thought you were tired," she said. "You told me you were 'utterly exhausted,' weren't those your words, Ike? Didn't you say you couldn't understand why I'd invited the whole *mishpocheh* up here on the one week you'd hoped to get some rest?"

"That's what I said."

"Well, for somebody who's so *tired*, Ike, so *ut*terly ex*hau*sted, you certainly leaped to that piano in a flash when Miss Bedford Village put her hand on your arm."

"She did not put her hand on my arm. Or anyplace else."

"She put her hand on your arm, and she put her face so close to yours I thought she was giving you artificial respiration."

"She merely made a request, Rebecca."

"What did she request? 'Roll Me Over in the Clover'?"

"She requested 'The Man I Love.' You *know* what she requested."

"So you played it."

"I played it. You heard me play it."

"And she draped herself on the piano and sang along. I thought you hated people singing along when you play."

"I do."

"But you didn't mind *her* singing along."

"I didn't even *hear* her singing along."

"You didn't? Well, well, I knew you were blind, but I didn't realize you were deaf, too. She sang along in a very horsy Wasp cooze voice, with her mouth an inch from your left ear; are you *sure* you didn't hear her? Maybe we ought to take you to Manhattan Eye, Ear, Nose and . . ."

"Rebecca, what is the point of this?"

"The point, Ike, is that I find the sight of a man tripping over his own cane in a mad rush . . ."

"I did not trip over any goddamn cane . . ."

". . . in a mad rush to get to the piano because some twirpy blonde stinking of horse sweat puts her hand on his arm and requests a goddamn song you hate to play . . . well, Ike, that is just plain dis*gust*ing," she said, spitting out the word so that it really did sound disgusting. "When a man your age . . ."

"What do you mean, a man my age?"

"You are thirty-one years old," she said.

"So what's that? What the hell is *that* supposed to be? Decrepit?"

"Everyone thought you made a fool of yourself."

"I did not make a fool of myself."

"Everyone thought so. Including me."

"The cooze from Bedford Village did not think I made a fool of myself."

"Go to hell," Rebecca said, and stormed out of the house, the screen door clattering shut behind her. I went into the bedroom and closed the door behind me, and lay on the bed. I thought of what my brother Tony had promised me on those long rides to the Bronx, when I was taking lessons from Federico Passaro, who was going to make me a concert star. *You'll have beautiful girls hanging all over you, rich girls in long satin dresses, wearing pearls at their throats, draped on the piano, and never mind that you're blind, that won't matter to them, Iggie.* Well, in 1957, though many beautiful girls in long satin dresses, wearing pearls at their throats, had draped themselves on the piano in more cities than I could count, I was still (Surprise, Rebecca! Stick around, I'm full of surprises) as virginal, so to speak, as my grandfather had been in 1901 when Luisa Agnelli, feigning sleep, had flashed her luxuriant crotch at him.

Mark Aronowitz had told me that in the entire United States he knew only one man who was not cheating on his wife. That man was Mark himself. Mark did not consider his frequent extramarital excursions "cheating." Mark was simply "advancing careers." And besides, his wife knew all about his penchant for young singers, which automatically implied tacit approval on her part, and therefore rendered meaningless the word "cheating"; you cannot cheat someone who *knows* she is being short-changed. I did not tell Mark that he could add a second name to his list—that of Dwight Jamison. Instead, I went along with the American fantasy (I thought it was a fantasy at the time; it is not) that anyone achieving celebrity status could call his own tune with members of the opposite sex (or the same sex, for that matter). Whenever Mark and I had breakfast together after an opening night someplace, and he asked over scrambled eggs and coffee, "Did you boff that gorgeous blonde last night?" I automatically answered, "Why, Mark, you know I don't fuck around," which he automatically took to be a sly and gentlemanly denial of the all-night orgy he knew had taken place. My masculinity had been preserved, Mark's suspicions had been verified, and in addition, he had been able to assuage any guilt he might have felt for his own unfaithfulness to Josie—who, by all accounts, was a devastatingly beautiful girl who had given up a promising singing career only because she'd fallen so madly in love with Mark.

382

In 1957, I still thought the bedrock of a successful marriage was fidelity, and whereas I was subtly flattered by Rebecca's jealousy, I also had to admit that my response to the Bedford Village blonde (I had not known she was a blonde till Rebecca told me) had been something more than innocent. To begin with, she had definitely *not* smelled of horse sweat, no matter *what* Rebecca later claimed. Instead, she had smelled of something reminiscent of Susan Koenig's perfume, which of course recalled countless hours of ecstasy spent in Susan's embrace. Moreover, when she rested her hand briefly on my bare arm (I was wearing an imported short-sleeved sports shirt, and hand-tailored slacks), I felt a response that seemed wildly out of proportion to her delicate touch, as though she had applied pressure to a particularly sensitive spot that immediately flashed a signal to my groin. She put her face very close to mine, I sniffed in Susan's perfume or something very close to it, and detected the admixtured scent of minty toothpaste and—what else? Was it the lingering aroma of suntan oil? Had she not showered after her day on the beach? This thought, too, was somehow stimulating. She told me that she just *adored* the way I played piano, and would I *please*, as a personal favor to her, though she was sure everyone asked me to do this, I was probably bored to *tears* with the same request over and over again, but would I *please* just do a *few* choruses of "The Man I Love," for which she would be eternally grateful, *please*? I rushed to the piano, more in self-defense (the slacks were very tightly fitted) than in eagerness to please. She followed me there, and sang into my ear as I played, almost throwing me off meter. She told me afterward that her name was Hope Coslett and that she was in the Westchester directory. "Hope is the thing with feathers," she whispered. Lying on the bed in the room I shared with Rebecca, I wondered what she'd meant. If I ever called her, would she do a dance with ostrich fans? She had excited me, no question about it. Rebecca had been right on target.

I heard voices in the kitchen. My son Andrew was exuberantly relating to Rebecca all the details of the fishing expedition with Papa Abe. They had caught a small sand shark, which was now proudly displayed on the kitchen table. Abe told his daughter he had never eaten shark meat in his life, and he wanted to try it now; he was willing to bet it was a rare delicacy. Rebecca sounded unconvinced, but we had a housekeeper with us that summer, and I guess she figured if Abe made a mess of the kitchen, the housekeeper would clean up after him. Besides, eight-year-old Andrew was begging her to *please* let them cook the shark (his whine was almost identical to Seth's except that he produced it in a high, piping voice, and usually accompanied it with a little nervous tap dance), and it would have taken someone stronger than Rebecca to have resisted both Abe *and* Andrew in the same kitchen on the same hot August afternoon.

They must have cut the shark open, preparatory to broiling it or frying it or whatever Abe had in mind for it, because the next sounds I heard were compounded of surprise, awe, and (from Andrew) delight. Apparently, there were three perfectly formed tiny sharks inside the one they had just cut open. Honest Abe ventured the opinion that the eviscerated shark had been feeding on smaller sharks just before they hooked it. But Rebecca, whose knowledge was encyclopedic, told her father flatly and authoritatively that some species of sharks were viviparous, and that what they'd caught and sliced open on her kitchen table was nothing more nor less than a pregnant shark. Her father wanted to know what viviparous meant (I was glad he'd asked the question because I was dying to know myself), and Rebecca told him viviparous meant bearing live young, and repeated that what he'd cut open on her kitchen table was a pregnant shark. Andrew asked what pregnant meant, and Abe said What the hell, it's only a fish, and they went about preparing to cook and eat the shark, as had already been planned, though I think Rebecca vetoed the idea of cooking the pups. The house rapidly filled with the stench of frying shark meat. Abe took one taste (he had style, the prick), told Rebecca it was the vilest thing he'd ever eaten in his life, promptly threw the whole stinking mess into the garbage can, and then went out onto the back porch, leaving Rebecca in a kitchen reeking of fried shark meat, and filled to bursting with a tap-dancing eight-year-old boy who wanted to know all about how the shark had got those babies in her belly. Quite calmly, Rebecca told him—even though I'm sure she hadn't the faintest idea of how sharks mated —that the mama shark and the papa shark had got together because they loved each other very much, and the papa shark had put his sperm into the mama shark, and the sperm had got together with the mama shark's egg, and the baby sharks had been formed inside the mama shark's belly. She made the mistake of adding, "Sharks make babies the same way people do."

"What do you mean?" Andrew asked immediately.

"People," she said.

"Is that how *I* got made?" Andrew asked.

"Yes," Rebecca said. "Why don't you go out on the porch with your grandfather?"

"You mean a sperm got inside your belly?"

"Yes."

"And got together with an egg?"

"Yes."

"An egg like in the refrigerator?"

"No," Rebecca said. "Well, yes. But not a chicken egg," she said. "A human egg."

"Yeah?" Andrew said.

"Mm," Rebecca said. "Now go outside and play."

"How did the sperm get inside your belly?" Andrew asked.

There was silence in the kitchen. It lasted at least a minute.

"The same way it got in the shark's belly," Rebecca said at last.

"What do you mean?"

"The papa shark puts the sperm inside the mama shark."

385

"Did Daddy put the sperm inside you?"

"Yes," Rebecca said. "Andrew, why don't you go outside and find your brothers? I think they're . . ."

"How did Daddy get it inside you?" Andrew asked.

When I heard this, I almost burst out laughing. I was delighted by my son's persistent questioning (so like his dear grandmother Stella's), and I was also tickled to death by Rebecca's discomfort. Good, I thought. See what happens when you falsely accuse Dwight Jamison of having responded to some dumb cooze from Bedford Village? Go ahead, smart-ass. Explain the mysteries of life to your eight-year-old son. You've probably memorized a lecture from some goddamn textbook, anyway. Answer the kid!

"Well," Rebecca said, and then took a deep breath, and apparently decided to go whole hog. "The daddy," she said, impersonalizing it so that it referred to daddies in general and not to Andrew's daddy in particular, "puts his penis into the mommy's vagina." She took another breath, and in a rush said, "And the sperm comes out, and that's how it gets in there."

"Yeah?" Andrew said.

"Mm," Rebecca said.

Andrew was thoughtfully silent for quite a few moments. I held my breath.

"That's how people do it, huh?" he asked.

"Yes," Rebecca said, and the confident tone in her voice indicated she thought the conversation had ended.

"Let's *do* it!" Andrew said.

His offer was so unexpected, his tone so exuberantly innocent, that I almost choked to death. I quickly covered my mouth with my hand. If Rebecca heard a sound from the bedroom, I knew she'd come in there with a meat cleaver. It was one thing to play "The Man I Love" for a dizzy blonde from Bedford Village; it was quite another to allow your own wife to flounder helplessly before the sexual inquisition of a bright eight-year-old.

"We . . . uh . . . can't," she said.

"Why not?" Andrew said. He sounded extremely puzzled.

"Well . . . uh . . . the mommy can only do it with the daddy," she said.

"Oh," Andrew said, and again fell silent. And then, with the spontaneous brilliance of pure inspiration, he piped excitedly, "Let's get Daddy!" and was running toward the bedroom when Rebecca's voice stopped him.

"Daddy's sleeping!" she shouted in panic.

"Let's wake him up," Andrew said.

"No," Rebecca said. "No! Now that's it, Andrew, I want you to go outside this minute."

I heard the screen door opening. But Andrew must have hesitated on his way to the back porch, because I heard him ask, somewhat suspiciously, "Is it really true?"

"Is what really true?"

"All that stuff you told me."

"Yes, it's true," Rebecca said.

"That's the way sharks make babies, huh?"

"That's right."

"And people, too, huh?"

"Yes."

"You mean everybody? Or just you and Daddy?"

"Everybody," Rebecca said.

"Then how come I never saw it on television?" he snapped, and I swear to God his voice had all the triumphant timbre of someone shouting, "Ah-ha, *got* you, didn't I?" I burst out laughing. Rebecca came rushing into the bedroom, and I covered my face defensively, expecting that single cleaver stroke that would smite my skull in two. But instead, she threw herself on top of me, and began kissing my closed eyes, and my nose, and my mouth, and my cheeks, laughing between kisses, and saying again and again, "Oh, you son of a bitch, you no-good son of a bitch."

Standing in the doorway, Andrew logically asked, "Are you doing it now?"

387

I took Rebecca to dinner alone that night. Davina and Seth had been invited to the home of a couple they'd met at one of the cocktail parties ("Who, me? I'm nobody but Dwight Jamison's sister-in-law"), and I prevailed upon Honest Abe and Sophie to sit with the kids. Abe protested at first. "We should *all* get out of here," he said. "The place stinks to high heaven." But he and Sophie stayed, and Rebecca and I enjoyed a quiet, candlelit shore dinner together. I apologized to her for the way I'd foolishly allowed myself to be flattered by the blonde ("It's beneath you, Ike, really," she said), and I promised it would never happen again, and we drank muscadet with our lobsters, and laughed over what had happened with Andrew in the kitchen, each of us telling the story from our separate viewpoints, Rebecca in the kitchen in a head-on confrontation, I in the bedroom as an eavesdropper. We laughed a lot that night, we reaffirmed our vows.

But I could not help secretly wondering what the blonde had meant when she'd whispered, "Hope is the thing with feathers."

❖

What you should be thinkin' about are the good things. And they got nothin' to do with makin' a lot of gold, or becomin' famous, or whatever. They got to do with the way playin' jazz makes you feel. . . . It's jumpin' in the middle of the ocean. It ain't swimmin' out gradually, it's jumpin' rght out to where you can't see no land no more, it's usin' everything you know to stay afloat and to swim however far out you think you can, and then like magic you get whisked right back there to shore again, and you wrap it all up with a big yellow ribbon, and there you are, and you feel good and clean and happy all over, and there ain't many things I know that can make you feel that way in life . . . there just ain't many I know of.

And at the piano, I feel that way. Always. I jump in with a four-bar intro, jump into water that's icy cold and deep, and instantly hear around me the vastness of the ocean closing over my head, darkness meeting darkness, the steady secret pulse of the bass and the high chinging tinkle of the cymbals, deeper and deeper until I know if I don't surface soon, my lungs will burst; there is terror in this knowledge, and exhilaration, and a sense of omnipotent control—I simply will not drown. Working against the water, and with the water, the water moving gelidly through my fingers, the steady reassuring life-line pulse of the bass thrumming in my ears, I glide in silvery ease to the surface high above, and explode from it in a dazzle of conflicting tactile sensations, sunshine shattering on my upturned face, frigid water sliding in rivulets from my naked body. Arching, hanging between sky and water for a weightless instant, I hold, I hold, and fall again. A bass drum explosion erupts in the deeps, and a flute is suddenly upon me, it glides wantonly by my side, we touch, we move apart, we touch again, the ocean yields to our deeper dive.

The sound of the cymbals trembles over the blackness, the pulse of the bass echoes somewhere very far above. There is limitless freedom in this void, nothing here to stumble upon, nothing to grope for, nothing to obstruct the abandon of our swift, clean descent. The flute has become my guide, and I follow fearlessly and trustingly, uttering small cries of encouragement and approval, marveling at the pure cold logic of our plunge through uncharted waters, delighting in the sheer beauty of the graceful acrobatics we perform together in this fathomless abyss. There are no restraints upon us, we breathe here more deeply than we did on the surface, and the mix we take into our lungs is pristine, a cleaning jolt that suffuses our slippery bodies and propels them recklessly toward the black sands below. At breakneck speed, we glide an inch above the ocean floor on wings of resonating sound. From above, we can hear the nervous consternation of the snare, the imploring whisper of the high-hat cymbals, the relentless bass fiddle pulse, as insistent as the tremor of the ocean itself.

There is no slow, steady, careful ascent, we have no fear of

389

the bends. An instant before, we were enveloped by deepest black, but now we are on the surface, in sunshine, and the muted trumpet lazily lobs fat globules of sound toward us as we skim the surface waves. Like playful and skittish children, we splash through the intricate bubble patterns the trumpet floats before us and behind, the ocean splintering as we dip below its cresting waves to surface again not three feet away, and dip again, and surface again. Dizzily we dive deep below the horizon and burst from the water in surprise. There is the scent of jasmine wafting from a distant shore, the sound of surf tumbling undiscovered sands. Twilight is falling, the trumpet exhales a brassy threnody, a bass string solo ripples the calm surface of the sea. Cool, the night winds are cool. The drum erupts in raucous exuberance, the flute soars upward into the sky like a startled shrieking gull. I follow, I follow and am suddenly alone, swimming in the blackness of a wheeling sky, falling again in headlong descent to the still water below, piercing the surface clean and straight and true, crashing jubilantly into the sea, and appearing magically on the shore not an instant later.

I am breathing hard, and sweating—but I am grinning. Beside me, the flute player says, "*Yeah*, man!" and I answer simply, "Yeah!"

❖

My grandfather was seventy-seven years old when he came to see my new house in Talmadge, Connecticut. I sent a Carey Cadillac to pick up him and my grandmother in Harlem. They were living on the corner of 120th and First Avenue, just across the street from the *pasticceria*. My grandmother wasn't feeling well; she was having trouble with her legs. She sat in the kitchen with Rebecca, sipping tea, while I showed my grandfather through the house. I knew every inch of that house by heart. I still know it. It is embossed upon my memory like the dots on a Braille sheet of music. I showed my grandfather the huge playroom, where special tables had been constructed for Andrew's electric train layout, and Michael's model raceway, and David's battlefield— he collects soldiers, I told my grandfather, he has these full-scale wars with them all the time.

"*Come tu*, Ignazio," my grandfather said, and chuckled. "Remember when you were small? Your soldiers?"

I took him into the living room, with the massive stone fireplace rising in the center of it, Thermopane sliding glass windows opening onto a terrace and gardens designed by a Japanese landscape architect. He was standing beside me, considering the fireplace.

"It's crooked," he said. "*Il camino è storto.*"

"It's supposed to be that way, Grandpa," I said. "The architect wanted one side of it straight and the other slanting."

"Ah?" he said. "*Sì? È vero?*"

As we climbed the stairs to the master bedroom, I said, "How's Aunt Cristie? Does she like the house in Massapequa?"

"Ah, *sì*, it's a very nice house, Ignazio. Not like this, but very nice. He's a hard worker, your Uncle Matt."

"And Uncle Dominick?"

"He's all right," my grandfather said. "You should call him. He was in the hospital a long time, you know. You never called him."

"I've been busy, Grandpa."

"Ah, *sì*, we are all busy," he said. "But your uncle had a heart attack, you should have called."

"I meant to," I said. "This is our bedroom. The Franklin stove was a gift. The builder gave it to us."

"It's very nice," my grandfather said.

"Grandpa," I said, "is Aunt Bianca all right?"

"Yes, yes, she's fine. She gives me a headache, but she's fine. She said to send you her regards."

"When I saw her at Pino's funeral . . ."

"Ah, *sì*."

". . . she seemed so frail," I said.

391

"Well, she's not a young woman anymore."

"Did you want to look at the boys' rooms, Grandpa? Or shall we go outside to my studio?"

"Where you work? Yes, I want to see that."

We put on our topcoats; this was October, and there was an early briskness in the air. As we walked down the slope behind the house toward where the studio was set in a copse of birch trees, I began telling him about the town of Talmadge, Connecticut, which he was not to confuse with Talmadge Hill, a nice small suburb of Stamford. "This is woodsy, *exclusive* Talmadge," I said, and smiled.

"*Cosa?*" he asked.

"That's what *Time* magazine called it when they were doing a cover story on one of our famous writers. 'Woodsy, exclusive Talmadge.'"

"What does that mean?" my grandfather asked.

"Probably nothing," I said. I went on to tell him there were two writers living in Talmadge, each more famous than the other, and both pains in the ass. "Why do writers want to talk about writing all the time?" I asked him.

"Who knows?" he said. "I don't know any writers."

I told him there were two of everything in Talmadge, it was like Noah's Ark, with everything that could walk, crawl, or fly being summoned to . . .

"What do you mean?" he said.

"Well," I said, "in addition to the two writers, we've also got a pair of aging actresses. One of them is dying of throat cancer and is supposed to be a dyke. She lives with a twenty . . ."

"A what?" my grandfather said.

"*Una lesbica,*" I said.

"*Sì? Una lesbica? Dove?* In this town?"

"Yes," I said. "They say she's living with a twenty-year-old girl, a Vassar . . ."

392

"*Che vergogna,*" my grandfather said, and clucked his tongue. "What else do you have two of?"

"Well," I said, "we have two interior decorators, and two art directors who win medals every year, and two . . ."

"For what?" my grandfather said.

"For art direction."

"What's that?" he said.

"They work for advertising agencies," I said.

"Ah," he said.

I was suddenly glad I had not mentioned that the two interior decorators were fags. One of them was named Theodore and the other Thomas, but they were called Tweedledum and Tweedledee behind their backs, or on occasion the Good Fairy and the Bad Fairy, though everyone kept forgetting which was which. A favorite party game in Talmadge was trying to figure out who was doing what to whom. Was Tweedledum the male in the marriage, or was it Tweedledee? All the women staunchly maintained that Tweedledee was bisexual. If not, why did he dance so close? "Does he dance close when he dances with you?" I once asked Rebecca.

"Of course," she replied. "He dances close with all the women."

"Does he get a hard-on?"

"No, Ike," she said. "Only *you* get the hard-ons."

"And what else?" my grandfather asked.

"Well, there are also two theatrical producers," I said, and went on to tell him about a Sunday-afternoon visit from one of them, a thirty-three-year-old *pisher* . . .

"A what?"

"*Pisciasotto,*" I translated.

"Ah."

. . . who was enjoying the success of a long-run musical comedy, his first hit in years. He had told me in all seriousness that he had done everything there was to be done with musical comedy (his last four shows had been total disasters), that this show of his, this magnificent entertainment he had conceived, and put together with the right people, and lavishly produced ("I don't produce cheap, Ike"), was the supreme realization of an art form that was distinctly American, and now it was time to be moving on to more ambitious projects, though America would keenly feel the loss since he and Hal Prince were probably the only true "creative" producers in the country, which by extension meant in the *world*, since nobody could do musicals like Americans, not even the English. He was thinking of running for the United States Senate. I listened to him, and wondered if he would ever become President of the United States, this thirty-three-year-old *pisher* stinking up my living room with the smell of his expensive panatellas. He asked me if he could sit in with the quintet one night. We were earning five thousand dollars a week at the time, and every record we made automatically hit the charts; the *pisher* had once played saxophone and clarinet in a dance band at Yale, and he wanted to sit in with us. "I haven't played in years, Ike," he confided. "Do me good to get the old embouchure in shape again." I told him the band's instrumentation was set (that distinctive Dwight Jamison sound, you know), and did not include a saxophone or clarinet. But I assured him I would most certainly vote for him when he ran for the Senate.

I laughed when I told this story to my grandfather, but he did not laugh with me.

"Well, here's the studio," I said, and I opened the door for him and showed him my record collection ("The ones on this shelf were Tony's," I said), and the new grand piano we had purchased, and my recording equipment (I explained that the entire place was soundproofed), and my Braille library, and he stood beside me silently, and then said, "It's very nice, Ignazio," and we went outside again.

We stood in the birch forest. He must have been looking up at the house commanding the slope, the house that had cost two

394

hundred and fifty thousand dollars to build, the house of glass and stone and wood, the house I now called home.

"È *precisamente come la casa del padrone*," he said. "In Fiormonte," he said. "Don Leonardo. *Il padrone*. He had a big stone house on top of the hill, just like this."

He was silent for several moments. I could hear the sound of falling leaves in the woods. He put his arm around my shoulder, and hugged me to him, and said, "So, Ignazio, you are a success now, eh?"

❖

Let me tell you about success. The two are inextricably linked, America and success, the left hand playing that inexorable chord chart, the right hand inventing melodies. I once asked a noted jazz critic, a man who'd written dozens of books on the subject, whether or not he related the improvisational line to the chord chart when he listened to jazz. He pondered this question gravely for a moment, and then replied, "No, no, I'm interested only in contours and shapes, the geography of the performance." I respectfully submitted that he was perhaps missing the point. I opened at a Los Angeles club the following week, and the critic respectfully submitted that I played lousy jazz. I try to stay very far away from music critics. But if any of you out there are "interested only in contours and shapes, the geography of the performance," then I respectfully submit that you are missing the point as well.

I reached the pinnacle of my success in 1960, when I recorded an album titled *Dwight's Blues* (Victor LPT-X3017). Its popularity was well deserved; the recording session had been inspired, and the quintet never played better. I don't know why a blues album caught on in 1960; maybe the country was bored to death and needed something to weep about, if only an LP record. The sound as it had been successfully defined on our first record (you do not mess with either Mother Nature *or* success) spotlighted piano and flute, with muted trumpet and rhythm section in the background. I had changed my personnel again just before we cut the record. On flute, I was using a twenty-two-year-old girl named Alice Keating, whom I'd hired straight out of the New England Conservatory of Music. On trumpet, I was using an old black jazzman named Sonny Soames. I'd had a lot of trouble keeping trumpet players. Their solos in my band were rare, and nobody likes doing donkey work. (A very well-known trumpet player once sat in with the quintet, and said to me afterward, "Well, Ike, it sure was nice not playing with you.")

I suppose I was spoiled rotten even before the album took off. Success is difficult to resist; it is exceedingly difficult to resist. It has been personified as female, the Bitch Goddess, but I firmly believe it is male in gender and exclusively American in origin. (John Wayne probably thinks of success as a voluptuous full-blown woman; what can I tell you, Duke?) I have seen this hairy male beast (success, not you, Duke) attack and devour the strongest men and women. He stinks of booze and fornication, his breath can knock you senseless for a week. He belches and farts in public, he uses obscene language, he is a braggart and a dullard, and he has but a single ear. Yet when he clutches you in his powerful arms and plants upon your lips a kiss that surely reeks of all things vile (it is the kiss of death, make no mistake), there is nothing to do but succumb. The Beast is too strong, he can break you in two, he can scatter your limbs to the four winds after he has picked them clean of flesh (he will do that, anyway), and it is better to suffer his crushing embrace (it's what you've wanted all along, isn't it?) and let him take you where he will.

It is no accident that America is the nation that pioneered the best-seller lists, the record charts, the best-dressed lists, the ten-best-movies-of-the-year lists, and (God help us) even the ten-*worst*-movies-of-the-year lists, a distinction in itself; if you cannot be one of the ten *best*, there is some satisfaction (but only in America) in knowing you are listed among the lousiest. In America, if you are eleventh, you might as well be dead. And if you are Number One, then you are exactly what America itself desires to be, ever and always. I do not wish to raise problems, forgive me. But what is so terribly wrong about being number two? Or (God forbid) number eleven? In 1960, *Dwight's Blues* was Number One on the LP record charts for more months than I can recall, and something began happening to me.

I was spoiled rotten even before the raging success of the album; I had, after all, been successful since 1955. I was used to making my demands known and having them satisfied, I had grown accustomed to deferential treatment from headwaiters and recording executives, music publishers and nightclub owners, hotel managers, airline hostesses, everyone. Everywhere I went, they asked, "Is everything all right, Mr. Jamison?" Yes, everything was all right. When I was a boy, my grandmother Tess had treated me like an Italian Prince, which is one step higher than a Jewish Princess. My brother Tony could sometimes escape her solicitous clutches, being blessed with vision and a pair of stout little legs that could carry him scurrying away from her advancing embrace. I *never* escaped her. "I'm going to *get* you, Ignazio!" she would say, and those loving grandmotherly arms would snatch me up, and her tongue would cluck in deep affection, and sometimes she would sing to me in Italian, and press me against her pillowy bosom, and tell me what a darling little boy I was. If I had been left solely to the care and training of my grandmother Tess, I would have grown up to be a hopelessly dependent vegetable. It was my grandfather who taught me to stand on my own, blind or not. But my grandfather was Italian, you see. And I was American. And starting in 1955, I was a *successful* American. And in 1960, I became a *ragingly* successful American, and the world was full of Grandma Tesses eager to tell me what a darling little boy I was, eager to turn me into a hopelessly dependent vegetable. And something began happening to me.

Maybe I only (only!) wanted to go to bed with my mother.

Maybe those tales of Charlie Shoe exploring her youthful quim had incited me to fantasize wildly about the joys to be experienced between those maternal thighs. Success had brought me power, after all, the power to command whatever I wanted whenever I wanted it. So why not now dismiss my father, who had peed his own pants when he was but a mere lad, and take my rightful place in bed beside my mother? Maybe that was it. Or maybe I had to prove to Jimmy Palmer that his own fumbling attempt at adultery (had there *really* been an Irish whore on Pelham Parkway?) could be topped by his famous blind son, show him I was not only a better musician than he was, but also a better swordsman, a man who could screw every beautiful woman in the universe without having the Virgin Mary appear to Rebecca, without getting *caught*, and certainly without leaving any telltale evidence about golden earrings with sapphire chips in my dresser drawer. That's another possibility. Or maybe, being blind, I just *naturally* demanded more of everyone—more and more love, more and more respect, more and more proof that I was not what I (and thirteen other little blind bastards) thought myself to be—nothing.

Whatever it was (and I certainly do not dismiss any of these quite respectable tenets), I began to think that since my *album* was Number One, then I *myself* was Number One. I had cut the album, hadn't I? I mean, after all, the album was only a mechanical reproduction of the music I had made, the music I had pulled from somewhere inside my head and my heart; the album was *me*. Now never mind whether or not I was a good father (I was), or a loyal and devoted husband (I still was), or a man who did not cheat on his income tax (I took advantage of legal loopholes), a man eligible for the Talmadge Good Neighbor Award, an upstanding member of the town board, a pillar of the community, or an all-around darling nice guy. Never mind any of that. Never mind what the *man* Dwight Jamison was. The man was the album. And the album was successful beyond my wildest dreams. They used to touch me. When I walked toward the bar after a set, they reached out to touch me, I could hear them whispering, "Here he comes," and then I would feel the cautious touch on the sleeve of my jacket.

Well, unless I wished to believe that America was a land of idol-worshipers bowing and scraping at the clawed feet of the hairy monster called Success; unless I wished to believe that the crowd reaching out to touch me as I walked from the bandstand to the bar was really reaching out to touch The Beast; unless I chose to come to grips with the painful knowledge that The Beast was something independently alive, standing behind my shoulder each night, leering out at the crowd and demanding adoration for himself, then I *had* to believe the cheers were for me and not for my success, the cheers were for Dwight Jamison, the cheers were, in fact, for Ignazio Silvio Di Palermo. And why not? I deserved them.

Yes.

Deserved! Because I was giving so much of myself to the public, yes, and it was only fair that I should get something more than money in return. (Christ, was that me? Did I really believe that?) Yes. Up there on the bandstand each night, I was reaching into my head and my heart and discovering somewhere in my own experience something I was willing to give to total strangers. It leaped from my fingers and into the room, and it became theirs, no longer mine, not even mine *and* theirs, but theirs alone. My past and my present, my joy, my anger, and my sorrow became theirs to push around on their plates with their leftover dinners while they signaled the waiter for another round.

I rationalized my promiscuity (which is *exactly* what it was) on two levels. First, I told myself I had already given of my head and my heart, so what would it matter if I now gave of my cock? Giving of my cock was really giving nothing; I was still being true to Rebecca. Secondly, I played a mental trick that can only in retrospect be considered schizophrenic. (Don't be so quick to

399

agree, Rebecca!) I told myself all these women really did love me and my shabby, dignified good looks, and my blond hair and sightless blue eyes, and my talent, and everything about me. But at the same time, I told myself they only loved the incandescence of my success, they only loved The Beast. I zippered on The Beast's hairy hide the way I would a gorilla suit, but at the same time I denied that he was me. All those women loved me for myself, yes, but *no*, they really loved The Beast. I was only the conduit through which adoration for The Beast flowed. The women were faceless; they would have been faceless even if I could have seen them. And I was faceless as well. The Beast was getting it all; I was only his boy. And yet I knew they adored me.

Mishegahss, I admit it.

I'd have to be *really* nuts (I *know*, Rebecca; save it) to pretend at the age of forty-eight that all that fucking around had been caused by a capitalized Beast relentlessly stalking the landscape of the American myth. But sometimes, when I'm alone and I remember with a start that after all is said and done I am only blind and only Ignazio Silvio Di Palermo, I wonder what it would have been like if I'd never been a big success, ma'am. Would you offer to blow me if you saw me stumbling along Broadway behind a Seeing Eye dog, with a sign advising HERE BUT FOR THE GRACE OF GOD GOES THEE?

❖

Jesus, the things I remember!

Jesus.

It is the summer of 1941, and my brother has taken me to the Friday-night dance at Our Lady of Grace on 225th Street and Bronxwood Avenue. We are walking home together afterward. There are roses blooming everywhere. They line the fences outside the two-story houses as we walk in the balmy, scent-laden night.

My brother picks a rose and gives it to me.

❖

The Masters At Forcing Independents to Acquiesce came around to see me in the fall of 1961. The man who ran the Chicago club in which I was playing was a hood. There are some nightclub managers or owners who tell you to play softer or louder or faster or slower or not at all, depending on what their drinking clientele is doing at any given moment, but Al Gerardi never bothered us. He was smart enough to know that we were riding a wave of popularity, and he wasn't about to mess with music that was causing his cash register to jingle along in counterpoint. I almost liked him. When he said he wanted me to meet a few of his friends, I honestly thought they were fans.

We sat in Al's office, and they introduced themselves as Arthur Giglio and Ralph Isetti.

"Is it true you're Italian?" Isetti asked.

"That's right," I said.

"That's what we heard," Giglio said.

"That makes us '*paesani*," Isetti said.

I said nothing.

"Your album's doing pretty good," Giglio said.

"It's a nice album," Isetti said.

"This guy Aronowitz," Giglio said. "He's your manager, huh?"

"Yes."

"Who else does he handle?"

"Well, he's got a long list of clients."

"But you're the biggest one, huh?"

"I don't really know."

"Sure, you're the biggest. What do you want to stay with him for?"

"We've been together for a long time now. He's a good manager. And also a good friend."

"They only look out for themselves," Giglio said. "The kikes."

401

"My wife is Jewish," I said.

"Yeah, we know," Isetti said, and this was the first warning I had that trouble was on the way. I felt my scalp begin to tingle.

"Well," I said, "I'd better get back outside."

"No, don't rush yourself," Giglio said. "Al's in no hurry. You ain't in no hurry, are you, Al?"

Al, who had been silent till this moment, now said, "No, everybody's happy outside."

"Everybody's happy in here, too," Giglio said.

"We coulda sold a shit pot full of that album," Isetti said. "That's a nice album."

"Victor's doing a fine job," I said.

"Victor who?"

"RCA Victor."

"Oh, the record company, you mean. Yeah, but maybe you ain't getting the right kind of jukebox distribution, you know what I mean?"

"We lifted three singles from the album, and they're all doing fine on the jukes," I said.

"They could be doing better," Isetti said.

"We got a few record companies of our own," Giglio said.

"We also got some hotels in Vegas."

"And of course we could guarantee very good jukebox exposure. Much better than you're getting now."

"I'm not sure I understand," I said. I understood completely. They wanted to get into the dry-cleaning business.

"We'd like to manage you, Ike," Giglio said.

"I've already got a manager."

"Kiss him off," Isetti said.

"I couldn't do that."

"Try. I'll bet you could do it if you tried."

"Why should I?"

"Because we can handle you better. We're Italian, we understand you better. We like the way you play piano, Ike."

402

"Well, I'm very flattered, but . . ."

"Don't be so fucking flattered," Isetti said. "We're talking business here."

"If you want to talk business, go see my manager."

"We will. As soon as we settle this with you."

"It's already settled."

"No, we don't think so. Not yet, it ain't settled."

"Al, we've got paying customers out there," I said. "If your friends are finished . . ."

"We ain't finished," Isetti said, "and the customers can wait."

"Sixty-forty is the deal," Giglio said.

"Look," I said, "I'm satisfied with Victor, I'm satisfied with my manager . . ."

"And I'll bet you're also satisfied with Alice Keating," Giglio said, and the room went silent.

"Yes," I said. "She's a very good flute player."

"Especially the skin flute," Isetti said, and the room went silent again.

"We've got pictures of you and Alice," Giglio said.

"You like broads, huh, Ike?" Isetti said.

"We'll get you plenty of broads, you like broads."

"It's too bad you're blind," Isetti said. "These are nice pictures." I heard the sound of something being slapped onto the desktop. "It must be a real drag being blind, huh?"

"You can't even see yourself in action when you're blind," Giglio said. "Take a look at those pictures, Al. Go ahead, open the envelope. We had them blown up eight by ten, Ike," he said confidentially. "Take a look at them, Al. They're nice pictures, ain't they?"

Al moved to the desk. He was silent for several moments. Then he whistled softly.

"Listen," I said amiably, "who do you guys think you're kidding?"

"Oh, are we kidding somebody?" Giglio said.

403

"Gee, I didn't know we were kidding," Isetti said.

"What do you think of those pictures, Al?" Giglio said.

"Those are some pictures," Al said.

"You got a nice *shlahng* for a blind man," Giglio said. "Ain't that a nice *shlahng*, Al?"

"Yeah, that's a nice *shlahng*," Al said.

"She goes down on it nice, too," Isetti said. "Almost like a pro."

"I'll bet your wife and kids would like to see how this girl plays flute, huh, Ike?"

"Maybe we ought to sign *her* too," Isetti said, and they all laughed.

"This is all bullshit," I said. "You haven't got any pictures, and you're . . ."

"We've got pictures, Ike," Giglio said, and I knew they had pictures.

"We own that hotel you're staying in," Isetti said. "You know that mirror across from the bed?"

"How would he know where the mirror is? The man's blind."

"Well, there's a mirror across from the bed," Isetti said. "It's a one-way mirror. Like the cops have. It comes in handy sometimes."

"You shouldn't ought to fuck in the daytime," Giglio said.

"We wouldn'ta got no pictures if you fucked only at night."

"Unless you kept the lights on."

"He's blind, what would he need the lights for?"

"What do you say, Ike?"

"Sixty-forty is the deal," Isetti said.

I decided to pull rank. If there's one thing Italians understand, it's somebody telling them exactly who he is. In Italy, it is not uncommon to hear people in every walk of life indignantly demanding, "Do you realize who I am?" In Italy, this has become a joke. Even a street cleaner will get on his high horse and say, "Do you realize who I am?" Rank was very definitely the thing to pull.

Who did these cheap hoods think they were fooling around with here? I was Dwight Jamison.

"Do you guys realize who you're talking to?" I said.

"Yeah," Giglio said. "We're talking to Ignazio Silvio Di Palermo."

"A 'paesano," Isetti said.

"A 'paesano who's going to pick up the phone, and call the police, and tell them . . ."

"A 'paesano who'll get his hands broken if he does that," Isetti said.

"You won't break my hands," I said.

"We won't, huh?"

"If you break my hands," I said, taking a cue from my grandfather, "I won't be able to play piano anymore. And sixty percent of nothing is nothing."

"So we'll find ourselves another piano player," Isetti said. "Meanwhile, you'll be on the street selling pencils."

"You won't break my hands," I said, but I wasn't so sure anymore.

"Anyway, who's talking about breaking your hands?" Giglio said. "What are you threatening the man for, Ralphie? We're about to enter a partnership here, and you're threatening the man."

"I wasn't threatening the man," Isetti said.

"What do you say, Ike?" Giglio said amiably. "Sixty-forty."

"No," I said, "I don't think so. I appreciate your interest, but . . ."

"Ike," Giglio said, "this is not a threat, please don't take it as a threat. But what we're going to do is mail those pictures to your wife."

"And maybe to a few newspapers, too," Isetti said.

"Nobody'd publish them," Giglio said, and laughed. "Not *those* pictures. Ike I got to tell you, those are the dirtiest pictures I ever seen in my life. What do you say? You want to be partners? Or you want your wife to see you lapping that girl's pussy?"

"If you mail the pictures . . ."

"Oh, we'll mail them, all right."

"Then you've got no hold on me anymore. I'll have nothing to worry about."

"You'll still have your hands to worry about," Isetti said.

"Stop it with the man's hands, will you, please?" Giglio said. "Ike, be sensible. You don't *really* want your wife to see those pictures, do you?"

"Look," I said, "what the . . . what are you bothering with me for? I'm just a piano player. There must be . . ."

"We like the way you play piano, Ike."

"We can make a lot of money from the way you play piano."

"What do you say, Ike?"

"Mail them," I said. "I don't give a damn."

"Okay," Giglio said, and sighed. "Ralphie, put the pictures back in the envelope and mail them to the man's wife. That's Rebecca Jamison, Old Holly Road, Talmadge, Connecticut."

"You're not scaring me," I said.

"Who's trying to scare you?" Giglio said. "We want to be partners."

"Go ahead and mail them," I said.

"We will."

"Is that it?"

"That's it," Giglio said. "For now. We'll see what happens next, huh?"

"Take care of your hands," Isetti said.

❖

They did not mail the pictures, if indeed the pictures existed at all. I kept waiting for an explosion from Rebecca, but it never came. Alice quit the band just before Christmas. She had met a Miami land developer while we were playing down there, and had decided to marry him. She asked me to promise never to tell anyone about the things we'd done together. I told her I never would, and meanwhile I kept waiting for that envelope full of pictures to be delivered to Old Holly Road in Talmadge. By February, I began to think I'd bluffed them out of the pot, just the way my grandfather had done back in 1937. An occupational hazard of playing jazz piano is beginning to believe that life is only an echo of jazz. If it had worked for my grandfather back then, maybe it was working for me now. He had played the head chorus, and I was playing the head and out. I was home free.

They caught up with me in March.

I was working in Detroit at the time. I was alone in my hotel room when a knock sounded at the door. It was close to eleven-thirty; the eleven o'clock television news was just signing off.

"Who is it?" I said.

"Danny."

Danny Sears was my new flute player. I opened the door. Two men came into the room, pushing me back and away from the door. I heard the bolt being thrown.

"Hello, Mr. Jamison," one of the men said.

"Who's that?" I said. "Who is it?"

"Don't panic, Mr. Jamison," the other man said. "All we're going to do is break your hand."

I turned immediately and ran for where I knew the phone was. I got almost to the night table beside the bed, when one of them clamped his hand onto my shoulder, and twisted me around to face him, and hit me in the gut. I doubled over. My dark glasses slid halfway down my nose.

"That hurts, doesn't it?" he said.

"Don't let us hurt you no more than we have to," the other man said.

"Sit over here, Mr. Jamison."

"Look . . ."

"Sit *down*, Mr. Jamison, this won't take a minute."

"Look," I said, "look, are you guys Italian?"

One of them laughed.

"Hey, come on," I said, "this ain't funny, you know? It may be funny to you guys, but it ain't funny to me." I suddenly realized I had fallen back into the speech patterns of my youth, the language I had used every day of the week in the streets of Harlem. In a recurring nightmare I've had ever since that night in Detroit, I dream I am standing on the curb in Harlem, waiting for a taxi. I am dressed in white tie, tails, and a top hat. A woman is standing not fifteen feet from me. As in all my dreams, she is only vaguely defined, a blurred shape, an uncertain presence. But she is a woman, I know this, and she is Italian, I know this too. She is standing on the corner waiting for a bus. I hear a vehicle approaching and, hoping it is a taxicab, I raise my cane to hail it. It pulls to the curb. I hear a man, presumably the driver, asking, "Where you going, Mac?" I answer, in the acquired speech I've been using for half a lifetime, "I'm Dwight Jamison, would you mind taking me to Birdland, please?" As I get into the taxi, the Italian woman cackles and says, "Who do you think you're kidding?"

They were both laughing now. Their laughter was mean, the privileged laughter of people sharing an inside joke.

"Well, come on," I said, "*are* you Italian?"

They *had* to be Italian, my infallible ear told me they were Italian. But why were they laughing if they weren't something very far removed from Italian? Were Italian racketeers now hiring black men or Poles or Jews or Irishmen to break the hands of Italian musicians. Ahhh, the American myth realized at last. But they were *my* hands.

"Let's talk," I said.

"It's late as it is," one of them said. They sounded almost identical. I could not tell their voices apart. They still sounded Italian. But then why had they laughed?

"Who sent you here?" I said.

"Mr. Jamison, it don't *matter* who sent us."

408

"Was it Giglio and Isetti? All right, here's what you do. Go back to them and . . ."

"No, we're not going back to nobody."

"I'm trying to tell you we can talk!"

"About what?"

"About sixty-forty, seventy-thirty, whatever the hell they want!"

"It's too late," one of them said.

"You're too late, Mr. Jamison."

"They ain't interested no more, Mr. Jamison. They got themselves another boy, Mr. Jamison."

"You're too late."

"You missed the boat."

"You coulda had yourself a sweet deal, but instead you got to get your hand broke. You understand?"

"That doesn't make sense," I said. I had put my hands in my pockets. I was trying to hide my hands. "If they're not interested in me anymore . . ."

"Yeah, well, lots of things in life don't make too much sense," one of them said.

"Which hand?" the other one said.

"You hear him, Mr. Jamison? Which hand?"

"What?"

"Which hand? They told us only one hand. Which one you want?"

Yes. Yes, that was what they had said when they came into the room. They were here to break my *hand*. Singular. One hand. And now they wanted to know which one. That was very considerate of them. They were behaving like gentlemen, inquiring which of my hands I preferred broken, or conversely, which I preferred left intact.

"Look," I said, "this is my livelihood. . . ."

"This is *ours*," one of them said.

"Which hand?"

"How much are they paying you for this?"

409

They both laughed again.

"I'm serious. I don't know how much they're paying you, but I'm sure . . ."

"Forget it."

"And make up your mind, you hear? Otherwise we'll break *both* fuckin' hands and get it over with."

"The right or the left? Which one?"

The right or the left? Which one, Ike? Which hand do you find most useful to the geography of your performance? Which of these precious appendages do you find essential to the definition of contours and shapes? Which of your eyes would you like plucked out, because these hands in addition to being your source of income are also your eyes, Ike, you have been using them to see with since the day you were born. Which could you most readily do without? Which one will you sacrifice? The left hand that strikes the chords or the more inventive right hand that creates new melodies? Which? Choose.

"Break them both," one of the men said.

"Wait a minute!"

"Then which one?"

"The . . . look," I said, "please don't break my hand. Please. Please, I . . ."

"This guy's gettin' on my nerves," one of them said.

"Which fuckin' *hand?*" the other one said.

"The . . . the . . . the left," I said, and I began to whimper.

One of them stood behind me, his hands on my shoulders. I heard the other one moving a piece of furniture over to where I was sitting. "Please," I said, "please," and he seized my left hand by the wrist and held it firmly to the top of whatever he had moved into place in front of me, and I said, "Please, no, don't, please," and I thought of Basilio Silese in the locker room of the Boys' Club, and I wished my brother Tony were there to rescue me as he had rescued Basilio, wished he would barge into the room and shout, "Hey, what are you doing there?" but my brother

410

Tony was dead, he had been killed in Italy by an Italian soldier. "Please," I said, "please don't, please," and the man standing behind me said, "Shut up, you cocksucker," and looped a folded towel or napkin or handkerchief over my head and into my mouth like a horse's bit, twisted it tight from behind with one hand while the other hand forced me back into the chair again. I tried to say please, please, please aro⸱ ᷉d the cloth, but the other man smashed something hard down on the knuckles of my hand, and then methodically and systematically and apparently emotionlessly— he did not grunt, I could not even hear him breathing heavily— smashed three of my fingers at the middle joint.

I passed out after the first finger.

The boys did not quite wreck my career, though I'm sure the oversight was unintentional. They left my pinkie and my thumb intact. This allowed me to play shells the way Bud Powell used to play them way back then when I learned to hate his style.

❖

My mother called the day before Rebecca and I were scheduled to leave for Europe. My hand was still in a cast. We had arranged for Sophie to stay with the children while we were gone; she would be assisted by our live-in housekeeper and a college student we had hired to chauffeur the children to their various activities. Sophie had arrived, with three valises, a week before our departure date. She told us she wanted to get accustomed to the routine, learn her way around the thermostats and the garbage disposal unit. I spent a lot of time hiding from her in my studio. It was there that I took the call from my mother.

"Hello, Ike," she said, and I knew instantly that something was wrong. My mother's voice is a delicate instrument. It can promise the hyacinths of spring or the gardenias of death in a single breath.

411

"What's the matter?" I said.

"Nothing."

"Is Grandpa all right?"

"Yes, fine."

"Then what is it?"

"Nothing," she said. "Are you all packed for your trip?"

"Yes, Mom. Mom . . ."

"Is Sophie there?"

"She arrived last Thursday."

"Give her my regards."

"I will. Mom, is anybody sick or anything?"

"No, no." She hesitated, and then said, "Aunt Cristie came to see me this morning. She came all the way from Massapequa."

"What is it?"

"Nothing," my mother said, but she was weakening, I was beginning to reach her, not for nothing was I her son, not for nothing had I listened to countless interrogations and cross-examinations conducted by Stella Di Palermo, Mr. District Attorney, in various kitchens I had known.

"Is Uncle Matt okay?"

"Yes, he's fine."

"Then what is it, Mom?"

"Your aunt wanted to talk to me," my mother said, and sighed.

"What about?"

"Nothing."

"Mom, she didn't come all the way from Massapequa to talk about nothing. Now what the hell is it?"

She hesitated for a long time. Static crackled on the telephone wires. Then she sighed again, and said, "It's Luke."

"What about Luke?"

"He drinks," she said, and fell silent again. "Do you know what I mean? He's a *drunk*," she said. "My brother."

I waited. I could hear the electric clock humming on my desk. My hand inside the plaster cast felt suddenly confined.

412

"I can't understand it," my mother said. "I just can't understand it, Ike. We used to have such fun together, Luke and me. We used to go to the movies together every week, oh, we saw everything, all the big stars, all the pictures, we had such fun. Just Luke and me. My father wouldn't let Dom go till he was older, and Cristie was too tiny, it was just Luke and me, he was so much fun, he was such a good brother. He used to have this very high, silly laugh, Ike. When Charlie Chaplin or Fatty Arbuckle came on, Luke used to bust out laughing, oh, what a laugh he had, and all the kids began laughing the minute they heard him, they knew it was him, they recognized that laugh of his. He was funnier than the movie, I swear to God, it makes me want to laugh just thinking of those Saturdays when we . . . when we . . ."

My mother sighed, and fell silent. I waited.

"I couldn't believe Cristie," she said at last. "When she told me, I just couldn't believe it. Luke? I said. Are you talking about *Luke?* Are you telling me Luke is a drunk? Yes, she said, yes, Stella. But, Cristie, I said, are you sure this isn't something like . . . like once at a party or . . . or with the boys or . . ."

She stopped talking. For a moment, I thought the connection had been broken. Then she said, "Always be a good boy, Ike. Luke was always a good boy, I can't understand it. Cristie told me he's so drunk sometimes he can't even stand up at the pressing machine. Do you know the big iron Grandpa has, the one he uses for hand pressing? Luke left it on a pair of pants the other day and burned a hole in the leg and almost started a fire in the shop. I don't know what to do. Grandpa will kill him if he finds out."

"No," I said, "he won't kill him."

"You don't know Grandpa," she said.

"I know him," I said.

"Oh, what are we going to do?" she said. "What are we going to do?"

I did not know what to tell her. Our plane was leaving for

Rome early the next morning. I finally suggested that she contact my Uncle Dominick, and asked her to please write me, she had the itinerary.

On our third night in Rome, Rebecca and I looked up an Italian saxophone player with whom I'd been corresponding over the years. He was playing in a nightclub on the Via Emilia. He recognized me the moment I came through the door, even though we'd never met. He introduced me to his sidemen and they played a set in my honor, starting it with "The Man I Love." They were not very good jazz musicians. I was discovering that hardly anyone in Italy played good jazz. But they were overwhelmed by my presence, and they tried hard. At the end of the set, they came to our table. One of them had a cousin in Chicago, and wanted to know all about Chicago. I had played there frequently, of course, but Rebecca had never been to Chicago. She became restless as we chatted in Italian, a language she found impossible to grasp, though it was simpler than the French she'd studied at Barnard.

They began asking me questions about famous American jazz-men, and since I'd played with many of them, including some of the old-timers, I was able to relate inside anecdotes, which they listened to intently. They were cautious about my blindness until I told them a story about Charlie Mingus and Lennie Tristano, who is a blind piano player, and a damn good one. Mingus and Tristano had got into an argument one night, and Mingus had said, "If you don't shut up, Lennie, I'm going to turn out the lights and beat hell out of you." The Italian musicians hesitated a moment, in puzzlement. It was the saxophone player who burst into laughter, and then explained the anecdote to the others— "*Tristano è un cieco, eh? Dunque, quando Mingus . . .*" They, too, began laughing. Rebecca was bored. She had heard all my stories a hundred times before, and was getting a headache from all the Italian babbling. She excused herself at 2 A.M. and took a taxi back to the Hassler. When I came into the room at four, she was still awake.

"Do you really want to go to Saint Peter's tomorrow?" she asked. "Frankly, I don't care if I ever see another church as long as I live."

"What would you like to do instead?"

"You're the big wop," she said. "You tell me."

I hired a chauffeured car to take us to Villa d'Este the next day. Rebecca told me that the hundreds of fountains there only made her want to pee, and she spent half the day searching for ladies' rooms. She could not get the word *gabinetto* straight. I told her to think of "cabinet." She answered that a cabinet was in her mind something very far removed from a toilet. "Then ask for the *pissoir*," I said. "Everybody knows what a *pissoir* is."

"Don't be so smart," she said. "If I can't understand the language, I can't understand it."

"You should have gone to Berlitz. You had plenty of time to go to Berlitz."

"What were *you* doing while I *planned* this trip?" she asked. "Besides getting your hand broken?"

"I was sitting around thinking how nice it would be to get away alone with you."

That night, we made love together. In the shuttered room overlooking the Spanish Steps, the sounds of cats and taxi drivers filtering up from the Piazza Trinità dei Monti below, we copulated on the oversized bed, and when I asked, "Did you come?" Rebecca testily replied, "Of *course* I came! Will you please shut up?"

We left Rome in a rented Fiat. Rebecca, of course, did the driving. She found it exhilarating at first, but long before we reached Florence, she was complaining that we should have spent the extra money for a chauffeur-driven automobile, which we could most certainly have afforded. I explained to her that having

415

a chauffeur along would be identical to sharing the trip with a stranger. She made no comment. In Florence, there was a letter from my mother. She told us that Dominick had spoken to Luke about going to Bellevue for a voluntary drying out, but Luke had refused. That evening we had dinner in a hotel outside the city. We ate outdoors on a terrace above the Arno.

"Do you remember the night we met?" I asked her. "In that Staten Island toilet? You were with someone named Martin. . . ."

"Marvin," she said.

"Yes."

"Yes, I remember," she said.

We stayed at the Excelsior Palace in Venice, at the beach, but it was still too chilly to swim. Rebecca bought little glass animals to take home to the children. I learned that *melanzana* was the proper way to say "eggplant" in Italian, and not *muligniana*, the Neapolitan pronunciation I had learned as a boy in Harlem. We bought a ring for Rebecca We visited the lace factory. We sat in San Marco's and listened to outdoor concerts. We drank a lot. On a gondola ride, we heard rats splashing into the canal.

In Stresa, there was another letter from my mother. Rebecca recognized the handwriting at once, impatiently said, "Your mother again," and tore open the flap. I waited anxiously while she unfolded the letter. My grandfather had found out about Luke, as of course had been inevitable. He had personally taken him to two meetings of Alcoholics Anonymous, and Luke seemed to be responding well, intent on curing himself, grateful for all the familial attention that was being lavished upon him. "I hope he gets better," my mother wrote. "I love him so."

"I wish she'd stop about Luke already," Rebecca said. "There isn't a word here about how the kids are." To the desk clerk she said, "Is that all the mail?"

"*Sì signora, è tutto,*" he answered.

"I told my mother to make sure they wrote," Rebecca said to

416

me. "They have the itinerary, we should have at *least* got a card by now." Her voice turned away. "The five bags there," she said. "The green ones. No, the *green* ones."

"*Signora?*"

"*Le cinque valigie verdi*," I said.

"*Grazie, signore*," the bellhop answered.

In the evening dusk, we sat sipping cocktails outdoors as Rebecca outlined the next day's journey. A road map was spread on the table before her, I could hear it crackling as she nervously traced out the route. She was fearful of driving through the Alps and the Brig Pass. A man's voice apologetically intruded. He said he couldn't help overhearing our conversation, and offered the advice that we could put the car on a train at Domodossola, if we liked, and then take it off again at Brig, though actually at this time of year, mountain driving wasn't all that bad. Rebecca invited him and his wife to join us. His wife said very little at first, she smelled of bath oil, and I envisioned her as small and dark. The man was a stockbroker. Rebecca immediately informed him that I was a jazz pianist, and though he had already heard my name in introduction, he asked again what it was, and I said, "Dwight Jamison," and he was silent for a moment, and then said, "You're *kidding!* Honey, this is Dwight Jamison! Jesus, I have all your records going back to the original quintet! Jesus, this is a real honor! Dwight Jamison! Jesus!" Beside him, his wife quietly said, "I love your records, too."

In the evening after dinner, we strolled beside the lake together, the man walking up ahead with Rebecca, the wife by my side. She told me she was unhappily married. She told me she had a lover. She told me she missed him terribly, and wished he were here with her, instead of her stockbroker husband.

"Are you and Rebecca happy?" she asked.

"Yes," I said, "we're very happy."

"I can tell," she whispered, and then sighed.

The bed in our room was a huge *letto matrimoniale*. I awakened in the middle of a nightmare, groping for Rebecca. I was shouting, "You can give it right back to the Indians!"

"Give what back?" she asked sleepily.

"Italy," I said.

On the drive through the Alps, Rebecca kept cursing the stockbroker for telling her there was nothing to worry about this time of year. She also confided that he'd put his hand on her ass while we were walking the town the night before.

"What did *you* do?" I asked.

"What do you care what I did? You probably had *your* hand on Miss Bryn Mawr's ass."

"No, Rebecca, I didn't."

"Sure," Rebecca said.

In Interlaken, we ate trout caught fresh from the river running beside the hotel, and Rebecca described to me the distant shrouded beauty of the Jungfrau. In Lausanne, there were hastily written notes from the boys, enclosed in a letter from Sophie. Rebecca read them to me as we sat on the terrace at breakfast in the morning sun, and flies buzzed around the jam pots. It was almost the end of May, the breeze was balmy. In the distance I could hear the delighted cries of children pedaling boats on the lake, and suddenly I missed my sons terribly.

"They seem to be fine," Rebecca said.

"What?"

"The children."

"Yes," I said.

The last letter from my mother was waiting for us at the Meurice in Paris. As we stood by the desk, Rebecca read it aloud to me. My mother informed us that Luke had disappeared. My grandfather had hired private detectives, and Uncle Matt had asked all his friends to be on the lookout. "I hope we can find him," she wrote. "I worry about him, Iggie." This was the first time she'd called me Iggie in years.

That afternoon, when Rebecca went to have her hair done, I took a taxi into Pigalle and wandered the streets alone, and at last stopped at a small bar, and ordered a double Scotch on the rocks, and sat sipping at it. The girl who took the stool beside me reeked of perfume reminiscent of what Poots had been wearing the night I first sat in with a band and was told to chop off my left hand. "Vous désirez, monsieur?" she asked, and immediately rested her hand on my knee. We chatted for a while, my Santa Lucia French was clumsy, she switched in desperation to English as we settled upon a price.

At the hotel she led me to, she whispered discreetly that the concierge expected a *pourboire*, and I fumbled in my wallet for the unfamiliar bills, and was not quite certain how much I handed her. In America, I carried only tens, and I took my change in singles, and kept the smaller bills in a separate section of my wallet. There were days when I came home with as much as fifty dollars in singles. Now I blindly paid the concierge, and then the girl, and she led me to a bidet in one corner of the room, where she washed first me and then herself. The bed was narrow and set against the wall. I touched the wall with the spread fingers of my right hand, and realized there was a mirror fastened to it beside the bed. I told the girl I wanted only *soixante-neuf*. She worked long and hard, she was a thorough professional, but at last she straddled me and brought me to reluctant climax inside her. I was vaguely dissatisfied when she left me on the street outside the hotel. I lifted the lid of my Braille watch. It was still early. Rebecca would be busy at the hairdresser for at least another hour.

I did not know what I wanted.

I wandered through Pigalle again. A breathless voice implored me from a doorway, and I hesitated and then approached. There was the aroma of perfume, the rustle of silk, the click of high heels as the girl shifted her weight. We bargained for several moments until I realized with a shock that I was talking to a man

419

in drag. I backed away in horror. *"Mais il y a des filles aussi,"* he explained, but I hurried to the curb, and held my cane aloft, and hoped a taxi would stop for me.

We arrived home during the second week in June. The children scrambled out of the house and rushed into our open arms. I held little David close, I stroked his hair.

"Did you have a good time, Daddy?" he asked.

"Yes, we had a marvelous time," I told him.

My grandfather called that night. He welcomed me home and then told me he had finally heard some word about Luke. According to the detectives, Luke was living in a hotel on the Bowery. I asked my grandfather if he wanted me to go down there, but he assured me this wasn't necessary.

The next day, he went down alone to talk to Luke, and tried to persuade him to come home again.

Luke told him to go to hell.

❖

Rebecca is shrieking, shrieking. I rush out of the studio, I trip on the rough stone steps leading up past the pool to the house, cross the patio, find her screaming still. "What is it?" I ask. "For God's sake, what is it?"

"Andrew," she says.

He is moaning near the pile of logs stacked alongside the storage shed. I search his face with my hands. There is an open wound over his left eye, I feel his blood hot and sticky on my fingers. Hysterically, Rebecca tells me he'd been trying to split the logs with an ax when a huge splinter hit him in the face. She goes suddenly limp in my arms and though I try to support her, her dead weight collapses her to the ground. My son is crying in pain now. I rush into the kitchen. Harriet dials the hospital for me, and it is she who drives Andrew and me to Stamford. He is bleeding profusely as she leads us into the emergency room. The

420

doctor takes five stitches over Andrew's left eye, and bandages it, and asks me if I carry Blue Cross. I can only think what might have happened if this had been Harriet's day off.

❖

My thirty-seventh birthday fell on a Tuesday. Honest Abe personally went to Harlem to pick up my grandparents, shrugging aside the very idea that I should send a Carey limousine for them. "What's the matter with an Oldsmobile? An Oldsmobile is no good? An Oldsmobile, if you want to know, is a *better* car than a Cadillac."

Abe was performing a familial duty. In October of 1963, we were one big happy family, you see. On Passover that year, my grandfather had read the four questions in the Seder ceremony to my youngest son, David, and if that had not been a fine demonstration of the melting-pot theory, then I have never understood the theory at all. (I sometimes think I never have.) From the page printed in English, my grandfather had read (quite dramatically, in fact), "Why issa *this* night of a Passove differ from all the *odder* nights of a year?"

And David, reading from the Hebrew side of the page, had answered, "*She-b'chol ha-lay-los o-noo och-leen cho-maytz u ma-tzoh, ha-lai-loh ha-zeh ku-lo ma-tzoh,*" and so on.

Even Honest Abe laughed.

The quintet was between engagements on my birthday. That is not a euphemism. My career did not take its nose dive till 1965, and I owe its longevity to the boys in Detroit. News of my "accident" had made modest headlines in most of the country's newspapers, and I'm sure the public's curiosity ("Is his hand all gnarled, or *what?*") accounted for the increased attendance wherever we played, and extended a career that should have ended in 1962, just as Biff had prophesied. Five, six years, he had said. Seven the most. By 1962, the rock shlocks were already making

421

inroads. By 1964, when the Beatles made it all respectable with their film A *Hard Day's Night*, jazz musicians, with a few rare exceptions, had all but had it. Listen, who can kick? I got ten years out of it. Remind me to send the boys in Detroit a bunch of roses. Or a case of crabs.

We sat around the rosewood dining room table in the house on top of the hill. My grandfather, as befitted a patriarch, sat at the head of the table, though he knew, as I knew, that he was no longer the patriarch; his own family was scattered to the four winds, Dominick in Brooklyn, Cristie in Massapequa, my mother on the Grand Concourse, and Luke only Christ knew where. With neither pomp nor ceremony, my grandfather had passed the scepter on to me, ignoring those next in the line of succession. His son-in-law, Jimmy, was affable but ineffectual. His eldest daughter Stella, was formidable (especially during inquisitions) but nonetheless a woman; he *was* Italian, you know, though by 1963 he had been a citizen of these United States for eighteen years. I was now the actual if not the titular head of the family, and though my grandfather occupied that chair at the head of the table, not a soul sitting around it doubted that we were here to honor the reigning potentate. Rotating clockwise from where my grandfather sat with his back to the draped sliding Thermopane doors, my kinsmen, my *compaesani*, my *landsleite*, and my devoted followers were:

1. Davina Baumgarten Lewis, blond and beautiful, thirty-one years old, who was wearing (according to the testimony of Reliable Rebecca, her doting sister) "a green jersey dress slit to her navel."

2. My mother, the indomitable Stella.

3. My oldest son, Andrew, who at the age of fourteen had taken to announcing each of his intentions to fart or belch. "I have to fart," he would say, and invariably would do so.

4. My mother-in-law, Sophie, who while baby-sitting with the children during the long trip Rebecca and I took to Europe in the spring of 1962 caught Michael innocently examining his penis

422

and told him about a woman named Sheine, who used to live on the lower East Side, and whom everyone called the Crooked Lady. "Sheine used to abuse her genitals," Sophie told him. When we got back in June, Michael asked me what his "generous" was.

5. The aforementioned Michael, who, at the age of twelve, was seeing a psychoanalyst in nearby Greenwich three times a week. Rebecca refused to believe that her mother's story about Sheine the Crooked Lady had only aggravated Michael's problems. "Your mother is a cunt," I told Rebecca.

6. Me, the thirty-seven-year-old birthday boy, my staunchest admirer, sitting in sartorial splendor (Rebecca supervised the tailoring of all my clothes) at the end of the table opposite my grandfather, shades covering my dead baby blues.

7. My grandmother, Tess, on my left. She was eighty years old, and complained constantly of arthritic pains. She also complained about there being thirteen people at the table; thirteen, she said, was a hoodoo jinx of a number. She walked with a cane these days. Welcome to the club, Grandma.

8. My youngest son, David, ten years old. David was the star pitcher of the town's Little League baseball team. When I told him my brother Tony had been a very good ballplayer, he said, "Is he the one got killed in Korea, Daddy?" Wrong war, son. Close, but no cigar.

9. Seth Lewis, Davina's husband, the noted certified public accountant, the least loyal of all my subjects, though certainly the most vociferous. He had predictably complained about the long drive up from Central Park West, where he and the fair Davina now lived, still childless. "That Merritt Parkway is a bitch," he said, the moment he stepped into the house. And belatedly, "Happy birthday, Isadore." He called me Isadore as a joke.

10. My father-in-law, Honest Abe, who, though never devoutly Orthodox or Reform, had come a long way toward becoming reformed—in his fashion.

11. Rebecca Baumgarten Di Palermo Jamison, my bride of

fifteen summers. Our anniversary would fall on a Tuesday this year, and we had already decided to take a long weekend away together, perhaps go back to Mount Pocono, where we'd spent our honeymoon—provided I was not playing in Nome, Alaska, or Kalamazoo, Michigan. She was wearing a green dress, too. I knew because when she took it from the closet she asked if she should wear the green. "The wearin' of the green will be fine, m'dear," I'd said in what I thought was a perfect Irish brogue. Rebecca had not laughed. She had not laughed when Davina came through the door wearing green, either. Rebecca did not laugh much lately. Had she seen the pictures, after all? Or were they only in her head—as they were in mine?

12. My father, Jimmy Di Palermo, who now stood up and banged on his glass. I knew it was my father, and I knew what was coming.

13. Francesco Luigi Di Lorenzo, my grandfather.

Three more than a *minyan*.

An all-American *minyan*, at that.

My father cleared his throat. "I have a little poem," he said.

"He *always* has a little poem," my mother said, and sighed.

"In honor of Ike's birthday," he said, unfazed.

"Read it fast, Pop," Rebecca said. "The roast is almost done."

"I like Jimmy's poems," Sophie said. "You write good poems, Jimmy."

"You do, Jimmy," Abe said. "Your poems are very interesting."

"*What* has he got?" my grandmother asked. In addition to the arthritis, she was going deaf in one ear. I put my hand gently on her arm and said into her good ear, "A *poem*, Grandma. He's going to read us a poem."

"Oh, good," she said, almost childishly.

My father's poems were always acrostics, the first letter of each word on every line combining vertically to spell out a message or a name. He tapped his glass for silence again, and then began reading:

Dear friends and family, relatives alike,
We gather today to honor dear Ike.
Ike, that is, of piano-playing fame.
Gather round, pay homage to his name.
He's thirty-seven years *young*, not old.
That's not so bad, if I may be so bold.

Jack Benny's already thirty-nine.
And he can't play piano half as fine.
Many people in the world enjoy Ike's sound,
I happen to know 'cause I've been around.
So let's raise our glasses—that's why we're here—
On this his birthday, to wish him good cheer,
Now and forever, for many a year.

"Happy birthday, son," he said, and handed me the shirt cardboard upon which he had hand-lettered the poem. I could not see the ornate lettering, but I knew he had probably worked on it for weeks.

"Thank you, Pop," I said.

"That was a good one, Jimmy," Abe said. "I think it was one of your best."

"I don't know what you mean by 'relatives alike,' " my mother said. "What's a family, if not relatives?"

"I had to make it rhyme, Stella," my father said.

"Yeah, but that's stupid," my mother said. "Relatives *are* the family. Isn't that right, Seth?"

"Well, he had to make it rhyme," Seth said.

"Pop, do you want to help me carve the roast?" Rebecca asked, rescuing my father.

"He tries to make it rhyme sometimes," my mother said, "and he don't make any sense."

"The artwork is so beautiful, though," Sophie said.

"Well, he used to design crochet beading, don't forget," my mother said.

"Do you need any help in the kitchen?" Davina asked.

"Wouldn't you know the *shvartzeh* would get sick on Ike's birthday?" Abe said.

"No, we're fine here," Rebecca called.

"Grandpa, would you open the wine?" I said.

"What?" my grandfather said, and I suddenly realized he had been silent for quite a long time.

"Open the wine, Papa," my mother said.

After dinner, they brought in the cake, turning out the lights first, even though the effect was lost on me. I beamed embarrassed approval while they sang to me, and then Rebecca put the cake on the table, and moved my hand toward the rim of the plate, helping me to locate it. I had already felt the warmth of the burning candles, and knew exactly where it was.

"Make a wish," Davina said.

"I already have."

My fingertips touching the edge of the plate, I positioned myself over the cake and let out my breath.

"A little to the right," Rebecca prompted, and they all burst into applause when I blew out the candles.

"What did you wish, Daddy?" Michael asked.

"That's a secret," I said.

"Tell us," Davina said.

"He's not allowed to," little David said. "Otherwise it won't come true. Isn't that right, Daddy?"

"That's right, son."

"I have to fart," Andrew said.

"Andrew!" my mother said sharply, and burst into laughter.

I felt arms encircling me from behind. A kiss touched my cheek. I thought at first it was Rebecca. "Happy birthday, Ike," Davina whispered. "What did you wish?"

"Can't tell," I said.

I had wished we could go again to Pass-A-Grille, and walk again in Rebecca's magic garden, and sit again in sunshine on a white sand beach while she read *Peter Pan* aloud to the children.

426

❖

David is throwing a rubber ball against the wall of the garage. I sit in sunshine on the patio, and listen to the steady rhythm of the ball thumping against the wooden doors. His brothers are away, there is no one to play with him. So I listen to the solitary game, and I sit in sunshine, and wish for all the world that I could walk out there to him, walk unerringly to where he is monotonously throwing the ball and catching it, throwing it and catching it, and say to him, "Hi, son, want to catch with me?"

I listen to the ball.

❖

The record sales began plummeting sometime in 1965. The drop was sudden and swift, no gradual tapering, no slide from popularity to relative obscurity in a slow descending curve. I was at the time demanding (and getting) $7,500 a week for myself and the quintet, and taking home, from personal appearances alone, somewhere between $3,500 and $4,000 a week for myself, fifty-two weeks a year (if I felt like playing that often). In addition, there were television appearances, and royalties from records and my *How to Play Jamison Jazz* books (Volumes I through IV) and from sheet music annotating my unique improvisations, and there were European tours, and a guest shot in at least one motion picture—there was, in short, the whole *shmeer*. I had hit the American jackpot, than which there is none greater. Even after paying four sidemen, and a driver for the band bus, and a band boy to help us load and unload the instruments, and a personal valet, and my manager, Mark Aronowitz, and a publicity agent, and an advance man, there was more than enough loot left to keep Rebecca and me living in the style to which we had become accustomed. (I was to dread the sound of those words every time

427

they came up during the divorce negotiations.) We had the big house in Talmadge, with a housekeeper, a gardener, and a chauffeur, a swimming pool and tennis courts (Rebecca played, and loved the game), and we also had a house in the Virgin Islands, which we visited on those rare winter weekends when I was not out there earning the big buck, and an eight-room *pied-à-terre* in the city—we had it made, friends. I was earning money by the fistful, and I was investing it wisely, and my investments made more money, and it seemed to Rebecca and to me (and probably to my grandfather, too) that I was indeed digging out gold from the streets, and the vein of ore would never be depleted, I would keep on working with my pick and shovel forever, the supply was inexhaustible.

And then in 1965, the new album came out (I've blocked out the title) in the spring sometime, I'm sure it was the spring (I've blocked out the month), and it simply refused to move despite a lot of newspaper advertising and radio ballyhoo from Victor. In the next two months, I dropped from number two to number eight in the polls, a nose dive that seemed absolutely inconceivable to me. A month after that, a gig in Miami was abruptly canceled, and a month after that Mark started talking about playing a series of one-night stands across the country— "Get a new audience for yourself," he said.

"What's the matter with my old audience?" I asked.

"If you're talking about your hard-core audience, you'll always have that, Ike. But the big bread comes from a floater audience, and jazz lost some of those people to folk, and now it's losing the rest of them to rock. It's your own fault."

"What are you talking about? *My* fault?"

"Not *your* fault personally. I'm talking about jazz musicians. You guys have become so intellectual, nobody knows what you're doing anymore. These rock groups get up there and start playing and there's a gut appeal. . . ."

"Mark," I said, "you give me any rock musician, and I'll put

428

him up against his jazz counterpart, and he'll be wasted in ten seconds flat."

"The jazz musician?"

"The *rock* musician! These clowns think they're making music if they can play two or three chords in sequence. They learn the I, and IV, and the V, and they teach them to another kid down the street, and turn up the amps, and that's it, that's supposed to be music. Have you heard some of these guitar players driving a single chord into the ground, playing the same boring lick over and over again? I'll put a guitar player like Joe Pass up against any one of them, and he'll kill them in a minute."

"Ike, what can I tell you?" Mark said. "Am I the arbiter of taste?"

"No, you're my manager," I said. "And my manager is supposed to get gigs for me."

"All I'm trying to say is that you need a new audience, Ike. Maybe you ought to add a folk singer to the quintet. Or fuse jazz with rock, come up with something. . . ."

"I'm not a gimmick musician, Mark."

"Who said you were . . ."

"What are you going to suggest next? That I do a *light* show next time I play?"

"That wouldn't be such a bad idea," Mark said.

"I'd rather retire gracefully than . . ."

"Oh, bullshit," Mark said.

". . . than corrupt the kind of music I've been playing for the past ten years."   . . .

"Okay, so go play it," Mark said. "Play it in your studio. Get your mother up there to listen to you. I'm trying to tell you it's impossible to get back an audience that's drifted away. You've either got to get a completely *new* audience or . . ."

"Or what?"

"There are other things. Maybe I can get you some work scoring a movie."

429

"I'm *blind,* Mark."

"So what? You'll listen to the actors talking, and some stooge'll describe the action to you."

"I don't want to score a movie. I want to play piano."

"Well, what can I tell you?" Mark said.

I felt nothing but hostility and contempt for rock music and the people who were making it. It seemed to me that most of the rock musicians were barely competent instrumentalists who got together in groups only so they could combine and organize their ineptitude to create a sound which, highly amplified, obfuscated their lack of talent. In 1964, when the intellectuals embraced the Beatles, I analyzed "A Hard Day's Night" (the tune, not the movie) in an attempt to discover why these four musicians who could not play their way out of a paper bag had suddenly captured the public's imagination. It was a mixolydian tune with a double tonic, and mildly interesting—certainly more interesting than much of what the other rock musicians were playing. But it seemed to me that even the Beatles were reducing a highly skilled form to something completely pedestrian.

And besides, they were putting me out of work, they were breaking my rice bowl.

❖

Michael has run afoul of a bully in his class, a boy who constantly taunts him about seeing a shrink, and makes fun of his stutter, which is one of the reasons the poor kid *makes* the damn trip to Greenwich three times a week. (The analyst tells me the stutter is only a symptom; the real trouble is that Michael feels overpowered by his "famous" father, a not uncommon phenomenon. When I ask him why my other sons don't stutter, he says, "They may be stuttering inside.") In desperation, Michael challenges the boy to a supervised fistfight in the gymnasium. The boy accepts immediately; he is twice Michael's size and certain he can

430

demolish him. That night at dinner, Michael asks me how to fight. He has never had a fistfight in his life.

I do not know how to advise him.

It is his older brother Andrew who tells him to make sure he gets in the first shot, just hit the other guy right off and keep hitting him before he can catch his breath. In the playroom, I hear them boxing, Andrew offering encouragement as Michael punches at his open palms. I am afraid for my son, but I cannot help him, I do not know how to help him. The next day, when the other boy asks him if he's sure he wants to go through with this, Michael punches him squarely and unexpectedly in the mouth, just as Andrew had advised, and keeps punching him across the length of the gym floor until the other boy begs him to stop. He describes the fight to us that night. "He was bleeding from the mouth and from the n-nose," he says excitedly, and then turns to Andrew and says, "Thanks, Andy."

I am losing them.

When they were infants, I held them in my arms at night, each and separately, and fed them their bottles and learned to change their diapers, though I was fearful at first of the safety pins. I bent over their cribs, and sniffed the sweet aroma of their baby smells, and powdered their bottoms, and listened to them giggling in wonder or surprise at each new discovery they made, and told them each and separately, over and over again, "I love you."

I love them still.

But they are becoming men too soon.

❖

At least once a month, and sometimes twice, Immigrant America came into our Wasp America living room in Talmadge. There was always good reason for these get-togethers. My mother's birthday was October first, and mine was the fifteenth. Honest Abe's birthday was in November. December meant Christmas.

Sophie's birthday was in January, Michael celebrated his in February. March was sometimes Passover and Easter both. Rebecca had been born in April and so had David (we had planned to name him April, if he'd been a girl). Mother's Day came in May, and Father's Day in June, and July 7 was my grandfather's birthday, and August was Davina's (we never celebrated Seth's, fuck him), and Andrew had been born in September, and on my block that added up to a full year of family reunions, such as they were.

Rebecca despised them.

ANDREW'S BIRTHDAY, 1965

So this is your birthday, huh, Andy Boy?
Well, let's all hope it's full of joy!
Everything bright and everything merry,
Everything just like a bowl full of cherries!
That's our wish for you today.

Sweet sixteen is the happiest day,
I'll bet you kiss all the girls today.
X is for xylophone, like in Daddy's band
That's the sweetest quintet in all of the land.
Everything you do should make him proud,
Even your mother should cheer out loud.
Now shout "Happy Birthday!" everyone in the crowd.

STELLA: He doesn't *have* a xylophone in the band.

JIMMY: I couldn't think of a word starting with X, Stella.

STELLA: Still, it don't make sense if that isn't what he has in his band. Ike, do you remember Goomah Katie in Newark, New Jersey? Her grandson got appointed principal of a high school.

SETH: You should get yourself a new tax lawyer, Ike. There are new gimmicks coming up every day of the week, and that *kahker* you've got working for you is straight out of Charles Dickens. You know those jazz books

you wrote? Did you know you can donate the manu-
scripts to a university library and get a big deduction?

DAVINA: Let me tell you what happened Friday. I got on the
subway at Fifty-ninth and Lex, and this little Puerto
Rican started, well, feeling me up, and I . . .

SOPHIE: You should have slapped his face for him!

DAVINA: No, what I did was reach behind me and take his hand
in mine. I held it all the way downtown.

ABE: He probably thought you were falling in love with him,
darling.

DAVINA: At least it stopped him.

JIMMY: Anyone want to play cards? Abe? Some poker?

SOPHIE: It's chilly in here. Do you find it chilly in here?

PASSOVER, 1966

Pray for us, Christians and Jews together,
And help us get through this stormy weather.
Sophie's passed on, we miss her bright laughter.
Sophie, dear loved one, rest well ever after.
On this day we praise God, and we offer him prayers,
Victims of grief, we must still be his heirs.
Ever respectful, even in strife,
Ready to face the rest of our life.

ABE: Well, frankly, Ike, I don't know what Becky's so upset
about. I figured with Sophie dead, may she rest in
peace, if anything should happen to me . . .

ME: I understand that, Pop. But Davina says you drew a
new will, is that right?

ABE: That's right.

ME: And you've left everything to her.

ABE: Well, yes. What's the matter with that? Seth isn't a
millionaire, you know. I figure you've taken good care
of Becky, *chas vesholem* anything should happen to

433

you. And I know you've got trust funds set up for the kids. . . .

ME: Pop, that isn't the point.

ABE: Then what's the point? I think I'm missing the point.

ME: The point is you're hurting Rebecca.

ABE: You're making this up.

ME: Why would I make it up?

ABE: How do I know? Maybe *you* want the money.

ME: Pop, you can shove the money up your ass, for all I care. I'm talking about the fact that you have *two* daughters, and you're hurting one of them by leaving everything you've got to the *other* one, to Davina.

ABE: Davina should have kept her mouth shut. I told her in private, and now she's causing trouble.

ME: Pop, *you're* the one causing trouble. Why don't you change the will?

ABE: If it means that much to Becky, I'll change it already. I don't know why it should mean so much to her. She's got plenty. You got plenty, the two of you together.

ME: Shall I tell her you'll change it?

ABE: It's not even that much money. What do you think it is, a fortune? It's a couple of thousand dollars, that's all.

ME: Shall I tell her?

ABE: Tell her, tell her.

ME: When will you change it?

ABE: I'll get around to it.

MOTHER'S DAY, 1967

Mother's Day wishes to the women here,
On this special day, we hold them all dear.
Though Davina gets to do the dishes,
Here's extending her, too, the best of wishes.

434

Eldest among us is dear Grandma Tess;
Regards to you, Grandma, we wish you the best.
Son Ike has his family, Rebecca's the mother.

Dear Becky, like you he won't find another.
And so let's thank God for another good year.
Yes, drink, and be merry, and be of good cheer.

JIMMY: Seth? Some cards? A little pinochle?

STELLA: Never you *mind!* This is Mother's Day. The *men* are supposed to do the dishes. Am I right, Rebecca?

DAVINA: Where's Harriet today? Did you give her the day off?

STELLA: Certainly. Harriet's a mother, too, right, Rebecca? We're *all* entitled to the day off.

SETH: Davina's not a mother. Let *her* do the dishes. Like Jimmy said in the poem.

JIMMY: Well, what's new, Ike? Anything new? Any new records or anything?

GRANDMA: Ike, play something for us. Come on, give us a little tune on the piano. You never play for just the family no more.

ME: Grandpa?

GRANDPA: Sì, Ignazio?

ME: Are you all right?

GRANDPA: Sì.

ME: Grandpa?

GRANDPA: That was nice of your father. To mention Tessie. In the poem.

SETH: What is it? Is the old man crying?

DAVINA: Rebecca, have you got a minute?

REBECCA: Sure. What's the matter?

DAVINA: Come upstairs, okay?

JIMMY: Seth? Some cards? Stella, I put a new deck of cards in your purse.

STELLA: He's crippled, your father. Get them yourself!

435

REBECCA: What is it?

DAVINA: Why didn't you invite Daddy here today?

REBECCA: I did invite him.

DAVINA: But you told him not to bring Donna.

REBECCA: I told him nothing of the sort.

DAVINA: Then what did he do, invent it? You know, Rebecca, for someone who's intermarried her*self* . . .

REBECCA: I have nothing against Donna.

DAVINA: Then why can't he bring her here?

REBECCA: I didn't say he couldn't bring her here.

DAVINA: He goes everywhere with her, you know. It's not as if it's a great big secret.

REBECCA: No, it's certainly not a secret. Mama's dead a little more than a year, and he moves in with a *shvartzeh* file clerk who . . .

DAVINA: She's very good for him.

REBECCA: She's twenty-four years old!

DAVINA: So what? Don't be such a prude, Rebecca. You want to know something? I think it was going on even when Mama was alive, what do you think of that?

REBECCA: I believe it.

DAVINA: So?

REBECCA: So let him do whatever the fuck he wants, but he's not bringing her to *this* house. Not yet, he isn't.

DAVINA: Then when?

REBECCA: How does eight years sound?

CHRISTMAS DAY, 1969

May all ye merry gentlemen,
Every lady gathered here, too,
Rejoice and sing a loud "Amen,"
Remembering Christ our Lord was a Jew,
Yes, just like Abe and Seth, and Davina, too.

436

X marks the spot of this, Ike's house.
May all in it be happy, even a mouse.
And as for the rest of us, what else can we do?
Say "Merry Christmas to all, and a Happy New Year, too."

ABE: Donna, you want some more turkey? Rebecca, is there more turkey in the kitchen?

REBECCA: Harriet? Would you bring in the turkey platter, please?

DONNA: The stuffing is delicious, Rebecca.

REBECCA: Thank you. Harriet made it. *Harriet!*

HARRIET: Comin', comin'.

STELLA: Why does Ike have to leave the table right in the middle of dinner?

REBECCA: It's an important call.

STELLA: What kind of call is so important he has to leave the table on Christmas Day in the middle of dinner?

REBECCA: It's something about scoring a movie.

JIMMY: Ike's going to be in another movie?

REBECCA: No, he's going to *score* it. Write the music for it.

JIMMY: Yeah? Maybe he can get a part for me in it.

HARRIET: Who wants the turkey, ma'am?

REBECCA: Donna would like some, please.

HARRIET: You the one, miss?

DONNA: Yes, please.

JIMMY: I could do my Charlie Chaplin imitation.

REBECCA: Well, Pop, all he's doing is writing the music for it.

JIMMY: Maybe he could put one of my poems to music.

STELLA: You and your poems.

ABE: He writes good poems. Didn't you think that was a good poem, Donna?

DONNA: Yes, it was very good.

STELLA: Thank God he didn't use "xylophone" again. That's 'cause I told him about it that time. He's got some memory, this one.

JIMMY: She takes credit for everything I do.

437

STELLA: Well, *didn't* I tell you?

ABE: Did you see that Christmas card from Harry James, Donna? Ike knows Harry James.

DONNA: There's one there from Count Basie, too.

JIMMY: Those bands are always repeating themselves. Ike never repeats himself. That's what I like about his band.

STELLA: What bands repeat themselves? What are you talking about?

JIMMY: Like Count Basie's.

STELLA: Sure, only *your* bands were good.

JIMMY: Did I say anything about my bands? I said *Ike's* band was good.

DONNA: I love "The Man I Love."

JIMMY: That was his best record. It was the first one, and it was the best one. I don't care what anybody says.

HARRIET: Ma'am, if the young lady's through, I'd like to start clearin'.

It amazes me now that everything remained so predictably constant in our Immigrant America. Aside from statistics—Sophie's death, Tolerant Abe's *shvartzeh*, this or that latest event in my all but invisible career—the voices, the cadences, the tonalities were precisely those I had heard in Harlem and Rebecca had heard on the lower East Side during all the days of our separate childhoods. When Rebecca repeated the conversation she'd had in the bedroom with Davina, I could have sworn I was listening to a similar conversation my grandfather once had with Grandma Tess, who'd refused to allow Aunt Bianca to bring her butcher boyfriend into the house. And in contrast to those seemingly endless Sundays we spent with the family, the times we spent with close friends and acquaintances were exhilarating. *They* were Wasp America— even though most of them were the grandchildren of immigrants or slaves. I don't know when Wasp stopped meaning **W**hite **A**nglo-**S**axon **P**rotestant. I feel certain that in the new American

438

lexicon, the acronym should more properly read **W**ealthy **A**nd **S**uccessful **P**rofessional. A Protestant ditchdigger is an Immigrant American, and Paul Newman is a Wasp American, and Camelot (when it existed) was divided between the folk who lived up there in the uppermost chambers of the castle and the folk who squatted in the castle keep below. Forget the fact that John F. Kennedy was the grandson of Irish immigrants, forget that he was a Catholic. Even my mother (who's American, don't forget) knows he was a Wasp. She knows it because she is an Immigrant American, whatever else she may tell herself.

In July of 1970, like all men who suddenly find themselves to be not only forty, but almost four years past it already, I began questioning everything—my success, my marriage, my family, *and* America. I had a lot of time to do a lot of soul-searching, navel-contemplating, and nitty-gritty investigation. This is what I decided. I decided everything was hunky-dory.

My success had lasted longer than anyone might have reasonably expected. I had enjoyed ten long years of popularity, and people still knew my name wherever I went; in fact, the house band would invariably break into the Dwight Jamison version of "The Man I Love" whenever I walked into a club. I'd already scored one movie, and Mark was certain he could get me other movie gigs. Every now and then he'd line up a weekend in a posh spot on the Coast or in Miami, and that was enough to keep my hand in. Alone in my studio, I would sometimes spend long hours listening to my jazz collection, and in truth I rather enjoyed the serenity of what could only be called semiretirement.

As for my marriage, I considered it quite carefully, and decided it was no worse and perhaps a lot better than most of the marriages around us. I no longer had the freedom I'd become accustomed to on the road, but I discovered there were a great many . . . well . . . "restless" women in the town of Talmadge, Connecticut, and that they were eager to exorcise their demons in various motels and country inns to which they were kind enough to drive me in their station wagons. I lied relentlessly and recklessly to Rebecca. Our chauffeur would drop me off at a record shop in Stamford, and I'd tell him I wouldn't be needing him till four o'clock, to pick me up in front of Bloomingdale's at that time, and then the transfer to this or that station wagon would take place, one or another willing matron transporting me first vehicularly and later physically. They all had different station wagons and different in-bed specialties, the most bizarre of which perhaps was . . . but I digress again. I would be standing in front of Bloomingdale's at the appointed hour, having first wandered into the record shop to buy two dozen albums at random, and when I got home that afternoon I would tell Rebecca I'd had a marvelous time record-hunting, not to mention a delightful Chinese lunch. Rebecca bought it. (I *thought* she was buying it.) And meanwhile, I figured this was what marriage in America was all about. I mean, if such and such a respected Talmadge matron was cheating on her husband with *me*, then it was reasonable to assume *he* was cheating on *her* with a respected matron somewhere in New York City, where he took his three-hour lunches. In a way, my explorations into suburban sex were more satisfying than the liaisons on the road had been. My fame had passed, you see; The Beast no longer claimed morsels from the table.

I told myself, too, that those euphemistic record-hunting expeditions, or shopping trips, or dental appointments, or fittings at the tailor's, or simply long walks alone in the Talmadge Reservation were helpful to the sex life Rebecca and I shared together. I had long ago decided that I simply *needed* more sex than she did (does that sound familiar, Mr. and Mrs. Phil Anderer?) and that she was getting no more and no less (well, perhaps a *teeny* bit less) than she desired. I remained convinced, too, that Rebecca was faithful to me, that whereas she immediately triggered desire in any man who mistakenly read her smoldering look, she would just as quickly turn on her green death ray and *zotz!*—a smoking pile of ashes from which could be heard the echoing traces of

440

an advertising man's voice oozing, "Do you ever get into the city?"
I told myself that what I was doing was not only American, it was
probably international or maybe universal as well. If I'd been a
successful (albeit fading) jazz musician in Italy, I'd have had a
steady mistress with whom I would spend weekdays in Porto
Santo Stefano, *shtupping* her before her own hubby came down
from Milano for the weekend. (During the week, *he* was up at
Lake Como, putting it to a Genoese lady whose husband was in
Portofino sticking a lady from Naples.) There were a lot of Little
Orphan Annies in Talmadge, and I found at least a few of them,
and we used each other to satisfy our separate needs, whatever
we told ourselves they were. Actually, I had no needs. Everything
was hunky-dory.

My immediate family was as hunky-dory as any of the families
surrounding us, or any of the families we knew in New York City,
fifty miles to the south, or New Haven, approximately the same
distance away to the north and the east. My youngest son, David,
was attending a private school in New Canaan, intent on getting
into Princeton—sixty percent of the kids who were graduated from
his school found themselves in Princeton afterward. He was a
bright kid who maintained a straight-B average, and who (like
every other kid in the world) was a member of a rock group; his
instrument was bass guitar. He played it as well as did any of the
bass guitarists in any of the successful rock groups; he was lousy.
I once told him all I had to do was pull out the plug and rock
music would go away. He told me I was old-fashioned. Actually, he
called me an *alteh kahker*; not for nothing was he half Jewish. My
middle son, Michael, had been accepted at Columbia University,
and was living in a rat-infested apartment on 119th Street near
Amsterdam Avenue. He shared the apartment with a girl two years
older than he was. She had not told her parents she was living
with a boy. She referred to Michael only as "my roommate"
whenever she spoke to Brighton, Massachusetts, on the telephone
her parents were paying for. If Michael ever chanced to answer the

phone when they called, he used one of a dozen different names and told them he was the superintendent come to fix the pipes (I suppose he *was*, in a way), or the *faygeleh* poet who lived down the hall, or the boyfriend of a girl who was visiting the girl he lived with —his inventions were varied and imaginatively deceitful; not for nothing was he half Italian. My *farblondjeteh* son, Andrew, was at the moment in India, having dropped out of three colleges in succession, and having discovered that his father was nothing but a nine-to-fiver in disguise, a money-grubbing, materialistic fink— "Who needs money?" he asked. "I can get along on pennies a day. Pennies!" (Yes, son, but they're *my* pennies; I busted my ass to earn them.) He had not written for three months, but many of our friends had wandering children, too, and we were all convinced this would pass, eventually they would settle down. In the meantime, Andrew was safe from the draft (he'd had cartilage removed from his knee after a skiing accident), and we figured if he had already survived the war in Vietnam, he might one day survive the war raging within himself. My immediate family, then, was what any of us successful Americans might have expected of our immediate families in the year 1970, by which time one president, one assassin, one separatist, one neo-Fascist, one civil rights leader, and one presidential hopeful had been murdered.

My Immigrant family was in pretty good shape as well—with the possible exception of my Uncle Luke, who had disappeared from the face of the earth right after my grandfather confronted him on the Bowery. Honest Abe had remarried—not his little *shvartzeh*, but a nize Jush lady from Miami. He was living down there with her and helping to run the gift shop she owned on Collins Avenue. My parents, though they seemed to be going to doctors and to funerals more and more often, were nonetheless happy in their apartment house on the Grand Concourse. Each time my father came for one of the family get-togethers, he brought one of his poems. Seth and Davina were still happily married, still childless, still living in the same building on Central Park West, though they had moved to an apartment four stories higher, overlooking a magnificent view of the park. My grandmother had died of a stroke the year before, and at the age of eighty-nine, my grandfather had finally been convinced to leave Harlem and to move in with my Aunt Cristie out in Massapequa. I saw him perhaps once a month, usually at my mother's house.

And my Wasp family was in fine shape, too, consisting as it did of successful Americans like myself, wealthy self-made men who were ready to swap ethnic jokes, and tell this or that intimate ancedote about one or another Broadway production or Hollywood film or celebrity more or less famous than ourselves, and exchange Christmas gifts, and do favors for each other, and embrace each other (an old-world affection) whenever we came into or left each other's company. One or two of us were also fucking each other's wives (though not my Rebecca! *never* my Rebecca!) and looking the other way while we swigged the booze and danced the wild *Tarantella* and greeted the sun or bayed at the moon. We were one great big Wasp American family, and we realized that nowhere but in the United States could we have scaled such dizzying and spectacular heights while managing simultaneously to cling to our spectacles, testicles, wallets, and watches.

As for the greater American family, the family at large . . . well, the country was in ragged shape, but it had been there before, and in 1970 we still clung to the hope (speak for yourself, John)—all right, I still clung to the hope that we'd somehow get out of the mess we were in. Somehow we'd manage to preserve what was good, true, and noble, we'd find new wellsprings of courage, and drink from them deeply, and replenish our spirit, and go marching arm in arm together into a bright and shining space-age future, brothers one and all, *including* the fucking black man who was dominating whatever was left of jazz in New York. In the meantime, I had grown accustomed to the fact that I was no longer Number One (or any number at all) on the charts, and no longer

443

mentioned in any of the polls, and no longer a Big American Hit. I was a man secure in the knowledge that he was loved by family and friends, and I gave to them my own boundless love in return. I was a man at peace with himself.

Why then, you may ask, did I go to bed with Davina Baumgarten Lewis on the afternoon of July 17, 1970?

❖

The seventeenth was a Friday. My schedule for that day (I still have the memo I punched out on my slate; I am a very organized fellow, except where it concerns my life) was as follows:

11:00 AM	Leave Talmadge
12:30 PM	Chipp's—final fitting
1:30 PM	Lunch—Mark Aronowitz
	Four Seasons
3:30 PM	Jeffrey Epstein
	MGM—29th floor
	1350 Avenue of the Americas
5:30 PM	Drinks—Davina and Seth
7:00 PM	Dinner—Sardi's
8:30 PM	"Fiddler on the Roof"
	Majestic Theater

I took the car and driver into the city that day. Rebecca planned to drive her own car (a $22,000 Maserati) to New Canaan later, catch a train to Grand Central, and then taxi over to the apartment on Central Park West. Our plan was to spend the cocktail hour with the Lewises, after which we would go our separate ways, Rebecca and I to dinner and the theater, Davina and Seth to a party in the Village. My afternoon meeting with the MGM executive was to be an important one; we were supposed to discuss the possibility of my scoring another film. I suppose that's why Mark had asked me to lunch. He was anticipating a fat fee on the horizon, and it does not hurt to be kind to the people who are

444

putting ten percent of *their* daily bread on *your* table. In retrospect, I'm amazed he showed up at all, or—considering what he had to tell me—stayed to pay for a lunch that did not promise future revenue. The first thing he said was, "We've been screwed, Ike. Here's the story. . . ."

The story was glum. I listened to it as I downed first one Beefeater martini, and then another. It seemed that MGM had changed its collective mind. They were having internal troubles, Mark said. They weren't even sure they were going ahead with the picture, but even if they *did* go ahead with it, they wanted to use the guy who had scored *The Wild Bunch*, had I seen *The Wild Bunch*?

No, I told him, I had not seen *The Wild Bunch*.

"So that's it," Mark said. "Epstein was supposed to fly in last night, but he canceled. They called me just a little while ago. I tried reaching you in Talmadge, but Rebecca told me you'd left early."

We finished lunch at a quarter to three. I walked Mark up to his office on Forty-seventh and Broadway, shook hands with him, and began walking crosstown and then downtown. I had no specific destination in mind. It was a reasonably cool day for July in New York, and I wandered aimlessly, wondering if I should fill the time between now and five-thirty by taking in a movie. There was a crowd on the corner of Forty-fourth and Sixth. In 1970, there used to be a very good hot dog stand on that corner; it has since been torn down. A lot of sidewalk hookers used to line up there for a late-afternoon lunch before starting their daily grind. I figured now, as I heard the buzz of the crowd all around me, that one of them was being hassled by a cop.

"What is it?" I asked someone who was standing beside me clucking his or her tongue, the repeated *tsk-tsks* falling like brushes on a snare drum.

"Oh, it's a bum," the person answered. She was a woman who sounded very much like my mother. I immediately identified her as Italian, though she spoke without a trace of accent.

"Is something wrong with him?" I asked.

"He's picking bugs," she said.

"He's what?"

"He's sitting on the curb with his shirt off, and he's picking bugs out of the shirt and stamping them dead under his shoe."

"Bugs?"

"Lice," she said. "You know. Bugs." She began clucking again, and then she said, "His back is all covered with sores. The bugs must've bit him, don't you think?"

At that point, the vagrant said, "What are you all looking at? Leave me alone," and his voice startled me for a moment because (I'm sure I was mistaken) it sounded exactly like my Uncle Luke, or at least my Uncle Luke as I'd last heard him in 1950, when I'd telephoned to ask him something—what was it I'd called to ask him? "Go on," he said, "get lost," and I was convinced now that the man sitting on the curb picking lice out of his shirt and stamping them dead under his shoe was my Uncle Luke (I'm positive I was mistaken), who had disappeared from sight eight years ago.

"What does he look like?" I asked the woman, but she was gone, and a man answered for her.

"Who?" he said. "The bum?"

"Yes."

"He's an old fart," the man said.

"How old?"

"Sixty, seventy? Who can tell with these bums?"

"Is he wearing glasses?" I said.

"Yeah," the man answered, surprised. "How could you tell that?"

I turned away swiftly. If it was Luke (It *can't* be, I told myself, though Luke if he was still alive would be in his late sixties, but no, it can't be him!), I didn't want to talk to him, I didn't want to hear him say again, "Hey, Iggie, how's the kid?" I tapped my way through the crowd, "Excuse me, excuse me, please," and found my way to the curb, and asked someone to help me across Sixth

446

Avenue. I walked east, still without a destination in mind (or so I believed), thinking about that man sitting on the curb killing lice, and telling myself over and over again that Luke was dead, he *had* to be dead, he'd been gone a long, long time now, no one had heard from him in years, of course he was dead. I turned left on Fifth Avenue and began walking uptown. It was not until I reached Fifty-seventh Street, and was standing outside the Doubleday's there, that I realized I was sweating and trembling. I walked to the curb and raised my cane, holding it aloft, hoping some passing vehicle would be a taxicab, hoping the driver would realize I was hailing him. As I waited, still trembling, I imagined a woman standing at the corner bus stop not fifty feet away, staring at me. I wanted to get away from her as quickly as possible, before she could say, "Who do you think you're kidding?"

A taxicab pulled to the curb. "Where you going, Mac?" the driver asked.

"Central Park West," I said, and I gave him Davina's address, and climbed into the back seat, and closed the door.

"You okay?" he asked.

"Fine," I said.

I heard him throwing his flag, and then he gunned the taxi away from the curb.

"You look familiar," he said. "Are you somebody?"

"No," I answered.

The doorman at Davina's building recognized me, but he called upstairs nonetheless to announce me. The elevator operator took me up to the sixteenth floor, and I tapped my way down the hall, and found the doorbell in the jamb, and pressed it, and heard the familiar chimes inside the apartment, and then heard the peephole flap being drawn back, and then the door being unlocked.

"You're early," Davina said. I went into the apartment. She locked the door behind me. "Is something wrong?" she asked. "You look . . ." She let the sentence trail.

"I think I need a drink," I said.

447

"Sure."

"My meeting was canceled," I said.

"You're lucky you caught me home."

"Were you going out?"

"Just to pick up a few things. Sit down, Ike."

I had followed her into the living room. I knew where the furniture was (unless she had rearranged it), and I found one of the couches, and sat, and heard Davina padding barefooted to the bar in one corner of the room, on the side with the windows overlooking the park.

"What would you like?" she asked.

There was the scent of lilac in the room. I suddenly thought of my Aunt Bianca.

"Ike?"

"Anything."

"Well, what?"

"A little Scotch," I said.

"Ice?"

"Please."

As she poured, she said, "Are you sure you're all right?"

"Yes," I said. "I'm fine."

She came back to the couch, put the glass in my hand, and then sat beside me. "What time is it, anyway?" she asked, and must have looked immediately at a clock someplace in the room, because then she said, "You really *are* early. Becky won't be here for at least two hours."

"Yes, well, I told you. The meeting was canceled."

"No problem," she said.

"If you have to go out . . ."

"I have to run up to Columbus Avenue for a minute. We're out of club soda, and I thought I'd pick up some hors d'oeuvres while I'm at it. Those little things you warm up. You can come with me if you like."

"No, I'd rather wait here."

"Well, excuse me then, huh? I want to get out of these dungarees. Would you like another drink?"

"Please," I said, and extended my empty glass.

She rose, took the glass, and went to the bar again. I heard the sound of whiskey being poured. She came back to me and put the glass into my hand. As she started out of the room, she said, "Shall I put on some records?"

"No," I said. "Thanks."

"Make yourself comfortable," she said, and went down the corridor to her bedroom.

I sat on the couch sipping my Scotch. For no apparent reason (I already knew what time it was, Davina had already told me Rebecca would not be here for at least two hours, which meant it was now three-thirty or a little bit later), I opened the cover on my wrist watch and felt for the raised dots. The first ten letters of the Braille alphabet also double for the numbers one to ten. The big hand was now on the G, the little hand was almost on the D; it was now precisely twenty-five minutes to four. At the Blind School, I had never had any difficulty translating letters to numerals; it was the imaginative jump *following* this simple task that threw me. I asked Miss Goodbody why the three was a three when the *small* hand was pointing to it, but a fifteen when the *big* hand was pointing to it. And why was the seven a seven, but also a thirty-five (Like when we say it's seven thirty-five, Miss Goodbody), and also a *twenty*-five (Like when we say it's twenty-five to four). That's a very good question, Iggie, Miss Goodbody answered. It was now twenty-five to four, and Davina was in her bedroom, which was at the far end of the apartment; I had placed my coat on the bed in that bedroom many times over the past several years. I decided to go into the bedroom to chat with her. I told myself I was a little drunk. Two strong martinis at lunch, a pair of Scotches now, I was just a little drunk. I got up off the couch, and banged my shin against the coffee table, and found my way down the corridor, past the bathroom I knew was on the

449

right, and the small room on the left Seth used as a study, and then knocked on the door to the master bedroom, and called, "Yoo-hoo, are you decent?"

"Ike?" she said.

"That's who," I said. "Are you decent?"

"Well . . . no," she said. "Not exactly."

I opened the door. "Who did you think it was?" I said.

"Hey!" she said. "I'm not dressed."

"That's okay," I said. "Who'd you think it was?"

"Come on, get out of here," she said. "I'll be with you in a minute. Go make yourself another drink."

"I feel like talking."

"Ike, get *out* of my bedroom," she said, and laughed, and came across the floor (she was still barefooted) to where I was standing just inside the door, and gently turned me around, and gently nudged me out of the room, and then closed and locked the door behind me. "I'll be with you in a minute," she said.

I went back into the living room. I found the bar and poured myself another drink, sniffing the lip of the bottle first to make sure it was the Scotch. Again, for no apparent reason, I checked the time. It was twenty minutes to four. I snapped the lid shut on my watch, went to the sofa (this time managing to avoid the coffee table), and sat. When Davina finally came into the living room, I said, "That was *some* minute. That was an *Italian* minute."

"You're not getting drunk, are you?" she said. "Becky'll kill me."

"Why don't you have a drink yourself?" I said.

"What time is it?" she asked.

"About a quarter to four."

"I'll have one when I get back," she said. "Ike, if the phone rings, don't bother answering it. It's out in the kitchen, I don't want you breaking your neck."

"Poor little blind bastard," I said. "What are you wearing now?"

"Just a little white cotton shift," she said. "And sandals."

450

"Aren't you allowed to wear dungarees on Central Park West?"

"Well, that's not it. I like to . . ."

"Are you wearing stockings?"

"With sandals?"

"What *are* you wearing?"

"I just told you."

"I mean *under* the shift."

"None of your business," she said.

"Is it what you were wearing when I came into the bedroom?"

"I was putting on my face when you came in."

"Yes, but what were you wearing?"

"Hey, Ike . . . cut it out, huh?"

"Do I smell lilac?"

"What? Oh, yes, I have some in a vase."

"I thought you might be wearing lilac under your shift. My Aunt Bianca used to wear lilac all the time. She ran a corset shop. They called her the Corset Lady. She made corsets, girdles, bras, everything. I used to handle a lot of bras in her shop. You wouldn't by chance be wearing a bra under your shift, would you?"

"Yes, I would by chance be wearing a bra."

"And panties?"

"Panties, too."

"Pity. Is that what you were wearing when I knocked on the bedroom door? Bra and panties?"

"Yes. Are we finished with my underwear?"

"Who'd you think it was?"

"I don't follow."

"When I knocked on the door."

"Well, I knew it wasn't Seth because he called and said he wouldn't be home till six or a little after. And my boyfriend only comes on Wednesdays," she said, and laughed lightly. "So it had to be you."

"Lousy tune," I said. "Why wouldn't you let me stay?"

"In the bedroom? Are you kidding?"

451

"Can't see a fucking thing, you know. Blind, you know."

"Poor little blind bastard," Davina said. "Listen, I'd better get going. You sure you don't want me to put on some records?"

"Have you got 'The Man I Love'?"

"Yes, shall I . . . ?"

"Dwight Jamison's version?"

"What else?"

"Hate it," I said.

Davina laughed.

"Don't you believe me?"

"I never know when to believe you," she said. "I never know when you're serious."

"You can believe me when I say I hate 'The Man I Love.' You can absolutely believe I'm serious when I say that."

"I believe you already," Davina said. "Is there anything else you'd like to hear?"

"No. Thank you."

"Okay. I'll be back in a little while."

"Did I tell you about Michelle?"

"No. Michelle? Who's Michelle?"

"A Beatles tune. Too many unpredictable chord changes in it. Goddamn tune isn't even logical. Probably the best thing they ever wrote, but useless to a jazz musician."

"I'm always fascinated by what you do with a song," Davina said.

"Thank you," I said.

"I really am. I think it's amazing."

"Thank you. It's a shame nobody *else* is fascinated these days, but thank you, anyway, Davina. I appreciate your fascination."

"I'd better get going," she said. "Are you sure you'll be all right?"

"Listen," I said, "why don't you forget the club soda? We're just beginning to talk."

"Well . . . Seth likes club soda."

452

"You can go for it later. He won't be home till six, isn't that right?"

"That's right."

"Isn't that what you said? Six or a little after?"

"Yes, that's right."

"So?"

"So?"

"So here we are. Alone at last."

Davina was silent for a moment. She walked to the bar. I heard her pouring herself a drink.

"Booze and the piano go together, did you know that?" I said.

"No, I didn't know that," she answered. "What is this, Ike? A pass?"

"Davina, I'm sure you would recognize a pass if . . ."

"Is it?"

"Yes."

"Are you drunk?"

"Sober as a judge."

"Then cut it out, okay? You're making me nervous."

"I notice, however, that you still haven't left the apartment."

"Well, I'm flattered, of course. . . ."

"And interested?"

"No."

"Curious?"

"No. Cheers," she said.

"Cheers."

"Do you do this often, Ike?"

"Never," I said.

"That's a lie. I know at least four women you've had affairs with."

"Would you like to be number five?"

"Nope."

"Time is running out, Davina. Time is tick-tocking along. Before you know it, the whole *mishpocheh* will be here, and then what? A beautiful afternoon wasted."

"You're really something," she said.

"Why don't you take off your dress?" I said.

"Who's Michelle?" she said.

"Did you hear me?"

"I heard you. Who's Michelle? One of the women on your list?"

"I have no women, I have no list. Davina," I said, "I really would appreciate it if you took off your dress."

"Why?"

"Because I would like to go to bed with you."

"Well, that's putting it on the table, all right," she said. I heard the ice clinking in her glass, she was silent for a moment, I assumed she was sipping the drink. Then she said, "I have to admit I've thought about it."

"So have I. I thought about it just a few minutes ago. And I asked you to take off your dress, but I don't see anything happening yet."

"Is that why you came up here?"

"I came up here because I thought I saw a ghost. But now that I'm here, I'd like to go to bed with you."

"So it shouldn't be a total loss, right?"

"What do you say, Davina?"

"No, Ike. Of *course* no."

"Okay," I said. "Nice seeing you." I stood up and banged my shin against the coffee table again. "You ought to move that coffee table," I said. "Blind people have a lot of trouble with it. I think I'll run down and take a look at Lincoln Center. Never *have* seen Lincoln Center; might as well take a look at it now. I'll be back around five-thirty."

"Sit down," she said.

"No," I said. "You've hurt my feelings."

Davina began laughing. "Sit down, you nut," she said. "Sit down and be a good boy."

454

"My mother told me I should always be a good boy. Like my Uncle Luke. My Uncle Luke was always a good boy. But now he's a drunk sitting on the curb squashing bugs." I sat. "May I have another drink, please?" I said.

"Uh-uh. If Becky comes here and finds you drunk . . ."

"You know what she used to call my Uncle Luke? Mr. Rumples! Met him once or twice, and right away decided he was too . . . *shabby* for her. Too . . . *shabby* for the goddamn Jewish Princess!"

"Why do you want me, Ike? Because I'm Becky's sister?"

"*Want* you? Now that is a very quaint way of putting it, Davina. I don't believe I've heard it put so quaintly since my mother told me about her flapper days."

"How would you put it?"

"I want to fuck you."

"Say it again."

"I want to fuck you, Davina."

"Why?"

"Because of your *mind*. I want to fuck your *mind*, Davina. I want to fuck you out of your mind."

"Why?"

"Because it's what *you've* wanted ever since we shook hands on Mosholu Parkway in the year . . ."

"Oh, boy!" Davina said, and began laughing again.

"That's the truth," I said. "And if it isn't, who cares? Everything's a lie, anyway, what difference does it make? Do you want to, or don't you?"

"I want to."

"Good."

"But I won't."

"You'll be missing a marvelous opportunity," I said. "I've been told I have a very nice *shlahng* for a blind man. I was told that by experts in the recording, hotel, and jukebox industries—not to mention the photography profession."

"I'm sure it's gorgeous."

455

"And I'm also a very tactile fellow. You wouldn't believe the things I can do with my hands."

"I'm sure your hands are heavenly."

"Then come here," I said.

"No. You come here."

"Gladly. Take off your dress."

"You take it off for me."

I found her, I pulled her into my arms and slid both hands up under the short white dress, she was dressed for a wedding, why was she dressed in white, didn't she know we were attending a funeral? "Easy, you'll rip them," she said, and I found her mouth, and placed upon her lips with donnish solemnity the kiss of death, my death, Rebecca's, the death of everything we had known. Davina pulled away breathlessly and said, as though reading my mind, "What about Becky?" and I answered, "What about her?" having already forgotten her, having already relegated her to a tattered mythic past of roller skate keys and Tom Mix shooters. I thrust my tongue into Davina's mouth, and again she twisted away, and tossed her head and laughed and said, "She's your wife," and I thought *Was* my wife, *was*, we are burying her today, and said only, "She's your sister," and kissed her fiercely. We sank together, sank locked in felonious arms to the floor, and Davina said, "Not on the rug, for Christ's sake," ever the Jewish housewife, were there newspapers on the kitchen floor on this bloody afternoon of *shabbes?* "Wait," she said, and, "Wait," again, and then said in false and foolish defense, "I'll tell her, you know." I answered curtly, "Tell her," and entered her, the *coup de grâce* of a marriage and a lifetime. Jaggedly we coupled on the thick pile rug, the rhythms of our murderous intent raggedly forcing a contrapuntal rhythm from between her clenched teeth, "*Tell* her you forced me, *tell* her you raped me, *tell* her you, *tell* her you, *tell* her you," a litany strangled when she came on a moan. I stopped, I withdrew immediately, I held back juices already climbing that homicidal shaft, as if even then it was not too late, even then I

456

had not committed myself finally to what was irrevocable. "You won't tell her," I said, and Davina whispered, "I won't have to."

❖

I was the one who told Rebecca, though that was not what Davina had meant. Lying spent and sweating beneath me, Davina had meant only that Rebecca would *sense* what had taken place, there would be no need for *anyone* to tell her she'd been slain on a living room rug. I told her at the end of August. She had suggested, apparently on the spur of the moment, that we drive up to the Catskills. When I asked her why, she said she just felt like taking a drive up there. I should have known there was a reason for the trip. ("Smart, smart, smart—but *stupid*," Rebecca used to say.)

She drove me up to the little town in which her Tante Raizel had rented the *kochalayn* summer after summer when Rebecca was a child. She took me down to the river where she and Davina used to swim while her mother sat watching them from the bank, her shawl wrapped around her shoulders. She took me to the drugstore, where the proprietor still recognized her, took me to the luncheonette, where she ordered a celery tonic and a hot pastrami on rye, the way she used to when she was a kid. And then we walked up into the hills.

This was August, the end of summer was almost upon us. Rebecca said she had been doing a lot of thinking about us and the family and the lives we were leading. She said she knew how important the family was to me—the kids thought of the family as a dynasty, that was a very good thing I had done for the kids, instilling in them such a strong sense of family. But now, she said, the kids are all grown up, Andrew is off in India someplace, he's almost twenty-one, Ike, I guess he'll find himself one of these days, I *hope* he finds himself one of these days, and Michael's at Columbia, he's got his own apartment in the city, I'm sure he'll be all right, though I know the city is terrible right now—would you like to sit, Ike?

We sat. The woods were still except for the incessant buzz of flying insects.

"I guess we could take David with us," she said. "There are good schools over there. He's seventeen, he can finish high school someplace over there, it won't hurt him. High school is a bunch of crap, anyway. He won't really be learning anything till he goes to college, if he decides that's what he wants to do."

"When you say 'over there,' what do you mean? Europe?"

"Yes."

"You want to go to Europe?"

"Yes. Maybe Italy. Maybe we could sell the house in Saint Croix and find a little villa in Italy."

"Well," I said.

"It's just that I think it's time we devoted a little thought to ourselves," Rebecca said. "You're not tied down with such a grueling schedule anymore. . . ."

"You mean I'm unemployed these days," I said.

"Well, whatever you want to call it. We're well off, Ike. We won't ever have to worry about money, thank God. So maybe it's time . . . well, we never had much time to ourselves. There was always the band and the children." She hesitated. "I'm forty-two years old," she said.

"Yes," I said.

"Yes," she repeated, "and I've noticed how bored you are lately. . . ."

"Bored?"

"Yes, and I don't want to find *myself* becoming bored, too. I think . . . well . . . there are a lot of bored people, bored women, in Talmadge. I . . . guess you know there are bored women there."

"Well," I said.

"Well, Ike, let's be honest with each other, okay? Let's for

458

maybe the first time in our lives be honest with each other."

"I've always been honest with you, Rebecca."

"Sure," she said. "Ike, I know there are other women. When you were on the road all the time, I could ignore what you were doing because you were far away, and . . ."

"Rebecca, I've never . . ."

"Ike, please. There were women then, and there are women now, but now they're very close to home, and I'm getting tired of looking the other way. I don't know how much longer I can go on looking the other way. I'm not blind, Ike . . . forgive me, I didn't mean to say that." She paused. I reached out to touch her face, certain she was crying. She shook her head, telling me she was not. "I want to start again," she said. "It'll be easier this time. We've got money, we're still healthy, thank God, we can go anyplace we want to, anyplace in the world. It doesn't have to be Italy if you don't want to go to Italy. We can go to Greece, if you like, I *did* enjoy Greece, Ike, even though the fucking colonels are running it. Or we can spend part of the year in Europe and part of it in the Caribbean; it's entirely up to ourselves, don't you see? We're free agents." She hesitated again. "Ike," she said, "I want to start all over again. Before it's too late."

"Rebecca," I said, "I don't know who's been talking to you. . . ."

"Nobody's been talking to me, Ike. I'm not stupid. Those long telephone calls you take in the studio aren't from Mark Aronowitz; he doesn't call that often these days. And I've had a few calls at the house, too, you really should caution your ladies to . . ."

"Rebecca, there aren't any . . ."

"Would you like me to provide a list? Please, Ike, I know *exactly* who they are; they all go out of their way to give me signals, they all want me to know that my husband is fucking them. Ike, I don't want to make this a . . . a . . . recriminating sort of thing. I really don't give a *damn* about your stable, I just want to get *away* from it. Can you understand me?"

"You're mistaken," I said.

459

"Your sons know, too," she said.

"My sons . . ."

"They have friends, their friends talk to them. Ike, some of these women, Ike, they're just *pigs*, really, it's so beneath you. Can't we please leave Talmadge? Can't we go to Europe or someplace, try it for a year? Ike, don't you see? There's nothing to keep us here anymore."

I thought, in the split second it took for me to steel myself for what I was about to tell her, I thought Yes, Rebecca, you're quite right. There's nothing to keep us here anymore. I'm tired of lying to you, Rebecca. I'm tired of lying to myself.

"The afternoon I was with Davina," I said. "The afternoon we were alone together . . ."

"I don't want to hear it," Rebecca said.

"I want to tell you what happened."

"I know what happened," she said. "I'm not a fool."

"Rebecca," I said, "Becky, Becks . . ."

"Don't say it."

"I want out."

"No."

"I'm tired of lying."

"Then don't anymore."

"It's too late," I said.

"I love you, Ike."

I took a deep breath.

"Rebecca," I said, "I don't love you."

❖

My grandfather was almost ninety-three years old when he died. He might have lived to a hundred and three if he hadn't been mugged on the Grand Concourse, in broad daylight, on the afternoon of June 16, 1973. My Uncle Matt had driven him from Massapequa the day before, and he had planned to spend the weekend with my parents; Matt was scheduled to pick him up again on Sunday night. On Saturday afternoon, having run out of De Nobili cigars, he had gone downstairs to replenish his supply. His attackers caught him as he was walking back from the candy store. He was never able to describe them to us; they had struck from behind, suddenly and without warning. They could have been white, black, tan, yellow, red, or any one of the myriad colors that had been tossed into the caldron that never boiled. They could have been the Irish he had feared and hated for most of his life, or the Jews he had come to partially understand, or the Italians he considered his own. Whatever they were, they were Americans. A woman from my mother's building recognized him lying on the sidewalk as a patrolman went through his pants pockets searching for identification. She ran upstairs immediately and knocked on my mother's door. By that time, an ambulance from Bronx-Lebanon was already on the way. My mother called me from the hospital, and I called a local taxi service and had them drive me to the Bronx. (The driver complained about having to go into the city on a Saturday night.) I got to the hospital at 7 P.M. My grandfather had just been brought down from the operating room. The surgeon explained that they had evacuated a subdural hematoma caused by the blows to his head. They had stopped the internal bleeding, and it now remained to see how he would respond.

My grandfather came out of the anesthesia at twenty minutes to nine. He was groggy, but he recognized my mother, and said to her, "*Madonna, che mal di testa!*" and then drifted off to sleep again. He awakened again at nine-fifteen. My mother, my father, and I were still in the room with him. We asked him how he felt. He told us he still had a headache, and then asked if he could have a cigar. The nurse told him no cigars, not yet. He chatted with us for about ten minutes, and then seemed to drift off to sleep again. At twenty minutes to ten, he began talking incoherently. The nurse summoned the doctor on duty, who recognized

461

immediately that my grandfather was in a semicomatose state. The doctor could not say whether his condition was a reaction to the trauma of surgery, or whether internal oozing had started again. My grandfather's vital signs were perfectly normal. There was nothing they could do but watch him very carefully. At ten minutes to ten, the doctor and my parents left the room, and I took up my vigil beside my grandfather's bed.

A great many people came into that room during the next fourteen hours. Some of them were real. Some of them were ghosts recalled in my grandfather's rambling narrative. Some of them were conjured by me, as I told him stories I was not quite sure he heard or understood. Some of them rushed only fleetingly through my mind as I listened for his breathing in periods when he was silent.

My three sons came to the hospital. Aunt Cristie and Uncle Matt came to the hospital. Their three children came, too. I hardly recognized their voices anymore; I had not seen them for more than twenty years. Uncle Dominick came in from Brooklyn with his wife Rosie and their married daughter. Aunt Rosie kept asking me if I remembered her sister Tina, and then went on to say she'd married a lawyer, too, and was living in Seattle. I told her I remembered Tina. My grandfather must have known I was sitting beside the bed because he kept addressing me by name as he told me, in scrambled chronological order, all the things he remembered. I don't think he knew he was dying, but he was summing up his life nonetheless, and trying to make some sense of it. And like a good jazz piano player feeding chords to a horn man, I filled the silences with reminiscences and thoughts of my own, and tried to sum up my life as well—and make some sense of it. My grandfather kept wondering aloud where Pino or Angelina or Aunt Bianca or Umberto the tailor or Grandma Tess or his sister Maria were. He was waiting for dead people to come to the hospital to visit him.

462

I kept expecting Rebecca to show up. I don't know why I expected her to show up.

I guess he expected her, too.

At one point, in the middle of the story he was telling me or telling himself about the day he had met Grandma Tess, he suddenly said, "Rebecca? *Dov'è* Rebecca?" and I told him again we were divorced now, Grandpa, we had been divorced since 1972, when an Italian boy had gone down to Haiti to sever all ties with a Jewish girl, and he said, "Ah, Ignazio, *che peccato*," and then went on to describe the girl coming to him across a picnic lawn, the girl with hazel eyes and chestnut hair.

And again, when he was recalling the day he had marched into Honest Abe's showroom to extend his personal welcome to the family, he interrupted his wandering narrative to say, "*Ma dov'è* Rebecca? She no comesa?" and then immediately asked, "Where'sa Abe-a Baumgart?" And I thought of the last conversation I had ever had with the Mad Oldsmobile Dealer, in September of 1970, three weeks after I'd left Rebecca. He called me from Miami, and I picked up the telephone in the living room of the house I had rented on the water in Rowayton, and he said, "What's this I hear about you and Rebecca?"

"I don't know what you've heard," I said. I had told Rebecca to keep the news of our separation secret until Andrew got back from India; a cable had informed us he was in Amsterdam, and we'd assumed he was on the way home. Now Honest Abe was on the phone.

"I heard you left her," he said.

"That's true," I said.

"You want my advice?"

"What's your advice?"

"Go back to her on your hands and knees, and kiss her ass. That's my advice."

I told my grandfather now, told him in a lull during his own

untiring monologue, still not certain that he was hearing anything
I said, told him I might have done just that, might have crawled
back to her on my hands and knees and kissed her ass, if only
Rebecca hadn't been so willing to forgive even what had happened
with Davina. Grandpa, I said, I know what I did was terrible, but
was it any worse than what I'd been doing all along? The first
time I went to bed with another woman, forgive me, Grandpa,
was in Malibu in 1960, she wouldn't take off the tiny gold cross a
lover had given her, I couldn't understand it, forgive me, please.
She told me I just missed looking shabby, and I laughed, and then
in bed she wouldn't take off a crucifix I couldn't even see. Ah,
Grandpa, that was the true death, the rest was only cremation. If
I'd had the courage then, I would have told Rebecca about that
woman whose name I can't remember, all I can remember is the
crucifix, the way I told her about Davina ten years later. Christ.
Ten years! Ten years of living a lie.

"Are you crazy?" my mother had asked on the telephone when
I broke the news to her. "What do you mean, you've left Rebecca? Are you crazy? Jimmy, do you *hear* this? Did he *tell* you
this? Are you crazy, Ike? You have *everything!*" she shouted, and
she began to cry.

"Grandpa," I said, "everything was a lie."

He began talking again, he was telling me now of what had
happened when he and the men walked into Charlie Shoe's shop,
and I thought of that day in the Catskills, the day of my belated
confession, thought of having told Rebecca I did not love her,
though I loved her still and loved the memory of what we once
had been. And she suggested as she wept that perhaps we could
make some sort of arrangement, lots of married people had different kinds of arrangements—but what the hell were we living
already, if *not* an arrangement? Could I allow her to forgive me
forever, until one day I took between my hands an actual stiletto,
no symbolic phallus plunging deep inside a weak and willing sister,
but an actual honed piece of steel, and plunged it into her breast

464

and ended it that way? I did not want forgiveness from her, I did not want absolution, I wanted freedom. I wanted *myself* back, whoever that person was in the year 1970.

"I am thirta-four years old," my grandfather was saying, "it is enough. I promise you, Ignazio, this time I go home because I have been no more I wish to have this terrible things that happen, where in Italy, no, it does not, I will go home, I will tell Tessie, I will tell you grandma, I will say *no*, Tessie, we go home, you hear me, Tessie, I take you home now, I leave here, this place, we go home *now*, we go."

And then, abruptly, he began laughing and told me about the time the barrel of wine broke in the front room, and I fell silent with my own thoughts again, and only half listened; I had heard this story before, I had heard it as a child when I was growing up and learning to be an American. I had learned quite well. On the telephone last December, Rebecca had said to me, "I don't care if the children spend Christmas with you. Christmas is yours."

Ah. And I had thought it was ours.

I had thought, in my silly sentimental notion of us and America, that everything was ours to share together. I had thought the gold in the streets was there for *all* of us to pick up, to pulverize, to toss over our shoulders like magic dust so that we could soar up over the tenements— Christ, her voice on that Pass-A-Grille beach as she read *Peter Pan* aloud to my sons, that Jewgirl voice I had first heard in a smoky toilet on Staten Island, and can still hear now in the dead of night when I awaken with a start and stare sightlessly into my bedroom and hear below the murmur of water against the rotting pilings of the old house.

Grandpa, I said aloud again (we were talking simultaneously now, I don't think either of us was hearing or listening), I still hate myself for having led Rebecca to the showers, and washed her clean, and stuffed her into a boxcar for transportation to the ovens, and later picked her teeth of gold. Grandpa, I think I stayed with her as long as I did because I wanted to prove to

Honest Abe that only in America could a Jew and a Gentile live happily ever after, show him he'd been wrong. But he was right, the prick, and I can't stop believing I've betrayed not only Rebecca and the kids, but also an ideal I loved almost as much.

"Ah, Ignazio," he said, "that Christmas Day, to tink of steal a chestnut? No, this wassa no right. I come out the house, I walk to where Pino lives, together we go on top the hill, we can see Don Leonardo's house, everything blows on the hillside, we talk about America. . . ."

"Grandpa," I said, "was I wrong? Should I have stayed? It *was* a lie, Grandpa, but where the hell is the truth?"

"And first," he said, "when I come here, I say to myself, I say to Pino, no good. We go home. We go back tomorrow the other side. What gold? Where is this gold Bardoni says? In the subway? In the mud? No, Ignazio, was terrible this America."

"Grandpa," I said, "don't die."

"And the noise. *Madonna mia, che rumore!* I tink I never get used. I swear, Ignazio, I woulda go back if I no meet you grandma. Ah, *che bellezza!* Oh, I see her, I fall in love. . . ."

"Please don't die on me," I said. "You're the connection."

We both fell silent then.

We were silent for a long time. The sun was up. I had not realized the sun was up. I snapped open the lid of my watch and felt for the time. It was a quarter to twelve. Had the sun been up that long?

"Ignazio?" my grandfather said.

"Yes, Grandpa?"

"Ah," he said.

"Ah," I said, and smiled.

I did not know where his semiconscious meanderings had led him, or whether or not he had reached any conclusions. I knew only that he was still alive, and his voice sounded strong, and that was good enough.

466

"Wassa time I no like this country," he said. "You believe that, Ignazio?"

"I believe it," I said.

"Wassa time I tink *Ma che?* I'm spose to make this place my home? Issa no gold here. Ignazio?"

"Yes, Grandpa."

"I'ma verra rich man, I have good life here. Wassa true what Bardoni told me in Fiormonte. *Le strade qui sono veramente lastricate d'oro.*"

He died in the next instant. A massive hemorrhage exploded somewhere inside his brain and killed him at once.

❖

Head and out.

I can do it on a piano. But there's no tying up half a lifetime with a bright yellow ribbon, there's no taking it home. I spend a lot of time wondering about it, but so far there've been no moments of truth, no dazzling revelations. Maybe those moments come only to people who can see. Or maybe it's enough to recognize the lies; maybe the truth will come in its own good time.

My son Andrew, when he was .in elementary school and kids were asking him what religion he was, used to answer, "I'm nothing." Then, when he grew weary of the response "You have to be *something*," he took to saying, "I'm a gorilla." When I asked him what that meant, he said, "It means the same thing; it means I'm nothing. Only this way, I don't have to explain."

I would like to explain. I owe an explanation. I've kept you here for hours now, and probably haven't entertained you at all. Anyway, my bag of tricks is running out, I haven't a fresh triplet in my head. So let me explain. Pretend you're a movie producer for a moment. Just read the synopsis, and forget the rest. It's the

467

chord chart that matters, anyway, and not the geography of the performance.

I still try to link them together all the time—the failure of my marriage, and the failure of the myth. I try to find a connection, but each time I think I've obviated my guilt by blaming the divorce on a success that could only have happened in America, I recognize I'm only telling myself another lie. I try not to lie to myself these days. So, for whatever it's worth (Rebecca, friends, enemies, relatives), *I* was the one who eroded the marriage, *I* was the one who left wife and family, *I* was the one who done us in. The butler is innocent. I'm the culprit. So much for that.

As for the rest . . .

Once upon a time, I wanted to be an American. I wanted to do all the things Americans in the movies did, especially if they could see. I wanted to come off my yacht and stroll up the dock wearing a blue blazer with a family crest stitched to the breast pocket. I wanted to come off the tennis courts after a vigorous set, I wanted to visit my polo ponies in the stables, and ski dangerous mountain slopes, and tell hair-raising tales in the lodge afterward while I sipped mulled wine or buttered rum. I wanted to throw enormous lawn parties, I wanted my wife to sit in a wide-brimmed floppy hat, gin and tonic in a pale white hand, children shouting in the distance as a governess discreetly cautioned silence, my beloved bride kissing one or another of her short-pantsed, knee-socksed darlings when he ran up to her, laughing him away with a "Run along now, dearest, Mummy's talking." I wanted family to be family, and friends to be friends, and friends to be family, and immigrants to be Wasps, and Wasps to be all those people who lived and loved within a six-mile radius of the luxurious house I had built of solid gold mined in the streets.

And I *became* American, more or less, though I never did any of the things sighted people can do, but that was hoping for much too much, really, wasn't it? Even this land of the free and home of the brave can do nothing for the congenitally blind, although

468

it can come a long way toward helping them to realize dreams. My own dream was vague but nonetheless glowing, and whereas I realize now it was *only* a dream, there were times when I thought it had leaped that uncertain line between illusion and reality to become a joyous fact. When I first heard "Ballad for Americans" in 1940, for example, it seemed to me the exultant, triumphant cry of a people who had finally come through. Even the "Czech and double-check" was an echo of an "Amos 'n' Andy" catch phrase. We had made it, I believed; we were ready to fulfill our promise of greatness; we were at last a true family. From that moment on, the grandsons of Russians would dance *la cucaracha* with the granddaughters of Norwegians; Negroes would sing the *Marseillaise* on Saint Patrick's Day as they marched up Fifth Avenue side by side with Swedes; on Columbus Day, in the bars along Third Avenue, Germans and Finns would toast the Year of the Butterfly, and croon gypsy lullabies; and on Christmas Day, Jews and Seventh-Day Adventists would give praise to Buddha, while atheists and agnostics carried gifts to the altar.

Dreams are lies.

If the gold Bardoni was talking about was merely an element whose atomic number is 79, atomic weight 196.967, melting point 1063.0 degrees centigrade, and so on—why, yes, *certainly* it was here in the streets to be scooped up in both hands. It's *still* here, in fact. Jazz, as you probably know, is enjoying a tremendous resurgence. Even Earl Hines is making a comeback, and if I chose to come out of what I prefer to call semiretirement, I'm sure I could get some good gigs, I'm sure I could start earning the big buck again. Somehow, the big buck doesn't matter to me anymore. Somehow, the joy of playing jazz disappeared the day The Beast tapped me on the shoulder, and advised me to pick up a shovel and start digging. But if Bardoni was talking about *another* kind of gold, a gold that is corrosion-resistant and malleable, you will not find it here, friends, you will not find it in the debris of

469

the shattered American myth. Moreover, you are a fool to search for it; it is only pyrite.

Sometimes, when I walk the main street of Rowayton, tapping my careful way back to the old wooden house on the water, I think of all those black (*or* white; it doesn't make a damn bit of difference) people out there who are America's huddled masses yearning to breathe free, the wretched refuse of *our* teeming shore, tired, poor, and hungry, fighting off rats with one hand while filling out correspondence-course lessons with the other, and I realize they are exactly what I *used* to be, back then in the thirties, when I was running through the guinea ghetto with my hand in my brother's. And I realize further (and this is what frightens me and causes me to stop short in the middle of the pavement) that what they want to be, what they are striving to become—is *me*. Dwight Jamison. And I do not exist. I am a figment of the American imagination. I am the realization of a myth that told us we were all equal, but forgot to mention we were also all separate.

The person I became was someone I did not know. No matter how many times I passed my hands over his face, I could not construct a mental image of who he was. I'm still trying to find out. I do not have the truth yet. But I know that when I said to my grandfather on his dying bed, "You're the connection," I was speaking something very close to the truth, unless I was merely denying the lie. He *was* the connection. He remains the connection between whatever I am and whatever I used to be. At the hospital, when I went back to pick up my grandfather's death certificate, one of the nurses asked me for my autograph. We began talking, and I recognized that voice, I recognized those cadences, and when she told me she was Irish, I was not surprised. She was twenty-three years old, and had been born in the Bronx— but she was Irish. Well, what *else* could she claim to be? American? Who or what is that?

An American is not the man I embrace in greeting at the cocktail parties I infrequently attend, but neither is he my Uncle Matt, eager to take me anywhere in his taxicab, for which he still does not have his own medallion. And where is Wonder Woman's cousin, the Wasp Woman I conjured as a child? She's not the art director's wife (is she?), chirpily telling her assembled guests, with appropriate innuendo, that her husband misses the 6:05 from New York too often for comfort. But neither is she my Aunt Cristie, offering me some nice fresh lemonade she squeezed herself. Where are the *real* Dwight Jamisons? Where, for that matter, are the *real* Jerzy Trzebiatowskis?

And yet, my grandfather, just before he died, told me he was a rich man, and I know he wasn't talking about material wealth. Sometimes, in my house on the water, sitting before a blazing fire the housekeeper has started for me, I listen to the crackling wood, and remember the fire Francesco Luigi Di Lorenzo made on Christmas Day in the year 1900, when he decided to come to this country. And I think of what he said to me just before he died—"The streets here are truly paved with gold."

And I wonder anew.

Although much of the preceding narrative is written in what might be called "first-person personal," it, too, is a lie. The characters, the events, and even some of the places are fictitious. And whereas the words attributed to real jazz musicians were actually spoken by them at one time or another, they certainly were never said to the fictitious character called Dwight Jamison. Marian McPartland, for one example, did make the comment about disappearing drummers—but it was an aside to an audience who'd come to hear her play jazz at the John Drew Theater in East Hampton in the summer of 1973.

I used many different sources while gathering information that would help me to understand music, and jazz music in particular. But I am especially indebted to John Mehegan—the jazz pianist, teacher, and writer—for sharing with me his own love for the piano, and his vast understanding of this unique art form. In a series of interviews taped over the space of two months, he gave to me tirelessly and graciously of his time and knowledge, and I am humbly grateful.

So, little book . . . good-bye. I hope you are a big success.

This is America, don't forget.

EVAN HUNTER

Pound Ridge, New York
February, 1974